About the Author

Ariane has French and Dutch heritage though she was born and raised in London. Having spent twenty-two years there, she now lives in Salzburg, Austria where she is closer to a landscape to that of the Four Flames.

The Four Flames: The Schumy War

Ariane Van Hoof

The Four Flames: The Schumy War

Olympia Publishers
London

www.olympiapublishers.com
OLYMPIA PAPERBACK EDITION

Copyright © Ariane Van Hoof 2018

The right of Ariane Van Hoof to be identified as author of
this work has been asserted in accordance with sections 77 and 78 of the Copyright,
Designs and Patents Act 1988.

All Rights Reserved

No reproduction, copy or transmission of this publication
may be made without written permission.
No paragraph of this publication may be reproduced,
copied or transmitted save with the written permission of the publisher, or in
accordance with the provisions
of the Copyright Act 1956 (as amended).

Any person who commits any unauthorised act in relation to
this publication may be liable to criminal
prosecution and civil claims for damage.

A CIP catalogue record for this title is
available from the British Library.

ISBN: 978-1-84897-820-1

This is a work of fiction.
Names, characters, places and incidents originate from the writer's imagination.
Any resemblance to actual persons, living or dead, is purely coincidental.

First Published in *2018*

Olympia Publishers
60 Cannon Street
London
EC4N 6NP

Printed in Great Britain

Dedication

To my brother, Alexandre, who was there the night I came up with the idea for the book and helped me to write the plot on little yellow post-it notes in our grandparents' attic.

Contents

I	11
II	19
III	25
IV	33
V	41
VI	50
VII	67
VIII	77
IX	89
X	100
XI	111
XII	123
XIII	135
XIV	146
XV	158
XVI	168
XVII	183
XVIII	197
XIX	209
XX	225
XXI	236
XXII	250
XXIII	260
XXIV	281
XXV	322
XXVI	340

I

Athena laid still in the middle of a large field in the countryside. It was her seventeenth birthday the following day and she told her parents she wanted to spend her last few days of being sixteen in the middle of the fields, laying on the dry grass, feeling the hot sun blaze against her pale skin.

Athena had, as Tomas always said, "an aura of such light surrounding her like a shield from the darkness of the world." Even though she lived in poverty, and her house was merely a shack of one room shared among three people, Athena was always cheerful and never let her misfortunes dampen her spirits. She spent every sunny day out in the fields dreaming away and often thinking of ways she could help her sick father. Athena had tried many things to heal her father. When there were thunderstorms, she would always place vases, open boxes and jars outside to collect the rain water. She would then collect the water and boil it with special herbs and give to her father as a healing potion. Nothing, however, can cure the malice that comes with old age.

Today, however, Athena was only dreaming of a fairy tale.

She caressed her long brown hair, untangling any knots on the way down until she felt her waist. She smiled as she remembered a fairy tale she had recently read: In a huge castle with high towers covered in ivy, a cruel king had locked his daughter away in the dungeons, teaching her a lesson that writing fairy tales was a load of nonsense and a waste of time, whereas learning how to sew and helping in the kitchens was time well spent. One day, while she was crying, a young knight emerged from nowhere and he suddenly...

'Athena, you must come NOW. Athena, NOW!' her mother yelled from afar. Athena opened her large blue eyes, quickly got up and ran as fast as she could towards her home.

'Agatha, we have to tell her now. We must tell her before I pass away.

We should have told her on her sixteenth birthday. Tomorrow, she will turn seventeen. We have waited far too long.'

'I can't bear this, Tomas. We have raised her like our own. What if she leaves immediately? What if you die straight way? I will be left all on my own. In one day, it will be from three to one. You should have never seen her that day thirteen years ago because then we wouldn't even be having this conversation!'

Agatha turned around, ready to unleash her usual flood of tears, but held them back as soon as she saw Athena running towards them.

'What's happening? Father, are you alright? Do you need any help? Tell me, I want to help. I need to help!' Athena said desperately, catching her breath as she leant against the bedpost.

Agatha and Tomas looked at each other but remained in silence. They didn't dare look at her. Athena, puzzled by their silence, started to worry even more.

'What is going on?' she demanded in a forceful voice.

'Athena, we both love you very, very much. We want you to know that. You must,' her mother finally replied, her voice gradually getting quieter.

Athena nodded, curious of what the following news could be.

'Athena, we should have told you this on your previous birthday but we couldn't bear it and with this illness of mine, I don't think I will survive much longer.'

There was a silence for the next few minutes. Athena was too afraid to break it.

'I found you near a river bank in front of the Naran Flame.'
'Have you heard of the Naran Flame before?' her mother asked.

'No, I haven't, mama,' Athena replied.

'Please, Athena do not call me that. I have always insisted for you to call me Agatha. I still don't understand why you never listen!'

Athena looked down and took a deep breath, feeling the lump at the back of her throat grow bigger.

'Agatha, I think you have said enough. Athena, come here and sit next to me.' Tomas said, patting the space on his bed next to him. Athena went and sat down, trying her best to fight the tears.

'The Naran Flame is one of the Four Flames. They are found past that field you spend a majority of your time in. To get to the Four Flames, you cross the field and you will see a gate. Past that gate, there are four big hills. By the time you reach the fourth hill, you will see an inn on your left, a small woodland on your right and a volcano directly in front. It is a few days walk till you will see two bridges. Choose the one you feel is right. After you have passed the bridge, you must not look back!'

'Father, why are you telling me all this? Must I leave?'

'Athena, you must understand this is very difficult for both Agatha and me. However, it is your right to know where you came from. You deserve to know where you were born and where you lived at the beginning of your life.'

'I don't understand. Are you trying to tell me that I was born in the Naran Flame?'

'Most probably. You see, there was a terrible revolt thirteen years ago. The Chamcoks tried to break through the Flame and they had somehow succeeded. They killed everyone in their path. I am not sure whether your real parents are still alive. I never saw them.'

Athena couldn't believe what she was hearing. Her eyes began to swell up and tears started to trickle down her cheeks, making their way down her neck.

'So, *neither* of you are my real parents?'

Agatha and Tomas didn't dare speak. They just looked down.

'I don't believe this. I truly cannot believe that you both are telling me this *now*. It's so...' her voice broke off, followed by a series of muffled sounds. 'Why did you find me there if you live all the way over here?'

'Ah well, at that time when I was fit and up and about, I was a messenger. On that particular day, I was asked to deliver a message to King Agalaya himself.' Tomas proudly replied.

'I remember it like it was yesterday. I was leaving the inn and a group of Blucks came up to me. They told me to deliver a letter to the King. I obeyed them and set off immediately. They gave me a horse and I got to the Four Flames in only two days!'

'Wait! I thought you said that the Chamcoks were the ones who-'

'Yes, they were, but you see the Blucks and the Chamcoks are part of the same army, except the Blucks are highly trained and skilled soldiers. The Chamcoks are less skilled and more barbaric. They are just men who came from poverty, knowing that if they didn't want to starve to death, they would have to join the army. That's what makes them so ruthless. They kill to survive.

Anyway, the Blucks and Chamcoks are allies and therefore work with each other. They have one aim: to destroy the King and his descendants and to take control over the lands.'

Agatha looked up at Athena and told her a different story from the same day. 'That day was the day my son was born.'

'You... you had a son? How come I've never heard of this before? What happened?' Athena asked, wiping the tears off her pale face.

'Well, there was no village doctor at the time, so when I was in labour, I had to wait till Tomas came back home to help deliver the baby. However, Tomas didn't come back in time.'

'Agatha, you never told me that you needed help to deliver the baby. If I had known that, I would not have left to the Four Flames!' Tomas replied, followed by a series of coughs.

'That's beside the point, but anyway... where was I?' Agatha mumbled to herself, ignoring her husband's coughs.

'You were at the bit about waiting for Tomas to-'

'Ah yes, I remember. When I was just about to lose all hope, a young man arrived at the doorstep. He told me that he could hear someone in pain and saw me in labour through our window. He very kindly helped to deliver the baby. All was well, until he stole the baby!'

Silence.

Finally, Athena plucked up the courage to ask, 'How can you steal a baby right in front of its mother's eyes?'

'I was utterly exhausted and I just gave birth for the first time. I wasn't exactly fit to run after a man, was I?' Agatha snapped, folding her arms crossly.

Athena and Tomas looked at one another. Tomas had tears in his eyes. 'How come this is the first time I am hearing about this? Thirteen years and you never told me the truth. You always told me that you had a stillbirth. That the child died the very moment it came into the world.'

'What was I supposed to tell you, Tomas? You came home with a little girl in your hands. You seemed so happy. I didn't want to make you feel guilty!' Agatha shouted out, turning red in the face.

After a while, Tomas replied, 'I don't know what to say!'

Athena, feeling slightly awkward, asked, 'So, what are we supposed to do now?'

Agatha and Tomas looked at each other and then to Athena. Tomas replied, 'That is completely up to you, my sweet. You may go to the Four Flames if you wish, or you may continue to stay here with us. It's your choice. We want nothing more than for things to go back to the way they were before. However, it's your decision, not ours.'

Athena, completely caught off guard from all this, was lost for words. She could go on the journey of her life and find more about her past. If she was lucky, she would find her biological parents. Yet, if she left, the chance of Tomas being alive when she came back was minuscule.

'I need to think about this alone.' Athena told them both and before they could reply she was already out of the door.

'Oh dear, Tomas, I really hope she stays here with us. Who else could help me with the cleaning and the-'

'Listen to yourself, woman! A young girl has a great opportunity to see the lands and hopefully meet her real parents, yet here you are being completely selfish, hoping she stays. Not because you love her but because you need help around the place!' Tomas said angrily.

Agatha looked away.

'You have no idea how it feels to have your child stolen in front of your very eyes. Watching that man just *steal* our son made me want to kill him. It took me hours to fall asleep, knowing that my son could have been in my arms if my husband had just turned up. But he never did! So, don't you point your fat little finger at me, blaming me for wanting a bit of help! You should really be pointing that old finger of yours to yourself because had you come straight home from the inn, we would have had a son!'

'Yes, but if I did come home, we would have never had Athena. She is special, Agatha. I know you've always been a bit hard on her, but there is a reason for everything. We were meant to be her parents.'

Agatha looked through the window to see Athena walking through the field, gazing up at the sunset.

'Every time I watch her play or walk or relax in the field, I imagine her brother being with her. It would have been nice for her to grow up with someone around her age. It would have made my heart full, knowing my son was here and that our family was complete.'

Agatha shut her eyes and pinched the top of her nose. She hated to cry. She found it a sign of weakness.

Tomas limped out of bed to kiss her hand.

'Agatha, you must stop mourning for the boy. He is alive and he will return one day. At least you *knew* that he was alive! I was always told that he was dead but that is not the point. We have Athena and although we do not share the same blood, she will always be our daughter. She loves us and at the end of the day, isn't that what each parent wants? To be loved by their child?'

Agatha looked Tomas in the eyes. Her hazel brown eyes were fixed onto his. After a while, she smiled and leant in to kiss him.

Athena, shocked by all this news, turned around to look at her home. She could see through the window that her parents were embracing.

She suddenly burst into tears. Why were her parents embracing at a time like this? Were they glad that she might leave?

'That's not possible. They told me I had the choice. No, I'm sure they want what is best for me. I know they have good intentions. They are just forgiving each other for the incident of their child.'

Athena finally laid on the grass in her usual spot, near the big oak tree. She looked up: The sky was navy blue, the stars were becoming more and more visible and the moon was almost full. She smiled. She would always try to count how many stars there were. It relaxed her.

Athena stayed there, thinking, not moving a muscle for more several hours. After those two hours, she picked herself up and sighed. She was still unsure of what to do.

'I'll just have to go back to the house and ask Agatha and Tomas!'

Athena ran back home, racing a hare that was also in the field. She couldn't help but smile as she watched the hare run past her. However, when she finally reached the door, her smile faded as she overheard Tomas talking about the Four Flames.

'Agatha, it really is the most beautiful place: the huge waterfall in the Forest Tatila, little rivers everywhere, the markets not far from the four large mountains. The Azul, Morado, Amarila and the Naran Flame which is the smallest. That's probably why it was easier for the Chamcoks to break in. Well, that and also the fact the Royal Family lived there.'

'It's always nice to see you talk about the Four Flames. It makes you so happy!'

'Well, what I'm about to say doesn't make *me* happy. The village doctor told me something on his last visit. I didn't want to alarm you, but since-'

'Tell me!'

'It's been confirmed that General Avran, the commander of the Seven Hundred Army, is planning to overthrow King Agalaya himself! Once again, as it was thirteen years ago, there is tension in the air. Can you believe it? We can't tell Athena anything about it though. It's not up to us to make her decision. Perhaps it is her fate to go back now. The revolt brought her here and-'

'The war will bring her back there.' Agatha concluded.

Tomas took a deep breath and nodded.

'I just don't want her to get into any danger. I tell you, if they see her then that's it for her! They will recognise her instantly. Anybody would. Her blue eyes give her away instantly!' Tomas told Agatha. He suddenly lowered his voice and whispered, 'I know they will be waiting for her.'

Athena ran back into the field. Why would they be waiting for her? How would they be able to recognise her?

She ran back inside and demanded, 'Why do they want me?'

Tomas looked bewildered. 'What are you talking about, Athena?'

'I heard you. I just heard you talking to Mama. You told her they will recognize me. They are waiting for me. WHY?'

'You have a gift, dear child. A gift that very few have!'

'I have no gift. I'm an ordinary child. There is nothing special about me!'

'You are deeply mistaken, my sweet.'

Agatha looked over to Tomas who continued to speak.

'Have you ever wondered why you were able to learn things quickly? How you have such a large range of vocabulary even though you have never been properly educated? How you always know how to say the right things at the right time? How you sometimes know exactly what I'm thinking, and then you say those thoughts out loud? You cannot call any of those things ordinary, can you now?'

Athena took a moment to consider this. She had never considered those things to be "special".

'I don't understand how they can still recognise me though! I was only an infant when they perhaps had a glance at me.'

Tomas looked at her and paused for a moment.

'Athena, they will recognise you. Your eyes are blue. Have you ever seen anyone with blue eyes? Agatha and I, along with the majority of the world have brown eyes. You are a special person, Athena, with a special gift. More special than you realise.'

'Should I go then?'

'You must do what feels right. You know how much we adore you. You know how well we know you. This is now on your mind. You will eventually leave and we all know it! So, I tell you to go now. Don't waste your time. Go, my sweet child!'

'Then it is settled. I'm heading to the Four Flames tomorrow!'

II

'I can't believe that General Avran actually threw me out of the army. It's absolutely absurd. I mean, what I did wasn't that bad was it?'

No response.

Malo was being dragged along the countryside path by two mounted soldiers. (His back was gliding through the muddy ground and his arms suspended up in the air by the ropes tied to the saddle of each horse.) They were under strict orders that under no circumstances were they allowed to talk to Malo. He was, after all, banished from the Seven Hundred Army and was therefore banished from its premises. They finally halted and both soldiers got off their horses and untied the ropes from Malo's wrists.

'There you go, scum. You are to *never* cross the bridges into the forest *ever* again. Otherwise, I will personally kill you!'

'Oh, you know that's never going to happen. Actually, I bet you four hundred rubies that I will be back here in less than a fortnight. Deal?' Malo proposed. Instead of a verbal response, he was spat on by the small but heavily built soldier. With that, they rode back to the headquarters.

Since he was recently tortured, Malo had difficulty standing up. His right leg was still bleeding and his left was already bruising. He felt blood trickle from his nose and he could barely see through his left eye as it was swollen.

'I hate that man,' he said repeatedly.

When he was finally up on his feet, he looked in all directions, wondering which way to go. He didn't really know where to go from here. He had no family and the army robbed him of all his personal belongings, including the only picture he had of him and his parents.

In front of him, he could see a volcano in the distance and behind him, past the two bridges, was the Forest Tatila and the Four Flames. If he went towards the volcano, he would just be going further into the countryside, but if he went back towards the Four Flames, he would probably encounter some soldiers patrolling the forest.

Malo took a deep breath and then grunted. He felt so conflicted.

Part of him knew he had to go to the Four Flames. It was the only place he would be of use with the upcoming war. However, he didn't want to go back there immediately. In his condition, he wouldn't be able to put up a fight against any soldier he would encounter.

It was time for a break. He didn't want to go back just yet, so he made up his mind.

After ten minutes of Malo standing in the same spot, thinking about life, he mumbled to himself, 'Right, let's climb the nice big volcano and see what we find.'

As he started to walk, he felt the ground tremor slightly. He slowly turned around. Sure enough, two horses were heading towards him. He didn't bother moving, knowing that there was no way he could outrun a horse.

'Oi! I forgot to do something.' the little man said, jumping off his horse and running towards Malo with his comrade right beside him.

Malo had no idea what the soldier was on about, but seeing that he was wounded, running would be pointless as they would easily catch up with him.

The little man came up to Malo and kicked him in the groin. 'That was from General Avran. He wanted you to have a proper farewell!'

He and the other soldier walked back to the horses, leaving Malo on the ground in a great deal of pain. It was only after an hour he could stand again.

It was midday and the heat was getting more intense. The soldiers had spent over a day bringing Malo far from their territory. On the way, they simply threw pieces of bread at him and gave him very little water, so Malo was feeling very light-headed and dizzy. On top of that, he had to endure the pain from his wounds and the heat from the sun.

'Hopefully, I can make it to the inn where I can just lay down and get drunk. That will definitely ease the pain!'

Over the course of the day, Malo managed to limp along the countryside path and make his way over the volcano. He carefully made his way around the rim of the crater. Finally, on the other side, he caught a glimpse of the inn by the foot of the volcano. He smiled and sighed with relief.

Athena was packing her bag, putting in a change of clothes and a few pieces of bread and mushrooms, along with nuts and berries.

She went to her parents and gave them both a hug and a kiss.

'I will really miss you. A part of me is feeling tremendously guilty for leaving you both. Especially you, Tomas! Are you absolutely *sure* you are fine with this?'

'I am sure, my sweet. I really am. You will regret it every day if you don't find out about your past. All three of us know it. Here, I have something for you.' Tomas said.

He revealed an old tin box. He opened it up and took out one hundred rubies.

'Oh no, you really don't need to!' Athena said, trying to give the money back.

'No. We will not take that as an answer. You jolly well will accept the money, Athena!' Agatha snapped.

'Mama, please-'.

'Oh, dear child, I don't mean to shout at you. I'm just rather nervous. That's all. You've never been allowed past the fields and I'm afraid you'll run into trouble. There are a lot of dangerous soldiers out there. Just don't run into trouble, all right? You're a very intelligent girl. Figure out a way to travel safely. There is only so much Tomas and I can do for you. We've given you money and food. The rest is up to you!'

Athena kissed her on the cheek. 'That's not all though, is it!'

'No, it's not. With you gone and him dying,' Agatha said, nodding in Tomas's direction, 'I'll be alone once and for all. I've been married to Tomas for over thirty years, and you've been with us for thirteen. So, I don't remember how it feels to be all alone. I don't think I can handle it.' Agatha explained as her eyes started to water.

Athena gave her one last hug and kissed her on the forehead. She then looked deep into Agatha's eyes.

'Mama, I promise, I will come back for you. For the both of you.' Athena told them as she looked over at Tomas. She picked up her bag and set off, walking through the field.

She finally reached the gate. The gate she was never allowed to open. Athena hesitated for a moment as her hand rested on the handle. She closed her eyes, took a deep breath and slowly pushed down.

She felt her heart race and her hands tremble, but she continued to stride forward. Athena knew exactly what she had to do and felt every part of her aching to meet her real family.

After a few minutes of walking, she could hear something.

A voice.

Athena looked around but there was no sign of anyone.

I wish, for once, my parents would let me go free, but no! My duty lies with the lambs, the cows and the fields. When I turn eighteen in a few months, I'm out of here!

Athena stopped and processed what she had just heard. How could she hear a voice and not see the person? They couldn't have been hiding because it was afternoon and the sun was still out.

I'm going to leave now. I can't take this anymore. They won't care. All they care about are the lambs, the cows and the fields!

Suddenly, a young man emerged from the woods nearby. All Athena could do was stare at him.

'Can I help you?' the young man asked.

'Were you just talking out loud? I think I heard you!'

'No, I wasn't. I was walking *silently* through the woods,' he said slowly, thinking that Athena was a bit strange.

'But I heard you! You're going to be eighteen in a few months and you're leaving your home because you're fed up looking after the lambs, the cows and the fields!'

After studying Athena for a moment, the young man realised. 'Oh my god. You're one of them!'

He quickly ran back into the woods.

Athena sighed. She shrugged her shoulders and decided to ignore the boy's comment and to continue walking.

'Right!' she told herself. 'I'm going to walk past those hills, and I'm going to try and find some place to stay. Perhaps the inn father was talking about! And tomorrow, I will walk over the volcano and try to reach the bridges.'

Athena snorted. She just thought of a joke which wasn't very funny, but since everything around her was still and silent, the only person she could amuse was herself.

She yelled, 'Nobody can hear me! I'm all alone!'

The word "alone" echoed several times, sending a chill down Athena's spine. She whispered to herself, 'I really am all alone.'

From then on, she decided to remain quiet till she reached the inn.

Meanwhile, Malo was trying to climb down the volcano. He kept falling over which made it harder to get up as time went on, especially as he always fell on the same part of his injured leg.

'Oh, Malo, do you really know what you're doing?' he asked himself. He answered his question in a different accent for sheer amusement with, 'No, I just hope to get drunk and meet someone to actually talk to other than myself!'

He was so irritated that he leant down and picked up a red rock and threw it afar, but he leant too far forward that he fell over again. This time, he didn't bother getting up. He just laid there, thinking of what he had done.

'Maybe I do deserve this. Maybe it's the Gods deciding to make me suffer. I mean, I'm so close yet, so far to the beer! This is another level of torture, for sure!'

He placed his arm under his head, making his position a bit more comfortable.

He looked up at the sky and stared for such a long time, that all the clouds merged into one. This led Malo to fall into a deep sleep.

Athena reached the top of the last hill and stood there for a few minutes. She closed her eyes and took a deep breath, smelling the rich and humid scent that came from the red volcano. Athena then cast her eyes over to the inn. It had two floors and was made of dark, red wood that almost matched the colour of the volcano. The windows on the bottom floor had dark green shutters, an empty wooden terrace as the chairs were folded up against the walls, and a quaint front door shaped as an arch with a green outline.

'Yes!' she cheered as she saw a bed through a window on the second floor. Her feet were aching and all she wanted to do was to jump on that bed and relax.

Athena rubbed her hands together and was shaking with excitement. She couldn't *wait* to meet new people. She always loved to read stories, but now, she was going to hear and learn the stories of others.

Athena looked down as she began to make her way down the hill, when she suddenly looked back up. Something had caught her eye. She could see something near the bottom of the volcano.

'I wonder what it could be.'

III

As Athena made her way closer to the volcano, she could see what it was. It was a man, and by the look of things, an injured one.

As soon as Athena realised that the man was badly hurt, she ran towards him as fast as she could. She bent down next to him and shook his shoulder.

'Hello? Are you all right?' she asked, unable to think of what else she could say or do.

Malo, who was in a middle of a reverie, suddenly felt as though his world was shaken. He tried to ignore it, but the shaking grew more and more violent and he decided to try and wake up. He heard a distant murmur and realised it was a girl's voice. So, he immediately opened his eyes.

At first, his vision was blurred but he could vaguely make out the shape of the girl. He suddenly felt something prickly on his face.

Athena, seeing that he was waking up, felt a sense of relief. His hand touched her hair. She thought he would continue reaching up to her face, but instead he flicked it away.

She realised that it was tickling him, so she tucked her hair behind her ears.

She then softly slapped his cheek to help him fully wake up, or at least talk.

After a few slaps, he suddenly grabbed her wrist.

'What are you doing?' he growled.

Athena jumped and quickly removed her hand. She studied her wrist and saw his red finger marks. She looked back up at Malo who was still laying down with his eyes closed. He looked perfectly kind. She could feel he didn't mean to hurt her.

'I am just trying to help you! I can see though that you are wounded and that you need some help so, I would appreciate you allowing me to do something rather than bruising my little wrist!'

Malo wasn't quite able to understand why this person was raising their voice at him. He had politely and softly asked what she was doing and now, according to her, he was aggressive. He gently touched her arm and now she was going to bruise because of his "firm" grip?

Malo decided to get up and talk to her before she made other accusations.

He slowly and carefully stood up, even though he was in a lot of pain, and introduced himself.

'Hello, my name is Malo. Hey, that rythmes! Anyway, I am deeply sorry about your bruised wrist. It was certainly unintentional and I didn't mean to hurt you.'

Athena gave him a sympathetic smile. She also stood up and examined him. He had light brown eyes and dark blond hair. He had quite a muscled body and he was just a few inches taller than her.

'My name is Athena and it's quite alright. May I ask what happened to your leg?' she said, quite alarmed as blood was trickling down his leg and onto the ground.

'Oh that! I fell over many times,' Malo replied, unbothered anymore by the blood.

'Maybe we should head towards the inn?' she suggested.

Malo nodded and started to make his way down. Athena picked up her bag and stayed close to him, in case he fell over. She offered her help along the way, but he continuously refused. This didn't stop her from keeping an eye on him the whole time.

When they reached the inn, Malo held out the door for Athena and said, 'Ladies first.'

Athena quickly walked through. She had never been inside an inn and had no idea what to expect.

A man limped towards them with a serviette on his left hand and an empty glass in the other.

'How may I help you?' he muttered, clearly irritated.

'We would like a drink and then some hospitality,' Malo firmly replied.

The man grunted and showed them to a table for two. He let Athena and Malo settle in before he came back.

'What can I get the happy couple?' he asked again with an irritable tone.

Athena immediately replied, 'Oh, we aren't together. We simply—'

'Listen, sweetie, I didn't ask for a long story, I just asked what you wanted to drink!' the man snapped back at her.

He shook his head. 'Honestly, some people...'

Malo banged his fist on the table and shouted, 'That's enough! We will both have beers and don't you ever use that tone again with my friend. Otherwise, you may wake up in the morning with a part of you missing!'

Malo reached out for his sword from his belt, causing farmers around the inn to stare.

The man bowed to them with a false smile and went to the bar to get their beers.

Malo drew away his sword and stared at Athena, who was putting her bag down by her feet and staying down there to avoid getting involved with the dispute.

When she looked back up, she saw Malo stare right at her. She turned around to see if he was staring at someone behind her, but then he would have been staring at a stack of broken chairs.

'Your eyes... they're blue. Blue!'

Athena nodded. Tomas had mentioned this to her earlier and as she looked around the inn, she couldn't see anyone else who had blue eyes.

Malo leant back against his chair, rummaging his fingers against his chin.

'That's very rare, you know?'

Athena, starting to feel uncomfortable, decided to change the subject. 'Why did you shout at him?'

'Well, he was drunk and I have a little patience with drunks. Therefore, I lost my temper with him.'

'How did you know he was drunk?' Athena asked shyly.

Malo laughed. 'He was limping yet he seemed to be in good shape to me. Haven't you ever seen someone drunk before?'

'No, I've lived a very enclosed life. I was only allowed on some fields near my home, but apart from that, I have never seen the outside world!'

Malo shocked, asked, 'If a strange group of men comes up to you and they surround you and they say, "Hello there sweet cheeks", what would you do?'

Athena smiled and answered, 'I would say hello back to them and ask how their day has been!'

Malo tutted and shook his head. 'You obviously don't know what dangers could happen to you. You're young and attractive, so I guess you're off to a great start in the real world!'

Athena blushed and smiled, looking away.

'Why are you blushing? This isn't very funny!' Malo replied, angrily.

'So what? So what if I can't tell what danger is? It's not like I'm going to run into trouble anytime soon, is it?

I'm ready to learn. I'll make some mistakes, but I will learn from them. How can you have that kind of knowledge if you don't have the experience?'

The man arrived with two beers on a tray. He dropped the plate onto their table and left immediately. He was clearly frightened of Malo and his weapon.

Athena sipped the beer at once, curious to try a new drink that wasn't water or tea.

Malo laughed at her as she coughed, and then took a huge mouthful at once.

'How do you do that? I can't really describe it but it's a bit...prickly?'

Malo answered her question, 'No, they are called bubbles which make the drink even more enjoyable in my opinion!'

'I presume you've had this drink more than once before?'

Malo spat out his drink all over her face.

'I'm sorry, Athena! That was just too funny. Yes, I have had this drink more than once before because this is all they give us in t...'

Malo was about to continue but realised he should stop talking before he would regret saying something.

'So, why have you decided to leave your enclosed life?'

'I found out yesterday that my parents who have looked after me for as long as I can remember aren't my real parents. I was found on a river bank close to the Naran Flame.' Athena said, looking down.

Malo spat out his drink and once again, it reached Athena's face.

'Okay, that is the second time in the last few minutes that you've spat on me!' Athena snapped.

'I'm sorry, but you're telling me that you are heading for the Naran

Flame? You do know that particular Flame is infested by Chamcoks?!'

'I heard my father mention those names before, Blucks and Chamcoks, but I'm afraid that I haven't heard a great deal about them. Where does one find them? That way, I will be sure to avoid them.'

Malo bit his tongue and eventually laughed.

'It's too late. I am a Bluck.' he said in a humorous tone.

'You... you're a *Bluck?*'

Malo smiled and nodded.

'I am a Bluck from The Seven Hundred Army.'

Athena raised her eyebrows. 'You seem so nice and young. Why are you involved with such monstrous affairs?'

'I'm not. Well, I wasn't. I left because I broke some of their rules.'

Again, Athena gasped and looked at his legs from under the table and her face suddenly popped up again.

'Were you tortured?' she whispered.

Malo didn't answer but merely nodded.

'How?' Athena asked, almost too afraid to hear the answer.

'General Avran had his guards drag me onto the stage in front of the whole army. Avran tied me to a chair, gave a speech on how bad a soldier I was, and then punched me until I was severely injured. Then the last thing I can remember from *that* room was a large pole stuck into my leg. I probably lost too much blood which is what probably made me unconscious. I then woke up on the floor of a dungeon cell. 'Reserved for torturing' they used to say.'

Malo stopped and chuckled. Athena gently touched his hand, begging for him to continue.

'Then they got the muser out and—'

'Wait!' Athena interrupted. 'What's a muser?'

'Oh, it's an object used to torture people. It looks like a wooden pole and what they do is barge it into any part of your body. They barged it into my leg, three times. Or was it four times?

Anyway, they also barged it into my stomach which hurt very much. I swear that was the first time I cried in my whole twenty-three years of life!' Malo said, pretending to faint for dramatic effect.

'You're only twenty-three?' Athena asked, surprised.

'Yes. Why? How old are you?'

'I'm seventeen today, but that's not the point. How long were you in the army for?'

'I joined four years ago. It was my decision. It would have been easier to join the Chamcoks but I was a very skilled fighter, so I decided to risk joining the *infamous* Blucks. And it worked! Anyway, you said you're seventeen today?'

Athena nodded.

'Well then, let's celebrate!' Malo said excitedly.

'Barman,' he yelled out, 'it's my lady friend's birthday today. Let's see some of your finest wine! And please, for all of our sakes, bring us some food! We're starving. Starving, I say!'

He glanced at Athena. She was smiling to herself.

'Wipe that smirk off your face, Athena. We're going to have a drinking competition. Seeing that we're going to have to stay here for the night anyway, let's make this more interesting. Whoever drinks the most gets the bed and the other has to sleep on the floor. What do you say?'

Athena laughed out loud.

'Yes, like I'm going to win!' she said sarcastically. 'This is the first time I'm drinking something other than water or tea and you drink this regularly. I don't really want to seem like a pessimist, but I think I'm going to lose.'

The angry barman brought over another tray and dropped it on the other tray the previous barman had brought.

'Enjoy!' he said, impatiently. On the tray was a large bottle of wine, two glasses and a plate of meat and potatoes. There was also a complimentary gift on the tray for Athena – a transparent pen with flecks of Amber inside.

'You know what? Whoever wins gets this pen.' Malo said, a bit disappointed that Athena didn't want to play his game.

She nodded and leant back into her ripped cushion.

'What are you doing? We had a bet!' Malo said, rather irritated.

'Yes, but I'm going to lose anyway so-'

'Fine, I get it! Look on the bright side Malo, more for you!' he said to himself.

Athena laughed and watched Malo drink a whole bottle of wine.

She could tell from his very competitive attitude that he must have had a hard childhood. It was a way to survive. This must have been true if he chose to join the army at the age of nineteen. A wonderful trait for a soldier, of course. Athena watched him intently as he drank the rest of the wine from the bottle. Even though they were complete opposites, she very much enjoyed his pleasant company.

'And that, ladies and gentlemen, is how it's done around here!' Malo said, pleased with himself.

Athena smiled as she shook her head.

'You shouldn't be proud of that, Malo!'

They both laughed.

'I reward you with this pen.' Athena said in an accent as she handed the pen over to him.

Malo laughed even harder and held the pen up towards the ceiling and said, 'I will cherish this pen until it runs out of ink!'

He then dropped the pen and started to cry. Athena, completely taken aback, asked what was wrong.

'I was thrown out of the army and I have no idea where I am going now. I have nothing left! I don't know what to do with my life!'

Athena felt sorry for Malo, but couldn't help bite her lip to stop laughing out loud. To see a very strong soldier suddenly burst into tears was certainly a sight!

However, she looked at the facts. He was drunk, tired and wounded. His life, just like hers, had been turned upside down. She could understand to a certain extent how he was feeling.

Before she could say anything else, Malo was already on the floor, unconscious.

Athena sighed. She called one of the barmen and had him carry Malo to their room. She gave the bed to Malo and made herself comfortable on the floor nearby.

She blew out the candles placed around the room and curled up as she was quite cold. She was only wearing a light blue dress that came just above her knee. She wasn't upset though. Quite the opposite.

She quietly stood up after an hour and took away Malo's pillow, hoping that would quiet down his snoring, but it only made it worse.

Athena gave up. She put the pillow back and returned to the cool, wooden floor.

'Happy seventeenth birthday, Athena!' she whispered to herself. She never imagined that this was a situation she would find herself in, especially on her birthday.

It was how it was, and Athena knew this was where she was meant to be. She turned onto her side, tried her best to fall asleep and to ignore Malo's snoring.

IV

'Malo, wake up!' Athena whispered into Malo's ear.
No movement.

Athena sighed and gently hit him on his arm, but this only made his snoring even louder.

'Avran... wrong... kill... Oliver...Council...'

What were those words supposed to mean? Athena shuddered. She was a kind-hearted girl and couldn't bear the idea of seeing someone get killed. However, travelling with Malo at her side, she knew she was going to see it sooner rather than later.

Athena looked down to his face. He seemed so fragile, yet he was in the most dangerous and feared army of all the land.

She looked at his leg which was gradually healing. She couldn't help but get some fresh towels from the bathroom and clear away the dry blood from the wound.

Ever since she was a child, Athena always felt guilty if she didn't help someone or left an unwanted chore to somebody else. So, this felt natural to her.

Athena suddenly looked over at the door. She could hear a voice.

I can't believe it's before dawn and I have to start making breakfast for those ungrateful creatures who are our so-called 'guests'. I'm not paid well at all and I am treated dreadfully. I hate this. Why was I born into a family that runs an inn?

Athena stopped dabbing Malo's wounded leg and made her way to the door. She slowly bent down to look through the key hole, and sure enough, there was a young man holding a bucket of eggs. He suddenly turned towards the door and opened it.

Athena ended up bashing her head against the iron door handle as the young man opened it with such great force.

'I'm sorry, young lady. Are you alright?' he asked in such a way that it was obvious it was a rehearsed line. Though, seeing a girl get hit on the forehead with metal did make him feel a bit sympathetic.

'I'm fine. May I ask, was that you talking?' Athena asked, hoping he'd say he did.

'Excuse me? I didn't say a word out there. Apart from you and me, no one else is awake in this hell... I mean, in this inn. No one was talking. It was silent.'

Athena nodded. She knew it wouldn't be wise to repeat the same mistake she had made with the boy from the fields.

'My mistake.' she said, smiling.

The conversation was followed by an awkward silence. The young man decided to break it.

'How would you like your eggs? I'm about to start breakfast!'

'Um, is it possible to have them... cooked?' Athena asked, unable to comprehend his question.

The man snorted. 'Of course you can have them cooked. I'm asking how?'

Athena laughed nervously. Agatha had always been in charge with the cooking. Whenever Athena even came close to the stove, Agatha would chase away and tell her to play outside or to stay with Tomas. So, Athena had no idea what any method of cooking was called.

She knew that she wasn't stupid. Of course she wasn't stupid! She just had a lot to learn on how things worked in the "real" world.

'What do you recommend?'

The man smiled, still not daring to look her in the eyes. A guest had never asked for his own opinion, so he answered eagerly. 'I personally like them poached.'

'Then poached it is!' Athena said, smiling back.

The man smiled back and finally looked into her blue eyes for a while. He soon realised he was staring so he quickly looked away.

'I suppose I'll be going now to make your poached eggs.'

He quickly left the room, trying to hide his flushed cheeks. He walked down the wooden stairs and halted. He leant against the wall and realised something. He saw her eyes. He saw her *blue* eyes.

Athena got up from the floor and went back to the bed where Malo was still asleep, and continued to wipe the dry blood off his leg.

'Oh, Malo. Why won't you wake up? I want to go to the Naran Flame and find out more about my past.'

Malo continued to snore. Athena looked up, gazing at the wooden ceiling with a few spiders hanging from the bottom of their webs.

She tapped Malo on his cheek, but again, she had no success.

'Fine! I suppose I should just leave for the Four Flames now, should I?' she asked, raising her voice slightly.

Of course, she wouldn't leave without Malo… or at least without talking to him! So, she just waited in the corner of the room, thinking. She knew Malo needed his sleep, considering he was exhausted and badly injured. She was annoyed with herself in wanting him to wake up just so she could go on her adventure. She was buzzing on the inside though. She couldn't *wait* to get outside!

It was after half an hour that Athena's stomach started to rumble, so she headed downstairs for breakfast, glancing back at Malo before she quietly shut the door.

She walked down the creaking wooden stairs and arrived downstairs where the young man was holding two plates.

'I heard you leaving your room alone. I thought that maybe you would like to have your breakfast with me if… if that's alright with you?' he asked, shyly.

Athena looked down at the floor and looked back at him with a smile. 'Of course, how kind of you to offer.'

The young man smiled and led her towards a table near the window.

He pulled out a chair for her and she gracefully sat down, following his eyes until he sat down opposite to her.

'So, where are you heading to next?' the young man asked, staring back at her.

'Towards the Four Flames.' Athena answered whilst she picked up her fork.

The man nodded and then introduced himself.

'I'm Olimm, by the way. I believe you are Athena?' Olimm said
'How do you-'
'I heard you say "Happy Birthday" to yourself last night. By the way, I hope you had a nice birthday. Try this poached egg I cooked for you.' he told her.

Athena smiled and tried it. She felt like she was tasting dirty water with some salt, but in a solid form. She didn't want to tell Olimm this in case he would get offended, though she could only imagine what Agatha would say.

'Wow. Well, it's certainly interesting!' Athena told him with a big grin whilst holding her breath, so she couldn't get the taste anymore.

Olimm laughed and told her that was why it was his favourite.

'So, why do you want to go to the Four Flames anyway?' Olimm asked out of curiosity.

At first, Athena hesitated to tell him but then she decided that there would be no harm in telling him.

'I found out that my real parents live in the Four Flames. So, I am going to try and find them.'

'Do you have a guide of some sort? The Four Flames is very far way away and it is very easy to get lost. It seems like the countryside here goes on for eternity. Everything looks the same.'

'I don't really see it that way. I find that-'

Suddenly, a wild animal in the woodland close by was making a very loud low-pitched noise.

'What is that?' Athena asked completely stunned.

'You've never heard that before? Those animals are called Greliks. They live in the Forest Tatila. I don't know why this one is so far out. They often make a sound like that. It means they are happy. The opposite of that sound, which is high pitched, means it is lost or sad, or that they are communicating with the other Greliks. You do not want to be near a Grelik when it's lost because when they are nervous they eat, and they aren't exactly vegetarians.'

Athena's eyes widened.

'Right.' she said, her heart beating faster. 'What do they look like?'

'They vary in size. They can be small and reach your ankle or they can be enormous and be twice your size.'

'That it is quite a big difference. What colour are they?'

'They are...' he paused and laughed to himself. 'Actually, they can be adorable. They have short black fur, a very small tail, razor sharp white teeth and big green eyes. They have four legs, but they stand up, like you and me, when they come across humans. I must warn you that these creatures are extremely judgmental and they can also see you from a mile away.

They also have unique ears which are able to hear every thought in your mind. It is very important to think of positive thoughts, and you must *never*, under any circumstance, think about negative ideas. If you come up with images in your mind that they do not approve of, they will unfortunately yet inevitably kill you!'

Olimm paused for a second, shuddering at the very thought of being chewed up by a Grelik.

'Is it possible to get through the forest or woodlands without getting killed by Greliks?'

'Of course it is!' Olimm snapped back. 'Where do you think I got these eggs? A tree? No, it's easier for a Grelik to like you than to get a Grelik to hate you. All you have to do is please one and make them like you and then you are fine. They are all somehow connected. When they see a human, they just know if they have been approved by a Grelik. They would even offer you their services!'

Athena nodded and smiled. She was looking forward to meeting one of them. Maybe she would be able to hear *their* thoughts!

'Are there any other dangers in the forest?'

'Yes! Greliks would be the least of your problems. They only come out at night and at dawn. They only leave their den during the day if they feel disturbances around their territory. They are indeed very sophisticated, but like I said, they are the least of your worries. You should be worried about the Blucks from the Seven Hundred Army and the Chamcoks. They like to cause trouble and they occasionally come here for a drink – or ten!

You should really stay away from all the soldiers in the Forest Tatila as they will bring you nothing but trouble!' Olimm warned.

Athena nodded, taking a sip of her water. She asked Olimm more questions, in hope that it would give Malo time to wake up and come downstairs.

'Is there any other way to get to the Four Flames from here?'

Olimm stared at the volcano and Athena's eyes followed his.

'Is there really no other way? What about the Forest Tatila?' Athena asked, slightly anxious about having to climb a volcano.

'The forest is not here. What you see around you are the woods. Only after you have passed the two bridges will you see it. Anyway, I know it seems like difficult work climbing up and down a volcano, but it's the fastest way by far!'

She looked down at her empty plate. She could see some of the leftover water from the dish. She could suddenly remember the taste of those eggs. She tried her hardest not to vomit. Even though she hated the taste, she had finished her plate. She was always taught it was impolite and a waste if she didn't. However, for the first time, Athena was afraid that she would be re-served. So, she admired her fork instead.

Olimm could see Athena was distracted – strangely by the plate and fork – but he wanted to have her attention as he liked gazing and getting lost into her hypnotic eyes.

'Athena, if you like, I could accompany you to the Four Flames?' Olimm asked her in his sweetest voice.

Athena looked up at him and saw him smiling down at her. She laughed nervously as she wanted to be nice, but she didn't want to go with him. She barely knew anything about Olimm and she could feel something wasn't quite right with his intentions. He was being nice. Too nice.

Athena shuddered. 'Thanks Olimm, but I'm going to go there with Malo. I'm just waiting for him to wake up and then we'll go.'

Olimm's expression on his face changed. From smug to humiliated.

'Look, Athena, let me come with you. I can see you want to go straightaway. You're practically on the edge of your seat! You want to wait for Malo to wake up? Trust me, soldiers who come in and drink as much as your *Malo* did last night, don't wake up till the late afternoon. You'll have to wait for hours just to see him change position he's sleeping in. Here I am, offering you to leave now so *you* can get to the Four Flames faster! I'm only thinking of you.' Olimm said. Though he tried to say all this with sensitivity, Athena was not blinded by the forcefulness in which he was saying it with.

She could hear the conversation she had with Malo in her head.

So what if I can't tell what danger is? It isn't like I'm going to run into trouble anytime soon, is it?

The irony was enough to make Athena violently bury her head in her hands. There was no way she could get out of this. She could either walk out with Olimm or be dragged out. He wanted something from her. She just didn't know what. Well, she couldn't *hear* what! The only way out of this was with Malo's assistance.

'Sure, you can come with me. Let me go and tell my friend upstairs,' she said, getting up.

Olimm, who was closer to the stairs, rapidly walked to the narrow staircase and blocked the passage.

Athena was looking down at the ground, making sure she hadn't dropped anything onto the floor suddenly looked up to see Olimm blocking the staircase.

She smiled and asked, 'Can I go upstairs?'

Olimm shook his head. 'It would be wiser to leave straight away. I don't like wasting time.'

'Okay, but I must go to the restroom which is upstairs.'

Olimm sighed and unwillingly let her pass. He watched her go up the creaking stairway.

He knew that Athena was an Agalit. He knew it since the day before, as word had gone out that there was an Agalit close by.

He knew that if he ever encountered an Agalit, he would be free from financial problems for the rest of his life. The Seven Hundred Army had been asking for Agalits for years now. Olimm remembered exactly what was written on the posters, placed around Oakrose:

Agalits wanted. If you see an Agalit, bind their eyes, ears and hands. In this way they cannot use their power. Reward is two thousand rubies.

Olimm smiled. He would have no trouble bringing Athena to the army's headquarters as it was en route to the Four Flames. She wouldn't even see it coming as the headquarters were underground.

His smile widened, knowing that he would never come back to this god forsaken place. He would have enough money to change his life. There was only one problem: which of the two bridges would he choose when the time comes?

Meanwhile, Athena looked back downstairs making sure that Olimm wasn't following her with his eyes. She nodded to herself when she saw he was facing the opposite way. She quickly crept into her room and saw Malo sleeping, rolled over on his back with his mouth open. Athena shook him very violently and whispered as loud as she could to wake him up.

No movement.

Athena sighed. She suddenly heard Olimm's thoughts from downstairs and understood his plan for her. She knew Malo would easily defeat Olimm, even in his wounded state. All he had to do was wake up.

Athena could feel her heart racing as she realised Malo was in such a deep sleep. Nothing she could do would wake him up.

She suddenly had an idea. She took Malo's pen, which she found on the floor, and wrote a message on his arm.

Olimm came into the room and took Athena by the wrist.

V

Malo suddenly woke up, panting and sweating from his flashbacks of his torture. He calmed himself down by taking deep breaths, and took a minute to realise where he was.

He looked around for Athena and even went down the stairs, limping, to try and find her. There was no sign of her anywhere.

He crawled back into his bed and laid there with his arms behind his head.

'Oh, dear Athena, I could have sworn you were real! I remember you so clearly, but it seems as though you've just vanished into thin air.'

Malo sighed and closed his eyes, trying to remember everything he could from the night before. He remembered Athena's laughter and how he had spat beer twice in her face.

This made Malo chuckle a little, but he quickly stopped as his leg was aching. He looked down at his wound and saw it was slightly moist.

He then saw damp towels on the other side of the bed. He picked them up, smelled them and recognised her scent.

'Where are you, Athena?' he mumbled to himself. Malo continued to look around the room to see if there were clues as to where she might have vanished or rushed to. He checked all the cabinets in the room and then finally saw a huge mirror on the table, leaning against the wooden wall.

Malo sighed and saw his reflection. His hair was all over the place and his shirt was torn. He finally noticed the message Athena had left on his arm.

He touched his arm while staring at his reflection and then quickly looked down to read the message.

Olimm is taking me to the Seven Hundred Army. We are going to go over the volcano and continue till we get there. Please hurry!

Malo read it over and over again until he memorised it. He quickly looked out of the window to see if there was any sign of Athena or this Olimm.

There wasn't.

Malo felt a rush of panic and checked he had his sword on him. He rushed downstairs and grabbed a bottle of beer on his way out.

Practically breaking the door down, he hurried to the volcano, drinking the beer.

Athena was staring at the ground, counting as many red pebbles as she could since they began to climb up the volcano. They had passed the crater and were now on their way down.

'Three hundred and thirteen…three hundred and fourteen and guess what? Three hundred and fifteen!' Athena chanted to herself. Olimm was staring at her. He wasn't sure what her gift was, but he would have to find out before they reached the headquarters.

Athena, hearing these thoughts, shuddered, but made sure she didn't give anything away. She continued counting.

'Three hundred and seventeen…three hundred and nineteen…'

'You do realise you miscounted?' Olimm told her, unimpressed.

'I know. I just wanted to make sure that you were listening. I'm a bit exhausted. Can we please rest for a while?' she asked, yawning, trying to give Malo the time he needed to catch up with them.

Olimm sighed and carefully examined Athena, making sure that she really *was* exhausted. Although Athena wanted to stop because of Malo, she was actually tired and the dark rings around her eyes justified that.

Olimm cleared his throat and told her that she could rest for a few minutes, but to spend those minutes wisely.

Athena sat down next to a small grey boulder right next to pebble three hundred and seventeen. She rested her head between her hands and inhaled deeply a few times, trying to convince herself that Malo would come.

Olimm stared down at the back of Athena's head. He wondered how he was going to find out her gift. He didn't want to be stern with her because he rather liked her.

Olimm groaned with frustration.

He didn't want to be mean to her, but if he carried on being nice, she would never reveal her gift and he would continue to live in poverty for the rest of his life.

He asked himself, if he were to be nice to her and gain her trust, then maybe she would tell him?

This was good enough for him.

'Athena, do you want to stay here for a little while longer?' he asked in a soothing voice.

'Yes!' she replied immediately.

Olimm smiled and sat next to her on the rock. 'So, you are obviously not a big fan of walking.'

Athena laughed but didn't reply as she looked around to stare at the view of the countryside.

Olimm saw her gazing at the view, so he decided to comment on it too, hoping to gain her approval.

'Oakrose is such a beautiful county. From those two bridges, past the inn and the four big hills and miles and miles of plain fields, it's the most uncultivated county of the lands. Did you know that? It's also the calmest county with no crime. Did you know that too? Also, we're in the poorest county with very few people living here, so everything is cheaper. That's why the soldiers from the army come as often as they can. It's a long way from the headquarters, but they get a few days off here and there. It's ironic, isn't it? That the poorest county is right next to richest county, Tatila. They have the forest, the Four Flames...'

Olimm was going to continue talking about the army but he was scared it would alarm Athena.

'Have you ever travelled?'

'No, unfortunately, I haven't. I've never even seen the sea!'

'Really? Once my grandparents came and brought me on a little tour around the lands. We went through Tatila into Clandon. At the far end of that county is the sea. The green grass gradually turns into white sand. It's amazing and the sea is crystal clear. Such a pure, light blue colour. Like your eyes!'

Athena gulped. Olimm felt a bead of sweat trickle down his neck. He was doing so well. He needed to carry on.

'But the water is freezing. Instead of going South to the Lowlands, we went North to the-'

'Highlands.' Athena finished for him.

Olimm pouted and looked away. That obviously hadn't gone according to plan. She wasn't yet charmed by his travelling story with his grandparents. He continued anyway. He needed to gain her trust.

'Do you know anything about the Lowlands?' he asked with a big smile.

Athena shook her head.

'The Lowlands begins as fields along the border of Oakrose, Tatila and Clandon, but then the ground slowly turns into brown soil and then there are huge mountains bordering the coast. It's a natural barrier from the other lands across the sea. In fact, the Lowlands is the most populated area of Fairoses after Tatila. It's where most of the food comes from. The soil there is so fertile that the crops grow even during the winter! Did you know that?'

'I heard about it. My father used to tell me stories and myths of the lands. Apparently the mountains in the Lowlands are so diverse that each one serve a unique purpose. I heard one mountain produces potatoes.'

'Exactly! The farmers there are very organised and efficient with their land. They know that each mountain has its own magical uses as well. So, they also produce special herbs that cure many diseases. There's one called Boldo, another called…'

Olimm continued talking, but Athena suddenly thought of Tomas the moment he spoke of diseases. She knew Tomas and Agatha would be angry with her if she didn't go to the Four Flames, but a small part of her wanted to change route and go down to the Lowlands to find a herb that would help her father. She wanted to find a herb that would bring him back to the time he was able to walk with her further into Oakrose. It was there that he would teach her about the different types of plants and herbs, the different species of birds and animals and many other things. They would spend hours together, walking for miles in the deep countryside and Tomas would tell her stories and myths. He would teach her about history and geography and as much as he could about other things. He devoted as much time as he could into teaching her everything he knew.

Athena knew most of the things Olimm had just said. Tomas told her so much about Fairoses, though he would always speak in vague detail about Tatila. Now, she knew why. He was worried that she would one day figure out it was the place she came from.

Olimm could see Athena was no longer listening to him. He stopped talking and drummed his fingers against his lips. It was best that he stopped talking about this. Athena could ask where he learnt this information and he didn't want to tell her that it was from the soldiers coming to the inn, giving him this knowledge. Why did everything lead back to the army?

'What to do next?' Olimm mumbled to himself extremely quietly.

'What was that?'

'Nothing. I just want to keep you entertained.'

Athena subtly rolled her eyes knowing that was a lie. She could feel a part of him was genuinely enjoying their conversation, but she couldn't stop reminding herself that he was just trying to make her reveal her power.

She clearly has no experience in life. Poor little duckling! For someone who hasn't travelled, she seems to know a bit. Or maybe... she can teleport. Maybe she has gone straight to these places without the travelling part. Or maybe she just read these things and she learns very fast. She's not giving anything away!

Athena laughed on the inside. He did, however, raise a valid point. Learning things extremely quickly was a strand from her power of hearing people's thoughts.

She turned around and looked at the top of the volcano, hoping to see Malo arrive in order to save her.

Olimm, watching every movement Athena took, saw she was staring at the top of the volcano.

'Are you wondering how you were able to climb up and down a volcano? Was it just me or did you find it harder going down?' Olimm asked, trying to start a new conversation.

'It was harder to go down, but could we stay quiet? My head has one too many thoughts.' Athena quickly said, still staring at the tip of the volcano.

In actual fact, she just really wanted to see if she could pick up some of Malo thoughts as she could somehow sense his arrival. However, with her intense concentration, she couldn't help but pick up on a few more of Olimm's thoughts.

Malo was already halfway up the volcano. He felt more pain in his bleeding leg with every step. He tried his best to ignore the pain and think of Athena who needed his help.

After a while, he reached the top of the volcano. He had difficulty breathing, and soon he fell to the ground. He looked at what damage the walking and running had done to his leg. It was bleeding. A lot.

'I swear it's more injured now than when I was actually being tortured. The things I'm doing for this girl!' Malo said as he tutted.

Suddenly, Athena could hear Malo's voice from afar and she shifted her body position upright. Olimm noticed this and realised that she could sense something. It was presumably something she figured out due to her gift, so he decided it was time to carry on.

'Come, Athena, we must leave now. We have stayed here for too long.'

Athena suddenly let out a yelp and exclaimed, 'I think I twisted my ankle! Could you help fix it?'

Olimm immediately walked towards her and cleared his throat. 'How can I help fix it?'

'Just press around my ankle and see if you can feel anything out of place.'

Olimm nervously bent down and took her ankle into his hands. He didn't want to press too hard in case he made the pain worse.

Just then, Malo came into view and waved at Athena. She smiled and told him to hurry down, using one arm to help express herself. Olimm looked up at her. She suddenly put her arm around her ear.

'I thought there was a bee in my ear. My mistake. Please continue!'

Olimm smiled curiously at her and then looked back down at her ankle. Malo took the opportunity of the steep descent to skid down, making it quicker and less painful to get to Athena. Of course, this created a huge cloud of red dust.

Olimm heard this and turned around, but before he could see anything, Athena held his shoulder and made him look at her.

'It hurts! Make it better!' she quivered.

He looked into her blue eyes for a moment and then immediately went back to business. Athena turned away smiling. She knew she was a terrible liar but every time she was actually able to fool someone, she couldn't help but smile.

She subtly looked up to see where Malo was. He had silently crept around Olimm and was ready to attack. Athena's eyes widened. Even though she wasn't so keen on Olimm, she still didn't want him to get hurt. She just wanted him to leave her alone.

Malo looked up at her and she gently shook her head, telling him not to hurt Olimm. He mouthed to her that he wasn't going to kill Olimm but just knock him out. He did this by silently flicking his forehead, rolling his eyes back and pretending to fall back.

Athena looked away and squinted her eyes. Before Olimm could even touch her face to comfort her, he was already knocked out by the pommel of Malo's sword.

I will have my revenge on you, Athena.

Athena felt Olimm's hand let go of her ankle. She quickly got up and shuddered.

'Malo, what happens if he wakes up and kills us?' she asked, her voice trembling.

'Yesterday, you didn't know what danger was and now, all of a sudden, you think everyone is going to kill you? Let's not jump to rash conclusions, dear Athena!'

She remained silent until Malo answered her question. He rolled his eyes and smiled as he took out a glass vial, shaped like a thunder bolt, from a chain he wore around his neck. Inside the vial was a pale yellow potion. Malo placed a droplet into Olimm's mouth.

'Is that poison?' Athena asked, almost too afraid to know the answer.

'Not exactly. It's a type of sleeping potion. It will keep him unconscious for a week. That will give us enough time to get away. If you want me to kill him, then all I have to do is add two more drops and that's it!' Malo said. He added in a diabolical voice. 'Bye-bye Olimm!'

Athena replied "no" in a very soft voice.

'Good, that's what I thought,' Malo replied.

He looked around and then asked, 'Now, dear Athena, what's the plan?'

'The plan, Malo, is...' Athena began but was too distracted by Olimm's unconscious body lying on the ground.

'The plan is to head towards the Four Flames.' she finished.

Malo nodded.

'And what exactly do you intend to do there?' he asked, knowing the answer, but was subtly giving himself more time to recover. The pain from his leg was becoming unbearable.

'I *intend* to find out who my parents were or are and find out if I have any brothers or sisters,' Athena answered.

She sighed and looked up. The sky was rather grey and she knew it would soon start to rain. She looked down at Malo who was breathing heavily, even though he was resting against the rock.

'Malo, are you alright?'

After a while, he took his hands off his bleeding leg.

'I'm fine. I think I opened up my wound again, but it's bleeding more this time.'

Athena walked back towards him and bent down to take a look at his leg.

She lifted up the torn piece of Malo's trousers covering his wound and sure enough, he was right. The wound had doubled in size.

'What on earth did you do for it to get to that size?' she asked, stunned.

'Well, let's see! I woke up this morning and couldn't find you. So, I looked around the whole inn. That also somehow involved me barging into the women's bathroom. I don't think I ever had such a loud wakeup call,' Malo said in a very amused voice which made Athena chuckle.

'I then went back to the bedroom, laid on the bed and found damp towels. I suppose it was you who used them to help my leg get better?'

'It was. I could see your leg needed a clean. There wasn't much else to do anyway...'

'Didn't you sleep?'

Athena laughed. 'You were snoring so loudly, it was quite hard to -'

'When I snore, throw cold water on me. That usually does the trick!'

'Excuse me?'

He looked at Athena, grinning.

'Yes. You throw the water on me, I wake up a bit, shake a little and then I stop snoring. I don't know why, but it just works.'

'But... but that's how you wake up pigs!'

Malo burst out laughing. 'It is! I didn't think of that. Well, dear Athena, imagine I'm a snoring pig and then you won't feel bad when you throw water on me.'

'Your words, not mine.'

'Actually, did you know that a pigs pregnancy lasts three months, three weeks and three days? It's so easy to remember.'

Athena gave him a cheeky smile. 'Don't you mean a sow?'

Malo squinted his eyes and cleared his throat.

'Touché! Well, anyway, back to the story. I went into the room and I started to look around for clues as to where you might have gone. I finally looked in the mirror and I saw you wrote a small note on my arm,' he said, pointing at the fading note on his arm.

'There was no paper and I knew that Olimm would enter the room any moment, and I noticed that silly pen on the floor and-'

'Hey,' Malo said, taking out the pen of his pocket.

'This pen literally just saved your life! It is *not* a silly pen. I won it fair and square!' he said, now serious.

Athena looked away and told herself, 'The pen is really mine.'

Malo, hearing these words, looked at Athena and cleared his throat.

'Alright, alright. Since it was originally a gift for you, it can be *our* pen!' Malo settled.

'Stop, you're being too generous!'

'In case one of us ever dies this could be a sweet memory for the person who stays alive,' he said.

Athena looked at him in disgust yet remained silent.

'What?' Malo asked, utterly confused.

'You shouldn't joke about that. What happens if one of us really does die? And all we have as a solid memory is a *bloody* pen?' she asked. She shocked herself by speaking just like Agatha.

Malo tucked the pen into her bag and then gave her a hug.

'It's okay. I promise I won't use it to graffiti your tombstone when the time comes.'

Athena gave him an unimpressed look. He winked at her and then started to slowly walk down.

He looked back at her, offered her his hand. 'Shall we start our adventure?'

VI

Malo and Athena had been walking for two days now. They were going at a very slow pace for the sake of Malo's wounded leg. Athena would also keep finding interesting things around her and then give Malo a long speech about the object in question, finished by a story from when she was younger. They also passed the time by sharing jokes and stories about their past.

Malo had described his life in the army while Athena was describing her life back in Oakrose where she was sealed off from the rest of the world.

He described how many drinking contests he had, while she counted the number of stars in the sky every night. He told her how he was trained in the army to shoot animals, whereas Athena told him that she helped animals deliver their offspring.

'We're so different in so many ways.' Athena stated.

'You know what? You may be just right! I mean, you're a girl and I'm a boy.'

'That's not what I meant but well noticed! I mean, you are trained to kill animals where as I help them come into the world.'

'It's almost as if you were supplying us with all these animals to kill!' Malo replied, looking over at Athena with a cheeky grin. Athena, however, was not amused and didn't answer.

'It's different. You *want* to help the animals, I *have* to kill the animals,' he responded in his defence.

'You don't *have* to do anything. In this subject you don't *have* to kill animals!' Athena said.

Malo laughed.

'That's not entirely true. The Seven Hundred Army is completely different to how you picture the world. The world isn't perfect you know, dear Athena! Things are born, things are killed. It's just the way life goes.' Malo told her. 'The circle of life.'

'It doesn't matter. Since you are no longer in the Seven Hundred Army anymore, you don't have to kill anything!'

He groaned.

'Are you alright? Does your leg hurt again? We can stop here if you want?'

'It's not my leg, but thanks for reminding me! No, I was groaning because if I don't kill an animal, then we won't have dinner and *no way* am I missing dinner!' Malo whined.

'We've survived the last few days on mushrooms and bread, we can manage a few more days on what we have left.' Athena said, looking through her bag to see how much food was left.

'We've survived the last few days on *disgusting* mushrooms which taste like fish and stale *black* bread!' Malo replied, correcting her.

Athena felt her stomach grumble and as soon as Malo heard it, he made it clear that they wouldn't walk any further for the day. All they had to do was find a place to rest and eat for the evening.

It took them a while to find shelter far off the main path, but after a long search, Athena could see a small cave with large bushes surrounding it.

'Okay, let's leave our things in there and then head off to find ourselves a nice meaty dinner!' Malo announced, salivating at the thought of having something other than mushrooms and stale bread.

Athena, who was still discontent about his decision, decided to stay quiet. She wasn't against eating animals, but she just didn't want to be a part of their death. She was taught to eat them once they had died of natural causes. They both knew that she wasn't keen on the idea, but she would never win the argument against a hungry, stubborn soldier! Besides, she was too hungry herself to argue.

They reached the entrance of the cave and had a look around to make sure it was safe. Malo noticed that there were some Rects in the dark cave but thought it wise not to tell Athena...just yet!

They left their belongings in the cave and began to start their hunt with Malo leading the way.

They walked in silence for a few minutes. They were both hungry and tired. All they could think about was finding food. They had no luck at first, but Malo didn't want to give up or complain. Instead, he just took a deep breath and looked up at the sky. It was beautiful. The top part was clear blue, yet the lower part was of a darker shade. The sun was in between the two shades of blue and it would soon set behind the hills and volcano.

'Hey, look up at the sky! Isn't it incredible?' Malo asked, still gazing in admiration. It had been a few years since he was able to look at the sky whenever he wanted, as the Seven Hundred Army headquarters were based underground. The only time he could see the sky was when he was in the training arena and there, you practiced your sword fighting. Gazing at the sky would have proven difficult while fighting in single combat.

This world is so beautiful.

Athena smiled at his thought. She didn't need to look up, even though she did. She had spent more than a decade in the fields and always laid beneath the huge tree, full of pink flowers to give her some shade. With the small brooke nearby, silently flowing through and changing the direction of the leaves from the willow trees, it was certainly her paradise. She would also always look up at the sky and watch the sunset in the summer. Only once the stars had been out for hours would Athena go back home.

She suddenly felt homesick, with sudden memories rushing to her head about her folks; Agatha and Tomas.

She took several deep breath to calm herself down. She had Malo now, and until she met her real family, he was her family.

'Why don't we go near the small lake we walked by not long ago? It might be easier to catch an animal.' he suggested.

'If we are going to a lake, why don't we just eat fish?'

'No way! We've been eating your way the last few days. Now, we are going to eat *my* way. I don't eat fish. I eat *real* meat like a man!'

'Like a *real* man!' he repeated as he turned to her and kissed his biceps.

Athena couldn't help but laugh. At the exact moment he turned to her, a deer ran by.

'Well, real man, you just missed a deer! It was behind you.'

Malo suddenly turned around. He managed to see which direction it went and ran after it, ignoring the pain from his leg. He wanted dinner and he wanted it now!

Athena went to collect enormous lily pads from the lake (so they had something to eat the deer on) while Malo was busy chasing the deer. She began to walk back to the cave when she heard Malo shout out her name several times.

Athena immediately placed the lily pads on the floor and ran back to the place where they originally separated.

She looked in all directions, but there was still no sign of Malo.

'Malo! Where are you? Are you okay?'

He didn't answer so Athena closed her eyes and concentrated very hard to hear his thoughts.

Boy, oh boy. Athena's going to get one huge shock. I'll creep up behind her and when she least expects it, I'll go 'boo' and she'll scream!

Athena, hearing this, sniggered, but then quickly stopped as she could vaguely hear Malo's footsteps. She stood still and waited for him to come closer.

Malo was looking down on the ground and making sure that he wasn't going to tread on any leaves in case it would make a sound.

Just as he was about to come out and yell "boo" at Athena, she turned around and screamed at him first. He fell over from the shock.

Athena started laughing at him. He also laughed a little, but was freaked out by the small insects creeping up both his legs.

'It's these stupid piro leaves. They gave me away!'

'Aww, don't blame the leaves.'

'I do! Piro leaves are so fragile that whenever you get close to one, they break, making a stupid noise.'

'Maybe you just have to be delicate when you touch them.'

Athena bent down and helped Malo up as he very carefully picked up a piro leaf.

'For you!' he said putting it in Athena's palm, gently closing her hand around it. She smiled.

'Every time you see a piro leaf, you have to remember me. Promise?'

Athena looked him in the eyes and nodded. She opened her palm and looked at the leaf. It had four petals, two of which were half the size of the others, creating a design of perfect symmetry.

'So, where's the deer?'

'I put it on a hanging branch on a tree over there, to protect it from the insects.' Malo explained, still trying to wipe insects off his torn trousers.

'I'm impressed that you got that deer up so high!'

'Excuse me, did you not see my muscles earlier?'

He was about to make her feel his biceps when she told him, 'Okay, let's get that deer down and head back to the cave!'

Malo walked to the tree and got the deer down by using a thick stick to poke it until it fell off the other side.

Athena watched the dead deer fall down right in front of her. Immediately after it fell, a few twigs and leaves fell on her head. Malo pointed at her and laughed. 'Your punishment for thinking I'm weak.'

Malo placed the deer on his shoulders and walked back to the cave, giving Athena a big tap on the back as he walked past. His strong tap made most of the twigs and leaves fall off her.

'Still think I'm weak?' he asked, winking.

Athena nervously laughed. 'Are you going to keep proving that you're strong until you punch me or something?'

'Expect the unexpected.' he called out as he strode ahead.

Athena stood still. Expect the unexpected. It made her think of her gift and how she could sometimes hear his thoughts. So, she would be expecting what he thought was unexpected.

Maybe he would then figure out her gift. Perhaps he already knew?

Athena began to feel dizzy from the anxiety this was causing her. What also caused her anxiety was the fact that she couldn't control her gift. If she concentrated very hard, then sometimes it would work. However, if this gift was supposed to be a part of her, then it should come more naturally.

'ATHENA!'

'I'm coming!'

Athena quickly made her way to the cave and saw the deer placed on a rock by the entrance. She went in to find Malo, and walked past the glowing Rects. She looked at them closely and saw the veins in their two wings were actually producing all this light. The animals were black, so they camouflaged with the darkness, making the light look like glowing patterns on the wall from afar.

'You are all actually beautiful.' she said as she looked at them with admiration.

'Athena, come here!' Malo said in a very serious tone.

She went deeper into the cave and saw him stare at an inscription written on the wall.

'Can you understand this?' he asked.

Athena studied the inscription and touched it softly.

'It looks as though a young child wrote it.'

'That would make sense,' Malo whispered back as he pointed to a small hand print next to the inscription.

Athena touched the writing. 'What sort of material is this? I've never come across it before.'

'Yoliytu. It's a specific type of red charcoal. It's only found in the Highlands.' he replied as he touched the material too.

'It's only used by the Striberosse.' he said as he left. Athena followed him out of the cave, afraid of staying alone in there.

Malo collected bark and twigs. He then started a fire by quickly and violently swiping a stick across his stubble.

'Doesn't that hurt?'

Malo looked at her with a serious face and shook his head.

'Why aren't you talking? You seem rather angry.' Athena noticed.

Malo continued to stare at her and finally answered back. 'It was the Striberosse who tortured and slaughtered my parents.'

Athena held his hand. 'I'm so sorry.'

'It happened when I was a boy. One day, my family and I were just playing games in the fields not far from here. It was the worst day of my life. I didn't even recognise the fields as we walked here. I blocked this whole place out of my mind.'

He paused and closed his eyes.

'While we were in the middle of playing a game, those monsters just came, tied us up and brought us to their camp. They sat me down on a rock and made me watch my parents die.'

Malo took a deep breath.

'They got my mother first and cut off all her hair with a long knife. Then, with that same knife, they slashed her shoulders and face. How they massacred her face, I...'

Malo's voice cracked and his lips trembled uncontrollably. He looked away as he wiped his tears from his cheeks.

Athena let go of his hand and walked to the other side to see his face and begged him to continue, but Malo no longer wanted to talk. He found it too hard.

He stood up and dragged the deer next to the fire. Athena watched him slice the deer open and cut out two large parts with a knife he carried on his belt next to his sword.

Malo then found three large sticks. He stuck two of them upright, parallel to one another, and violently stuck the third one in between them above the fire.

Athena took out the lily pads and Malo placed the cooked meat on them.

He let her choose which piece she wanted and then they ate in silence.

After they finished, Malo said he was so tired that he wanted to go to sleep as soon as he could. Athena whispered goodnight and turned around. She wanted Malo to have other thoughts that didn't just include the deer.

I really want to tell her more. I've never actually told anyone about this, but in the army they used to say, it's better to let it out than in... well, in most cases!

Hearing this made Athena smile. She felt her arm go numb as she was leaning her head on it, so she turned over and faced him.

'Malo, please continue your story. I really want to know what happened.'

Malo looked down and tried to continue the story, but just thinking about it made his lips tremble again.

Once again, Athena leant over to him and held his hand. Malo looked down at her blue eyes and with the fire's flame reflecting off them, it really helped him remember what happened that tragic day.

'After they slaughtered my mother, they moved on to my father. My father was in shock. He couldn't move. He just watched his pregnant wife die in front of him. She was six months pregnant, by the way. It made things even more tragic.'

Malo paused, took a deep breath and suddenly tightened his grip on Athena's hand. After a while, she couldn't take the pain anymore and took her hand out of his.

'Ouch, Malo!' she whispered, massaging her hand.

Malo stared at her and then looked away, yet he still continued his story. 'They pushed my father up against the tree that my mother was laying by, and tied him to it with his front facing the trunk of the tree. They grabbed their knives and all started stabbing him numerous times.'

Athena gasped in horror.

'But my father had the heart of a lion and survived that part. The next part he didn't. They handled two Greliks and blind-folded them. Greliks are nice creatures generally, but they were in a frenzy. So, they used all their anger and strength against my father who didn't know what was going on.'

Athena suddenly felt sick. How could such events happen in such a peaceful place? The Striberosse sounded incredibly dangerous and if it was really them that made those markings at the back of the cave, then perhaps they were close by.

'Those monsters!' she said, outraged.

'Monsters is an understatement. These men are just about ready to kill anything. They are probably nearby as well.'

'Okay, Malo, I really don't think I can sleep now!'

'Why? If you think they're going to kill you, then you're wrong. They have this policy, you see, that forbids them from killing the young as they are the future generation! That's why they didn't kill me when they killed my parents.'

Athena turned back the other way and rested her head on her hand, her eyes still wide open.

'Well, for what it's worth, I am glad you are alive. It means you are destined for something big if you survived that.' she said as she held his hand for a moment before withdrawing it.

'Malo, are you still awake?' she whispered after a while.

He suddenly snored very loudly. It was his way of saying he wasn't in the mood to talk.

Athena sighed. She couldn't sleep, so she decided to go to the back of the cave to take another look at the inscription.

As she made her way into the cave, huge bright lights were suddenly produced by the Rects' wings. At first, they caught her by surprise, but then she realised she felt safer with them around, even if their beady black eyes did make her feel a bit uneasy.

Athena reached the inscription and studied it very carefully. She realised that, although the writing was written by a child, it was quite high up. Even Athena wouldn't be able to write that high.

She looked around the cave to see if there as anything that she could step on to get a closer look at the engraving.

'Wait a minute!' Athena told herself. She looked through her bag for the pen. Athena then grabbed a long and flat stone from the ground and then copied down the inscription onto the rock.

A Rect also followed her which was rather ideal for Athena as she needed some source of light. She let the Rect rest on her shoulder as she read her copy of the text.

After a while, she finally understood one thing. This was not written by only one child.

'Rise and shine, dear Athena! Athena, Athena, Athena. ATHENA!' Malo yelled into her ear, yelling louder and louder every time.

'O... Okay... OKAY I'M UP! Malo stop, that really hurts,' Athena said, grasping hold of her ear.

'Oh no! Your ear isn't going to bruise, is it?'

Athena got up and walked over to Malo who now had his back to her.

She crept up to him and pinched his waist making him jump a few inches off the ground.

'Ouch! That hurts!'

Athena smiled and replied, 'Oh no! You're not going to bruise, are you?'

'Very funny!' Malo replied, rolling his eyes.

Athena was about to reply, but then she could sense something was coming towards them. It was coming from behind.

Malo thought he hurt Athena's feeling as she didn't answer back at him and she turned around.

'Athena, I was only joking. Please don't...cry?' he said, not knowing how to end his sentence.

'Athena, ple—'

'Ssshhh!' Athena hissed back at him.

She grabbed hold of him by his tunic and dragged him behind the nearest bush with great difficulty.

'What on earth are you doing?'

'People are coming and I can hear that they don't have good intentions.' Athena blurted out.

Malo was unable to speak, making weird faces but then was able to say, '*How* do you even know that?'

'I'm an Agalit.' she told him impatiently, now able to feel the vibrations coming from the horses.

'Well, I know that! Ever since I saw your eyes. So, that's your power; to hear people's thoughts?'

'Yes.' Athena whispered.

'You do know that hundreds of people are looking for you?!'

'I know!' she whispered, seeing the men on horseback come closer to them. 'They're here.'

'What are they thinking?' Malo asked, looking straight at her.

'They're going to perform sacrifices here. Like your parents. The Striberosse. They're here,' she whispered, unable to hide her fear. Not for her, but for their chosen victims.

Athena pushed him down and dropped to the ground too.

Don't move, dear Athena.

They both suddenly felt a huge thud on the ground, followed by high-pitched screams.

'No, please don't kill her. SHE IS MY WIFE!' a man was yelling. It was impossible to not hear the sound of desperation in his voice.

'I don't care! You're going to die too! I'm doing her a favour. She's not going to watch you die, so stop complaining,' a Striberosse yelled back.

'SHE IS MY WIFE AND SHE IS CARRYING MY CHILD!'

A tear fell down Athena's cheek. Malo saw this and felt the same way. Neither of them could see what was happening, but they didn't need to. This was an exact repetition of what happened many years ago to his parents. He was unable to do anything about it back then. However, now he could!

Malo turned around and past the twigs and leaves, he saw the man's wife tied to a tree. Her husband was held back by two soldiers, and a young girl was tied to a rock, forced to watch her parents suffer and die.

Athena, I'm going to help that family. Don't speak, move or do anything. Just stay there!

Athena obeyed. She knew that he would be able to stop them and that he needed to do this in order to gain some inner peace.

Malo silently got his sword in his hand, ready to fight.

He took a deep breath and quickly rose from the ground, making as little sound as possible. He crept around the whole scene and went behind both soldiers who were holding the man back. Malo firmly gripped his sword and stabbed one soldier in the neck.

The soldier let out a cry, but Malo covered his mouth until he fell to the dusty ground. The other soldier, seeing this, let go of the man to help his comrade, but Malo also stabbed the soldier in his neck once, killing him instantly.

Meanwhile, the man ran to his daughter and untied the rope and quietly told her to hide in the woods, and to only come out when he called her.

This made Athena smile, knowing that at least the daughter was safe.

Malo signalled the father to come towards him and the man obeyed. Malo picked up a sword that fell from one of the soldiers and handed it over.

He pointed to the three other soldiers who were harassing the mother. Malo whispered to the husband to kill the furthest one to the left.

The man nodded and slowly crept up on the soldier who was laughing and insulting his wife. This angered him so much that he stabbed the soldier in the neck until he fell to the ground. The soldier next to him drew his sword out and started to fight the man.

At the same moment, Malo became his victim's shadow. However, unlike his comrade, this soldier turned around and stabbed Malo in the arm.

Athena shuddered. She could tell that particular soldier was the leader. He had the power and strength to kill Malo, so she quickly got up and ran towards him.

'Oh no!' Malo said as he saw Athena running towards him.

The soldier followed Malo's eyes and saw Athena. He smiled and drew back his sword.

'Well, hello there, sweet cheeks. How are you on this fine day?' the soldier asked in a sweet voice.

Malo sniggered. He couldn't believe that the soldier was actually *flirting* with Athena.

'Hello, I'm lost and I noticed that you seem to...' Athena suddenly stopped and stared at the scared woman tied to the tree.

'Jolie?' she asked in amazement, pretending to know the woman. Athena quickly ran to her and hugged her.

Both the soldier and the father who were fighting each other suddenly stopped, very confused.

Malo seized the opportunity and got a hold of his sword and stabbed the soldier in the leg.

The husband, seeing this, followed Malo's example and stabbed the other soldier in the stomach. He fell to the ground, shaking. His death was going to be a long and painful one. The husband had no military training, but his will to protect and save his family made him even more ruthless than the Striberosse.

'I'm here to save you! Your daughter is in the woods. Go to her!' Athena whispered to the woman and quickly untied the rope. She pushed the woman in the right direction. As she passed her husband, he picked her up and embraced her tightly.

'Aurore, you can come out now. It's safe!'

The young girl emerged from the forest.

'I thought they were going to kill you!' she told her parents as she ran towards them. She hugged her mother.

'I really thought they were going to kill you!' Aurore told her mother with tears falling down her cheeks.

'It's alright, sweetheart. It's alright.' the mother gently told Aurore, stroking her hair.

Everyone suddenly turned around as they heard a shriek from the last remaining soldier that Malo was strangling.

Athena ran to them and kneeled next to Malo.

'He's the one who killed my parents. I recognise him. The scar on his cheek was given to him by my father. When they grabbed us in the fields, my father grabbed his knife and slashed this hooligan across the face.' Malo growled, tightening his grip.

Athena looked at him in the eyes.

'Do you really want to kill him? Or do you want to have answers?' she softly asked.

Malo very slowly loosened his grip.

'What's your name?' he asked harshly.

'Hister, sir.' the soldier croaked.

'You were the one who killed my parents, weren't you?' Malo hissed at him.

Hister didn't dare to reply. It was only when Malo, drew his sword out did Hister speak.

'Yes, I helped kill your mother and yes, I was one of those who stabbed your father.'

'You knew my mother was pregnant, yet you still slaughtered her. You were going to kill this man's wife, yet you knew that she was pregnant. Do you have a wife?'

'Yes.'

'Is she with child?' Malo asked.

'No. She can't have children.' he explained.

'Do you want children?' Malo demanded.

'Very much. I want a daughter!' Hister declared.

'Were you planning to keep this girl after you killed her parents?' Malo asked with his hands around Hister's neck once more.

'Yes.' he spat out.

Malo tutted. 'Wrong answer.'

He punched Hister in the face. Athena shuddered.

'No, Malo.' she said, still in a very calm, soft voice.

Malo's tears by now fell onto Hister's face. He continued to punch Hister in the face.

'You killed my parents in front of me. You killed them. They are gone and I will never see them again.'

Athena couldn't help but feel Malo's pain. She silently cried, putting her hand on his shoulder. Malo stopped punching Hister as he brought his hands to his face to wipe the tears away.

'You're lucky Athena's here, otherwise you would have been gone by now!' he whispered into Hister's ear. He then stood up and went towards the horses.

Athena watched him go and then her eyes were on Hister's.

'You're an Agalit.' he whispered as he breathed in. For the first time, she could hear fear in his voice.

'That cave over there.' Athena pointed towards the cave. 'There is an inscription on the wall. What does it say?'

'Each symbol was written by a different child. The children we successfully collected after we killed their parents. There was, of course, the occasional child who managed to escape, but no more that I can't count on my fingers,' and with that Hister showed his hands that were missing three fingers in total.

Athena took out the flat rock and counted each individual symbol.

'You did this to fifteen families. Since when?' Athena asked, fighting back the tears of just the thought of fifteen children being forced to watch their parents die in front of their own eyes.

'We travel to different counties in Fairoses where we do our sacrifices every year. We come from the Highlands, but we rotate county every year. So far, we have killed thirty mothers and fathers in the last eight months. That inscription you saw? It's the only one visible. We conceal all the others from previous years with grey Yoliytu.'

Athena looked away and closed her eyes. How could he say all this with no remorse?

'What about that small hand print next to the symbol?'

'That was an accident. One child was able to untie the rope and it got in the way of our...business.'

Athena gritted her teeth. 'So, you killed that child.'

'It wasn't me but it was still a shame.'

Athena shot a glance at Hister and started to raise her voice.

'Why do you do this? Why do you kill parents and take their children?'

'We want to raise them like our own children. To be part of the Striberosse tribe. We want to expand our tribe all over Fairoses.'

'Why?'

'They are the future.'

Athena could feel a lump form in the back of her throat, making it painful to swallow.

'You will never kill anyone anymore. Do you understand me?'

Malo, hearing Athena in distress, decided to intervene.

'What's wrong?' he asked.

'I'm telling Hister he will no longer kill any more parents.'

'You're right. He won't!' Malo confirmed. He took out his vial filled with the pale yellow potion.

'One drop will send you asleep for a week. Two drops will send you asleep for a few months. Three drops will send you to sleep... forever!' Malo explained to Hister, swinging the vial side to side, putting Hister in a hypnotic trance.

Hister gulped.

'How about three drops?'

'No...please. I promise I won't kill anymore!' Hister pleaded.

'Fine, two drops it is!' Malo declared and forced two droplets into Hister's mouth. Athena never knew whether the third drop was added unintentionally or on purpose.

'That will give you time to think of what you've done.' Malo said to Hister, patting him hard on the cheek.

'Thank you so much for saving my family, Athena... and Malo,' Aurore said sweetly, while giving them both a kiss. She blushed right after she kissed Malo on the cheek.

'No problem.'

Malo smiled at the small child, holding her hand. He then turned to the father.

'I hope you and your wife are happy. Having another child, I mean!'

'Yes, we cannot thank you enough. If you ever need anything...any place to stay, we will be happy to look after you.'

'There are four horses. We will be happy to share them with you!' Athena declared, counting the horses which belonged to the Striberosse.

'That is very kind.' the mother replied.

She bent down to Aurore and asked, 'Do you want to choose a horse, sweetheart?'

Aurore's blue eyes lit up with such glee. She ran towards the black horse.

'Of course she chooses the stallion!' the mother said, grinning.

'She has blue eyes just like you. She is the first in our family to be an Agalit. It's what makes her extra special to us.' the father said, grinning.

'What's her power?' Athena asked.

'We're not completely sure. She only turned four years old recently. I think, however, it may be to produce force shields. When we were playing with her the other day in the fields, we had to find her, and we weren't able to physically touch her because she was barred by an invisible force shield.'

'That would be an incredibly useful power to have in the future.' Malo thought out loud.

The parents nodded as they watched their young child manage to get on top of the black stallion.

'She is so small and innocent. I don't see how she can handle such a big power!' the mother said.

'What is your power, Athena?' the father asked.

'She can hear thoughts!' Malo answered for her. He turned to Athena and winked at her.

Don't worry, dear Athena! I'll protect you from anyone who wants to harm you.

'What a beautiful gift. I hope we cross paths again. We should be getting on our way now.' the father said as he held his wife's hand.

Before the family was about to ride off on their two horses, the father turned around to Malo. He rested his hand on Malo's shoulder, leant in and whispered, 'I should warn you that they tried to take Aurore because she's an Agalit. With the war coming, everyone is more and more desperate to get their hands on them. Take extra care with Athena when you reach the Forest Tatila.'

Malo gave him his word that he would protect Athena with his life.

'Malo, before we go, there is something I need to see.' she said after they waved farewell to the family.

She walked back to the cave and went straight to the place with the inscription. Athena took a step back and examined the whole wall. There was nothing out of the ordinary. It just looked like a normal grey wall.

She had an idea.

'This might take a while but I just need to see this.' she warned Malo. He looked at her with a serious frown.

'You do whatever you have to do. How can I help?'

Athena went over to the deer's corpse and told Malo to cut off two large pieces of skin that would be used as towels. He did as he was told. Afterwards, they walked to the lake to make their towels damp. They then returned to the cave and began wiping the wall, washing away all the grey Yolyitu.

Once they finished, they took a few steps back and looked at what they had unveiled. The whole wall was covered with inscriptions. Some even overlapped others. The wall had been used over and over again, and layers of Yolyitu had to be removed. Who knew how many years this had been going on for?

Malo turned to Athena.

'Promise me, dear Athena, that when we are finished at the Four Flames, we destroy these people. Promise me?'

He looked at her with such intensity and determination. However, with the pain and tears in his eyes, she couldn't help but feel this was the young Malo talking. The young Malo who was forced to watch his parents die.

Athena held his hand. 'I promise.'

VII

Athena and Malo both mounted their horses and continued with their journey. They headed towards the Forest Tatila and were on their way to the two bridges.

'So, when did you know you were an Agalit?' Malo asked out of curiosity.

'The day before I met you, actually!'

'I still can't believe that your gift is to hear thoughts. It's so ideal for me since I'm the only other person here.'

Athena laughed.

'Great, now I *really* don't have any privacy!' Malo replied, laughing on the outside, but crying on the inside.

'I know you're worried about it but I don't want to hear your thoughts all the time. I mean not that you're not interesting or anything...' Athena said, a bit stuck on what to stay.

'No, it's fine! I'm not an interesting person anyway.' Malo replied.

Silence.

'That's when you are supposed to say "No I find you very interesting!" or something like that!' Malo said imitating her voice.

'Well, you say you're not interesting, but in your head you know you are. You're just fishing for compliments!'

Malo looked away, pouting.

There was silence for a while. Athena decided to distract herself from her thoughts (and his thoughts!) by looking around and really appreciating the oncoming scenery.

She studied the Four Flames from a distance. They were four huge mountains, and although the Naran Flame was the smallest of the Flames, it was still impressive. However, nothing compared to the incomparable grandeur of the Azul Flame.

'Wow, the difference in size between the Naran Flame and the Azul

Flame is incredible!' Athena gasped in amazement.

'Sure! The King Agalaya lives in the Azul Flame.' Malo replied.

The word Agalaya somehow seemed familiar to Athena.

'Agalaya? That is the name of the King?' Athena asked.

'Yes. There is only one family which has the name Agalaya. The Royal Family. They are all Agalits.' Malo began to explain.

'Wait! Does that mean... I'm part of the royal family?' Athena asked, rather excited.

'Well, let's not jump to rash conclusions, dear Athena! Gifts can also come randomly. Mutations. Like Aurore. You are the second Agalit I've met. I met the first one when I was younger. The village I lived in when I was a small child had a boy that was an Agalit, but everyone tried to avoid him. Even his own parents!' Malo explained.

'That's so harsh! Why?'

'Well, his gift was to burn things. Especially when he was angry or scared, he would burn anything.'

'That's quite extreme! So I suppose he burnt homes, trees and things like that?'

'Exactly! We both shared the same teacher and this teacher made us gifts. He made us wooden swords and one day, this boy accidentally burnt his. He saw me play with mine and he got so jealous that he burnt it. That's why I have a small scar on my finger.' Malo said, showing Athena the small scar at the tip of his second finger.

'It's so small. I can barely see it.' she said, smiling.

'Just like I can barely see your bruises. Interesting, isn't it?' he said as he stroked his chin.

Athena tried to punch his shoulder, but almost fell off her horse in doing so. Malo caught her just before she was going to fall flat on her face.

'How old were you?' Athena asked, her heart still pounding.

'I was around six or seven years old.'

Athena nodded and smiled. Malo mimicked her exact reaction, making them both laugh hard.

They both returned to silence for a few moments, but then Athena asked, 'How old were you when the Striberosse killed your parents?'

Malo suddenly turned serious. 'I was nine years old.'

'What did you do between their death and joining the army?'

'I was supposed to go with the Striberosse, but there was no way I was going to spend time with the people who had just murdered my parents!

So, I told them I needed to stop for a while. A soldier was assigned to wait for me while the other soldiers continued on because they were on a strict schedule or something like that. Anyway, I waited till they were out of sight, and then I grabbed the soldier's sword when he wasn't looking. Then I stabbed him in the leg!'

'Malo, you were nine when you first stabbed someone? You violent boy!'

'Well, I didn't kill him, did I? Anyway, as soon as I stabbed him, I ran for it. I never ran so fast in my life, and even though I could hear the other soldiers chasing me, I continued to run. My heart was pounding so fast, but I was able to carry on running because I knew if they ever caught me, my punishment would be nothing more than three slashes!'

'You've been slashed before?' Athena asked in horror.

'Oh yes! I was slashed about three times a month before then!'

'Why?' she asked in complete shock.

'Well, you said it yourself, I was a violent child. I always challenged my teacher to a duel. I got carried away one time and I ended up breaking his leg,' Malo said proudly.

'You shouldn't be proud about that! Anyway, what did you do after you escaped from the Striberosse?' Athena asked once again.

'Well, nothing really. I didn't want to go back home. I never liked it there. Also, it would have been too painful to be there without my parents. It was the perfect opportunity to leave. So, I lived for two years in the forest and survived by begging for food from people passing by.'

'You did that for *two* years?'

'Yes, that's what I just said.'

'What did you do after those two years?' Athena asked, ignoring his comment.

Malo laughed. 'I joined Ciwoon!'

'Ciwoon? I've never heard of that.'

'Ciwoon is a group of fighters who teach young teenagers to fight. That's how I was able to enter the army because of my excellent skills in fighting. Otherwise, I would have had to join the Chamcoks.' Malo told her. He shuddered at the thought.

'And how long did you do that for?' Athena asked curiously. She agreed that Malo had excellent skills when it came to fighting.

'Around six years. After I left them, I travelled to many places around the whole of Fairoses to fight in duels and competitions. I owe much to Ciwoon. Without them, I would have nothing. I would *be* nothing.'

'And then you did that for two years before you went to the army.' Athena concluded.

'Exactly.'

Then there was another silence.

I think I can see the two bridges from here. I really believe it's the left one, but if we're both so stubborn, it's going to take a while. I mean if worse comes to worst, we go on different brid... she can hear what I'm thinking! Hello, dear Athena.

Malo smiled, turning all red.

Athena grinned. 'Hello.'

'Being an Agalit. Do you have any other powers as well? I mean, abilities that ordinary people don't have?'

'I think so. I learn things very fast.'

'That's nice! I wish I could learn very quickly. So, if you read a book, you remember everything?'

'More or less. If I read about a language, I would be able to quickly learn it.' Athena answered back, shyly.

'Wow!' he said, rather impressed.

'Have you ever heard of the language Dertiym?' she asked.

'Isn't that the old language of Fairoses?'

'Yes. Well, for my tenth birthday, my father gave me a book on Dertiym and it took me a week to read the big book and by the end of the month, I was able to speak Dertiym fluently... well according to Tomas anyway,' Athena explained.

'That's impressive. When I read a small book it takes me months to finish, and by the time I get to the end, I already forgot everything! So, I just save myself time and don't read in the first place. There's only one book that I've had to learn and remember. It's a book the army gives each soldier when they join. It talks about the lands and their history and geography.' Malo said.

'Is that why Olimm knew so much? He was talking in detail about the different counties and-'

'But he's not a soldier!'

'No, he's not, but a lot of soldiers come to the inn and I guess they all talk about it.'

'I never went to that inn. Too much effort to cross the bridges. In case you would come back on the wrong one, it would take *so* much longer to get back to headquarters.'

'Where would you go then?'

'I would go to the markets by the Four Flames. I have a good friend there called Roderic. I would also change parts of my uniform so people wouldn't run away.'

Athena smiled. 'How did you meet Roderic?'

'I was at the Four Flames for my last tournament before I headed off to the army. I won the tournament, and at the time, Roderic was serving drinks in the arena. He was really nice and wished me luck. I came back the next day to have a drink at his stall and we became friends. So, when I see him on my days off, we eat together. He sells fruits now. I don't think my liver would be able to take any more beer. The great thing about these fruits though is that they have an after taste of beer. It's great!'

Athena laughed. 'You and your beer...'

'It's a love story for the ages!'

They finally reached the end of the path. The time had come for them to choose. Both bridges were about two hundred yards apart.

They got down from their horses and just stood still for a moment, studying what they saw in front of them. This decision had to be made wisely.

The soil between both bridges changed. The left bridge was still very much in character with the path Athena and Malo had spent days following. The soil was of the same brown colour and there were green bushes and peach trees surrounding the start of the bridge as well. The bridge itself seemed very secure. The planks they would walk on were made of a thick wood and were placed close to one another. The risk of falling would be much smaller. The ropes on either side they would hold for safety were tightly wounded and didn't seem to move too much from the wind. It was strong and therefore reliable.

Then they turned to the right bridge. It was no longer brown the soil, but a light grey. Light grey with hundreds of thousands of little pebbles. The bridge had no bushes or trees near it. Everything was bare. It was beautiful the bridge, no doubt, but it didn't even compare to the safety of the other bridge. The archway that lasted until the other side would make them feel like royalty. How could it help though? It was resting on the wooden railing that looked like it could barely hold its own weight. The planks they would have to try and walk on were set far apart and some had even fallen off, while others were dangling down, waiting to fall. The distance between the cliffs was about a hundred yards. Having no problems on a faulty bridge seemed very unlikely.

Athena turned to Malo. He looked at her with a big grin and said, 'We should move closer.'

They cautiously walked towards the edge of the cliff and Malo told Athena to look down. She carefully took two steps forward and peered over. She knew what to expect as she could hear it.

A river.

The brown and grey soil separated all the way down the valley and then all the way back up to the top of the opposite cliff. Only at the top was the soil all brown again. (Only by the very edge of the cliff because the moment one walked down from the bridge, one was immediately in the Forest Tatila.) Even through the clear blue river at the bottom of the valley, Athena could see the separation of the two colours.

She took a few steps back. 'What do you think, Malo?'

'I think it's beautiful. I'm also thinking that we should take the left bridge.'

Athena rummaged her fingers across her chin. 'You are going to disagree with me, but I feel like the right one is the bridge to choose.'

Malo sat down on the ground. 'You are going to have to give me a very convincing speech to cross that death bridge. I'm waiting. In fact, I'm looking forward to this.'

Athena smiled.

'Alright. Well, I want to cross the left bridge as well. I do! It looks so much safer, BUT I know that the right one is, well… the right one! I thought about it. You said that no one ever knows which bridge to choose because it changes with magic? Or people forget? Well, you weren't so clear about that-'

'It's because I don't know, dear Athena. Nobody does. It's a mystery. That's why nobody can figure a way. It's pure chance.'

'What if it's not? If you say it's to do with magic, then there must be some sort of unconventional logic behind it.'

Malo raised his hands to the sky.

'I know nothing about magic. I'm human. I don't have to deal with that. I think in a logical way because that's how my brain works.'

'Exactly! This whole journey so far, we have been saved because of you–'

'Well, you also helped solve things in a way I wouldn't have… wait a minute. You're an Agalit. That's magical in a sense.'

'How many Agalits have crossed this bridge?'

Malo laughed. 'I have no idea. Not very many, I can imagine. Agalits are so rare. Meeting that little girl, Aurore, was a complete fluke!'

'Maybe it takes something magical to understand magic. Stand up!'

Malo did as he was told. He towered over Athena, casting a shadow over her and said, 'Human to Agalit. What do you need?'

'Do you remember the grey pebbles? Do you remember the archway? It's so beautiful, it's not something you could forget.'

Malo scratched his head. He was trying to remember.

'Truthfully, I don't remember the grey pebbles. Or the archway. I remember light green pebbles. They were so light you would think they were transparent. Wait!'

He bent down and put his hand in a small pouch within his left boot. It was there he always hid a small knife. When Malo was being dragged along the ground a few days ago, he felt rocks, pebbles and dirt cover his clothes and body. He tried his best to get rid of it all, but he thought, if there was anything left, it would be stuck in this little pouch. Sure enough, he was right. There was a little pebble but it wasn't green-it was grey.

'What the-'

'This makes sense. The reason why people don't know which bridge to choose is because the soil and bridges change their form. That's what helps keep the secret. The green pebble turned grey because it's the magical bridge. So, it's the right one. In every sense of the word.'

'It must have been enchanted by the Wueltins. The magical beings from around here. They can cast spells on people to forget things. Maybe they enchanted the right bridge.'

'Most probably. From what you've said though, it's not the biggest disaster if we take the wrong path. You will recognise the territory of the army earlier than anybody else. We would then go off the path and into the forest and just-'

'Wait a minute! If you thought about that the whole time, why did you give a whole speech?'

Athena smiled. 'You wanted an explanation. I wanted to figure it out. Now, I've learnt what you think about magic AND about Wueltins. We both learnt something new today.'

Malo laughed.

'Yes. I learnt that magic makes even less sense now. Okay, let's go! We'll have to leave the horses here. It would be a death sentence for them if they have to cross this bridge.'

Malo led the way to the right bridge. Before he began praying for his life, he turned around to Athena. 'I never thought that I'd reach a point in my life where somebody six years younger than me convinces me to walk three hundred feet over ground on a bridge that can barely hold its own weight. Actually, it's three hundred and twenty-six feet. How do I know that? IT WAS IN THE ONLY BOOK I'VE EVER READ!'

Athena couldn't stop laughing. She could sense Malo's fear. Usually, she would comfort him, but she just knew that nothing would go wrong, so to see him panic was rather amusing.

'I need to read more. I need to learn more.' he was whispering to himself.

Athena patted him on the back and offered to go first.

'No, dear Athena, I'll go first. I'll make sure it's safe. When I call you, start walking over alright?'

Athena nodded.

Before he took his first step, he looked around to calm himself down.

He looked up at the sky which was of a hazy light blue shade with a hint of orange. He then looked ahead. He could see that the Forest Tatila covered the entirety of the land between the cliff edge and the Four Flames.

The strip of forest which separated both bridges was just as wild and exotic as it was further in. The area was filled with so many trees and bushes that made it impossible to look far ahead. Malo took note of the exotic red and green ivy draped over the cliff edge. If the bridge collapsed, the ivy would be his last hope.

'Don't think of such things, Malo. It won't come down to that. I promise!' Athena said.

He started walking with his heart skipping a beat every time he stepped onto an unstable wooden plank.

He held onto the rope very tightly, and was able to feel his own sweat making the rope slightly moist.

He looked down those three hundred and twenty-six feet to see the river silently flowing by. There were many sharp-angled boulders directly below him, and just next to the river, Malo could make out a group of resting Greliks.

The wooden plank he just stepped on fell off and landed in the river. This made Malo's heart race. He didn't want to disturb the Greliks or gain their attention.

He was finally near the end of the bridge, so he signalled Athena to come over.

Everything was fine, until she reached the middle of the bridge when, all of a sudden, both horses started to fret. Distressed by the group of Greliks heading towards them at full speed, the panicked horses kicked the huge wooden poles which supported the bridge.

Athena quickly looked at Malo with panicked eyes.

Run. Run now!

The horses carried on kicking the wooden poles with such force until they collapsed, bringing down half the bridge with them.

'Run as fast as you can!' Malo yelled as loud as he could as there was the chaotic background noise of the horses neighing and the Greliks producing a very loud and high pitched scream.

Athena ran as fast as she could and didn't look back. Malo was watching her in horror. He could see that if she wasn't fast enough, she would fall. A part of him felt like he was going to throw up from the anxiety for her, but he kept a straight face as she came towards him. He didn't want her to panic even more.

Athena ran so fast that she ran into Malo, knocking him on the ground.

'That was *so* close!' she whispered.

The Greliks looked at them from the other side of the valley, but now they had calmed down and were resting by the edge.

Malo stood up and then helped Athena up. He gave her a big hug and let out a huge grunt.

'You make me feel like an old man, dear Athena. My poor heart can't take all this anxiety.'

He kissed her head and then gently pushed her forwards to make her start walking.

'Let's hope we have a few hours of rest before we almost die again.'

'I'm sorry that-'

'Don't be sorry. Let's move on and just be thankful we are both still in one piece!'

'Alright.'

After a few moments, Malo began to laugh to himself.

'What?' Athena asked, starting to giggle a little too.

'I think you've actually made me bruise!'

VIII

As they walked into the Forest Tatila, Athena could understand the beauty it was renowned for. There were many different types of bushes and flowers which covered the ground. There were tall, thick trees with branches that sometimes intertwined with those of other trees. There were many different types. There were oak trees, cotton trees, wisteria trees, gum trees, dragon blood trees and many other exotic looking ones.

Malo turned to Athena and told her, 'Do you know the story behind the forest?'

Athena shook her head, still looking around in awe.

'Well, they say that thousands of years ago, every country from the East came to Fairoses to create relations for the first time. They all saw how beautiful the lands were. So, when they arrived back to their home, they sent back seeds from their most magnificent and unique trees. Can you imagine? All those seeds from those countries were scattered across the area that is now the Forest Tatila. All these exotic trees have brothers and sisters on the other side of the world. Isn't that incredible?'

Athena turned to him in admiration. 'That is incredible! *This* is incredible,' she said as she waved her arms around her. 'I've never seen anything like it before.'

'So, you jumped out of the lake because you were afraid that Alex was going to set the boat on fire, because you punched his brother, and you did this because you thought he was bullying your friend, Pavle.' Athena said, summarising the whole story Malo spent a long time explaining.

'Yes. I hated Alex. He always used his gift to scare me. I mean, just because he was able to set everything on fire...'

'But it worked!' Athena pointed out.

'That's not the point. Nobody should use violence to scare others.'

Athena was about to reply back, but then she heard several voices.

'That General Avran is absolutely bonkers! How can he think we can take over the Azul Flame with only seven hundred soldiers and those stupid Chamcoks from the Naran Flame?'

'I don't know, but he has never failed before. He has the brains of something else.'

'You're right. Now, let's get out of here before it turns dark!'

'Why? You afraid of the dark?'

'No, but soldiers who are out after dark and aren't on night-patrol get ten slashes on the stage!'

'Of course. That doesn't sound pleasant at all!'

'Doesn't it?'

And with that, both soldiers headed back to headquarters.

'What is it?' Malo whispered, unable to hear anything.

'Soldiers from the army. It's fine, they're heading back to the headquarters.'

'Why are they heading back?' Malo asked curiously.

'If they stay out after dark they would get-'

'Ten slashes,' Malo remembered. 'Boy, I do not miss those ten slashes one bit.'

Athena suddenly looked at him.

'You were slashed in the army too?'

'Slashed, beaten, almost drowned, almost burned to death, starved, deprived of water, locked in the dungeons for three days straight without any food or water and branded... that's about it!'

Athena wasn't able to speak, but her eyes said it all.

'Yes. All in the space of four years! Quite an achievement I have to say,' Malo said with pride as he looked at his nails.

'What mark did they brand you with?' Athena asked, afraid to know what the answer was.

'They branded me with words in the old language. I was never able to find out what it was. Nobody I know, including myself obviously, can understand it. Maybe you could tell me?' he asked, looking very excited.

'Where's your mark?'

'We can do it when we find shelter because it's getting dark.' Malo said, looking up at the dark red sky.

'I just realised! You chose the right bridge, dear Athena! Otherwise, we'd be at the marshes by now.'

'Then how come there were soldiers out here?'

'I guess as the army is searching for Agalits, soldiers are sent deeper into the forest, just in case…'

'In case any Agalits are wandering about.'

Athena stopped walking. Malo looked back at her.

'What's wrong?'

'What can you tell me about Agalits?'

'Well, tell me how much you know and then I will fill in the gaps.'

'I know that I have a power. That's it.'

'Right. Well, you don't know much then. Have you ever seen your own blood?'

Athena thought for a moment.

'No.' she realised.

Malo took out his dagger and cut his finger deep enough for red blood to trickle out.

'Your turn.'

Athena shook her head. 'No! I'll bruise!'

'Athena, do you want answers or not?!'

'I do.' she replied quietly, and offered him her hand.

He put his dagger away, and bent down to get a small knife from the pouch in his boot.

'After this, it won't be of much use.'

He opened up her palm and looked her in the eyes.

'Do you trust me?'

She nodded. He kept eye contact with her as he stabbed her hand.

'Look down, dear Athena.'

She quickly looked down at her hand. There wasn't a scratch on her hand. Nothing. The blade, however, had completely crumpled.

Athena took the knife from Malo and stared at it.

'How is that possible?' she gasped. 'Am I immortal? Can I not die?'

Malo bit his lip and tried his hardest not to laugh, but he couldn't help himself.

'No! Your gift is to hear thoughts… here and there… you need to have lessons on how to control that. Anyway, your skin can't be penetrated by a blade. A simple metal blade. However, that's not an excuse to be careless. Everything else will kill you all the same.'

'Why do I bruise then?'

Malo shrugged his shoulders. 'You're just *special*, dear Athena. Do you know what colour your blood is?'

Athena shook her head.

'Green. You look like a human but you just have green blood and a unique power. I think that's enough to keep you thinking for the next few hours.'

Athena smiled. 'For sure!'

'We should hurry up now and find a place to rest overnight. The guards on night patrol will be out here soon.'

He threw away the useless dagger as they walked on.

'Look, I think there is a small cave near those huge trees over there.' Malo whispered, pointing at a vague somewhere.

Athena nodded and they quickly walked towards a large group of exotic-looking trees surrounded by honeysuckles.

'It's so beautiful,' Athena said as she looked around.

Malo nodded. 'The Forest Tatila is like this everywhere: Bushes with berries, green trees all year round, brooks and many other features. It's known for its beauty and magic!'

They both sat underneath one of the exotic-looking trees and rested for a few minutes. Athena turned her head and looked up at the tree. The thick trunk was very colourful. It was as if a painter put all the colours on his palette and swirled them around. Over the years, the brightness and intensity of the colours had calmed down, but the different textures and patterns created were still visible. The branches grew longer and drooped more as the tree grew higher. At the tree-top, they were so long that they would reach the first branch. The crescent-shaped leaves which were small in size but large in number were glowing green as the night grew darker.

'It's just so beautiful.' Athena said as she followed the colour purple around the trunk.

Malo went to go and find some dinner while he told Athena to find some wood for the fire.

'Deer?' Malo suggested.

'Yes?'

'No, I mean, do you want to eat deer?' Malo asked, a bit embarrassed.

'Oh... yes.' Athena replied, even more embarrassed.

Silence.

'Well, I'll go this way,' he said, pointing left.

'Okay.' Athena replied immediately.

That was awkward.

'I heard that!' Athena called out, smiling.

Malo suddenly turned around to Athena.

'Right, I forgot you can hear me.'

He turned around again.

I've really got to be careful what I think now.

'I heard that too!'

There's just no escaping you, is there?!

Athena laughed.

'Is it wise to make a fire with soldiers so close? Won't they see it?'

'No, the trees block the view from the outside. Trust me, they won't come here.'

Hearing the confidence in his voice, Athena trusted him and set off.

They both arrived back at the same time.

'I've got the wood!' Athena said, with the wood in her hands.

'I found two rabbits. No deer tonight.' Malo announced, holding the two well-fed animals in his hands.

Athena laid the wood down a few yards away from the tree.

'Here you go,' she said, passing Malo a small twig.

He dropped the rabbits and snatched the twig from her hand.

'Thanks,' he replied as he violently and quickly scraped the small twig across his ever growing stubble, making a small flame appear.

'It actually causes me pain to see that. I almost feel the sensation on my cheek,' Athena said, as she took the twig from Malo's hand, and threw it in the middle of the other sticks, piled together.

The fire suddenly roared upwards. Malo grabbed his knife and cut the rabbits open.

'So, where is your mark?'

'On my back. Do you want to tell me what it says?' Malo asked.

Athena nodded and slowly lifted up the back of his shirt. When she lifted it high enough, she was able to see the brand. The shape was circular with two words.

Athena touched the mark gently with her fingertips.

'It's so deep!' she gasped.

'Yes, I know. I was there.' Malo said, laughing.

'Right! Sorry.'

'No, don't be. Just tell me what the mark says.'

'Alright! Well, I know what the first line reads, but the second... I'm not quite sure.' Athena honestly replied.

'Well, what does the first line say?' he asked impatiently.

'It says: You will die.'

'Well, that's not a very nice thing to permanently write on someone! What else does it say?' Malo asked.

'I'm not quite sure. The second line could mean 'Before you expect it'? I'm not quite sure. The markings aren't quite clear. It's almost as if they've changed.' Athena said, incredibly confused.

'Magic has to be involved. Its logic can never be quite understood. Oh well. At least we have half of it!' Malo said.

Athena took a breath in and was about to say something, but she could feel that he didn't want to talk about it anymore, so she exhaled and remained quiet.

'Dinner is ready!' he continued as he pulled down his shirt and saved the rabbits from being completely burnt.

'Here you go.' he said as he wrapped a huge orange leaf around the cooked rabbit. He carefully handed half of it over to Athena.

'Thank you!'

They both began to eat and couldn't help but feel excited and enchanted from their surroundings. Even though Malo had lived so close to the Forest Tatila, he never had the chance to just venture around.

'Is something wrong? You haven't said a word for a few minutes. Not that I'm complaining.' Malo said, winking at her as he continued to eat.

'I'm fine. I'm just wondering...why did you leave the army and why were you branded? If you don't mind me asking?' Athena quietly asked.

Malo tutted. 'Don't ever waste your time wondering, dear Athena. Just ask me what you want to know straightaway. Of course, I will answer any question you have.'

He took the water flask Aurore's parents gave them out of her bag. He poured himself a drink and then handed it over to Athena.

'Okay. Why did you leave the army?' she asked sweetly.

'I didn't leave. I was forced to leave, because I talked back to General Avran when he was yelling at someone else.'

This sounded so ridiculous to Athena, that she couldn't help but laugh.

'I'm sorry, what? Because you spoke back to this man, you were thrown out?'

Malo nodded.

'Why was he yelling at the person in the first place?'

'The man he was yelling at was called Fiju. Fiju was working in the dungeons where we keep prisoners. One of these prisoners was extremely violent. He had serious issues. He would kill someone just because he *felt* like it. According to General Avran, it didn't really matter if he did. Many men try for the army, so they would be easy to replace.

Anyway, this prisoner saw Fiju coming his way to give him his dinner, but the prisoner was already hungry and had no patience. So, when he saw the food arriving, he grabbed Fiju's arm and pinched his nose and forced all his food down Fiju's mouth.'

'Wait a minute! This prisoner was suffocating Fiju, yet he was the one being yelled at by General Avran? This general sounds really-'

'Horrible, inhuman, the devil reincarnated?' Malo said, giving suggestions.

'Cruel. Anyway, carry on,' Athena said.

'Well, I was on Guard duty and I saw Fuji suffocating. So, I tried to push this prisoner's hand back into the cell, but he was too strong.'

'So, what did you do then?' she asked, taking a sip of water.

'I cut off two of his fingers.'

Athena spat her water out.

'You cut off two of his fingers?' she repeated.

'Well, he was choking my friend. What do you expect me to do?' Malo asked.

'You could have-'

'Told him to stop it?'

'Yes! Well, you could have started off with that.'

Malo laughed.

'My dear Athena, this man would kill someone he didn't even know, because he felt like it. Do you honestly think that if I stood there, pointing my finger at him, saying, "Now, stop it right there, young man", he would have listened?' Malo said smiling.

'Good point. Anyway, why did Fiju get yelled at? He didn't do anything wrong!'

'When General Avran saw the prisoner's wounded hand, he ordered all the guards in the dungeons and Fiju up in the courtroom. He then ordered all the other soldiers to come as well. He found out that there were only three soldiers working in that particular area of the dungeons, so he ordered us up onto the stage.

He saw Fiju, still panting, since he almost died. He leant down to Fiju's height, looked him in the eyes and smiled. He thought it was Fiju that chopped off his fingers, but then Fiju ratted me out. He told General Avran that it was me who had cut off the prisoner's fingers.

The general then came towards me and started yelling at me and when he yells, he spits! Anyway, I talked back to him when he had finished talking.'

'What did you say to him?'

'I told him that the prisoner was suffocating Fiju and that he was a terrible general and should have never even been given a place in the army – even as the slave of a servant.

This got him in a very bad mood as you could imagine. He turned around and tried to punch me in the face. I saw it coming, so I blocked his hand and punched him back...but with his own fist.'

Athena gasped, bringing her hands to her mouth and then laughed.

'I can imagine he was in a *really* bad mood after that!'

'You could say that. After I punched him, he said "How dare you punch me?", and I replied "General, technically you punched yourself!"

He had quite the little tantrum after that. It was even more humiliating for him as the whole army was there to witness this... entertaining scene, shall we say.'

'And that's when you were tortured.' Athena concluded.

'I was given dinner as it was dinner time, but then I was forced back onto the stage and that's when it started.'

'Oh dear,' Athena said, bringing her hands to her mouth once again.

'I know.' Malo said, grinning.

Athena remembered the rest of the story from the first night they met, so she left it at that. It wouldn't be nice for him to have to tell the story again.

'Well, that's all behind you. You don't have to worry anymore. No more torture, no more near-death experiences like this afternoon, no more-'

'You were so sure that nothing bad would happen.'

'Well, I was right in a way. We are both still alive. We're going to make it to the Four Flames. I just feel it.'

'You think it's fate?'

'I really do!'

'Well, fate isn't going to carry us there! We need to stay alive until we get there and then fate can do whatever it does. I don't even believe in fate. Why are we even having this conversation?'

'Because I was just trying to reassure you that you are safe now.'

Malo chuckled. 'We're so close to the enemy. Let's pray that *Fate* keeps us out of their hands. I sure hope you're right and we do make it to the Four Flames in one piece.'

'I'm sure. Alright, good night, Malo. We have a long day ahead of us tomorrow.'

He turned around to fall asleep, still chuckling. He knew that he'd have to make it to the Four Flames.

There was someone over there that he had to meet.

'Do you think they can see us?'

'No, you nugget, they are clearly asleep.'

'Well, let's grab them while they are still sleeping.'

'No, you nugget, it won't be as much fun!'

'But we will have the element of surprise!'

'We need them awake!'

'Why?'

'Because, you nugget, General Avran won't want two people asleep in his prison cell, would he now?'

'But, they would w-'

'Just go and wake them up you nugget!'
'Stop calling me that! My name is Twit.'
'Well, you look like a nugget to me.'

Athena suddenly opened up her eyes.
    'Malo, wake up! Some soldiers are here.' Athena said, shaking him.
    Malo shook her off and turned around, snoring louder.
    Athena shook him even harder.
    'Malo, wake up!' she hissed into his ear.
    Malo started mumbling. 'It's early in the morning and I'm tired.'
    Athena rolled her eyes.
    'Come on Malo. Now!'
    She didn't want to throw water on him, so she pinched him.
    He suddenly sat up and held his ear.
    'Ouch! Athena, come on, that's not funny,' Malo said.
    Athena smiled evilly. 'Malo, there are soldiers right over there. They can see us, hear us and they want to take us as their prisoners.'
    'Well, why didn't you say so?!'
    He quickly got up. They gathered their things up and ran as fast as possible.
    'Wait a minute. Why on earth are we running away from a couple of soldiers? I could easily take them down,' Malo said, dropping all his things on the ground. He casually drew out his sword and walked back, yawning.
    Athena went after him, grabbed his arm and tried to force him back the other way.
    Malo laughed at her. 'What are you doing?'
    'You can't kill them, tie them up or whatever! If they go missing, then more soldiers will be sent out to look for them. *Then* what?'
    Malo took a deep breath and asked, 'What do you suggest we do then?'
    Athena smiled at him. 'I have an idea. We are going to trick them!'

'Nugget, they got away. Run after them immediately!'
    'I'm tired. Why can't we just take our horses and ride after them?'
    'NOW!'
    'Why was I assigned to be with you?'
    'Because you're lucky. I should be the one complaining about...why are

we wasting time here? Run after them!'

'Look, they're coming back.'

'You better be right about that!'

Athena ran towards them with some mud on her cheeks. Both soldiers gazed at her.

'Why hello there, sweet cheeks! How are you on this fine day?' the dominant soldier asked, sweeping his hair back.

'I'm doing terribly! There is a dangerous man over there who says he is my husband but, really, he isn't! He is *obsessed* with me! He follows me, ruins my relationships with other men!'

Athena came closer to the soldier and whispered, 'Is that really fair?'

The soldier gulped and shook his head. 'Not at all! Would you like me to catch him and bring him to dungeons of the army's headquarters?'

'You're part of the army? *The* Seven Hundred Army? My friend always told me that she found soldiers ugly men with cold hearts!'

Athena leant even closer to him.

'She stands corrected,' Athena said, looking at the soldier straight in the eyes.

'Thank you very much-'

'Hello, my name is Twit,' the other soldier began but before Athena could even reply, the dominant soldier shoved him backwards.

'Sorry about him. He's a nugget. Now, would you like me to seize that man?'

'That would be wonderful!'

Both soldiers ran towards Malo, who was standing stationary.

'Oh no, what a surprise! Two soldiers coming this way. Whatever should I do?' Malo said in a high pitched voice, clasping his cheeks.

The two soldiers quickly reached him. Twit stopped as soon as he recognised Malo, but the other soldier drew his sword out and pointed it to Malo's neck.

'Well, look who it is! You just couldn't stay away could you, Malo?' the soldier said in a very serious tone.

'Benny! How have you been?' Malo asked, gritting his teeth. He had always despised these particular soldiers. They were always paired up and funnily enough, they were the ones who dragged him out of the headquarters premises.

'I've been great. Actually, I helped the general choose your replacement. The man we chose is huge. He is certainly already more of an asset to the army than you ever were.'

Malo just looked into Benny's eyes with a huge smile. He knew Benny didn't like that.

'You see that pretty girl over there?' Benny said, pointing his sword towards Athena.

Malo nodded.

'Well, she says that you have been following her, harassing her and claiming that you are her husband. I don't know if I believe that, but any excuse to seize you would do!' Benny announced and had Twit bind his hands.

'Oh no! Where are you going to bring me?' Malo asked sarcastically.

Benny looked at him. 'What on earth is wrong with you? We are in the Forest Tatila. Where do all the prisoners go? The dungeons, you imbecile!'

Malo gasped but suddenly started laughing. Athena's plan was amusing him. Acting so naive and innocent was actually quite fun.

Benny and Twit started to walk Malo back towards Athena. She hugged Benny.

'That's him.' she confirmed, acting scared.

'Alright. Twit, let's bring him to the dungeons and as soon as we arrive, inform General Avran. I'm sure he will be more than thrilled to see Malo again.' Benny smiled, showing all his yellow, rotting teeth.

Malo smiled at Athena. Everything was going according to plan.

IX

They had been walking for a while now and Benny spent every one of those minutes talking to Athena. It wasn't often that he met a young woman.

'So, Athena, how old are you?' Benny asked, staring at Athena's blue eyes.

'I'm twenty-six,' she replied, looking away.

'Really? I'm twenty-six too!' Twit said.

'Twit, nobody asked for your opinion.' Benny snapped. He turned back to Athena and flashed her a smile.

'I'm twenty-eight! You know, everyone says to make a healthy marriage work, the husband has to be two years older,' he said.

Athena suddenly cringed. 'I've never heard that before.'

'Yes, Benny, *I've* never heard that either,' Malo said, grinning.

'Shut up! You have been interrupting my conversation with the lovely Athena this *entire* time,' he said, glaring at Malo.

'Poor you! While you're flirting with my wife, I'm tied up here in these ropes!'

Benny asked Athena, 'Would you like me to give him a potion that would paralyse him physically, including his big mouth?'

Athena shook her head very calmly. 'That won't be necessary. I'm sure he now understands how important it is not to interrupt our conversation.'

Benny smiled at her and said, 'I see your point but I have known Malo for a few years now. If there is one thing that I've learnt, it's that he is too stubborn to change his own ways. No matter how harsh the consequence.'

Malo rolled his eyes.

Benny took out a vial, quite similar to Malo's, but instead of a pale yellow potion, it was dark navy. Twit pinned Malo to the ground as Benny knelt down and poured one droplet into his mouth.

'That way you can't move, talk or interrupt for a few hours,' he said, patting Malo's cheek.

Athena's heart started to race. How was her plan going to work if Malo couldn't even move a muscle?

Benny suddenly glanced at Athena who changed her look from despair to relief.

'I'm sorry you are against this. It's just that I know Malo's type. He's dangerous,' Benny said as he held her shoulder. 'It's for the best.'

'Alright, I believe you,' Athena said, trying her best to hide her distress.

Benny looked her in the eyes and played with her hair. Malo, seeing this tried to groan, but it was hopeless. He tried to kick Benny but he had no control of any of his movements any more.

This plan might not work anymore, dear Athena! You have to run now. That's all you can do.

Athena subtly shook her head.

You have to escape. You have a bigger chance of escaping whilst you're still in the forest. Once you are in the headquarters, it will be almost impossible.

Athena just ignored him.

'You see the crater over there, Athena? That's where the Seven Hundred Army is based. It's down there.' Benny told her.

Athena could see the enormous crater in the middle of a plain field. Circling the crater itself was a series of trees with rope, linking one to another. Marshes encircled the field making it almost impossible to escape, as there were always security guards on duty. By the time one would reach the marshes, it would be too late. Around the marshes, tall yet thin trees kept the area enclosed from the rest of the world.

Green, spiky Aloe Vera plants were seen around the premises. Benny explained to Athena that the army used the plant as a basis for each and every potion.

'What are those for?' Athena asked out of curiosity, pointing at the ropes that joined from tree to tree.

'Those are our training facilities. When you apply for the army, you have to get from tree to tree using the ropes. It's very tough! That's why all the soldiers have very strong upper body muscles,' Benny said. He looked over at Twit who was day dreaming and bumping into trees.

'Well, most of them.'

Past the tall trees, they reached a barbed-wired fence that surrounded the marshes.

My dear Athena, I'm warning you! This is your last chance to escape. Once you are in the field, there is no way of coming back out, unless you have General Avran's consent. Go now! I mean it. Leave and save yourself!

'No, I'm not leaving you!' she muttered angrily through her teeth.

Benny looked at Athena.

'What did you say?'

'Um... I'm not leaving *you*!' Athena said, smiling at Benny.

'Of course you're not! Even if you wanted to, I wouldn't allow it!' he said, holding Athena's hand tightly.

Twit walked up to the guard by the entrance of the fence and told him that they had found two prisoners for General Avran.

The guard immediately opened up the gate for them. As Athena passed him, she noticed how his face was completely scarred.

She couldn't help but stare at him and the guard didn't like that one bit.

'Stop staring!' he growled, and with that he punched her in the stomach.

Athena quickly clutched her stomach and groaned.

This infuriated Benny, so he punched the guard in the face and threw him on the ground and continued kicking him in the stomach. He finally spat on him.

'Are you alright?' Benny asked, turning back to Athena.

Athena forced a smile on her face and nodded feebly.

'Don't worry. His punishment will come soon enough,' Benny said as he glared at the guard who was lying on the ground.

'Don't you think he has been punished enough?' she asked, feeling pity as she looked down at the young guard's scarred face.

'No! Here in the army, you would be lucky if you didn't get that every day. He hit an Agalit. He hit *you*.'

Athena gulped. She let herself forget for a moment that she was important to them.

'Come on. Let's go! Our duty is almost over and the general will be waiting for the prisoners.' Twit warned.

'Come, Athena, I will carry you,' Benny declared. He took a hold of Athena's legs and carried her over his shoulder.

Athena would have carried on walking by herself, but her stomach was hurting so much, she wasn't even able to walk.

'What am I supposed to do with Malo?' Twit asked in despair.

'Drag him for all I care,' Benny said.

'I'll carry him. Unlike *some* people, my heart isn't made of stone.'

Once they had reached the marshes, Benny carefully helped Athena onto the ground.

'Are you able to walk now?' he asked.

Athena tried to get up and although her stomach was still in pain, she pretended as though she was better.

'How do we get through the marshes?'

'Well, we need to jump quite far! Can you manage that?'

'Sure. I'll give it a go. I mean, what's the worst that can happen?' Athena asked, smiling.

Benny and Twit stared at each other.

Twit replied, 'Well, if you fall, then you will sink. It will be fine as long as either Benny or I are close by– to help you out!'

Athena nodded but then looked over at Malo.

'What about him?' she asked.

'Twit will get a rope and tie it around Malo's wrists to his waist. Twit will be fine, I can assure you,' Benny confirmed.

That wasn't the response Athena had hoped for, but she decided not to ask any more questions in case Benny or Twit started to get suspicious.

Benny jumped first and reached the other side without any problem. Then, it was Athena's turn. She took a deep breath and jumped as far as she could. She only made it by a few inches. She lost her balance and instead of falling back into the marshes, she fell into Benny arms who caught her.

'Good jump!' he whispered.

Athena flinched again and subtly tried to get away from Benny's embrace, but he was too strong.

It was Twit's turn to jump over. Twit was one of the best soldiers at jumping and that was why he was always assigned to gather prisoners. Even with the extra weight, he always managed to land safely on the other side of the marshes.

Twit reached Athena and Benny with the rope tightly tied across his waist. He quickly removed it, only to see the huge red marks left.

'Doesn't that hurt you?' Athena asked moving closer to Twit to touch the mark.

'No, it doesn't hurt that much,' he replied, feeling his ears burn up as she touched him. He couldn't remember the last time he was this intimate with a girl.

'Athena, come,' Benny said, quickly moving Athena away from Twit. Benny suddenly turned around and shot a glare at Twit.

Twit mouthed back "what", but Benny just turned around and ignored him.

Athena asked Benny, 'What about Malo?'

'Don't worry! Twit will carry him until we reach General Avran's accommodation.'

'Then?' Athena asked.

'Then he will go in the dungeons and stay as a prisoner,' Benny replied.

'What about me?' Athena asked anxiously.

'Depends,' Benny said.

'On what?' Athena asked slowly.

'Your behaviour,' Benny said, smiling at her, once again, and flashing his yellow rotting teeth. He held her hand very firmly that way she wouldn't be able to let go.

As soon as I can move my arms and legs again, I'm going to beat the arrogance out of him!

Athena smiled.

It's so fun having a conversation with you without talking. I can say whatever I want without exercising my mouth. It's a dream come true!

Benny tugged at Athena's hand and told her it was time to move on. She had no choice but to follow him.

It took another ten minutes to walk from the marshes to the entrance of the huge crater.

The trees up close were very big. Each tree trunk was hollow with a few indents on the inside so the soldiers could climb up.

'Is that how the soldiers get up onto the rope?' Athena asked.

'Yes!' Benny and Twit answered at the same time. Benny turned to Twit and snarled at him.

'Why do you keep doing that?' Twit asked, irritated.

'Because she's mine!' Benny hissed.

'So what? I'm not allowed to talk to her?' Twit asked, completely stunned.

'That would be great.' Benny replied and turned back to Athena.

'Athena, would you like to go up the trees?' he asked in a sweet voice.

Twit rolled his eyes.

'Yes!' Athena replied immediately as she was curious of how the soldiers did their training.

Benny brought her to the closest tree. She went inside and looked up. She was able to see the sunlight coming from the top. She went up, placing her feet in the small holes. They alternated which made it easier to climb up.

As soon as she reached the end of the footsteps, there was a hole that had the rope in sight.

Athena went through the hole with little difficulty, but would have fallen off if it weren't for the rope.

'Hold onto the rope only with your hands and let your body drop,' Benny called out from below.

Although she was a bit terrified, Athena found it all very exciting. She took hold of the rope and felt the wind gush across her face.

'This is amazing,' Athena yelled out.

'I told you,' Benny screamed back at her.

'I wasn't talking to you,' she yelled back.

'Oh no!' she muttered. She offended Benny.

Benny scowled. He turned to Twit and slapped him with all his force against his face.

'Ow!' Twit screamed, 'What was that for?'

'Athena was talking to you, wasn't she? Have you and she been doing things behind my back? You *have*, haven't you!' Benny yelled.

Twit suddenly started laughing.

'You are *so* into this girl, she's actually driving you insane. We've all been together since we first met her. We couldn't have done anything behind your back,' Twit said in his defence.

'You're right, you're right Twit, but what should I do? She's not interested in me,' Benny said, scratching his head very fast in irritation.

'Well, she's not interested in me either,' Twit said.

'She *can't* be interested in Malo,' Benny said.

'Well, it would make sense if she was! I mean, they were together in the forest...'

'Now I detest her. How could she choose *Malo* over me? I'm just so...'

'Perfect?' Twit suggested.

'Yes, perfect. So darn perfect, yet she chooses this scum over perfect Benny!'

Twit started sniggering.

'What's so funny, nugget?' Benny asked, not amused.

'It's just... you sound ridiculous,' Twit said, now crying of laughter.

'Hello, who am I? Why, I'm Perfect Benny! Why am I called Perfect Benny? Because I'm just so darn perfect,' Twit continued in an accent.

Benny pursed his lips and then slapped Twit again.

Twit howled. His face was now bleeding.

'Why did you do that again?'

'Because I'm just so darn perfect,' Benny said, imitating Twit with his accent from before.

'No, you see, it's not funny when you do it.'

Benny pushed him backwards.

'You have crossed the line this time...' Benny warned, about to punch Twit in the stomach.

'How do I get down from here?' Athena quickly shouted out to save Twit from the unnecessary pain.

Benny immediately changed his facial expression and started smiling as he looked up at Athena.

'You can either go on to the next tree or if you want to stop now, you can just let go,' Benny said, beaming.

He is such a freak, a drama queen and is just the biggest psychopath I know.

Athena nodded in agreement.

'You couldn't be more right.' Athena murmured.

Athena jumped down from the high tree without any problem. By now, the pain from the punch was gone.

'What should we do now?' she asked Benny and Twit.

'How about we go and meet General Avran.'

'I'd rather not! I've heard bad things about him.'

'That wasn't a question, Athena,' Benny replied, still smiling.

Fear immediately overcame Athena and she found herself running.

She ran towards Malo and asked, 'What do I do now?'

You can't do anything now! The best you can do is act stupid and ruthless. That way we could have a good chance of being in the same prison cell, but you have to be very insolent to get there!

Athena nodded and whispered, 'Alright.'

Benny picked Athena up and ordered Twit to drag Malo across the ground.

They walked around the edge of the crater. Athena peeped down and saw five white pillars in the middle of the cave, training arenas and stables in the corners.

'Where do the soldiers eat and sleep? Where are the dungeons?' Athena asked, unable to spot them.

'There is another storey beneath that. In fact, it's like a whole other world down there. What you see before you is only the beginning. It goes much further down into the ground than you could ever imagine. It's going to be a long walk.'

Athena subtly turned around to see Malo who was being dragged along the ground by Twit.

This is horrible!

Athena felt very bad but there was nothing she could do, so she turned around. They were now at the top of the narrow staircase leading down to the arena. Athena noticed how uneven the stairs were.

'What happens if I fall off?' she asked, looking down.

'Then you break your neck and die,' Benny said, bluntly.

Athena gulped. She wasn't afraid of heights, but she was afraid that Benny was going to push her off. However, hearing his thoughts, those were not his intentions.

'You can go down first, Benny,' Athena said.

'Sure! If you want.'

'That wasn't a question,' she said, suddenly smiling.

Benny grabbed her ear violently.

'Careful not to cross the line,' he said aggressively, as he let go of her ear.

His stared at her for a few moments before he turned around and started walking down.

Are you all right? I swear as soon as I can start moving again, I'm going to really punish him!

They started walking down the stairs carefully. Benny turned around, ignoring Athena who was right behind him, and said to Twit who was putting Malo on his back, 'You can drag him down!'

'What? No! That could kill him,' Twit said, completely outraged.

'Don't talk back to me. Do what I say otherwise it will be two days in the dungeons for you!'

Twit sighed and got the rope out again.

'I'm sorry, Malo. When you can start feeling your arms again, pinch my leg and I'll untie your wrists. Then, you can beat up Benny. Beat him up enough for the both of us, will you?' Twit whispered.

'Athena, get to the front NOW!' Benny ordered.

Athena was so afraid of Benny, tears came to her eyes. Her hands were shaking violently as she tried to wipe those tears away.

'Stop crying and do as I say.' Benny hissed.

Athena quickly rushed past Benny but almost fell as she tripped over a rock on an uneven step. Benny caught her but told her to watch it.

Athena went to the front, unable to look at Benny as she was so disgusted by his attitude.

Athena tried to look around, but Benny's thoughts were too loud.

How could she not like me? I'm not being nice to her anymore! I'll leave her to General Avran. If he is in a good mood, he will keep her to himself...but if he is in a bad mood, he will lock her in the dungeons with the other prisoners. I hope he does that. She is just insolent and rude and should be put to death immediately!

Athena gasped.

'Benny, I don't think I can drag Malo any further,' Twit said, panting and looking at Malo.

'Why not?' Benny snapped.

'He's getting too many cuts.' Twit explained.

'I don't care anymore. Do what you want, nugget! He'll be dead before sunset anyway,' Benny replied.

'What?' Athena asked, slowly turning around in horror.

'Malo is despised by General Avran! I highly doubt he would let him leave this place alive,' Benny said, laughing.

'You're a monster,' Athena whispered.

Benny scowled. 'Just keep walking!'

'Yes, just keep walking to my death.' Athena said.

Benny nudged her and told her to keep quiet.

Athena looked around. She felt as though she was really walking down to the Underworld. There was no source of light apart from the sunshine, beaming down onto the whole crater. She could imagine after sundown, this place really did turn into the Underworld. Athena decided to study the area more. She could make out five pillars put in a particular order to form a large circle. Within that circle, the ground was covered with mosaics with many different shades of blue. The light blue pieces were put together to make two swords, touching each other at the tip.

It was truly magnificent especially as the sun shone on the two swords. Around that huge arena there were much smaller practice arenas for duels.

Further away, in the corners, there were huge stables filled with many dark brown horses. Athena spotted a single black stallion that presumably belonged to General Avran.

Suddenly, Malo pinched Twit's leg. Twit carefully turned around and smiled at the sight of Malo moving his legs.

He subtly bent down and untied the ropes on Malo's wrists. Malo finally got up, but almost tripped down the stairs. Luckily, Twit pulled him back in time.

'Wait till we get to the bottom of the stairs. If you push Benny off the stairs, he might take your girlfriend down with him,' Twit whispered very softly as Benny was in front of him.

They finally reached the bottom of the stairs. There was no one in sight.

'Where is everyone?' Athena asked, a bit anxious.

'At lunch.' Twit replied.

Benny turned around.

'How many times do I have to tell you not to talk? It annoys me!' he yelled as he turned around, but then suddenly saw Malo stand in front of him, blocking the sunlight. Benny stepped back a few paces.

'You're not supposed to be up yet!' he said, completely amazed.

'I got lucky, but unfortunately the same can't be said for you.' Malo said, cracking his neck as he moved forwards.

'What's tha... that supposed to mean?' Benny asked, failing to hide his fear.

'It means I'm going to beat you up so much, you might want to take a few drops from your vial *now* to stop the pain!'

'Why?' Benny asked, acting completely innocent.

'Why? Because you flirted with my wife. You harassed her. You insulted her *and* you hit her!' Malo yelled back.

'I didn't hit her.' Benny replied truthfully.

'Yes, that's right, but you pinched her ear, and now it's going to bruise. In my books, that definitely counts as a hit,' Malo replied. Athena bit her lip to restrain herself from smiling.

'Now, I want you to apologise to Athena.' he continued.

'*What?*' Benny asked, widening his eyes.

Malo walked up to him and looked down at Benny, pointing his finger at Athena.

Benny sighed, knowing he didn't have a choice.

'I'm sorry!' he said quietly.

Athena nodded.

Malo punched him very hard in the stomach and across his face which left Benny on the ground.

Malo rubbed his hands together. He looked around. 'Now, where's General Avran?'

X

'Now, everyone is to eat in silence so Drake can have some time to think about the mistakes he committed today,' General Avran said as he walked up and down the stage, staring at the young soldier who was lying on the ground, shaking.

'Get up, boy, and eat your dinner. Then we will decide your fate!'

'Yes, General Avran! Thank you, General Avran!' Drake replied and slowly limped down from the stage and made his way to his assigned seat.

'Luckily for you all, I am in a very good mood as today is the day we turn our newest soldier, Sedty, into an Agalit!' General Avran announced.

There was a round of applause and the enormous man stood up. He was a huge muscular bald, black man with piercings all the way up both of his ears. He was, by far, the tallest soldier in the army.

His eyes were very dark brown.

'This will be his last meal for...'

Suddenly, Malo galloped into the room on the stallion with Twit at his side on a brown horse and Athena behind them both, also on a brown horse.

'General Avran,' Malo proudly said, sitting up straight.

'How dare you mount my horse!' he yelled, all red in the face.

'Oh, this is *your* horse? I'm sorry. Well, I don't think you would mind if I cut off a bit of his mane?' Malo asked, knowing what the answer was.

'You wouldn't dare!' the general said, articulating every syllable and pointing his finger towards Malo.

Malo mouthed the words as the general was speaking which made a few soldiers laugh.

'I would. You know me,' Malo said in a happy tone, drawing out his dagger and cutting a short piece from the horse's mane.

'Oh Malo, you do like to make an entrance!' a soldier murmured.

'How dare you! Guards arrest him immediately!' General Avran yelled.

'Oh yes. I hope you don't mind but I sent your guards to sleep,' Malo said, looking down at his small vial.

'After all, they did seem rather... tired,' Malo said, looking back up, smiling evilly.

General Avran decided it was no use losing his voice on a silly boy so he lowered his voice.

'What do you want?' he asked.

'I want to leave this place and have your stallion,' Malo said.

The general suddenly laughed which echoed through the courtroom.

'You can't have my horse! Trida was given to me by the Council when I was nine years old. I have had that horse for a decade,' General Avran said, utterly irritated.

Malo dropped the hair and tucked his dagger back in his belt. He looked up at the general.

'You are only nineteen years old yet you have control of the best army in the world.'

'Exactly.' General Avran replied. Malo sighed, with a smirk at the corner of his mouth.

'Well, you've had this horse for a decade. It's been long enough and I like Trida. So, I will be leaving now!' Malo announced.

Once again, the general's laugh echoed through the room once more.

'Alex, Piout, Fiju! Seize them!' the general said, ordering the three soldiers nearest Malo, Twit and Athena.

'And bring Trida here!' he added.

The three soldiers had no problem seizing them. Athena didn't try to fight back when they took her off the horse. Twit knew that there was no escape and therefore didn't fight back either and Malo didn't want to admit defeat so he got off the horse and sent Trida to the general himself.

He patted Trida on the side which made her run down the hall and even onto the stage.

'A simple "thank you" would suffice!' Malo yelled across the hall to the general who was stroking Trida on the nose.

'You are out of your mind!' he replied.

'At least I gave you your Trida back like you asked. I asked to leave but you're not giving me that so everyone in this room will now know that it is me that has won this battle, acting like the bigger man... even if I am the one who ends up in the dungeons,' Malo said, humiliating the general in front of the army once again.

'General, which dungeons should I lock them in?' Alex asked.

'Don't put them in the dungeons just yet. Escort them to the operating room!'

Alex nodded and led both Twit and Athena out, while Fiju and Piout dragged Malo out.

Athena looked around but all she could see were uniform rows of dark blue tents that surrounded the courtroom.

'Why are we going to the operating room?' Malo asked Piout.

'They're turning Sedty into an Agalit this afternoon. I suppose he just wants an audience,' Piout replied.

Athena's eyes widened. She didn't want to watch someone being operated on.

'Do we have to watch?' she asked wearily.

'Well, you have to be there. You can close your eyes,' Alex said.

'Wow, you're the second person I have ever met to have blue eyes,' he continued.

'Really? Who's the first?' Athena asked.

'General Avran,' Alex answered.

Athena had never met someone with blue eyes before Aurore. Maybe she and General Avran were more alike than she knew.

'Okay, down we go,' Alex said. Athena looked down the stairs that led to the operation room and General Avran's makeshift house. She started to make her way down.

There were many Rects at the corners of the bottom storey. Their wings were glowing white light; the only source of 'natural' light this far down in the ground.

Athena turned around to see if Malo was following, and sure enough he was.

Man, I hate this place! As soon as we enter the operating room, don't freak out.

Athena took this into account and continued walking down the stairs with caution.

I'm sorry your plan didn't work. It was good I have to admit, but leaving them at the gate asleep for a few hours was a long shot. At least we're still both alive!

Athena finally reached the bottom of the stairs. The ground was hard, black and rocky. The ceiling was extremely high, which made every spoken word, echo.

'Over there,' Alex said, pointing in front of them.

Athena smiled at him out of politeness and continued walking.

'So, Fiju, how have you been? I mean, I am the person who saved your life, yet you still handed me over to Avran like fresh meat! Let me tell you this; if you are in any danger ever again, don't rely on me to save you!' Malo warned him.

Fiju gulped, 'I didn't mean to rat you out, Malo. You know how Avran intimidates me. I get all nervous. I'm sorry!'

Malo breathed deeply but remained quiet.

'In you go.' Alex said to Athena while opening the door.

Athena went in. Her heart raced uncontrollably the moment she saw huge, transparent rectangular containers which were placed along the wall facing the door. They were filled with a bright green liquid.

Agalit blood.

There must have been at least twenty litres of it.

Athena saw a man strapped onto a flat board. His eyes were closed.

'Is he dead?' Athena whispered.

'Yes, he was already sick from... um' Alex began.

'Being an Agalit.' she finished.

'Yes, we were liberating him from a burden,' Alex said.

Tears came to her eyes. 'You think being an Agalit is a burden?' she whispered, turning to him.

'Well, I don't know! It's just what General Avran said,' Alex replied.

Malo suddenly came in with Fiju and Piout either side.

'Wow! There are more containers since I was last in here which was only a few months ago!' Malo noticed.

'Yes. We found one female Agalit a few weeks ago and we found this Agalit,' Piout said, nodding at the body, 'a few days ago. We're lucky!'

Malo laughed. Athena shot a glance at him so he quickly stopped.

'What is so funny?' Fiju snapped.

'It's just that... nothing,' Malo said, still grinning.

'What would you do it you found an Agalit right now?' Malo asked out of curiosity, glancing at Athena.

'Nothing. We have the amount required now. Enough to produce five Agalits of our own!' Piout announced proudly.

'So, you kill Agalits only to re-create them?' Athena asked.

'Yes! And with Renyu, we can give them any ability of our own choosing,' Fiju continued.

'What ability has General Avran chosen for his future Agalits?'

'The soldier you will see in a few minutes will be turned into an Agalit with the ability to be the strongest Agalit alive. He would be able to break anything. Metal, force shields-'

'Shut up, Fiju!' Piout ordered.

Suddenly General Avran entered with Sedty to his left.

'Piout, call Renyu now. We should not waste any time!' General Avran ordered.

'Right away, general!' Piout said and left to another room connected to the operating room.

General Avran sighed.

'If anything goes wrong Sedty, you were my favourite soldier!' he declared, patting Sedty on the shoulder.

'Oh please! That's what you said to Patrick before you murdered him. That's what you said to Killian before you pushed him down the stairs,' Malo said.

General Avran groaned. 'Why do you always have to defy *everything* I say?'

'I'm sorry! If you would like me to send you flowers and chocolates, just tell me! I would do anything for you!' Malo said, fluttering his eyelashes.

General Avran sighed.

'You are such a difficult child. That's why your parents chose to die, instead of spending the rest of their lives with you!' he blurted out.

'It is a shame that my parents died, because if they hadn't, I would have never met you!' Malo replied, used to the insults that were thrown at him.

'Yes, it is a shame that you came along and made my life a living hell!'

'I am four years older than you yet you treat me as a child when in fact it is you being a child, Nicolas!' Malo replied, now raising his voice.

General Avran paused for a moment.

'How dare you call me by my first name!' he exclaimed and spat on Malo.

Malo was about to lunge on him as his hands were tied back but then Renyu and Piout arrived.

'General. Is it already time?' Renyu began.

'I'm afraid so. Fiju, remove the former Agalit from the board!'

'Yes, general.' Fiju said.

General Avran was watching Fiju remove the body but then Athena caught his eye.

Athena didn't know what to do but she wanted to study his blue eyes. They were exactly like hers which drew her into his eyes even more.

General Avran looked down and moved towards the operating board.

'The body has been removed. Should I help Sedty onto the board now, general?' Fiju asked.

'Yes.' he ordered.

Before Sedty sat on the board, General Avran grabbed his shoulder and shook his hand. Sedty nodded and then laid down on the black board.

Renyu securely strapped him in and then removed one of the many containers off the wall.

He unscrewed one of the metal caps at one end of the container, took out a huge syringe and inserted some of the green blood. He then removed the syringe and placed the metal cap back on. He made sure he did it quickly just to make sure no blood leaked out. Every drop was incredibly valuable.

'This will sting very much, but at the end it will all be worth it. Just imagine it! You being the strongest man in the entire world!' Renyu said, trying to calm Sedty down as his heart was racing.

Suddenly, another man came in.

'Renyu, you have remembered to insert the mutation in the base S-Y?' the little man asked, distressed.

'Of course.' Renyu replied, completely relaxed, still tapping the air bubbles out of the syringe.

'What does he mean? What is he talking about, Renyu?' General Avran asked.

'We are just discussing about the mutation I changed in the Agalit's blood. The mutation changes the power. So, in this case, the ability from shattering glass to immense strength.' Renyu explained.

'Good, good. Continue with the procedure.'

Renyu smiled and cut open Sedty's tunic with scissors. He then put the scissors down and made a mental note of where Sedty's heart was so he could aim precisely. He had aimed perfectly in every other operation. It wasn't an option to fail for his last operation.

'Now, this will sting very much,' Renyu warned as he pierced into his heart with the huge syringe filled with Agalit's blood. The needle, if that even covered the word, was so thick that it covered the full surface of the heart. There was no point in giving him anesthetic. There was no medicine strong enough to help with the process of being turned from a human into an Agalit.

Sedty yelled as loud as he possibly could. He felt the blood fuse through his veins, capillaries and arteries.

Soldiers who were working in the stables stopped and heard his uproar. Those who were practicing in the arenas also stopped to hear Sedty.

'Poor man.' a soldier muttered.

The cry was so loud in the operating room that they all covered their ears expect for Renyu. He continued to inject the blood.

The container had a third left but Renyu could feel Sedty's pain so he stopped the infusion.

However, Sedty continued to scream.

'Why did you stop?' General Avran demanded to know.

'We may have put too much in him. I may have to take some out!' Renyu yelled back.

'No! It has to work!'

'Well, if we put too much in him then he will die. There is only so much blood a human can uphold.'

'He isn't human anymore. He is an Agalit!' General Avran yelled back.

Soldiers from all over the headquarters could hear this and felt more pity for the huge soldier who was in excruciating pain.

'Make him stop yelling!' General Avran ordered.

'I can't! I haven't produced any medicine for Agalits. Everything I use on him is now useless. His skin is too tough now. He will break all needles except for this one,' Renyu explained, indicating the immensely huge needle he was holding with difficulty.

'How long will he keep yelling for?'

'I have no idea! It changes with every person. For such a big man, he has a surprisingly low pain threshold.'

Athena couldn't bear the pain Sedty was in.

Can someone help me? Please! If only they could hear me. If only they could pull me out of this misery.

That was it! Athena rushed towards him and held his arm. She felt so much empathy for him, she had tears streaming down her cheeks.

Sedty suddenly opened his eyes.

His blue eyes.

He stopped yelling as all his pain flooded away onto Athena.

'That's amazing!' Renyu gasped, coming closer to Athena. However, before he could take another step, she collapsed onto the ground.

Her vision gradually turned blurry, but she could still see General Avran was walking over to her. His blue eyes were the last thing she could see.

'Why are you doing this to me?' Malo exclaimed.

'It's what you deserve you mean, insolent child. You are lucky that your friend Athena is still here because otherwise you wouldn't! I put you in the same dungeon as the prisoner you took two fingers from. I hope you will find your justice there!' Alex said, reading out the letter that General Avran had handed over to him.

'So, I'm supposed to rot here?' Malo asked, trembling.

'I'm sorry! They are not my orders, they are Avran's. If I could do anything, I would at least change you to a different dungeon cell!' Alex replied as he saw the prisoner stroking Malo's hair.

'I really would!' Alex whispered, feeling sorry for Malo, unlike the other soldiers who were all pointing and laughing at him.

Benny limped over to him with a black eye.

'Well, you finally get your justice. I paid your friend ten rubies to beat you up every hour for at least three days,' Benny said with a strained laugh.

Malo started laughing as well.

Benny suddenly frowned. 'Why are you laughing? If anything, you should be crying!'

'I'm laughing because you're really going to be dry on money this month!' Malo explained.

'What do you mean?' Benny asked, vexed.

'Allow me to refreshen your memory. When you dragged me out of the army's premises a week or so ago, we bet that if I came back in less than a fortnight, you would give me four hundred rubies. So, come on, pay up!' Malo said, grinning.

Benny couldn't speak for a while but then said, 'I only have eleven hundred rubies left! How would I be able to live?' Benny asked, exasperated.

'Well, you can start by giving me the four hundred rubies! Or when I get out of this dungeon, I'll kill you and then take all of your money.'

Benny sighed. 'I don't have the money on me right now!'

'That's fine. Give it to me when I leave!' Malo demanded.

Benny sighed nodded and then left.

'Your name is Malo! I will kick you where it hurts!' the prisoner said very slowly.

'Well, that's just... great.' Malo replied sarcastically, knocking his head repeatedly against the metal bars.

Athena suddenly woke up. Renyu was next to her, sitting on a chair.

'Ah, Athena. At last. You're awake,' he said, smiling.

Athena scratched her head. 'How long have I been asleep for?'

'Just for a few hours,' he softly replied.

'What happened?' Athena asked. She suddenly sat up and looked around. Everything was unfamiliar to her. 'Where am I?'

'First of all, you are in General Avran's makeshift house. He has very kindly offered you his room. To answer your first question, you touched Sedty's hand and then you fell to the ground.'

Athena remembered it all now.

Renyu took off his glasses.

'There is one thing I don't understand about you!' he said.

'Oh yes? What's that?'

'I'm not sure whether you are an Agalit or not.'

'Oh.'

'You see, there are very rare cases where a human can be born with blue eyes. When I saw you in the operating room, I really thought you were an Agalit. But then, over the last few hours, as I have been staring at you, I begin to doubt if you really are an Agalit.'

'What makes you say that?'

'I have noticed a few bruises on your wrists. Agalits have very tough skin. Therefore, they should not bruise. That is the only thing that has stopped me from believing that you are an Agalit. I have done research on Agalits my entire life and have read a handful of cases about Bruising. However, scientifically speaking, it's just not possible. So, are you just an exception? Are you a human outcast? Or were you made into an artificial Agalit? Were you sent from somewhere else as a spy?'

They were both an inch away from each other. Athena was grinning as was the scientist.

'You are telling me that you do *not* believe I am a real Agalit?'

Even though Athena was sure she was one, there was a little pain in her chest.

'Do you have a power, Athena?'

Athena didn't reply.

'Well, perhaps I will inform the general about my concerns!' Renyu threatened. 'Bruises and denial. I have enough reasons.'

'How would you do it?'

'I will get one of those painfully huge syringes and pierce your heart with it. If red blood comes out then you are human but if green blood trickles out, then you are an Agalit. Only once green blood pours out of you will I have no more suspicions.'

Athena looked him in the eyes. 'You wouldn't dare.'

'Oh, wouldn't I?'

'No. It won't happen, I can tell you that,' Athena said with such hostility.

'Do not underestimate the influence I have over General Avran, girl. One word out of my mouth and he would be ready to send his army unequipped to battle. That is how much trust he has in me.'

Renyu stood up and left the room.

Athena knew there was nothing else she could do. She could hear guards outside her room and besides, where would she go?

Athena stood up and looked around the room. There were pictures and paintings of General Avran.

He was so young in all the pictures. His face was pale with big blue eyes and light brown hair.

'No... is it possible?' she whispered to herself.

Athena took a deep breath and looked closer just to be sure. General Avran looked just like her when he was a child.

XI

Renyu suddenly entered the room.

'General Avran has given me consent to operate on you. He, too, is intrigued by you!'

'Well, you most certainly do not have *my* consent!' Athena said, harshly.

'I don't need your consent. You are under my authority now!' Renyu said, laughing as he grabbed hold of Athena's wrist and pushed her back into the operating room.

'Stop it! Somebody help!' Athena yelled out.

'Nobody can hear you nor do they care! No one can help you now,' Renyu whispered.

Athena's eyes widened. He pushed her onto the board and violently strapped her in.

'Please don't do this Renyu! It's not you! You are an intelligent man, and you ought to know that this-'

'Oh, do shut up!' Renyu snapped.

He took a huge empty container, and once again, inserted the huge needle into the container, making it able to take out a few litres of blood.

'I will only take out a bit of your blood,' he said.

'Wow! Thanks a lot. I feel so much better now!' Athena replied sarcastically.

General Avran suddenly walked in. 'Are you commencing the procedure?'

Renyu nodded.

'Maybe it's not the right choice after all.'

General Avran turned to Athena. 'I will believe you if you tell me the truth.'

'General, that may not be the-'

'Be quiet! This is between Athena and me!'

'But she won't tell you that she -'

'I will not ask you again, Renyu. Be quiet!'

'But, general, she is-'

'Do not question my authority!' General Avran said, raising his voice.

Renyu remained quiet.

The general looked at Athena and waited for an honest response.

'Yes, I am an Agalit. I have a gift, I promise! Please, don't operate on me,' she pleaded, with tears in her eyes.

'Very well! Renyu, release her.'

'General, how do we know that she is not lying?'

'I just can. Like you said, she has blue eyes. Now, remove the straps immediately!' General Avran ordered.

Athena took a deep breath and smiled. Renyu sighed and unwillingly freed her.

'Come with me!' the general said as he opened the door.

Athena jumped off the board. Renyu quickly took out a knife from his lab coat and stabbed Athena on her back. Her skin bent the knife.

The general told her to go back to the makeshift house. Athena obeyed and left immediately. He then turned to Renyu.

'How dare you defy me! She's a helpless girl, and you just couldn't wait to get your hands on her blood. I can't stand the sight of you!' the general said, and with that, he left, violently shutting the door behind himself.

'That girl will pay for that!' Renyu snarled.

'Thank you for stopping him,' Athena said, smiling at the general.

He nodded, but continued looking down. They were both back in his room. Athena made herself comfortable on the chair, whilst he was leaning against the wall.

'Where do you come from?' he asked, looking up.

'Oakrose. Pass the hills over the volcano.'

'I can imagine it's a nice life in the countryside! Not much to do there though. Any brothers or sisters?'

'No. None that I know of.'

'So, you are not sure?'

'Where do you come from?' Athena asked, turning the conversation around.

'I have lived here for most of my life.'

'In this terrible place?'

'Yes! That's why I was appointed general at such a young age!'

'Do you have any brothers or sisters?'

'Yes.'

'Which one?'

'Sisters!'

'How many?'

'At least two.'

Athena nodded.

General Avran sighed, looked down and then looked back up at Athena.

'You're one of them, Athena!'

She looked up at him, but didn't say anything for a few moments.

'When I saw those pictures of you,' Athena said, touching the picture frames, 'I thought you looked exactly like me!'

General Avran sat on the bed. 'I knew you were my sister the moment I first saw you.'

'How?'

'I feel a strong connection with you. A few Agalits have been captured and killed here. I'd ask them questions with Renyu before they died. To know their power, know their story, ask where they came from. I never felt anything. It's different with you. As you just said, we look alike. We have the same colour hair, same nose, long upper and lower eyelashes, thick eyebrows, similar bone structure... I mean, the list goes on.'

Athena felt her eyes look at those particular points as he listed them. She smiled and realised he was right.

'So, how old were you when you arrived in the army?'

'The Council says I was six years old.'

'I'm seventeen, so that-'

'You're seventeen? Twit told me you were twenty-six! I couldn't believe him because you look so young. Seventeen makes a lot more sense. I like you even more now! I'm not the youngest one here anymore,' he said with a big grin. Being the youngest person was the hardest thing for him to deal with in the army. Demanding authority from men who were older than him was something he always found challenging and stressful.

'Anyway, if you arrived here at six years old and now you are nineteen, then you have been here for thirteen years. Thirteen years ago, I was taken from my family. That must mean we were both taken at the same time. We were both taken during the Chamcok revolt.'

Nicolas couldn't help but grunt at the word "Chamcok".

'Well done for counting up to thirteen.' he said as he gave her a slow clap.

Athena tried her hardest not to smile at that because she didn't want to encourage such sarcasm. She had quite enough of that from Malo.

'This means we were taken away from our family! Our family of Agalits. I wish I knew all their gifts. What is your gift?' Athena asked, trying to calm down as her mind was bombarding her with questions.

'When I was eight years old, they removed all my blood and then inserted human blood straight away.'

'How is this procedure even *possible*? Don't you die without all your blood-'

'Well, it is possible. You saw what just happened with Sedty. I was the first person to have the operation. I was turned into a human, not the other way around.' he explained.

Athena didn't dare respond. What could she say to that?

'I don't remember what my gift was.' he whispered, his voice cracking.

'What's your first name? Is it really Nicolas or was Malo just winding you up?'

'It is Nicolas, and how did you meet Malo anyway? He's one nasty piece of work!'

'He really isn't. He is just incredibly stubborn!' Athena grinned.

'Well, he has done pretty awful things here.' Nicolas explained.

'Like what?'

'Well, to begin with, he cut off two fingers of a prisoner!'

'Yes, he told me that.'

'Well, unfortunately, I didn't understand him then, and I still don't understand him now. At this moment, he is in the same prison cell as that prisoner. A double punishment!' he said, grinning.

Athena gasped. 'He'll get killed if he stays there.'

'No, he won't. I wouldn't allow it!'

'How do you know what's happening in the dungeons right now? For all we know, he could already be dead!' Athena warned.

'He's fine. I told the prisoner not to lay a finger on him.'

'Did you offer this prisoner a deal? Will you give him something in return?'

Nicolas snorted. 'Of course not, he's a prisoner!'

'That's exactly my point, Nicolas. He has nothing to lose. I want to see Malo now!' Athena said as she stood up, stamping her small foot against the ground.

'Fine,' Nicolas said, sighing.

'I also want to leave with Malo immediately!' Athena declared.

Nicolas clenched his jaw. 'You want to leave? You just met your brother, and you don't even want to stay for a meal?'

'I want to meet my family. I want to meet my parents. You're not what I imagined. I would be happy to have a meal with you and spend time with you elsewhere. Like the Four Flames! Not here though. It's horrible and evil and I need to leave as soon as possible. Please. Let me go.'

'*You* may leave, but Malo may not! After all the disturbances he has caused here, he would have a twenty-year sentence minimum. Truth be told, I would have killed him today if it weren't for you.'

'He doesn't deserve a twenty-year sentence, yet alone a death sentence! You expect me to stay here to get to know my brother? All I see in front of my eyes is a boy who has a complex with authority, and wants to see the only person who has saved my life more than once in the past week die! I love the idea of having a brother, but I also hate knowing that the most evil person in the lands is related to me. You can change my opinion about you if you let Malo go. That's all it takes. Let one man go.'

Nicolas sighed. 'It doesn't matter anyway. I only decide on half of the matter. The other half is decided by the Council.'

'I want to see him *now*!' Athena exclaimed.

He rolled his eyes and brought her to the dungeons.

Athena rushed into his dungeon as soon as Nicolas opened it up.

'Malo, where are you?' she asked in exasperation, as Malo was now where in sight.

Suddenly, she heard a groan from behind the door.

Athena closed the door and saw him with blood trickling down his mouth. The prisoner was behind him; picking at Malo's hair like a mother baboon does to her baby.

'What did you do, you monster?' Athena demanded, talking to the prisoner.

'I was paid ten rubies to beat him up every hour. That is what I have done for the last eight hours.'

Athena turned around to Nicolas who was also in the dungeon.

'He's fine. I told the prisoner not to put a finger on him'

'Are you out of your mind?' Athena asked, restraining herself from shouting.

Nicolas took a deep breath.

'How was I supposed to know someone was going to pay him to-'

'It's too late to hear your excuses.'

She pulled Malo up with difficulty and headed for the door.

'You can't do that,' Nicolas said, holding her arm.

'Why ever not?' she asked angrily. She had had enough.

'Papers have been signed and sealed. He's not allowed to leave for another twenty years. I'm sorry.'

'Then get rid of *that* prisoner!' she demanded, pointing at the prisoner who was sitting in the corner.

'That can be arranged, but unfortunately, there are rules to respect. Malo cannot be in a dungeon by himself. He needs an inmate.'

Athena looked around the dungeon. It was surprisingly big. There were two adequate beds at the end of the room, and a small table in the middle. In the corner, there was a single toilet surrounded by blue curtains.

'I will be his inmate.' Athena announced.

Nicolas laughed.

'Why would you do that?' he asked as he folded his arms, rather amused.

'Because I'm all he has and he's all I have. I *refuse* to leave without him.'

'You can be Malo's inmate if you wish. I'm just saying, it's not a very wise choice.'

'I'll take my chances.'

Nicolas sighed and was about to argue back, but knew there was no point.

'As you wish,' General Avran said and left the room, returning a few moments later with two guards.

'Put him in another dungeon.' he ordered.

The two guards obeyed and lifted the large prisoner up, tied his hands together and brought him out of the dungeon.

'I don't know what else to say.' Nicolas said.

'Help me bring Malo to the bed, and then leave if you can't help us.' she snapped.

General Avran looked over at Malo. He was barely conscious. Even in that state, Nicolas couldn't help but feel his hands and jaw clench. Every part of him hated Malo.

'Nicolas, help me!' Athena ordered as she waited for his help.

For the first time since he could remember, Nicolas swallowed his pride, and went over to help his sister. Together, they carried Malo over to the bed. Without saying a word, Nicolas turned around and left

'Are you alright?' she asked, bending down.

Malo groaned.

'He beat me up. My face is nothing compared to my stomach,' he said and showed his stomach to Athena.

She gasped. It was already bruising on the edges and the middle was completely bleeding.

'How did he do that?' she asked completely outraged.

'He removed one of the legs from the table.' Malo said, looking over at the table.

Athena turned around and could see red blood dripping onto the stone ground from one of the table legs.

'What else did he do?' Athena asked.

'Well, he punched my face, stabbed my stomach and kicked me on the back of the knee caps!'

'Malo, we're going to get out of here first thing tomorrow morning. I promise!' Athena said.

'How?'

'Well, we could try and get one of the guards to give the key?'

'It won't work! Guards just don't give out keys to prisoners. They would be killed straightaway in front of everyone in the courtroom!'

'Can we bribe someone?' Athena asked.

Malo's eyes widened. 'Yes!'

'Who?'

'Benny.'

'*Benny?*' Athena asked in disgust.

Yes! He owes me four hundred rubies, and I know that he can't afford to lose that much money. I'm sure he would be willing to co-operate.

'We're definitely leaving tomorrow then!' she announced as she sat down on the other bed.

I'm starving!

'Me too! We haven't eaten today.' Athena realised, as her stomach was grumbling.

Dinner will be soon, don't worry.

'Why aren't you speaking out loud?' Athena asked.

It hurts when I move my mouth. Besides I prefer not talking.

'Hey, you just said it hurts when you move your mouth, yet you just grinned!' Athena noticed.

Malo turned to her and winked.

After a few moments silence, she got up.

Where are you going?

'To ask what time it is.'

She walked to the door and looked through the metal bars, which were placed in the middle of the metal door.

'What time is it?' Athena asked.

A guard came towards her. It was Alex.

'Athena? What are you doing in a dungeon? I'll let you out,' Alex kindly said and pulled out his keys to unlock the door.

He finally found the right one and unlocked the door.

'Why are you here?'

'I don't want to leave this place without Malo, but General Avran says that he has to stay here for another twenty years.'

'That's a long time. So are you going to stay here for twenty years?' Alex asked.

'No, I need someone to give me the key to our dungeon that way we can escape!'

Alex slowly walked back a few paces.

'I can't help you! I would be sentenced to death if I helped a prisoner escape!'

'It wasn't you I had in mind. It was Benny.'

'Benny can't help you because he isn't a dungeon guard. I just spoke to him, actually. He didn't say very nice things! He said that you were General Avran's mistress, yet you claim that you are Malo's wife. Is that true?' Alex asked.

'No, of course not! He was angry at me because I didn't like him.' Athena replied honestly.

'I believe you for some strange reason. If you really were General Avran's mistress, then I would have seen you around, unlike another woman who only comes here to see him…'

Athena shuddered. She didn't want to think of who this other woman was.

'Would you be able to send Benny down here tomorrow morning?' she quickly asked.

'Yes, I can try, but I don't think he will help.' Alex said.

'We'll see about that! By the way, when is our dinner arriving?' Athena asked, but then suddenly saw a soldier carry two trays full of food.

Alex smiled, and Athena went back to her prison cell.

'Look! The food is here at last.' Malo said, looking at his tray on the table.

'Oh, you're talking now?' Athena asked, smirking.

'Yes, I have to move my mouth to eat, so I may as well talk to you too! Can you please bring my food over?'

Athena took their trays to his bed and sat next to him.

'What is this?' Athena asked, as she handed a tray over to Malo, and pointed to one of the dishes on it.

'It's called Simbuy. It's a type of vegetable stew with tomatoes, sweet potato and spinach. It's boiled and then turned into a stew. The colour is quite off putting but it actually tastes very good! Look, there's also fruit and a nice slice of steak. General Avran has been kind. I've never seen him offer this to any prisoner. If you weren't here, he would have just given me nuts.' Malo explained.

Athena laughed and agreed. 'He really doesn't like you. It's so bizarre to me.'

'Sshhh. Don't ruin my dinner. Let's just eat in peace. We deserve this after such a long day.'

'Benny will come tomorrow morning,' Athena confirmed after a few minutes of silence. 'How would he actually let us out? He isn't a dungeon guard. What is your plan, Malo?'

'Well, we can first tell him to give us four hundred rubies to let us out. I'm sure he won't accept, so we wait until we find a price that works for both him and me. Maybe even down to the price of one hundred rubies...

But then, if he is caught he would be sentenced to death. Paying one hundred rubies and then being sentenced doesn't seem too nice, even for Benny!' Malo said, thinking out loud.

'Well, we could tell him that after we've escaped, he can be the one to tell General Avran. Surely Nicolas wouldn't suspect him!'

Malo looked at Athena with admiration. 'You are clever, dear Athena, you know?'

'Well... I have my moments.' she said, flicking her hair over her shoulder.

Malo winked at her. 'You're learning. Anyway, where do we plan to go after we escape?' he asked.

Athena got up and looked around, but then suddenly turned around to him with a cheeky smile.

'We could carry on going to the Four Flames?' she asked, shyly.

'Yes, I know that, but *how*?' Malo snapped.

'What do you suggest?'

'We could always take the river that runs through the Forest Tatila. It's quite narrow and many willow trees dip into it, but it is the quickest way through the forest and we won't have to walk.' Malo said smiling.

'You are so lazy.' Athena laughed out as she jumped back onto her own bed.

'Excuse me?' he exclaimed, pointing down his wounded body.

Athena put her arms up. 'I'm joking.'

They both laid back on their separate beds and began to close their eyes and drift off to sleep.

'Do we have an emergency exit in case we can never use the stairs back up to the marshes?' she suddenly asked, giving Malo a small fright.

'For goodness sake, do you ever stop thinking? None that I can think of right at this moment. There is always the tunnel used for soldiers to leave by horseback, but that would be the most obvious way. Also, there is a coded gate at the end of the tunnel. I don't know the new code. We will find a way, dear Athena, don't worry.' Malo replied, yawning.

'Alright, good night.'

Malo turned to his side to look at Athena.

'No. I don't believe that you will stay quiet. Tell me everything now, so you don't wake me up later. So, what happened after we separated in the operating room?'

'Well, Renyu finds out I'm an Agalit, he then tries to operate on me, but Nicolas saves me. Then I find out that he is my brother, then I'm stuck in a dungeon eating Simbuy which I don't even like!' Athena exclaimed, all in one breath.

Malo looked stunned, his mouth hanging open.

'What?' Athena asked.

'You don't like the Simbuy? How could you?'

Athena smiled at him but still looked worried.

'I'm joking. The part I'm really shocked at is that you and General Avran are siblings. Are you sure? I mean he is the worst person I've ever met, and you are the nicest person I have ever met! How is it even possible?'

'Well, I know he is my brother. He said it himself! Blue eyes run through families and it is extremely rare to have blue eyes. He has been in the army since he was six, and I was four when I was taken to Agatha and Tomas!' Athena explained.

Malo took a while to reply back.

'If he is your brother and both of you are Agalits, then what is his gift? That's one thing I have always tried to figure out.'

'He explained to me that his gift was removed, just like that Agalit we saw Fiju remove, before Sedty went onto the operating board.'

Malo nodded. 'So, do you know what his gift was?'

Athena shook her head. 'He doesn't know himself.'

Malo grunted. 'I actually feel sorry for him. Just a tiny bit. Stuck in this horrible, dark place since the age of six is just inhumane. Still, it doesn't excuse him from all the terrible things he has done in his past!'

'No, it doesn't, but you can understand,' Athena said, defending her brother.

'Alright. We can go to sleep now!' Malo said as he saw Athena yawn. He turned over to his right side and found a position that didn't aggravate his new wounds.

'Malo?'

'No. Malo is asleep. Please try again in the morning.'

Athena smiled and soon fell asleep herself.

XII

Athena woke up in the middle of the night. She heard a knock at the door so she walked over.

Nicolas was on the other side.

'I want to talk to you,' he whispered.

Athena sighed. 'About what?'

'You.' he whispered.

It was completely dark, but Nicolas's blue eyes glowed in the dark, as did Athena's. She nodded.

Nicolas smiled and unlocked the dungeon to let Athena out, and then quickly locked it up again.

'We can leave the dungeons if you want?' Nicolas suggested.

'No! Let's stay here.'

'Alright.'

He sat down on a long metal bench nearby, and Athena joined him.

'I want to know a bit more about you. For example, if you lived all the way out in Oakrose, why did you come by foot?'

Athena hesitated for a minute.

'I wanted to go to the Four Flames. My folks who looked after me, told me that they found me abandoned by a river bank near the Naran Flame.'

Nicolas looked away.

'What is it?' Athena asked at once.

'You shouldn't go there.' he warned.

'Why not? I have the right to find our family, don't I?'

Nicolas looked down.

'Athena, why are we turning five of our strongest men into Agalits? We are planning a war. Stay away from the Four Flames if you want to live. Many people will die. It would be a shame if you or anybody close to you like Malo died.'

'What happens if you kill our mother? Or our father? Wouldn't you feel incredibly guilty?'

Nicolas spat on the ground and clenched his fists.

'Our father. Our *dear* father. I would kill him on the spot. That man betrayed us! If he did love me, then he wouldn't have let me come to such a dreadful place like this,' Nicolas said, looking around.

'How could you even think that?' Athena gasped.

'How could you *not* think that? It's easier for you to forgive him than for me. You grew up in a safe environment with parents who loved you. Nothing ever happens in Oakrose. You were probably playing in the fields all day and sleeping all night. I wish I had that life, rather than this one. Living underground your whole childhood and adolescence...it's not right. It's not fair. I know this sounds very childish of me, but I just wished our father would have saved us. I hate it here, Athena. Don't you understand?'

A tear dropped from his cheek, and soon Nicolas burst into a sob. 'I haven't cried like this in years. Forgive me!'

His lips trembled, and he couldn't stop crying. Athena gave him a hug, and they embraced for several minutes, in silence.

I don't remember the last time somebody gave me a hug. I wish she knew how happy I am that she ended up here.

Athena felt the lump at the back of her throat come back. She looked up in order not to cry. She knew the last thing anybody needed when they were crying was to see or hear somebody else cry.

Athena whispered, 'Have you heard from our family?'

Nicolas gulped. She sat back and looked him in the eye. Their eyes were the only source of light in the otherwise pitch black corridor.

She could tell from his body language, he most certainly heard from at least one of them.

'Who was it?'

Nicolas wiped the tears from his cheeks and cleared his throat.

'Our mother.'

'Our mother? How is she?' Athena asked, almost jumping off the bench. 'Is she well? Where is she?'

Nicolas looked down once again.

'What is it? Tell me!' Athena asked.

'I killed her.' he said bleakly.

Athena remained completely still. 'You killed our own mother?'

'Yes. She was captured in the Forest Tatila. My soldiers brought her back to the headquarters and down to the operating room. I was in my room, working on a plan for the war, when they told me that they found an Agalit.

I gave them permission to remove all the blood from the Agalit, leading them to an inevitable death. I finished my work earlier than expected, so I decided to go down to the operating room. She immediately recognised me and I, her. I begged them to stop the operation, but it was too late. She was almost dead. It was even worse as her last words were "Nicolas, my son. What have you done?"

It was truly devastating.'

As Nicolas continued to tell the story, tears slowly trickled down Athena's pale face.

'Since then, I made sure I was at every operation, just in case another one of my relatives were on the board. That way, I would be able to stop it.'

'How long ago did this happen?' Athena asked, with tears running down her neck.

'Seven years ago.'

Athena suddenly froze and felt a chill down her spine.

'You have been planning this invasion since you were twelve years old?'

Nicolas nodded.

'This will be the last war Fairoses will ever know. It will take place in exactly one month. That is why I have decided I cannot let you leave this place; in case you go telling King Agalaya what you have seen. Also, it will be safer for you down here, rather than out there.' Nicolas explained.

'You can still stop this. You still have some humanity in you, so to speak. Use it! Stop it, stop everything. You just told me how terrible your life has been without our family. Why would you purposely do that to many other families? Why would you make children grow up without their own father? You suffer, therefore, everyone else must suffer too? Just hearing the Seven Hundred Army turns a whole village to fear. You know this, I'm sure. Just please, don't do this!' Athena pleaded.

Nicolas stood up, straightened up his uniform and opened up her dungeon door.

'Even though you were brought up to destroy, your true self just appeared for the past few minutes. I pray to the Gods that when the time comes, this will be the person to make the ultimate decision.' Athena whispered, and then returned inside the dungeon with Nicolas shutting it violently behind her.

Malo quickly woke up for a moment and mumbled some words, but then fell straight back asleep.

Athena waited until she could no longer hear her brother's footsteps to go back to bed.

She carried on crying, because the only reason why she set out on this journey, was to find her parents. To learn that her mother was killed by her brother made Athena feel like she was going to be sick.

'Athena, wake up, Benny is here!' Malo said, shaking her violently.

Athena turned around to Malo, and said, 'Wow, you're waking *me* up! That's a first.'

'Come on, dear Athena, he's outside our dungeon with the key. Hurry up!' Malo said, limping as fast as he could to the door.

Athena quickly rolled out of her bed, grabbed her bag and headed towards the door as well.

She looked through the barred window of the metal door, only to see Benny trembling and holding the keys which were rattling.

'Come on, all you have to do is unlock the door. You can do it. Come on, come on.' Malo said encouragingly, like he was teaching a baby how to walk for the first time.

'I can't! I will be sentenced to death. I don't like death, Malo. Really I don't!' Benny replied, with a few tears in his eyes.

'Don't be a coward, Benny! Besides, we have a proposition for you. Seeing that you already stole the key from Alex, I will only make you pay me one hundred rubies if you unlock the door. When we are finally out of your sight, you can go and personally inform the general that we have escaped. He won't suspect you. How does that sound?' Malo suggested.

'I'm not a dungeon guard! He *will* suspect me. In fact, he'll see right through your little plan!'

'Benny, we all know that Nicolas doesn't recall everything that goes on in this place. He probably doesn't remember or care where you work.'

Benny hesitated for a few moments but then rolled his eyes. 'Please, hurry up and leave this place.'

He took one hundred rubies out of his pocket and looked side to side, making sure no one could see the crime he was about to commit. He then quickly unlocked the dungeon door.

Athena and Malo rushed out, and as Malo past Benny, he grabbed the money from his hand.

Benny ran the opposite direction and headed towards General Avran's makeshift house.

'General, general!' Benny screamed as he entered his house.

Malo turned to Athena.

He spoke too soon. We might not make it out of here. Damn it, Benny!

'Who dares enter?' General Avran yelled, coming out of his room, dressed up in his uniform.

'General, it's an emergency. I was walking past the dungeons this morning as I wanted to annoy Malo-'

'You went to Malo's dungeon to annoy him? You are not allowed to go there. You are not even a dungeon guard!' General Avran yelled, holding Benny's collar, lifting him up from the ground.

'General, they have escaped!' Benny said with difficulty.

General Avran suddenly released him and ran out to the floor above, where all the soldiers were having breakfast.

He barged into the courtroom and told all of them to search for Malo and Athena. 'Whoever finds them will be rewarded one thousand rubies! An extra five hundred rubies for the girl, untouched.'

All the soldiers froze. They then looked at one another, and then they all made for the doors to search for their prize.

'Malo, they are everywhere! I can hear them. The whole army is looking for us!' Athena said, panicking.

'Well, we won't be able to make it all the way up the stairs!' Malo said, looking at the stairs, leading up to the sky.

'Why are you so relaxed? What do we do?' Athena asked, almost shrieking.

'I'm so relaxed, because last night, I remembered that there was a secret passage.' Malo said, smiling.

'Lead the way!'

'Okay.' Malo said, as he awkwardly skipped towards one of the stables. His leg was healing fast.

Skipping is surprisingly easier than walking when you've had wood barged into your leg.

Inside this particular stable were twenty horses. Malo and Athena went past them till they reached the very back.

Malo carefully bent down and started banging on the floorboards with his fists, creating a lot of noise.

'What are you doing?' Athena whispered as she could hear soldiers coming closer.

'I'm looking for the secret door.' Malo said and suddenly he heard a hollow noise. He looked up at Athena and gave an evil smile. He removed all the hay and gravel he put there on purpose to cover the trapdoor. He finally managed to open it.

Athena looked inside. It was pitch black.

'I'll go in first,' Malo said as he carefully lowered himself down.

Once Athena went in and quietly closed the trapdoor above her, she couldn't see anything.

'Malo, where are you?' she whimpered.

'I'm in front of you, dear Athena. Don't fret,' he whispered in a comforting tone.

Athena's heart stopped racing as fast, as she felt a bit safer.

'Where does this place lead to?'

'Close by the river bank in the Forest Tatila.'

'Wait a minute! Doesn't that mean that the tunnel goes upwards?'

'Yes, but you won't really feel it. You'll just feel as though you are walking in a straight line, but the last part of the tunnel does get rather narrow. We'll have to crawl later on. I will remind you when the time comes.' Malo explained.

They continued moving forward in silence for almost an hour.

'We are more than half way there.' Malo said after a while.

She put her hands out to see how wide the tunnel was, but as soon as she put her hands out, they touched the walls. There was only an inch or two between her and the wall.

'Malo, what happens if someone is rather fat?'

'Well then, they're stuffed!'

'General Avran, we have searched the entire perimeter. There is no sign of them.' a soldier confirmed.

'That's not good enough! They can't have gone that far, unless...'

'Unless what, general?'

'Unless there is a secret passageway that I am unaware of,' the general said. He immediately ordered all the soldiers back into the courtroom.

It took only a few minutes for every one of them to assemble in complete silence.

'It has come to my attention that there must be a secret passage built somewhere in the headquarters. That's where the prisoners must have gone. Now, whoever admits to their helping in the making of this tunnel, please come forward!' General Avran said, with an ice-cold stare.

Not one soldier moved a muscle. Even those who knew nothing of the passageway felt their hearts beating uncontrollably.

'Let me make this clear: Whoever comes forward will be given the one thousand rubies for practically handing the prisoners over to me.'

After a minute of silence, two soldiers came forward and went onto the stage. They stood before the General Avran.

'I would have thought it was you two! Piout. Alex. You were always assigned with Malo.'

The general moved closer to them, making Alex and Piout shake even more.

'Now, you two will help me capture them! Do you know how?' the general asked, in a slow monotone voice, treating them like children.

'By showing you where the tunnel is?' Alex asked.

'Yes, very well done!' he said, gripping Alex from his hair.

'You will do that. You will then come back. The Council and I will then decide your fate,' the general started, but then took out his sword. 'As for you Piout, you have failed to co-operate!'

He stabbed Piout in the heart.

'No!' Alex cried.

'Let me guess? He was *like* a brother to you?' the general asked, smiling down at Alex.

'He *was* my brother!' Alex said, bending down next to his brother's body.

'Go and show me where the secret tunnel is!' General Avran ordered.

Alex didn't move from his brother. General Avran rolled his eyes and then kicked Alex off the high stage with great force.

Alex groaned. The general jumped off the stage and landed right in front of him. He bent down and looked Alex in the eye.

'Tell me where this tunnel is.'

Athena and Malo were almost at the end of the tunnel. Athena suddenly felt the walls closing in.

'Malo, what's happening? Why are the walls closing in?' Athena asked in a panic, suddenly feeling hot and light-headed.

'Oh, I forgot to tell you! I was crawling all the way since the beginning! Easier to crawl than to bend down with the injuries from yesterday.' Malo told her.

Athena sighed and immediately got down on the ground, but then stopped.

She could hear a few voices at the beginning of the tunnel.

'Malo, do other people know about this tunnel?' Athena whispered.

'Of course! Alex and Piout know about it. You think I could have built all this on my own? I'm flattered.' Malo said, chuckling to himself.

'Is there a small possibility that they might have told General Avran about it? Because I can hear voices at the beginning of the tunnel!' she hissed.

'Well then, we better hurry up.' Malo warned, now crawling quicker.

'Run through the tunnel. Find them and come back with the girl. Leave Malo injured there, and then we will deal with him later.'

'Very well.' the soldier replied. He unwillingly climbed down the trapdoor and started to run along the pitch black tunnel.

Nicolas ran his fingers through his hair. If the Council were to find out that the prisoners had disappeared, he would be deemed unsuitable for leading the army. If he was to be demoted, then his name wouldn't be remembered in history as leading the most powerful army to victory over Fairoses.

'General, will he be able to catch them up? They've been missing for almost two hours!' another soldier said.

'He is the fastest soldier in the army. He will be able to catch them up. I have a meeting with the Council now,' he said as he walked off, his hands trembling.

'Malo, they're sending their fastest soldier after us!'

'It's alright. We're almost at the end,'

Sure enough, he was right, as Athena could see a faded light at the end of the tunnel.

She sighed with relief. 'Where will we find a raft?'

'I don't know. If we can't find one, then we can always make one,' Malo said. He turned around and was about to ask Athena if she had ever made her own raft, but then saw her eyes glow in the dark.

'Athena... Athena, your eyes are glowing!' he pointed out.

'I know.' Athena said looking down, ashamed.

'I would love to have eyes that glow in the dark!' Malo said, trying to make her feel better.

'Oh no!' Athena said looking at the end of the tunnel.

'Seriously! It must be great to have eyes that glow! I'm just surprised with myself that I haven't noticed it earlier. I guess it's because you sleep with your eyes closed... obviously. I'm such a-'

'Ssshh!! Malo, turn around. There is a *huge* Grelik at the end of the tunnel!' Athena whispered.

Malo turned around only to see a huge Grelik a few yards away. Its large green eyes were staring at them both.

Whatever you do, dear Athena, don't think of anything bad. Don't be scared, because if they smell your fear, they eat you straight away!

Athena froze.

Malo turned around and asked, 'What are you doing?'

'They won't eat us up! Don't think that,' Athena said in a panicked state, knowing it was partially true because it was thought with such conviction in his mind.

'Don't worry, dear Athena! Trying to lighten the mood,' Malo explained. 'Don't be scared because it *will* be able to sense your fear, read your thoughts and learn many things about you just by looking at you.'

Malo was quite scared himself as he never had a Grelik "approve" of him.

'Malo, what happens if they don't approve of us?' Athena asked.

'Well, they kill you!' Malo replied bluntly. 'Now, stop talking. They can hear everything we say!' he said, smiling at the Grelik as they were getting closer.

They finally reached the end of the tunnel, and Malo was only a few inches away from the Greliks nose.

'Athena, the Grelik is blocking the path. What do we do?' Malo asked, smiling on the outside, but crying on the inside.

Athena thought out to the Grelik:

Please, Grelik, we would greatly appreciate it if you let us out. You can interrogate us out there.

The Grelik obeyed and allowed Malo and Athena to leave the pitch black tunnel and into the sunlight. It took a few moments for Malo's eyes to adjust from the darkness to the brightness of the sun.

Athena smiled as she could hear the river close by.

They quickly got up from their knees, and looked the Grelik straight in the eye.

A child of Hera and a son of Zeus. Excellent, I am quite hungry!

'Please, don't eat us! We are both young adults heading towards the Four Flames. Even though we haven't been accepted by your kind, we are good people.'

You! Child of Hera! You can hear my thoughts?

'Yes, I am an Agalit. My gift is to hear thoughts from humans... and now animals I guess!'

The Grelik whined at a very high-pitch.

'Athena, what did you do to upset the nice Grelik?' Malo asked, still forcing a smile.

The Grelik moved towards Athena, his forehead against hers.

I am no animal! I am a Grelik. There is a vast difference between the two. Greliks are sophisticated, intelligent and are able to read minds. Animals are the complete and utter opposite. Do not compare me to an animal, Athena!

Athena continued staring into the Grelik's green eyes as he took a few paces back.

'I am very sorry for offending you.'

Now, why do you want to go to the Four Flames?

'I plan to go and find my father!' Athena said out loud, so Malo had an idea of what she and the Grelik were talking about.

But not your mother.

'No. I have recently learnt that she was killed several years ago,' Athena replied, looking down at the ground.

She loved you very much, Athena.

'How would you know that?'

I thought you could read minds. I see you have not yet mastered your gift. Your mother was a beautiful Agalit. So very beautiful and kind. We have missed you, Athena! You were too young to be approved. Better late than never. Welcome back to Tatila!

Athena smiled and thanked him.

'I've been approved!' she told Malo, winking at him with a cheeky smile.

'That's good! Now it's my turn,' Malo said as his heart began to sink.

They both saw the Grelik run a few yards ahead, with its small, fury black tail was moving side to side. The Grelik suddenly let out a low-pitched howl.

A few seconds later, there were thousands of low-pitched sounds coming from all over the forest.

The Grelik came back.

You have been approved with all the other Greliks. We are now at your service, but first, I must examine Malo.

The Grelik leant his forehead against Malo's and listened to all of Malo's thoughts.

What is going on? I'm actually quite afraid, but to be honest, I can't wait to build that raft. I used to make them with my father when I was younger. Ah, the good old days!

This sufficed for the Grelik as he could sense it was all true, and none of his thoughts were of a bad nature.

Once more, the Grelik made a loud low-pitched sound which was answered by all the other Greliks in the forest. He then turned to Athena.

Your friend, Malo, has also gained my approval. If there is anything I can do at your service, young Agalit, it would be an honour!

'Can you tell me more about my family? If you knew my mother, tell me where the rest of them are! Are they still alive?' Athena asked with such desperation.

No, my child. I cannot tell you anything. You will find out soon enough. You have waited thirteen years. You can wait one more day. Anything else?

'Actually, the Seven Hundred Army are trying to capture us again! It would be wonderful if you could make sure that *doesn't* happen.'

Of course! I can hear an unapproved soldier coming further up the tunnel and from the sound of things, he will be my lunch!

Athena laughed with the Grelik even though she felt very uncomfortable at the idea of it eating a whole human.

'Well, we should get going,' Malo said, breaking the awkward silence.

'Yes.' Athena replied immediately.

'Thank you very much for not eating us.'

The Grelik laughed in its own way, tail wagging and his large white teeth showing.

Athena and Malo quickly headed towards the river, following its magical sound.

XIII

'No, dear Athena, you have to tie the rope around the corners of the raft and *then* tie a double knot on every other log around all four edges.' Malo explained.

Athena and Malo had found fallen logs in the water, which they used for the main body of their raft. They also had rope which they took from the Striberosse.

Athena had never made a raft, nor had she read about them, so it was all completely new to her, and she was having difficulty with it.

'No! That is *not* how you do it!' Malo snapped as he dropped his rope and grabbed hers to do it himself.

'There you go!'

'I can't do it,' she moaned.

'You *can* do it, you just need practice.'

He placed his ropes in her hands and he held her wrists.

'All you have to do is make a small loop around this log,' he said, helping Athena's hands make a loop.

'It's working!'

'You see? You can do it.'

Athena smiled and finished her task.

'Alright, I think we can put the raft in the water now.' Malo said, tightening the ends of the rope one last time.

They both carried the raft and placed it onto the river bank.

'Athena, get on!' Malo said sternly, handing her bag over.

Athena obeyed and steadily sat down on one side of the raft.

Malo swiftly pushed it into the river, except the river's current was moving much faster than he had anticipated.

The raft, along with Athena, was already a few yards ahead of him.

'Malo, swim!' Athena called out as he was standing stationary on the riverbank.

Malo quickly dived into the water, ignoring the pain from his stomach injuries, and tried to swim as fast as he possibly could towards the raft. He finally reached it.

Athena pulled Malo onto the other side of the raft. His eyes were closed.

'I know you aren't dead. You're still thinking!' Athena laughed out, but Malo still didn't flinch.

'Come on, Malo!' she said, shaking him.

He still didn't move.

'Malo, it isn't funny anymore,' Athena said, now worried.

'You are just too easy to scare. Of course I'm not dead! Though, with all the anxiety you are giving me, I feel like I'm ageing ten years each day I spend with you.' he murmured, flashing her a smile.

Athena jokingly hit him. In one moment, this small action resulted with Malo falling off the raft. The imbalance in weight led Athena to also fall in and for the raft to float ahead.

Athena quickly sank, and Malo quickly went to bring her up to the surface.

'What do you think you're doing? Don't you DARE tell me you can't swim?!' Malo screamed, wiping the water away from his eyes with one hand and holding Athena's arm with the other.

'I can't swim!' she said, gasping for air.

'You never read about swimming? Well, you could have told me that earlier!' Malo yelled.

'When? When I suddenly fell off because you created an imbalance on the raft?' Athena yelled back.

'That was your fault. You pushed me off!' Malo screamed even louder as it started to rain. Thunder and lightning quickly took over the skies and dark, black clouds were emerging from nowhere, covering the blue and white skies.

'Look, it's turning dark early. It's thundering, it's raining. We can't argue now.' Athena pointed out.

'Fine! Climb onto my back and try to be as light as possible,' Malo growled, aggressively helping Athena onto his back. He quickly started swimming towards the raft. Athena did as she was told and tried to put as little weight as she could on his back.

'Are you alright?' she asked after a while.

'I can see the raft. I am now!' Malo replied, still looking forwards. Luckily, the raft had got stuck between two rocks further down the river.

'Would it help if I got off your back?'

'And let you drown?' Malo asked, confused.

'No. If you held my arm and-'

'No! Once we reach the raft, I'll hold it and then you climb over me and get on,' he said, firmly.

'How would you get onto it?'

'I won't. Once you are on raft, I'll drag it onto the river bank further ahead to where it's safe.' he said. 'We're almost there. Start climbing over my head!'

Athena obeyed and started climbing over his head. When she had her hands on his head, he reached the raft and securely held it down.

'Now, climb on!' Malo shouted.

Athena climbed onto the raft and fell flat in the middle of it. Malo dragged the raft towards the riverbank further ahead, where there weren't vine leaves and thorn bushes by the water.

After Athena had quickly climbed off the raft and onto the riverbank, she helped Malo drag the raft up towards a huge red exotic tree. Then, he dropped flat onto the grass.

'I'm sorry,' Athena said, as she sat beside him with her arms wrapped around her knees.

Malo didn't respond. He just laid there.

'I mean, if I hadn't push you off, then none of this would have happened. I feel terrible.'

Well, it was a terrible thing!

Athena couldn't help but feel terribly guilty.

'I'm joking, dear Athena!' Malo said, putting his hands up. 'I just feel like every situation gets even more dangerous. I feel responsible for you. I'm not just looking after myself, I also have to look after you too. It's so much work! I feel like I have adopted you as my child, and I have to hold your hand every step of the way, otherwise you'll manage to find some way to... die! When we meet your dad, I almost want to take your hand and put it into his. Pass on the responsibility, because I'm getting too old for this!'

Athena grinned.

'Oh, my poor heart.' he said in an old man voice, closing his eyes.

Athena looked around in silence as Malo took a few moments to relax. The sky was very dark, and she could still hear the thunder. She remembered she once read in a book, that when it thunders, it's very dangerous to be near a tree.

'We should find a cave.' Athena whispered.

Why?

'We need to sleep and it's dangerous to be near trees when it's thundering.'

'Sleep? But it's only the afternoon,' Malo said, yawning.

'We're both exhausted. We can sleep now and wake up very early. In this way, we could be at the Four Flames by this time tomorrow!' Athena said, excitedly.

Malo frowned. Although Athena could be careless, she was very agreeable to be with, and if they went to the Four Flames and she found her family, then he would be alone again.

'Malo, you can't think like that!' Athena said as she touched his shoulder.

Well, what would I do if you do find your family?

'You would be able to stay with me, but it's quite unlikely that I do find my family. General Avran killed my mother, remember?'

'I'm truly sorry about that, but I'm not surprised. It is in his blood to kill.' Malo said, expressing his opinion.

'No, it's not! He was just brought up as a killer. I'm sure if he meets our family again, he would... he *could* return back to normal.'

'My dear Athena, people can change, but General Avran isn't really a person nor is he an Agalit. He is a *thing*. He has no mercy, no remorse and he certainly has no kindness.'

'That's not true! When he was with me, he seemed different. He was himself. He just puts on an act to scare people and to get things done.'

'I don't believe that! I promise you, everyone is in the courtroom listening to him terrorize a poor soldier!' Malo said with confidence.

'We should really find shelter now,' Athena said as it was starting to hail.

Alright! How though?

Athena suddenly called to all the Greliks with her thoughts.

Please, can you help us?

Suddenly the ground began to quake.

Malo's eyes widened. He looked over at Athena.

'Please, dear Athena, don't tell me that you called the Greliks!' he frowned, knowing the answer.

'Well, who knows this place better than the Greliks?'

Malo grunted. 'I hate Greliks!'

Meanwhile, at the Seven Hundred Army headquarters, all the soldiers were in the courtroom.

'It is exactly four o'clock Alex. You promised me that I would have them back in the dungeons by one o'clock at the very latest!' General Avran said, calmly pacing up and down, in front of Alex who was placed in the centre of the stage. He was tied to a chair with his hands bound behind his back. His hair was all sweaty, and his face was covered with blood as General Avran spent the last hour torturing him.

The general suddenly turned to all the lugubrious soldiers.

'Unfortunately, I am going to cancel your dinner as well,' he announced with a smug grin.

There was a groan of discontent passing around the soldiers once more.

'Nobody will be able to eat until the prisoners are put back into their dungeon.'

Suddenly, the doors of the courtroom opened. Every soldier in the room watched the short, fat man run onto the stage.

'General, perhaps that isn't the wisest idea! These men are going to fight in the most important war ever known in Fairoses! They need food and energy if we are to have a guaranteed victory,' the man whispered.

'They need to understand the huge mistake they have committed.'

'It was done by maybe one or two soldiers, yes, but you must not punish the entire army. The Council is against it. Your actions are unacceptable. Letting the Agalit go, and now starving your army. I'm sorry, but we have now decided all your actions must be passed onto us, and it must have our consent.'

General Avran turned and looked down at the man.

'I own the Council. It was advised for me to have one when I was nine years old. Ten years have passed, yet you still treat me as that nine-year-old. No more. Now, leave!' he said, raising his voice.

'General, that is a very unwise decision. You don't have the authority, and you certainly do not have the knowledge to-'

'Do *not* question my authority, Mark! You are dismissed, the whole Council is dismissed. Now, leave and take your Council elsewhere!'

Mark looked at the general in the eyes.

'You have changed, young Nicolas. Why have you chosen this moment to change your attitude? The war is coming. Now, will the army have the same ruthless general that they have always known, or the new general who is now facing the war alone in an indecisive manner?'

'Mark, leave my stage, leave my premises and never show your face again,' the general yelled out, yet still keeping a calm face.

Humiliated in front of the whole army, Mark sighed and then turned to the soldiers.

'My friends, this man who calls himself General Avran has changed. He has lost all sense. He doesn't know how to make intelligent decisions anymore. Now, gentlemen, is this the man you want leading the Schumy War, with uncertainty in his mind? Or would you rather have the Council lead you to victory?'

Soldiers yelled different answers.

'Council!'

'General!'

'Neither!'

In the end, the general was so furious with Mark that he shouted out, 'Mark! You have defied my authority with the Council, and now with *my* army.'

He drew out his dagger and ruthlessly cut off Mark's right hand.

At first, Mark tried to contain his pain, but it quickly became unbearable. He screamed out in anguish.

'Leave now. and tell the others that if they don't leave the army's premises by sunset, it will be their heads,' General Avran warned.

Mark ran off the stage, his left hand holding his right. 'You will regret that, Nicolas!' he yelled, hunched over.

Nicolas rolled his eyes and then turned to the army.

'You see how ruthless I am! However, I have changed my mind. I will not kill Alex,' he said, looking over at the wounded soldier, 'and I will let you have your dinner early tonight. In fact, I will order a feast, as later tonight, every single soldier in this army will set out to find my two prisoners!'

Every soldier remained quiet, but the same question all came to mind. What was happening to their general? Nicolas was, in fact, asking himself the same question. As he walked off the stage, he felt a bead of sweat drop down his forehead.

'Well, I don't think we would have ever found this place alone!' Athena said looking down.

'Yes! Those Greliks are out of control.' Malo commented.

'Well, at least if soldiers come and try to find out where we are, they won't think of this place!'

'Absolutely. When I was in the army and I had to capture people General Avran demanded, we always looked near the river banks and the caves... but never here!' Malo explained.

'Yes, it was very kind of the Greliks to let us climb on their back and over their head!'

'It was quite strange when I accidentally put my foot in its eyes,' Malo said, shaking his head, smirking.

Athena laughed. 'That would explain why the Grelik said that you were out of place.'

'They are actually very kind though, even if they do scare me a tad.'

'Yes, and to also give us our dinner and clean water was also very nice!' she also commented.

'Deer stew *and* it was warm!' Malo exclaimed.

'Alright, don't get over-excited. I don't want you to fall off... again!' Athena added.

'That wasn't my fault. The Grelik's nose was tickling me!'

'Alright.'

'Seriously!'

'I believe you, but we should get some sleep now.'

'Fine, but if you hear soldiers coming, wake me up!'

'I don't want to throw water on you. I'll just pinch your ear again.'

'Well, whatever you do, don't push me off the tree! It would be quite a long trip down,' Malo commented, peeking down.

'Alright.' Athena said, yawning as she laid down.

Malo also laid down and then closed his eyes.

'Athena? Can you open your eyes? I forgot where I put my dagger!' he said, grinning.

Athena's eyes suddenly opened.

'Hurry! I want to sleep soon!' Athena complained.

Malo grinned. 'I know exactly where my dagger is. I just like to see glowing eyes in the dark!'

Athena immediately shut them again.

'Come on! I was joking, Excuse me, I had to carry you along the river, and now I ask you to open your eyes for a few minutes and that's too much? My, oh my, aren't we a little princess tonight?!' Malo said laughing.

'Goodnight, dear Malo!'

Malo turned the other way and pouted.

'Mark, why did Nicolas do this to you?' the head of the Council demanded.

'I dared to question his authority in front of the army,' Mark truthfully replied, still groaning from the pain.

'Fetch Mark a damp towel,' Oliver told Nerona, the councillor on his right.

She immediately left and Oliver turned back to Mark.

'He refused to let his army eat?' he repeated, completely astounded.

'At first, but as soon as I left the stage, I heard him say that he was going to move their dinner earlier and turn it into a feast.'

'Any reason why?'

'He told them that every soldier was to leave immediately after dinner to find the prisoners who had escaped earlier on today.'

Oliver nodded and started pacing up and down the dark, gloomy hall.

'These prisoners presumably have some value to him,' Oliver pointed out.

'I agree. If he was willing to let his army starve for an entire day, then they must be extremely important.'

'It seems as though our young Nicolas is falling apart. These prisoners must have something to do with this.'

'You can be certain about that!' Renyu said, as he suddenly walked into the Council's chambers.

'Renyu, we haven't heard from you in a while.' Oliver said, staring at the councillor.

'I was just performing an-'

'Operation,' Oliver said, finishing his sentence. 'Who was the last victim? Sedty was meant to be the last one, no?'

'Yes, but we decided to do one more because we had enough Agalit blood to do another operation comfortably. His name is Lupol. His ability is to produce an immense amount of wind. He'll be able to create full-blown hurricanes as soon as he has had enough lessons with our Agalit experts from abroad. All the Agalits will have mastered and controlled their powers by the end of the month. Those experts thought they were invited here to learn of our latest technology. The fools!'

'Did Nicolas attend?'

'He was aware of the procedure, but no, he didn't show up.'

Oliver nodded but remained in silence.

'Head of Council, is something bothering you?' Renyu asked as he quietly walked over to his large stone seat.

'I'm just wondering why Nicolas is acting this way. Eleven years, and now minutes before this great war...I just don't understand what the Gods are telling us!' Oliver replied as he stopped pacing and started spinning the large marble ball with the whole world imprinted on it, placed in the centre of their immensely huge, dark and cold circular chamber.

'It's the girl, Athena! They have a close bond of some sort. I saw it with my own eyes. The first time he paid attention to her, there was green electricity between them,' Renyu explained.

Oliver suddenly stopped spinning the marble ball and turned around to Renyu.

'A green connection? Are you sure?' Oliver asked in distressed.

'Yes! Definitely green. None of the others saw it. They were too distressed from the operation, but I saw it. I am certain.' Renyu replied back.

'Athena must be his younger sister. Of course, she is *the* Agalit that escaped.' Oliver gasped, widening his eyes. There were quiet murmurs around the chamber.

'Silence!' Oliver hissed. The councillors immediately obeyed but one.

'Head of Council, how do you know for certain that Athena is the boy's sister?'

Oliver went back to his seat which was the largest in the triangle of seats where the councillors shared ideas. Oliver, being the head of the Council, had the seat that was at the tip of the triangle.

'When we took our young Nicolas from the Naran Flame when he was six years old, he had green electricity attached to him. Magic, of course. Let's not even try to understand the logic there! Anyway, this was the only time in my life I saw anything quite like it. I decided to follow where the line of electricity ended,' Oliver said but then paused.

'It ended with a little girl who was sitting on the river bank, a short distance from the Naran Flame. She was crying and kept yelling for a "Nicolas". When we finally approached her, her eyes suddenly opened. She must have known that he was close by.

Nicolas suddenly ran towards her, fell down to the ground and hugged her. The green electricity encircled them, and every time I tried to grab Nicolas, the electricity would electrocute me. Five times I tried to grab him. Five times I failed. I called for him, threatened to kill his mother, but he didn't hear me.

I must admit, it was quite a sight: two young children on the ground embracing each other, on the river bank, surrounded by the trees with a thin yet deadly green electricity enclosing them from the rest of the world.'

The Council remained silent, not knowing what to say although they were all thinking the same thing. Finally, the same councillor who had asked the previous question said, 'How did you get him out of the circle?'

Oliver continued the story but still looked up at the small circular window above the marble ball, allowing a few beams of sunlight to come through.

'Another girl ran past me and ran straight into the circle without even being stung by the electricity. She whispered something to Nicolas and Athena, and then immediately ran out of the circle. But I grabbed hold of her.

I told her to get Nicolas out, otherwise I would kill her mother. She had tears in her eyes as she walked back towards her siblings. She was a clever child though! She never came back out of the circle.

When I thought I would never be able to reach Nicolas that night, another girl was about to run into the circle, but then I suddenly called for her. She slowly walked towards me. I picked her up and asked her if that was Nicolas in the circle. She nodded. I told her that her father had sent me to bring Nicolas to him.

She immediately ran to Nicolas and told her the news. Nicolas, innocently, ran towards me. It was as though he had forgotten who I was. Stupid child! But he was finally mine! It's a shame how I turned even the nicest boy into the most evil soul in just the space of a few years.'

Once again, the chamber was left in silence.

'Nicolas wants us out of the chamber and the army's premises by sunset, otherwise he will cut off all our heads.'

Oliver looked at him as if he had just woken up.

'What did you say?'

'If we are still here by tomorrow morning, Nicolas will have us all killed!' Mark said, raising his voice.

'Well, let's just wait and see if he's prepared to do that.' Oliver said, with a daunting laugh.

'Mark, assemble the Council!' Oliver demanded. 'We're going to find Athena!'

'General, I have just checked the Council's chambers. They have left with their horses.' a soldier told General Avran who was already mounting onto his stallion.

'Excellent! The only way to get things done is by using fear!' General Avran answered and then he kicked his stallion, Trida, on its sides. Within a minute, he was galloping through the Forest Tatila at full speed.

'Full moon. Excellent.' Nicolas whispered as he glanced up at the sky. He turned around and his whole army was right behind him in assembled order.

XIV

'Where are they? I know you know! Lead me to them immediately!' General Avran ordered the Grelik.

The Grelik, though he knew the bad intentions General Avran had, couldn't actually stop him as he was accepted from all the Greliks when he was five years old at the Four Flames-the youngest age to be approved.

'Lead me to them now.' he demanded again, drawing out his sword.

The Grelik groaned and then unwillingly led him to Athena and Malo. 'You are lucky I didn't kill you, animal!' he hissed.

The Grelik suddenly turned around. He was so very tempted to kill Nicolas right there and then, but he knew that was against the Grelik Rules. The penalty for going against the Grelik Rules was death.

The army is here and they seek Athena and Malo! I need them to be protected as we promised them that we would. I will lead this Agalit some place nearby.

There were suddenly high-pitched whines around the entire forest.

We will help Athena and Malo.

We will block the army from entering the Forest Tatila any further.

'What did you tell your other animal friends?' Nicolas demanded.

The Grelik didn't even turn around, but continued leading him deeper into the forest at a very slow pace.

'Who here has been accepted by the Greliks?' Oliver asked.

Out of the other twelve councillors, only three put their hands up. Oliver turned to them.

'We will go together to a Grelik and order it to lead us to Athena!' he said.

Mark and the other two nodded.

'The rest of you will stay hidden behind trees! Remember, any Grelik will be able to detect you and read your thoughts,' Oliver warned them. He climbed onto his horse and both he and his fellow councillors galloped through the forest with Mark calling for a Grelik.

One suddenly emerged from a bush and jumped in front of them.

'Grelik, lead us to Athena!' Mark said with confidence, though he tried to hide his slight fear from the formidable beast.

The Council are also searching for Athena. I have the only four who are accepted. Go to all the others who are hiding behind the trees like cowards.

The Grelik told this to all his brothers in a high pitched whine.

A few Greliks suddenly ran past their brother and headed straight for the other members of the Council.

'I can't wait to get my hands on Athena and Nicolas! It would be torture for either one of them to see the other die!' a councillor whispered to another. Suddenly, a gust of wind made his hair fly back. A Grelik had quickly ran past him. As the councillor turned around to see what had just past him, another Grelik pushed him over with its two hind legs.

The councillor fell on the ground and groaned. He then looked up, only to see a Grelik jumping towards him with its razor sharp, white teeth showing.

Athena suddenly opened her eyes. She could feel and hear the disturbances around the Forest Tatila.

'Malo! Malo!' she hissed in his ears.

Malo turned around and continued snoring. Athena was about to pinch his ear but then a Grelik climbed up the hollow tree. It entered the small room built within the intertwining branches.

Athena, hundreds of people are searching for you in the forest at this very moment.

'The Seven Hundred Army!'

Yes, and also the Council.

Athena looked up.

'The Council?'

Yes, they are part of the army but they now have separate intentions from General Avran. They want to kidnap you and kill you in front of your brother. To torture him.

Her eyes widened.

'The other Greliks aren't leading them to us, are they?'

Unfortunately, that is the case. They are leading him close by. It is your choice.

Would you like to stay here where I will protect you or should I bring you to the Greliks den?

Athena looked over at Malo who was in a deep sleep. She knew he was rather scared of Greliks, and that he was absolutely exhausted and that sleep was needed. She knew that they were high up in a tree, and if her brother *did* find them, he would have to find a way to climb up the huge tree. He would also have to get around the big Grelik.

'It's fine, we will stay here. Malo needs to rest. Stay close to the tree and make sure General Avran is not able to get to us!' Athena said firmly.

Very well!

The Grelik climbed back down and circled the tree along with another Grelik.

By now, Nicolas was a few yards away from the tree and the Grelik that was leading him to Athena finally stopped and ran away.

'Where are you going? Come back, you animal. I cannot see *my* prisoners!' Nicolas snapped.

The Grelik continued running, ignoring Nicolas. He had, after all, led the general to them.

Nicolas sighed and then looked around. He saw two Greliks circling a huge tree. Nicolas walked towards them. One of the Greliks stopped circling around the tree and charged towards Nicolas.

'I am looking for Athena and Malo!' Nicolas told the Grelik. The Grelik was only inches away from Nicolas's face, breathing heavily on his face to intimidate him, but this didn't bother Nicolas one bit. After a minute of silence of looking each other in the eye the Grelik looked at the tree, showing Nicolas their hidden location. He knew he couldn't go against the Grelik Rules.

'Thank you... animal!' Nicolas said.

The Grelik growled but remained calm. Athena saw Nicolas coming towards the tree.

'Quick, Malo, wake up!' Athena said, shaking Malo very hard.

Malo shrugged her off. Athena pinched his ear and he woke up.

'What is it?' he asked wearily.

'Nicolas is by the tree!' Athena said pointing outside.

Malo peeked out and saw Nicolas looking up at him. He suddenly caught sight of Malo.

'Um...'

'What is it?' she whispered.

'There may be a possibility that he saw me!' Malo said in an innocent voice.

'What?'

'Read his mind! What is he saying?'

'I can't hear his thoughts,' Athena said, trying hard to hear his thoughts.

'You can't hear his thoughts? Why not?' Malo asked.

'I am not sure! Maybe because he is an Agalit as well? I really don't know! I can't control my gift, it comes and goes,' Athena said, panicking.

Nicolas suddenly heard her voice and looked up at the tree. He could see a small hole inside the tree with a few blankets.

'Athena, I know you're there. Show yourself!' Nicolas called out as he couldn't see her.

Athena and Malo remained quiet as they leant against the side of the tree which blocked them from Nicolas's view.

'Athena, I saw Malo and I know you're together!' Nicolas said, raising his voice as he started to lose his patience. The only source of light was coming from the full moon through the grey clouds.

Silence.

Nicolas went to the Grelik who was circling the tree.

'Grelik, bring me up to them now!' he ordered.

The Grelik didn't move.

'Bring me to them otherwise you will be put to death according to the Grelik Rules!' Nicolas threatened.

The Grelik made a high pitched whine but still unwillingly brought Nicolas up. The Grelik looked up at Athena and told her with its thoughts:

Athena, look under the blankets.

Athena quietly lifted the blankets up and she saw a trapdoor.

Get in. Right now.

Nicolas, who was on the Greliks shoulder, was almost at the top of the tree.

'Malo, I'm going in!' Athena said as she opened up the trapdoor and jumped into the hole which turned out to be the opening to a long, slippery slide that went down into the ground.

'What?' Malo asked but then saw the huge hole. He shrugged his shoulders.

'I hate it when it's the full moon. Something bad *always* happens.' he sighed and then went into the hole.

Nicolas suddenly entered the room at the top of the tree. There was no one there.

'Where did they go?' Nicolas demanded, turning around at the Grelik, but it had disappeared.

He looked down from the top of the tree but still didn't see the Grelik.

'Sedty!' Nicolas roared across the forest. For a long moment, nothing happened. Then, gradually, the ground started to tremble. Nicolas could see trees suddenly disappearing. Sedty suddenly arrived at the bottom of the tree.

'General!' he called out in a very deep tone.

'I can't get off this tree. Chop it down!' Nicolas demanded.

Sedty nodded then moved back. He sliced the bottom of the tree with his hand and it collapsed immediately.

Nicolas jumped off right before the tree fell to the ground.

'Well done, Sedty! You have proven yourself to be a true Agalit,' Nicolas commented.

'Thank you,' he replied.

'Now, any sign of the prisoners?'

'No, general. There is absolutely no sign of them. All the soldiers have confirmed with me that there are no traces of them whatsoever.'

General Avran was about to speak back but then suddenly stopped.

'Is there something wrong, general?'

General Avran stared at him.

'All *my* soldiers reported to *you*?' he asked in disgust.

'Yes! Is that a problem?'

He decided to not say anything too drastic as he needed Sedty on his side. Besides, if he offended Sedty, he could be killed.

'No, Sedty, there is no problem!' he replied, with a small smile.

'Very good! Now let's find the rest of the army. We should give up finding the prisoners. They are nowhere to be seen!' Sedty declared.

'No! I still give out the orders and my order is to continue searching for the prisoners!' Nicolas snapped.

'You are wasting your time, General Avran! All the soldiers are together, assembled and ready to head back to the headquarters.'

'I suppose you gave them that order.' Nicolas sighed.

'Yes. I thought I was helping you.'

'No, Sedty, you are not helping me. The army is mine to order, not yours. I need you in this army, this war, but it cannot happen if I do not have complete authority over my men.'

'I am not trying to replace you permanently, *general*, but I am in charge when you are not there. When I was giving these orders, *you* were stuck at the top of the tree. If it weren't for me, *you* would still be stuck up there,' Sedty replied, looking up at where the tree stood a few moments before.

General Avran sighed. 'Where are my men?'

'They are not far from the headquarters.'

'Tell them... tell them to go deeper in the Forest Tatila! I saw the prisoners here in this very tree,' General Avran explained, looking down at the fallen trunk.

'I won't. They are exhausted. They should retire to their tents.'

'One more look around the forest!' General Avran snarled.

Sedty breathed deeply but then nodded. 'I will inform them immediately!'

General Avran suddenly grinned and then looked around the tree. There was no sign of anyone.

'I really thought I had you, Athena!' Nicolas whispered and then got back up again and went towards his army.

'I never knew there was anything like this! I would come here *all* the time!' Malo screamed with the wind hurling him forwards.

'I know, but we have been in here for a while now!' Athena screamed back.

'So? I could do this forever!'

Malo and Athena were in a large tunnel, which went underground so they could see nothing around them. They were sliding down at a very fast pace which made it quite difficult for both of them to breathe.

'I think we went deeper in the ground!' she called out.

'I don't!'

Malo was right as the next second, Athena could see the end of the tunnel which allowed her to see the dark sky with the full moon right in front of her.

'I think we are about to go up into the sky!' Athena said, rather scared.

With an extra gush of wind blowing with them, they flew out of the tunnel high up in the air.

'Wahoo!' Malo yelled.

Athena laughed but then suddenly fell downwards.

'Ouch!'

'Oh no! Please, don't bruise,' Malo said, smiling.

'Don't worry I won't because I fell on you!' Athena grinned back as she got up, clapping her hands together to get rid of the soil on them. As Malo was a lot heavier than delicate Athena, he fell to the ground first.

'Are you alright?' she asked as she helped him up.

'Yes. That was fun! Do you think we could do that again?' Malo asked as he limped over to where the tunnel ended.

'That's strange, the tunnel isn't there anymore.' he noticed.

Athena walked over to Malo and looked around the ground.

'That *is* strange!' she agreed.

A Grelik came up to them.

Are you both safe?

'Yes, thank you very much!' Athena said, smiling.

'Where is the tunnel?' Malo asked abruptly, pointing to the place they flew out of.

It disappeared in case anyone would have followed you. The Forest Tatila has many unknown features about it. Most never even hear about half of them by the time they die.

'He says that it disappeared in case anyone followed us.' Athena explained to Malo.

Malo nodded and smiled at the Grelik, still feeling a bit uneasy as Greliks scared him. This Grelik, in particular, was almost double his size.

Your friend is afraid of me.

Athena nodded.

'He is not used to seeing such creatures. Big and large.'

The Grelik growled.

'I'm sorry if I offended you,' Athena said, now feeling a bit uneasy.

You did not call me animal, therefore I will not be tempted to eat you!

She wasn't sure whether it was being sarcastic or humorous but either way Athena smiled.

'Thank you, once again!' she said as she moved away, bringing Malo with her.

The Grelik went the other direction but then rapidly turned around.

Remember, the army and the Council are still in the forest. Be cautious, young Agalit!

'General, we have searched the forest. We cannot find them. Can we leave now and retire to our tents?' a brave soldier asked on behalf of his comrades.

'No! We cannot leave without them.'

There was heavy sighs across the army. Sedty walked towards the general.

'General, we have searched miles and miles. Two prisoners, especially with one being a girl, would not have been able to walk that far. Let the soldiers return to their tents!' he strongly suggested.

General Avran looked at him in amazement, then leant closer to the Agalit who was two heads taller than him.

'This is *my* army. I am the only one who gives out orders. Do *not* defy me!' he exclaimed.

'Men, to your tents!' Sedty roared across the whole army.

There was a cheer among the soldiers as they gradually returned to the headquarters.

'It seems as though I can give out orders too!' Sedty said smiling and then joined the rest of the soldiers.

After a few seconds, Nicolas was the only one left in the forest with no horse and no soldiers.

'Sedty is really going to pay for that,' Nicolas said to himself and then called for a Grelik and ordered it to bring him back to the headquarters.

'Why, oh *why*, is this Grelik stopping *here*?' Oliver asked Mark.

'Maybe Athena was here?' Mark suggested.

Oliver rolled his eyes and then looked around to the other councillors but then realised one was missing.

'Where is Nerona?' Oliver asked, suddenly turning towards Nikhil.

'Nikhil,' he snapped, 'You were assigned with Nerona! Where is she?'

Nikhil looked down on the ground, his shoulders shaking. Oliver walked over to him and pushed him backwards.

'Look at me when I talk to you!' he yelled.

Nikhil shook even more violently. He then looked up at Oliver.

'She was eaten by a Grelik!' he whimpered.

Oliver looked up at the black sky.

'Why have the God's turned their backs on us now?' he said out loud. Councillors looked at each other. What were they to reply?

'Mark! You and I will continue looking for Athena. As for the rest of you, return to headquarters!' he barked. None of the councillors moved.

'Why aren't any of you going?'

'We don't have anywhere to go. By now, the headquarters will have many soldiers surrounding it,' Nikhil replied, looking down at the ground.

'Go back to the Councils chamber *now*! We will meet again.' Oliver demanded.

Nikhil sighed but still nodded and then left, followed by all the one other surviving councillor apart from Mark.

Mark turned to Oliver. 'Where should we look?'

'The Grelik brought us here so we should look around, *obviously*.' Oliver snapped.

Mark turned to the tree after a while and called Oliver over.

'This tree was cut down recently. You can still smell the fresh sap coming out of the purple branches. Look! It was broken by someone as the bottom of the tree is sliced perfectly.'

'A human could not be so strong to break a tree like this!'

'It was an Agalit. It was Sedty!'

'Perhaps Nicolas was here and told Sedty to cut the tree. Maybe he thought Athena was in the tree?'

'Why would he want to even risk killing his little sister?'

'Maybe he has much trust in Sedty.'

'I doubt that! Nicolas has no trust and faith with anyone. Maybe he was... stuck in the tree?'

'Then he called for Sedty to cut down the tree.' Mark realised.

'But then how does Athena fit in this theory?'

Mark was silent while he was thinking then he suddenly jumped. 'Maybe he thought he saw Athena in the tree!'

'*In* the tree?'

'Yes, look closely. The tree is hollow. He then got a Grelik to bring him up the tree to Athena but somehow she wasn't there and the Grelik left leaving him stuck and-'

'And then he called for Sedty.' Oliver finished.

Mark nodded.

'Where is Athena now?' Oliver asked. Mark looked around but there was no sign of anyone. They were all alone in a dark part of the forest. There were no trees nearby that had glowing features.

'I have no idea.'

Oliver sighed and started walking further ahead. Mark followed him with his eyes.

'Where are you going, Oliver?' he asked with a hint of annoyance in his voice.

Oliver turned to him.

'We are going to continue to search for Athena!'

'It's dark and we have no idea where she has gone and the other councillors are waiting for us!'

Oliver shook his head. 'We aren't returning to the Council, Mark.'

'But the others have gone there. You said we will meet again.'

'In the afterlife, yes.'

'You sent them to their death?'

'Yes. Let's be honest, there are only three councillors who are indispensable; you, me and Renyu. The others can die for all I care. Though it is a shame about Nerona. We are so close to the war. After that, everything will change. There is nothing else they can contribute at this point. What we need to do now is find Athena! Without her, we have nothing to blackmail Nicolas with. We need to go into this war with the ruthless Nicolas we created. Decisions, weapons, organization. Nicolas needs help with all of that. We can win and the Blucks and Chamcoks will reunite and take over the whole of Fairoses. Nicolas is different now! None of this matters to him. If we lose the war, there will be *nothing* left for us.'

'When I was younger, my father and I went in the forest to hunt. We found a huge horse, but it was different from any other horse so we brought it home. We didn't cook it but we offered it to our mother!' Malo whispered to Athena.

'That is so sweet. When I was younger, Tomas and I went on a long hike. We saw many animals and he explained everything we passed. The animals, plants, cures from plants. It was great fun!' Athena whispered back.

'Athena? I think there is a huge insect on my leg.' Malo screeched, not daring to look down.

Athena and Malo were laying on the ground next to a huge exotic bush, as big as a small tree, with white leaves and purple flowers which had glowing petals. Athena turned around to look at his leg.

'You are just so cute!' Athena said in a very high pitched voice.

'What? What is it?' Malo asked very quickly.

'It's a white cat,' Athena replied, leaning over to Malo's leg to reach out for the cat. It allowed Athena to pick it up and stroke it. Malo looked over.

'That *is* a cute cat.'

Athena looked down at the cat. She wanted to hear its thoughts. She knew a cat wouldn't be wandering around the forest for no reason. The animals that occupied the forest were Greliks, Rects, small animals and insects.

Athena closed her eyes and listened to every small detail around her. Malo's heartbeat, her heartbeat and the cat's heartbeat.

'Talk to me.' she whispered.

I am a cat sent from the Azul Flame. I have been sent to find you, Athena. Your father has been waiting for you for quite some time.

'My father? He knows I'm coming?' Athena wasn't able to stop.

Yes. You will meet him tomorrow.

'Why tomorrow?'

Tomorrow, you will reach the Four Flames and you will learn and understand everything about your past. Then you will have four weeks to decide whether you want to be a part of the war.

Athena opened her eyes and stared at the cat.

'The war will be so soon.' Athena realised.

Indeed. It has been known for centuries that this will be the Schumy War. The war that will decide the fate of Fairoses.

Athena nodded and then the cat suddenly leapt from her arms and ran away. Athena followed the cat with her eyes until it ran down the steep hill.

'So? What did the cat tell you?' Malo asked, all excited. He laughed to himself. He never imagined he could say such a sentence, completely sober.

Before Athena could respond, Malo jumped. 'Wow!'

She looked at him, alarmed. 'What?'

'I now know how hard it is to be you! Having to keep quiet for a few minutes. I didn't want to disturb you and the cat. I honestly don't know how you do it, dear Athena!'

She squinted her eyes at him and decided to ignore his sarcasm.

'I will meet my father tomorrow and the Schumy War will take place in a month.'

'Well, that is exciting news for us both! I'm glad we meet him tomorrow. That means this old man can get a few days of rest. I need to get some sleep now if I am to look presentable for your father!' he said as he winked at her before to turned around to fall asleep.

Sleep tight, dear Athena. Tomorrow is when everything changes.

Malo drifted off to sleep. His wounds healed faster when he was asleep and relaxed rather than awake and fighting to keep both him and his dear Athena alive.

Athena, on the other hand, was more awake than ever. She couldn't help but imagine how it was going to be to meet her family after all this time.

XV

'So, are you sure that the cat headed this way?'

'I'm sure, Oliver!'

'Then we shall go the opposite direction. Perhaps the cat saw Athena and led her the way to the Four Flames.'

'I saw the cat a while back. Maybe we missed her.'

'Maybe she is still asleep,' Oliver said, grinning.

Mark smiled back but then frowned as he saw the steep hill.

'We have to walk all the way *up* that, steep, rocky hill?'

Oliver looked up at the hill and nodded. Mark sighed and then started to walk.

'So, the cat went *that* way?' Malo asked, pointing towards the hill that went down.

'Yes!'

After a few hours, Malo woke up and saw Athena wasn't sleeping. He decided it would be safer if they made their way to the Four Flames sooner rather than later, in case there were soldiers still searching for them.

'Excellent! Do you know what would make things more fun?' Malo said, trying to contain his excitement.

'I don't know? Tell me, tell me, I say!' Athena answered, matching his optimism.

'We need to get flat rocks and stick them under our feet with rope. Is there any left?'

Athena looked through her bag and handed the remaining rope they had over to Malo.

'Great! This will be really fun, you'll see!' he promised and then quickly found four big flat stones by the nearby bushes.

'So, what do we do now?'

'Come here and I'll attach them to your shoes!'

Athena walked towards him and Malo put one rock under each shoe. He then took the string and tied it around the rock and her shoe and did the same with the other foot.

'Now, try and walk around while I do mine,' Malo advised.

Athena walked around and found it incredibly easy. It felt as though she was walking barefoot.

'I like to call these rockels! Alright, I'm ready. Now, we have to both run up the hill *as fast as we can* and jump up as high as we can when we finally get to the top. Then, you do nothing else. You just fly. It's so much faster to do this than walk. So, we save time AND have fun!'

'This sounds quite dangerous to me.'

'*This*, dear Athena, is danger in a fun way!' Malo said, laughing.

'If there is nothing left for me to do after the war, I could always advertise these at the markets by the Four Flames.'

Malo started running and Athena followed but as soon as they were a few yards away from the peak of the hill, both Oliver and Mark appeared.

'Keep running! And don't forget to bend your knees when you fall.' Malo called out. Athena obeyed.

'Mark, try to trip her over while I grab her!' Oliver ordered.

Athena heard this and then went as fast as she could to make it more difficult for them to capture her.

Malo jumped off the hill first. Athena was about to jump off, but Mark loosened the rope around her rockel. Sure enough, the rock fell off the hill as she jumped.

'Don't forget, once you start falling, bend your legs!' Malo shouted out to her.

'Malo, one of the rocks fell off!' she had to yell out as she felt the wind gush against her face. He turned around and looked.

Athena, I'm going to fall down now so I can help you when it's your turn. Try and stay as long as you can in the air, if that's possible!

Athena gulped as she saw Oliver and Mark running down the hill.

'I can't believe we climbed all the way up this hill just to go down straight away.' Mark complained.

'Bend your legs, NOW!' Malo roared from underneath.

Athena looked down at him and tried to bend her legs but she couldn't. She started to panic with her heart racing very fast. Suddenly, an idea came to her head.

Athena bent her leg to untie the rockel and dropped it in front of Oliver and Mark.

She then started to run in the air. Malo gazed up at Athena while he was still sliding down the hill.

'This has to be magic.' he whispered to himself, with admiration.

Oliver and Mark suddenly stopped running. Oliver looked at Mark and asked, 'Is she really flying in the air?'

Mark turned to him.

'I think so.' he replied and they both looked back up, watching her.

Athena started to smile in amazement. She only untied her rockel in order to jump a bit further ahead. Her flying, however, was controlled by a greater force. It was another power she could feel that was allowing her to flee from Mark and Oliver. She could feel the strong wind blowing on her face. Her legs felt free and her heart was beating with adrenaline and excitement.

Malo, after realising his mouth was wide open, could see her flying by. He quickly ran as fast as he could to catch up with her.

Even though she was being controlled by something beyond her, she knew it was there to help her. If she wanted to stop and return to the ground, she would be able to. She bent her legs and came down. Malo had finally caught up with her a few moments later. She quickly stood up, grabbed his hand and they both started to run.

'Run faster!' Oliver demanded.

'I can't, I'm exhausted!' Mark said, panting and gradually stopping. Oliver turned around to Mark and stared at him.

'You disappoint me, Mark.'

'I'm sorry.'

'No, you're not. If you truly understood how important catching Athena was, then you would have carried on running even if the soles of your feet were bleeding and blistering. I realise now that you aren't any different from the other councillors. I am the only, *true,* councillor who is really trying to make us win this war!'

He ran after Athena and Malo, leaving Mark alone.

'Oliver, wait!' Mark yelled.

Oliver turned around with a small grin on his face.

'Wait!' Mark repeated a bit softer, running towards him. Oliver folded his arms, waiting for an apology.

Mark knew exactly what he wanted to hear. Oliver had the personality of a cat which needed to be stroked and complimented in order to roll over and let you pass.

'I'm sorry, Oliver, I'm sorry. I promise I won't delay us anymore.'

Oliver nodded and then allowed Mark a few moments to fully regain his breath before heading off again.

Athena turned back and saw Oliver and Mark in the distance. She stopped running.

'Why did you stop?' Malo asked.

'They are far back. I need a break!' Athena said, holding her waist and gasping for air.

'Alright.'

Athena took a deep breath and looked up at the sky. It was dawn. The moon was slowly retreating and a beautiful dark pink sky began to appear. She then started running again. Malo glanced at her and saw that she was already a few yards ahead.

'Wait for me, dear Athena!' Malo said, in a high voice, skipping towards Athena.

She turned around and had a look on her face. 'What are you doing?'

'I'm bored and when I'm bored I pretend to be a fairy!'

'You are *very* strange, Malo!' she said, giggling.

'I know.' he replied, winking.

'What happened back there, by the way? When I said it was possible to fly, it is usually only for a few moments. What happened with you lasted minutes!'

'It was something else. It wasn't me or the rockels. Sorry to disappoint!'

'Well, when I try to sell these, I will use your story to make people buy them.'

'But I just said, it wasn't me or-'

'Sshh! Nobody needs to know.'

Athena shook her head, laughing. 'Anyway, it was magic. I could feel it.'

Malo grunted. 'Magic. I won't even try to understand the logic there!

It's something that completely baffles me.'

'Well, something that baffles me is how you've managed to live this long in Tatila without being approved by a Grelik.'

Malo shuddered. 'Even hearing their name gives me the chills. Well, I always did my best to avoid them. Believe it or not, I am usually quite good at keeping my head down and not attracting attention to myself. Except when I'm fighting in duels. In that case, I'm the biggest drama king you'll ever meet! Anyway, I have seen a few Greliks but never up close. They're sensitive creatures. I'm sure they have looked into my mind before, but know that there is nothing too evil in me. Some soldiers, however, have been killed in the past by them. In general, we all stay away from each other. Keep the peace between species in a way.'

Athena smiled. She imagined how he would be in a duel. Being a drama king. She didn't have difficulty believing that.

They continued walking in silence. Athena looked up and could see the pale blue sky with little pink clouds coming from the East.

After a while, Athena could hear some voices coming from ahead.

'Do you hear that?' she asked.

'You mean the voices in your head? No!'

'Can you hear people talking? Listen carefully.'

'I don't like that colour, Patrick. Exchange it immediately! I ask you to do one small thing. Honestly, next time I shall have Jane buy my clothes!'

'I'm sorry, mother! Give me one more chance. I'll buy you a gown with my own money. A gift!'

'Fair enough, but this time I shall choose which ever gown pleases me and I shall be ignoring the price. Mark my words!'

'Of course. Anything to please you, mother.'

Athena looked at Malo.

'I think we've reached the markets!' she said with light in her eyes. She looked ahead and vaguely made out the little markets behind the tall trees. They had finally reached the end of the Forest Tatila.

'Do you have the money?' Malo asked.

Athena looked through her bag and brought out the one hundred rubies Tomas had given her and the rubies from Benny.

'What can we get with two hundred rubies?'

'Depends on what you want to buy.'

'From what I just heard, women here wear dresses and gowns and men probably wear suits.'

'A gown usually costs four hundred rubies.' Malo sighed.

'Is there any way we could change prices? I mean if we work for an owner of a stall, they could reduce the price of the clothes'

'No, dear Athena, it doesn't work like that. We have to haggle.'

Athena felt her ears prick up. She suddenly turned around and saw Oliver and Mark in the distance.

Malo followed her eyes and saw Oliver and Mark charging towards him.

'Oh, the dear Gods above!' Malo screeched and ran as fast as his wounds allowed him towards the market, grabbing Athena's hand and pulling her closer to him.

'Mark, run faster! We almost have her in our grasp.' Oliver exclaimed, with hunger in his eyes.

Mark took deep breaths over and over again, gradually catching up with Oliver.

Athena and Malo reached the markets and paused at the sight.

There were so many people. Women wearing long, colourful gowns while men wore black trousers and long white tunics with laces at the top, circling their necks.

Each stall was surrounded by crowds of people who had their attention drawn to the products. There were stalls set up everywhere. Countless of small stalls were set up within a huge square.

'Hurry!' Oliver yelled over to Mark.

Athena and Malo suddenly turned around only to see Mark and Oliver only a few yards away.

Athena and Malo quickly began to run again.

'Get your purses here, Azulian purses!' a man was shouting from his stall. Athena glanced at the purses. They were all different types of colours. Her eye caught the light blue purse with shiny transparent beads beaded on.

'Look there!' Malo said as he pointed at a stall selling huge fruits.

'The sacks? That's a great idea!' Athena said, listening to Malo's thoughts.

They ran even faster to the three big empty sacks on the ground by the counter. Malo helped Athena into one. He then tied her sack up and went to the sack next to hers and climbed in quickly. He looked around one last time to see if Oliver and Mark were in sight. They were only a few yards away but were looking in a different direction.

Mark turned around and saw Malo, one leg in the sack, gawking at him. Mark glanced at the closed sack next to Malo, but then quickly turned back.

'Oliver, there's no sign of them. Perhaps we should head towards the Four Flames?' Mark suggested, patting his shoulder and leading him onwards.

'Mark, I was wrong. You do care about capturing them. You finally understand how important it is that we catch Athena!'

Mark nodded in agreement and started to walk towards the Four Flames with Oliver.

Malo just stood there, not moving a muscle until a plump, middle-aged woman barged into him.

'I'm sorry, young man, it...'

The old woman suddenly stopped talking. She looked Malo up and down and then looked back at his eyes and gasped.

Malo's eyes widened. 'No, no, I am not from the army. I left. It's a bad place. Very, very bad place. I have come here to join the King's army,' Malo said, very fast.

The woman lifted her head up, looking smug.

'Well, if that is the truth which I truly hope it is, then you should change clothing immediately if you do not wish to attract attention to yourself,' she said, throwing gold coins at him.

Malo watched her leave and then went over to Athena's sack. He untied it and helped her out.

'What was that you said earlier? You don't attract attention to yourself?'

'My uniform isn't usually a problem as I change it to make it *not* look like a uniform. Did I have time to do that this time? No, because we were being chased!'

'That's true. I'm sorry! Well, that woman was very nice. Run after her and say thank you,' Athena said, pointing to the direction she was heading.

Malo immediately ran after the woman and gave his thanks.

Athena bent down and collected the coins, but then heard someone's thoughts and felt their hand touch her shoulder.

Athena, I know what you are, what you are doing, where you are going. Be careful. There are many out there that wish you dead.

Athena immediately got up and stared up at the man. He was one of the men that were chasing her.

She tried to run towards Malo but the man grabbed her hand and pulled her back towards him.

'Listen, I know you think ill of me, but I just act like that. The other man I am with, Oliver, is the Head of the Council. I am Mark, his advisor. I saw your friend Malo and I could have told Oliver, but I didn't. I will do everything in my power to protect you, Athena.' Mark promised her as he strode back to Oliver who had his back to them.

'Did you find your child a gift?' Oliver asked.

Mark shook his head and then started walking away with Oliver following him.

Athena gazed at Mark but then heard Malo's thoughts. She turned back and saw him right in front of her with his hands behind his back.

'You were right for me to say thank you to her. She gave me another four hundred rubies!' Malo exclaimed as he revealed all the golden coins piled up in his hands.

'That woman is very generous. All together she gave us one thousand rubies!'

Malo looked back at the woman.

She must be one of the wealthiest women here.

Athena put all the money in her purse. Malo looked at her and asked, 'What do you want to buy?'

'Shall we just buy you new clothes and get some food?'

'You don't want anything for yourself?' Malo asked, slightly shocked.

Athena shook her head. 'We need to save as much as we can.'

'Your choice.' Malo said, walking to a stall that sold fruits.

'I'm choosing what you are going to eat. I want you to try foods they don't have in Oakrose. Let's meet my friend, Roderic.'

'Malo, it's been a while!' Roderic said.

'It has indeed!' Malo said, shaking Roderic's hand.

'How have you been? I've not seen you in months!'

'Well, things have changed since we last met. I was thrown out of the army and I met Athena. I'm helping her find her family here.' Malo said.

Roderic looked at Athena.

'Nice to meet you.' Roderic said as he gave her a big smile.

'Likewise! I've heard nice things about you.'

'How long are you staying for?' Roderic asked Malo, looking back at him.

'It depends. We are here to find Athena's father.'

'Do you know where he lives?' Roderic asked Athena.

'I don't.'

'A white cat came yesterday and told us that we will meet her father today,' Malo explained.

'Interesting. White cats are usually from the Royal Family. There are only two Flames that I would go to—'

'The Azul and Naran Flame.'

Roderic nodded. 'If I were you, I would first try the Naran Flame. It's smaller than the Azul Flame and so it would take less time to search. Be careful with those rotten Chamcok soldiers though,' Roderic warned.

'Urgh, Chamcoks. Thanks for reminding me. Okay, let's have some of your delicious fruit!' Malo said, rubbing his hands together in excitement.

'How about a red melon for you?' Roderic offered, handing over the huge fruit over to Athena.

'Thanks.' she replied looking at the circular red fruit. It was so big that it had to be held with both hands. The surface was rough with little white seeds all over it.

'So I am supposed to... eat it just like that?' Athena asked.

'Absolutely! You don't have to buy it. Consider it a gift from me.' Roderic said while handing Malo a small black circular fruit.

Athena slowly bit into the red fruit. It tasted like red berries but with an after taste similar to beer.

'Wow, it's really nice!' Athena told them. She remembered Malo telling her that he loved the fruit. She now understood why that was.

Malo and Roderic both looked at each other and then suddenly burst out laughing.

'My dear Athena, your teeth are red and so is the skin around your mouth.'

Athena placed the fruit on the counter and wiped her mouth but the red wasn't fading away.

'Here you go!' Roderic said, still giggling, handing a small transparent goblet with yellow liquid inside.

Athena was about to drink it but then Malo and Roderic at the same time yelled "no!!".

'What's wrong?'

'You are not supposed to drink it, dear Athena! You would die otherwise. You have to put some of the potion on your fingers and wipe it across your mouth. Then the red will go.'

'What about my teeth?'

'I was joking. It's only around your mouth. That was mean of me. I'm sorry!'

Athena quickly dipped her fingers in the potion and wiped it across her mouth.

'Is it gone?' she asked, her heart still beating fast.

Malo nodded as he took his last bite of his fruit. He suddenly banged his fists against the counter.

'Well, Roderic, nice seeing you again but we have to go. I need to change uniform.'

'Good seeing you too! Try to stay out of trouble, won't you?' Roderic said and waved at Athena.

I always do.

Athena smiled back at him and quickly left with Malo following her.

'For only three hundred rubies, that was money well spent!' Athena said.

'I especially love the leather boots,' he exclaimed, stroking them.

Athena looked at him. His long-sleeved white tunic had no laces and was tucked into his black trousers. He also wore leather boots that reached up to his ankles.

'I feel bad that you didn't buy anything though. Once we find your father, I will bring you back here and help you find something fairy-like to wear.' Malo offered.

Athena laughed. 'Deal! Now, let's go to the Naran Flame.'

XVI

'How are we going to get in?' Athena exclaimed, lifting her arms high up in the air and then folding them together behind her head.

They were walking towards the Naran Flame and could see there was a high black fence, guarding the front of the Flame.

'How do the people who live here get through?'

'They go through the main gate that only covers the front of the Flame. They're stupid enough to not protect the whole perimeter. But, anyway, why would they need to? Nobody would want to come here unless they really needed to.'

'I have an idea. How about we walk around the shield and see if there is a small hole that we can creep through?' Athena suggested.

'Of course! How could I have forgotten? My brain is all over the place today! When there was the revolt thirteen years ago, that's how the Chamcoks succeeded into entering this Flame.'

'You told me they were really stupid. How could they have figured-'

'They are, but they had help from the inside. This is my plan, dear Athena. We have nothing to lose by trying the main gate. We pretend we were sent here by General Avran. If the plan doesn't work, then we can always sneak around and find that infamous hole and creep through it. Agreed?'

'Agreed.'

They continued walking towards the main gate.

'How was there a hole in the first place?' Athena asked.

'I heard something from Alex who was friends with a soldier that was in love with Nerona, a member of the Council who knows everything, that there are very rare objects around the world that can break the "magic ways of life". There are instruments out there that can break force shields, remove powers from Wueltins or kill Agalits.'

'Kill Agalits? What?'

'Don't worry, for a long time we all thought these instruments were a myth. Something humans created to scare off arrogant Wueltins, I suppose. But they are so rare. This was the first time in history that an instrument of the sort was used in Fairoses. That's why it was such a shock when someone used it to let the Chamcocks in. Nobody could have imagined such a thing was possible. Not even the King!'

'How interesting.'

'Okay, there are Chamcoks everywhere. The gatemen are Chamcoks, servants are Chamcoks, citizens are married to Chamcoks. Just be vigilant, dear Athena.'

These men are worse than the Blucks. When Roderic talked about them, they were just words to me! I was too hungry to even think properly. These people aren't assembled in an army. The last time the Chamcoks tried to be put together as an army... well, let's just say, at the end of the day, three quarters of the army were killed by their comrades and it all started because one person didn't like his food!

'They'll never believe General Avran sent me here.' Athena said in a panic.

Malo laughed to himself.

'What?' she asked him, unamused.

'You could pretend that you work for me?'

'You mean, pretend that I am your slave? Or your cook?'

Malo was about to answer back but then considered Athena's suggestions.

'You know what? That isn't such a bad idea. Athena, my personal cook!'

Athena rolled her eyes, unable to not smile from the idea.

'What do you want?' the gateman asked, picking up his sword whilst spitting on the ground.

'I need to get through.' Malo replied, standing straight and avoiding eye contact with the gateman.

'Who says?' the gateman asked, spitting once more.

'General Avran. Leader of the Blucks. He wants to make sure that your men are ready for the upcoming war.'

The gateman looked Malo up and down.

'You are not a soldier. You are not dressed as one!'

'I had to exchange my clothes in order to buy some food.'

The gateman grunted and then looked at Athena who was looking down at the ground.

'Who's she?'

'She's my cook.' Malo replied.

The gateman was about to let them through but then stopped.

'If you have a cook, why did you have to exchange your clothes for food?'

Malo's eyes widened. He didn't know what to respond.

Say something!

'How can a cook, cook without food?' Athena asked in a very philosophical manner.

The gateman grunted once again and let them through.

Athena walked through and Malo was about to as well, but the gateman blocked his way by putting his sword to Malo's neck.

'Why did you bring your cook here? Are you insinuating that our food is terrible?' he asked, offended.

'On the contrary, it is known throughout the Seven Hundred Army that your food is exquisite.'

'Then why did you bring a cook?'

'I have allergies.' Malo said. He regretted saying it the moment he heard it.

'The army has strict rules against soldiers having allergies, illnesses and disabilities!' the gateman snarled.

'Well, I was the exception I guess. Lucky me.'

'Hold your tongue, boy!'

Malo nodded and the gateman lowered his sword and him walked through.

That was a close one!

They were now at the purple force shield. Athena touched it with her fingers. It was liquid, in fact, and it was only a few inches thick. Her fingers went through it and were now on the other side.

'This is such a weird sensation.' she whispered.

'I know. You just have to go through it slowly.' Malo said, and with that, he walked through with his eyes closed.

Athena stuck her hand out, then her arm and gradually she went through the shield as well.

They both walked up the mountain at a fast pace. The steps were equal in size and a long orange carpet was rolled from the entrance of the Flame up to the top of the mountain where there was a big castle. There were small, abandoned houses on either side of the road leading up the mountain. The habitants lived further up the Flame.

'We must not go in the castle no matter what!' Malo advised.

Athena agreed. She suddenly stopped as she caught sight of a painting inside a house.

'That painting!' she gasped, pointing at it. Malo put her arm down.

'Don't point, dear Athena. Chamcoks see that as a very rude gesture.'

'Sorry.'

'Now, the painting inside that house reminds you of something?' Malo asked.

Athena nodded. She continued to stare at it. The painting showed the landscape both she and Malo had crossed on their journey to the Four Flames: The volcano, the two bridges, the Forest Tatila, the black sky and the full moon.

'Do you think we can go in that house?' she whispered.

Malo looked at the house. It seemed to be deserted. There was nothing else visible in the small house apart from the painting and an old chest.

'The house is only one floor but it seems like a wreck. I guess the Chamcoks don't like it.'

'Is it safe to go in?' Athena mumbled already walking towards the door.

Malo looked around. There were only a few women and children.

Go in, quietly.

Athena nodded and tried to open the door but it was locked. Athena tried to kick the door.

'Ouch, that hurt!' she whispered, hopping around, holding her injured leg.

'My dear Athena, are you really going to complain about that after everything I had to go through?' he said, winking at her.

Athena gave a guilty look. 'Sorry,' she mumbled.

Malo laughed and pulled the door handle upwards. He looked at Athena and gave a cheeky grin as the door opened. She put down her leg and limped through the door with a small smile, but refused to look up at Malo.

'This place is so old. When was the last time somebody even set foot in here?' he noticed, stamping his foot and unsettling the thick dust from the floor.

Athena went straight to the canvas and realised it wasn't a painting, but a drawing. She recognised it. It was definitely her who drew it. She was sure of it.

'Malo, can you help me take it down from the wall?'

Malo carefully walked over to Athena in case more dust moved around the room.

He took a deep breath and placed the drawing onto the chest, which was directly underneath it.

'Wow, this frame is so heavy!' Malo screeched, leaning against the wall and rubbing his eyes as the dust was irritating them.

Athena immediately turned the frame around and saw another drawing.

'Look, Malo, there's another one!'

Malo leant over, took a closer look and said, 'The first drawing is much better. The one facing upwards.'

Athena smiled and replied, 'I think so too.'

She delicately unhinged the nails which made the frame fall apart, creating a loud thud.

'Whoops! That was my fault!' Athena said, looking over at Malo who was making a face.

'You can't make too much noise! If the soldiers hear us snooping around a house that isn't ours, then that will be the end of it!'

'I'm sorry.'

Athena carefully took out both pictures from the glass sheet that separated them from each other. She looked at the back of the first drawing.

'What is it?' Malo asked, looking away from the window.

Athena showed him the blank side of the paper that read:

Athena, aged three, 23rd March.

Malo grabbed the piece of paper and then looked up at Athena and said, 'You were *three* when you drew *this*?'

'Probably. Let's look at the other drawing.'

Athena turned the other drawing around and looked down at the blank side.

She paused.

'What is it?' Malo asked looking up at her.

'This isn't mine.'

'Well, I knew that because your one is amazing and this one is absolutely dreadful. I understand why it was placed backwards. Nobody should have to look at that!'

Athena looked at Malo, her eyes watered because of the dust.

'This drawing was done by Nicolas.' she said, showing him the blank side.

Malo put down Athena's drawing and grabbed Nicolas's drawing from her hands.

'Nicolas, aged five, 29th June, Athena's birthday,' he read out.

Athena continued looking at Malo.

'That means my birthday isn't in August but June,' Athena whispered.

Malo didn't know what to reply.

'Um... let's look in the chest,' he suggested and with that he removed the frame and drawings, placed them on the ground and opened up the chest.

As soon as Malo opened it up, a cloud of dust went straight into his face.

He suddenly coughed.

'Wow, that is a *lot* of dust,' he said, choking. Athena walked over and bent down next to him, and together they looked through the old leather chest.

'Papers, flowers, lots of dolls, drawings and more drawings,' Malo said as he went through the belongings.

'What's this?' Athena asked herself as she saw a doll. It somehow seemed familiar to her.

'What? That thing that seems to have been torn apart then sewed back together?' Malo asked in disgust.

'It's more than that!' Athena said as she stroked the pink dolls blonde hair.

Athena stared at the doll's face. It was true. The neck had been torn apart from the rest of the body, but then it was sewed together with brown thread.

'I remember this doll. It was mine.'

'How did you get it?'

'I... I don't remember.'

Suddenly a group of Chamcoks came by. They were all holding their swords.

'You there! What you doing? That's a haunted house. Get out. We want to talk to you!' a young man yelled as he pressed his nose against the dusty window. His friends were sniggering behind him.

Athena looked at Malo.

'What do we do?' she asked in a panic.

'We have to run through the door. You kick, I punch and we will be able to get away,' Malo said as he got up.

Athena stood up as well.

'You aren't serious, are you? There are at least ten men out there. I would barely be able to get away from one of them,' Athena said, panicking.

'I'm dead serious. Chamcoks are no match for a Bluck. Now, come on. I'll creep over to the door and open it very quickly. You run out. I will be right behind you,' Malo explained as he drew out his sword.

Athena did as she was told, but quickly tucked the doll and drawings in her bag.

'Ready?' Malo asked, already at the door.

She nodded. As soon as he opened the door, she stood up and ran as fast as she could.

The men were all looking the opposite way, but as soon as they heard the door creak open, they turned around and held their swords out.

'The girl's getting away!' one of the men pointed out.

'Never mind the girl, it's Malo we want!'

Malo took a deep breath and ran outside and stabbed the first man he saw in the thigh. The man screamed so loud that it caused everyone on the mountain to hear his shriek.

'You will pay for that, Malo!' another man scowled.

Malo was about to strike another Chamcok but then suddenly stopped. 'How do you know my name?'

'Was it not the famous Malo who stole my medal and rubies from that duel competition four years ago?' the leader of the gang recalled.

'You have been waiting for me for four years? Wow, you don't get out a lot, do you?'

There was a crowd that had quickly formed since Malo had stabbed a man in the leg. The leader cracked his jaw. He turned around.

'Everyone step away. Me and Malo are-'

'I believe it is Malo and I?! Not only is your sword fighting a bit rusty but so is your grammar. At this rate, you will never find yourself a girl.'

There were a few laughs amongst the crowd that now seemed to be the majority of the Chamcoks.

'Malo and I will have a duel. Step back everyone!' the man yelled.

Malo remained still.

'Fight me. Or are you too afraid?'

'No, I'm not afraid, I just don't like wasting my time fighting amateurs. Besides, there isn't a prize.'

'There is a prize.'

'Really? Where?'

'Right over there!' the man replied, pointing with his sword towards Athena who was brought to the front of the crowd, being held by two men.

'Her? She doesn't deserve to be my prize. Kill her if you want, but I will still leave if there isn't any other prize,' Malo called out.

Athena stared at Malo.

I'm bluffing, dear Athena. He won't hurt you and if he does, I'll kill him first.

Athena remained quiet.

The man sighed. 'Well, what prize would you want then?'

'How about your fancy sword? It's gold and shiny. The pommel and cross guard have emeralds on them. That will be the prize. Your sword. Well, we can throw the girl in too!'

The man nodded.

'By the way what is your name again? I forgot.'

'Andrew. Now, let us fight and I will show you who should have won that competition years ago!'

By now, the crowd had encircled them and all eyes were set on Malo and Andrew.

Andrew and Malo were only a few inches away from each other. They saluted, turned around and walked back four paces, as was the general etiquette in duels.

They both quickly turned back and Andrew ran towards Malo with his sword pointing at him straight away.

Malo quickly moved an inch to the left which left Andrew running into the crowd.

'Won't you ever learn?' Malo asked out loud, making the crowd laugh. Malo put his hand to his ear to make the crowd cheer even louder.

Andrew grunted and retrieved his sword from the cobbled ground. He stood up and ran towards Malo once again. He drew out his sword, and as soon as Andrew reached him, Malo bent down and lunged onto him. They both fell on the ground. Malo took his sword and was about to make Andrew forfeit by pointing the sword at his throat, but Andrew kicked it out of Malo's hand and then punched him in the face.

'My, oh my, you *have* improved.' Malo said as he was getting up from the ground.

'I have practiced six hours a day for the last four years!'

'So *that's* why you haven't found yourself a wife yet!'

Andrew kicked Malo's sword out of his way and then kicked him in the leg. His injured leg.

Malo groaned but didn't fall to the ground as Andrew had thought, but instead he ran to his sword and picked it up.

'You are going to pay.' Malo said as he wiped the blood from the edge of his mouth. He gritted his teeth and bit his tongue from the pain he felt in his leg.

Malo knew the weak points on the human body because when he was a child, a man had taught him these skills. Besides, he was getting fed up. This duel was a waste of time. Andrew was no match for him and he wanted to help Athena find her family. With the Council searching for them, Malo knew that if word got out there was a duel going on in the Naran Flame, the Council would be the first to come. For Athena's security, this had to end now.

'What's that over there?' he asked, looking east.

Andrew followed Malo's gaze and Malo took this opportunity to kick him behind the knee. He didn't like using this method. It was cheating in a way, but whenever someone was dumb enough to fall for it, he would forgive himself.

He fell down to the ground. Malo gave him time to stand back up, but Andrew was unable to do so.

'Do you surrender?' Malo asked him, still wiping his mouth.

'Never!' Andrew hissed. He grabbed his dagger from his boot and aimed it towards Malo's thigh.

Malo drew his sword and reflected the dagger, which landed between Andrew's legs.

Malo stumbled over to him and once again asked him if he was going to surrender.

'No!' Andrew squealed as he tried to reach for his sword but Malo kicked it away.

The tip of Malo's sword was pointing at Andrew's throat.

'I will ask you one last time. Do. You. Surrender?' Malo hissed.

After a few moments of hesitation, Andrew nodded. He could see there was no way out of this.

'Say it.' Malo snarled, now making his sword touch Andrew's throat.

'I surrender!' Andrew shouted, all red in the face.

Malo smiled and withdrew his sword. He gave his hand to Andrew to help him up.

'I suppose you would like my sword!' Andrew exclaimed, still panting.

'Yes... and the girl.' Malo said, pointing at Athena.

Andrew clicked his fingers and the two men immediately let go of Athena.

Athena walked towards Malo, holding her bag very tightly.

'The sword, Andrew.'

Andrew picked up his sword and slowly handed it over to Malo.

'But I will keep the girl!' Andrew said, grabbing hold of Athena.

'She was part of the package. I won her!' Malo said in the most aggressive tone.

'I changed my mind. You didn't want her at the beginning, so what makes you change your mind? Besides, at the duel four years ago there was a girl there who you were in love with. What happened there? You almost didn't care about your prize because you were so fixated on her. Did she reject you in the end because she came to her senses? Is that what happened?'

'Leave her alone!' Malo snarled, walking towards them, his blood boiling. In his mind, he was talking about both Athena and the other girl he had met years before.

Andrew picked up his dagger and held it close to Athena's wrist.

'No! I am keeping her. She would make an ideal wife.'

Malo paused and then started laughing. Andrew loosened his grip and Athena elbowed him in the stomach and ran behind Malo.

'Come back here, girl!' Andrew groaned.

'She only listens to me.' Malo grinned. He then turned to the crowd.

'Does it not degrade the whole society of Chamcoks that *this* man,' Malo shouted out, pointing at Andrew with his new sword, 'is one of you? If I found out that this man was part of the Blucks society, then I would take care of him myself, but that's just me. Now, you have all seen that I have won the duel. So, my prize and I-'

'Don't you mean my prize and me?' Andrew whimpered.

Malo looked at Andrew and tutted.

'Your grammar will never really improve...just like your fighting skills.'

'That isn't true! I have progressed a lot in four years. You said it yourself!!'

Malo bent down and looked at Andrew straight in the eye and whispered, 'Don't you think that if you have practiced that long and you *still* haven't managed to defeat me, then you are not talented at all? Perhaps you should try being a cook, a servant, a slave?'

Andrew spat in Malo's face.

Malo got up and continued to face the public. 'As we have all witnessed, Andrew really is the scum of your society. I trust that you will change that.' Malo shouted out.

He took Athena's hand and they both left, watching the Chamcoks move in closer to Andrew.

I don't think your father lives here to be honest. If he's related to you, then he must have some intelligence. No one in their right mind would stay in that Flame with all those imbeciles.

They quickly made their way down the mountain and decided to go through the main gate. They decided that there was no point in creeping through the hole. Besides, Malo had lost his patience. He wanted to get out as fast as possible, but knew he had to go through the purple force shield with grace. Athena held his hand which calmed him down and together, they went through the shield.

They reached a different gateman this time, who stood up the moment he caught sight of them.

'Passes please!'

'We don't have passes.'

'No passes, No exit. That is the policy.'

'I came here on an urgent quest from General Avran,'

'I don't care.'

'Fine! I have thirty soldiers in the market. If they find out that I am not able to leave, they will have you killed!' Malo threatened.

'Once again, I DON'T CARE!' the man said, raising his voice.

'Right. Can you hold this?' Malo asked, handing Andrew's sword over to the gateman.

The gateman grunted, but grabbed the sword anyway.

Malo coughed, looked at the gateman and then punched him in the face. The gateman went backwards, hitting the metal gate, opening it up.

'Thanks!' Malo said, as he took the sword from his hand and walked through the gate with Athena.

'So, we're still going to the Azul Flame, right?' he asked once they were far away from the Naran Flame.

'Yes! I have a few questions though. Do the Chamcoks leave the Flame? I didn't notice any in the markets. Do people enjoy living in the Naran Flame with soldiers on every street? How do the other Flames protect themselves from them?'

'The other Flames are quite far away. And besides, they don't have anything there that would interest the Chamcoks. The Azul Flame, on the other hand, is hard to enter. Because it is next to the Naran Flame and also because it's home to the King and several noble families. There are two gates there. One surrounding the Flame, and another gate inside the Flame.

The Chamcoks don't leave the Naran Flame because everyone despises them, even the Blucks. But we need a fighting society who can join us as an ally when it comes to battle. Anyway, they don't like moving a lot.

Surprisingly, there are many people who still live in the Naran Flame. Even with this infestation of Chamcoks. However, even though they are stupid and reckless men with swords, they are still somewhat respectful to the people who live there. They don't bother each other. Your family would have been smart enough to get out of it, I'm sure. The more I think of it, the more I know they are in the Azul Flame. They have to be!'

'I think so too. I mean, I wouldn't feel safe living there at all!'

'I don't think you would last very long anyway because you're an Agalit. They would turn you in to the Seven Hundred Army straight away. Anything to get the approval of your brother.'

'Why didn't they notice I was an Agalit?'

'They would never look in your eyes. They are too cowardly! Besides, they were interested me in, dear Athena,' Malo said, fluttering his eyelashes at her.

Athena burst out laughing. They continued walking for a few minutes in silence. Then Athena had to ask.

'Malo, you never told me about that girl Andrew was talking about.'

Malo chuckled. 'I *knew* you were going to ask about that. I think I'm also beginning to read minds!

Well, Andrew told most of the story. I met her at the duel competition. It was the last round and whoever won was the winner of the entire competition. As I was getting ready for the duel, a girl approaches me. She looks at me with her beautiful and tantalising eyes and bravely kisses me on the forehead. She then just looks at me in all her beauty and charm, and smiles. The moment she smiled at me, I knew she was the right one for me. I've always been a charmer with the ladies, dear Athena,' he said as he gave her a nudge with a cheeky smile, 'but all that changed as soon as I saw her. I can't explain it, but I felt like I breathed for the first time in my entire life. All the sorrow and torture I had once endured left my heart, and was replaced just by pure love and happiness. After that happened, I fought in the duel and it was the best I had ever done. That is why I have created such a reputation for myself here. It was because of her! She gave me that missing element I needed in order to be invincible!'

Athena gazed at him in admiration for a long moment before talking.

'Wow, Malo, this is a side of you I haven't seen yet! That is such a beautiful story. So, where is she now? What's her name?'

'I can't answer either of those questions. That was the only time I saw her. We didn't even speak. I just knew that was it. If I see her again, and that's all I pray for since that day, I will marry her.'

Malo paused for a moment and smiled to himself.

'Since meeting her, I haven't been with one girl or even thought about another girl in that way. I love her. No matter how many beautiful girls are around me, she is the only one I keep in my heart and stay faithful to.

All I can say more on that enigma of a woman, is that she was truly the most beautiful girl I had ever set my eyes on. When she came up to me, she was surrounded by such a warm yet powerful Aura and it was impossible to be anything *but* happy around her. Truth be told, when I used to be tortured in the army, I would always think of her. I would imagine us meeting and as soon as I managed to focus only on her, all the pain I was enduring would numb away. It was as though both my emotional and mental state of mind had completely defeated my physical state of being. I was able to endure all that torture, dear Athena, because of that girl I had met for only a few minutes.

You're the first person who knows about this last part actually. I've never spoken to anyone else about it.'

Athena had tears in her eyes. This was the sort of love she had read about. It touched her so much to actually hear it from a person who had *felt* those incredibly strong emotions than from the pages of an old book which only explained *how* those feelings were felt. This was the real-life story and not just a fairy-tale. It was much more beautiful, in Athena's opinion.

'She was my light in shining armour,' he finished off with a big smile.

Athena laughed. 'What a line.'

Malo scratched his ear and smiled as he looked down. Athena just looked at him with so much admiration.

'After we find my father, I'm going to help you find her, Malo.'

For the first time since they had met, Athena had never seen Malo smile with so much light in his eyes. 'Nothing in the world would make me happier, dear Athena. Nothing.'

He picked her up, hugged her and squeezed her tight. After he put her down, he continued beaming.

'So, how are we going to get into the Azul Flame if we have to pass a grumpy gateman? Actually, I don't even care anymore. I'm very excited. I just feel that he will be in the Azul Flame. I'm going to finally meet my father, Malo! And any other brothers or sisters I may have. I wonder if they will be as excited to see me as I am to see them!'

Malo gave her a big grin and put his arm around her shoulder as they continued walking.

'Here.' he said, handing over Andrew's sword to her.
'Even though his skills were dreadful, this is a very good sword!'

'Really?'

'Yes, someone will eventually have to teach you how to fight. You might as well have a nice sword. It is a shame, though, that the stones aren't turquoise but emeralds.'

'Why do you say that?'

'I saw you looking at that blue, shiny purse,' Malo said smiling.

XVII

'Mark, you tricked me. They are nowhere to be seen!' Oliver snapped.

'Oliver, I told you, I assumed that they would be in the Amarila Flame. I heard people say they came here!'

'That is not good enough. Lead me to another Flame immediately!'

'We can't leave without a pass.' Mark explained.

'How long does it take to *have* a pass?'

'Three days.'

Oliver groaned.

'So, you are telling me that we are stuck on this mountain for another three days?'

'Yes. It's usually easier to get out of the other Flames, but look at us! We are dressed as soldiers. This is the most peaceful yet strictest Flame. We can't sneak out.'

'If I were you, I would rent a makeshift house!' the gateman suggested.

'Shut up!' Oliver hissed as he started walking up the second largest mountain once again.

Athena and Malo walked from the Naran Flame to the Azul Flame, which had taken them at least half an hour.

'I thought that the Four Flames were all very close together?'

'Yes, apart from the Naran Flame. The will of the Gods I'd say for putting those Chamcoks as far away as possible from everybody else. Magic, eh? Logic-'

'That you will never understand. Why do you say that? Why are you against magic?'

'I'm not against it. It's just a different dimension, a different mindset, a different everything to what I'm used to. In the army, we all say that. When something happens that cannot be explained, we just say it's logic we can't understand. I just understand the basics of certain species such as

Agalits because it's in the book the army gave us to learn. But that's it! It's just something that doesn't interest us. We are soldiers. We kill. We keep the peace. That's what makes the Seven Hundred Army famous. We are seven hundred soldiers who fight at the highest level, and then the scientists in the army are the most advanced in the world because they have managed to fuse together reality and magic.'

'I really would love to read this book.'

'I don't have it and I don't need it. It's in here,' he said, grinning and pointing to his head. 'Anyway, are you ready to meet the King?'

'Excuse me?' Athena asked, her eyes widened.

'I forgot to tell you about my plan. I would have thought you heard it!'

Athena sighed. 'That happens to me often. I can't hear your thoughts and those around me but I can hear them at other times. When I was in the market that man who was following us spoke to me.'

Malo turned to her.

'The short one or the tall one?' he asked in distressed.

'The short one. His name is Mark.'

'I know what his name is. What did he say?' Malo snapped.

'Well, he said that he knows what I am. He said he is on our side.'

'What did you reply?'

'I didn't have time to say anything. He quickly left.'

'Well, we can talk all about this with the King. Anyway, my plan is for us to pose as messengers! We have to find some black cloaks at the market though. If that doesn't work, then I will just be honest and say I've left the Seven Hundred Army and want to join his side.'

'Are you sure that is going to work?' Athena asked.

'The people in the Azul Flame are very different to those in the Naran Flame. They are really nice and friendly. Everyone is nice here.' he said, pointing to the bustling scene of the people moving around the markets.

'Okay. If everyone is so nice, why do we have to wear black cloaks?' Athena smiled.

'We want to meet the King! Last time I came here, I didn't have the chance to meet him.'

'Maybe he could help me find my father.'

'That was also my plan. Wow, you're really missing out by not listening to my thoughts! You two would have plenty to talk about. Both being Agalits. You can tell him about your power. Maybe he could help you control it.' Malo suggested.

'What is the King's power?'

'He is immortal, though I've heard he looks no older than forty.'

Athena nodded. Was that really a power?

They both joined the hustle and bustle of the markets.

'Cloaks, cloaks...' Athena repeated over and over again, looking around for cloaks.

'Hey, Roderic, where can we find long, black cloaks?' Malo asked, leaning against Roderic's counter with a charming smile.

'On the other side of the market. You should see a section just for costumes. Not far from where you bought yours!' he replied, pointing at Malo's new outfit.

Malo posed for Roderic in a fairy-like way.

Roderic laughed. 'You are a strange one, Malo!'

'But you already knew that. I know where they are, dear Athena!' Malo said, holding her hand.

They hurried across the market. Malo kept barging into people and Athena apologising on his behalf.

Her head began to spin with too many thoughts streaming into her mind. She suddenly fell to the ground, with her hands covering her ears.

Why won't my son love me?

Can't my child be born today?

I love my clothes.

My stall needs to be painted again.

I hate my baby sister. She gets all the attention.

I hope my cat feels better. These herbs will help him.

'What's wrong?' Malo said, kneeling down on the ground.

'My head hurts!'

'Because you can hear everyone's thoughts?'

'Exactly.'

Malo sighed and then jumped back up again. He whistled so loudly that everyone stopped what they were doing.

'Can everyone just stay still for two minutes, please! My wife is with child and she's feeling very sick at the moment,' Malo yelled out.

He bent down and helped Athena up, and together they walked through the motionless crowd. Even though they still had many thoughts running through their heads, Athena felt much better as they weren't talking out loud as well.

That girl doesn't look pregnant!
She seems too young to have a child.
She's all bones on skin.

Once they reached the costume stalls, Malo yelled out, 'Thank you.'
Everyone continued with their day as if nothing happened.
'How can I help you?' the friendly stall owner asked.
'We would like two long black cloaks!' Malo said firmly.
'Very well,' she said as she knelt down and took out two black cloaks from a small chest under the counter. She handed them over to Malo.
'That will be two hundred rubies!' the plumpy young woman said. Athena took out the coins out of her bag and passed them to the woman.
Athena and Malo walked out of the market and started heading towards the Azul Flame.
'Why did you say that? That I was pregnant?' Athena asked, puzzled.
'Well, people here have great respect for pregnant women. They treat them like the Gods. So, I knew that if I said that you were pregnant and that you needed some quiet, they would all be silent immediately!'
'Interesting!' Athena said, smiling evilly and putting her cloak on.
'Are you *sure* this will work?' she continued.
'After everything we've been through? This will be a walk in the park! I'm sure it will work. We've been lucky…so far.'
'What will we say to the King?'
'The truth! The war coming in four weeks, the-'
'Shouldn't he already know that though? He is the King, after all.'
'I know, but everyone knows that his army is very small. They don't force people to join the army and nobody wants to fight here.'
'But you will definitely join? No matter what?'
'Of course. I could even become general. Can't be that hard.'
'Careful now. I don't want you to trip on your-'
'General Malo does sound catchy, don't you think?'
'Of course.'
'Really?'

'No.'

Malo gave her an unimpressed look.

'I think it's about time you have some rest, old man! You're becoming delirious.'

'Time with me has certainly turned you into a feisty one. I like it! Anyway, when we get to the gate, we have to say we are both messengers from the Seven Hundred Army and that we have a message for the King concerning the war in four weeks. Agreed?'

'Agreed.'

'But depending on the circumstances, I might make up a story on the spot. No matter what I say, stay by my side. Agreed?'

'Agreed!'

Malo looked ahead and saw the biggest mountain in front of them with the breathtaking, almost transparent, purple force shield shaped as a flame.

'It really is magnificent up close,' Athena noted.

'Definitely,' he said as he looked all the way up the top of the mountain.

'Can you see the castle at the top of the mountain?' Malo asked Athena, pointing up.

'Yes. It's huge! I'm quite surprised that the tip of the mountain can support such heavy weight!'

'Magic. Logic-'

'You could never understand.' They said together. Athena burst out laughing.

'Alright, dear Athena, control yourself. The gateman can see us now.'

'Hello,' Malo started.

'Why, hello there, young man. How may I help you?' the gateman asked with a friendly smile.

'We are messengers. We have an urgent message for the King Agalaya, concerning the war.'

'Ah yes. The King is greatly distressed about that matter. Hopefully, you would be able to send him good news.'

Malo nodded.

The gateman pushed opened the impressive metal black gate and gave them a piece of turquoise stone, which allowed them to pass the force shield.

'When you get to the next gate, give those stones to the guards. Seeing that your stay is not permanent, we do not want to take the risk of you two giving them to either the Chamcoks or the Blucks. So far, this system has been working well. Have a pleasant afternoon!'

'He was very nice.' Athena smiled.

'Yes, but we have to be careful because we have the force shield and two more barriers; the next gateman and the King's Guard.'

Athena and Malo both stopped talking and went through force shield slowly. They both closed their eyes and felt themselves pass through the very faint yet powerful thick line. Athena put her hands out and felt the violet liquid flow into her hands, where she was holding the stone. It was a much more pleasant experience than the Naran Flame.

They both reached the other side.

'Did you feel the liquid?' Athena asked, excitedly.

'Yes, but only for a few seconds.' he said in an impatient tone as he walked towards the guard.

'What are your intentions in the Azul Flame?' the gateman asked, putting on his blue hat, which was part of all the gatemens' uniform.

'We are messengers. We have a message concerning the Schumy War.'

'The King is worrying enough on that matter. I cannot allow you here if you will worsen the matter.'

Malo took a deep breath and closed his eyes, then he quickly opened them up.

'Listen to me-'

'Wait! You are right. We aren't allowed in if we are to worsen the matter. We both completely understand, but we bring great news to the King which will lift his spirit,' Athena said.

The gateman looked at Athena. 'You don't seem like a messenger. Where do you come from?'

'I grew up in Oakrose. I lived in a small shack close to six hills.'

The guard's eyes widened.

'You mean a small shack next to a huge oak tree and the four hills past the volcano?' he asked all in one breath.

'The very one,' Athena replied slowly, examining the very young man. His hair was black, his eyes were dark brown and he was the same height as Athena.

'A fortune teller told me that I was kidnapped as a baby. As soon as I was born actually. She gave me a description of my home where I was conceived. I was brought here and my father helped my biological mother give birth...'

Athena's eyes widened. 'Do you know what your mother's name is?'

'The fortune teller did give me a name!'

'Well, what was it?'

'It could be wrong...'

'Is it Agatha?' Athena asked with a huge smile on her face.

'Wow! Are you a fortune teller too?'

'No. What is your name?' Athena asked, with tears in her eyes.

'Yan,' the gateman replied.

'Your real father's name is Tomas. Both Tomas and Agatha are waiting for you to return to them one day.'

'How should I know that you aren't making this up on the spot? There isn't enough evidence.'

'Yes, there is! A fortune teller describes your home. She even gives you the name of your mother and you are thirteen. That should be enough evidence for you, Yan!'

Yan paused for a moment.

'How did you know my age?'

'You were born on the fifth of August. You are thirteen because you were born the same day I was brought to your house. Your kind father found me on the river bank, not far from here!'

Yan stared at Athena and started smiling.

'May we go through?' Malo asked, interrupting the silence.

Yan continued staring at Athena. Malo cleared his throat to get his attention.

'Of course!' Yan said, hitting himself on the head. He quickly opened the gate and took their stones.

'Have a nice and wonderful time in the Azul mountain. The mountain of Agalaya!' Yan recited.

Malo walked straight pass but Athena remained still.

'Are you planning to meet your real parents?' Athena asked, with a hint of hope.

'Of course. I was planning to leave straight after my fortune teller told me about my past, but my father told me not to. He said I shouldn't have found out. It was his place to tell me, not a fortune teller. Until he tells me I can leave, I will have to remain here.'

Athena shook her head.

'Why don't you fight him on it? You have the right to meet your real parents!' Athena said, feeling her blood boil.

'He isn't an ordinary man. He is a Wueltin. I cannot fight him on this. I trust and respect him. I will be fine. You must go now. There are other people coming to my gate in a few minutes,' Yan croaked, looking pass the force shield and seeing a family approaching the shield.

'Alright. When I visit Agatha and Tomas in a few months, I hope I will see you there as well.'

Yan nodded and gently urged Athena onwards.

'You will! Don't worry,' he said, smiling.

They walked away from the gate, but Athena kept staring back at Yan. Malo began to get impatient so he lifted her up and started carrying her away.

'My dear Athena, we have to go to the King!' Malo said, continuing to carry her up the mountain. He would rather suffer from the added strain on his legs rather than carry on listening to her conversation with Yan.

'He is *so* young. He is only thirteen and he has a nice job.'

'Being a gateman. Great job!' Malo said in a sarcastic way.

Athena hit his arm with her bag. Malo suddenly dropped Athena and grabbed hold of his arm.

'Why did you do that?'

'I didn't want to make you tired, walking me up a huge mountain.'

'So, you decided to hit me on the arm?' Malo asked, very confused.

'Well, if I hit your arm you wouldn't be able to carry me.'

'You could have said, "Malo, put me down!" but instead you hit me on the arm? You are a very disturbed Agalit, indeed.'

It's also because of what I said about Yan, isn't it?

Athena winked at him. 'You know me so well.'

Athena got up and started walking, with Malo following her. 'What was in that bag anyway?'

'You mean apart from a doll and two drawings?'

'Don't make me sound so weak. Do I need to show you my muscles again?'

'Don't worry. There were about fifty gold coins in there, Malo. Don't beat yourself up.'

'No, I'll leave that honour to you.' Malo said, winking as he continued holding his arm.

'This place is much nicer and more welcoming than the Naran Flame.' Athena noticed as everyone they passed smiled at them. There were small cottages on both their sides with small chimneys letting out blue smoke.

There were small shops everywhere and stalls, crowded by children, that were selling different types of sweets. There were shops that sold rare books, others which sold meat and vegetables and others that sold flowers.

'This place is incredible! There's everything you could possibly want.' Athena gasped as she passed a man, surrounded by a small crowd, handling two wooden sticks burning with blue fire.

They continued walking up the very long blue carpet which ended at the very top of the mountain. There were small fountains everywhere pouring out transparent water landing on pink flowers in the basin.

There were white cats wandering together in groups and everyone treated them with great respect, stopping to let them pass and stride across the wide road in pride.

'That is quite strange!' Malo said, looking at the cats, which suddenly looked up and stared at him.

'Why are they staring at me?' he whispered to Athena.

'They can hear what you say.'

'I'm sorry, cats. I didn't mean to offend you.'

'That is quite alright!' one cat said in a very low voice. They all continued to move as a group.

Malo's eyes widened. He suddenly looked at Athena.

'Did that cat just speak out loud?' Malo asked.

'Yes! I didn't know that these cats could speak out loud either.'

'And here I was, thinking I knew a lot about the Four Flames. I just forgot the fact that cats can speak here!'

'Woah! Did you just see what that man did?' Malo continued, looking at a man that they just walked past.

Athena looked back and saw a man juggling three white cats. He then threw them through a ring of blue fire.

Athena gasped. 'That's so dangerous.'

'I don't think the cats mind. After all, they are trained to do that. I don't think they'd do that if there were risks. Those cats are very intelligent.'

'So, what are you planning to do once we meet your father?' Malo asked curiously.

'Well... um... I was planning to stay with him, but with the war coming, I'm not quite sure anymore.'

'If we don't find your father, we can find a cottage to live in.'

'Where would we get the money?'

'The King would give you anything because you are an Agalit.'

'That's generous.'

'On the other hand, what happens if your father is a very rich nobleman? Would you live with him then?'

'We'll see. With the war coming-'

'Would you be upset if I died during this war?' Malo asked, knowing the answer.

'I can hear what you are thinking now, you cheeky person! You know I would be upset. It would be absolutely horrific if you died.' Athena replied truthfully.

Malo smiled.

'Why are you smiling?' Athena asked, also grinning.

'You care about me!' he said in a very girlish voice.

'Of course I do! Like I care about Tomas, Agatha and my brother.'

'You care about General Avran?' Malo asked in complete disgust.

'Of course I do. When we were alone together, he acted completely different.'

'How?' Malo asked, completely shocked.

'He acted as though he genuinely cared.'

'That's ridiculous! His only emotion is anger.'

Athena smiled but still looked ahead.

'No, Malo, he has *several* emotions: hatred with you, caring for me and anger with Renyu.'

'Why Renyu? General Avran almost worships that mad, old scientist.' Malo asked slightly puzzled.

'Renyu tried to operate on me. He was so determined to find out if I was a real Agalit. Nicolas didn't appreciate that.'

Malo was about to reply but he saw two Greliks being held by a large man. Malo walked over to him.

'Are we allowed to ride these Greliks?'

'Yes. Would you like to? They can bring you to the top of the mountain in only twenty minutes!' the man explained.

'That is quite impressive!' Malo said, stroking one of the huge Greliks with extreme caution.

'Do they mind if we ride them?' Athena asked, walking over.

'Of course not. They wouldn't have come to me otherwise.'

'Can we ride them to the top? Can we, can we? My legs are getting so tired!' Malo explained.

Athena rolled her eyes.

'If you really want to, Malo.' she said, exchanging looks with the large man, stroking the two Greliks.

'Yes!' Malo whispered to himself. He quickly climbed onto the Grelik he stroked.

Athena paid the man one hundred rubies and slowly climbed onto the other Grelik.

Athena is very light!

Lucky you. Malo is extremely heavy.

'Are you two brothers?' Athena asked.

Oh my Grelik! You can hear us!

'I'm an Agalit. My gift is to hear thoughts.' she whispered.

What about Malo? Is he an Agalit too? Because if he were, I bet you it's being the heaviest man alive!

Good joke!

They both banged each other's heads while laughing.

'Stop fighting!' the man shouted.

We aren't fighting, deaf human!

Both Greliks looked at the man and said it together in unison.

'They aren't fighting!' Athena sniggered.

'They are! Every time I climb on one of them, they bash their head against the other!'

That's because you are SO heavy!

'I'm sure they are just having fun.' Athena said, unable to contain her laughter.

'Alright. Greliks to the top of the mountain now!' the man ordered.

Both Greliks remained still.

Are you loving this?

I'm loving this!

When should we go?

Until he turns red in the face.

Friend, we are off in five, four, three, two, one...

They both waited till the man turned red from embarrassment.

'I'm so sorry.' he said to Athena and Malo, turning red.

Off we go!

They both started running at top speed up the mountain.

Athena suddenly saw everything as a blur.

'We... are... going... so... fast...' Malo yelled as he felt the wind smack against his face.

'How fast are we going?' Athena asked her Grelik.

Very fast. We are both two of the fastest Greliks.

I am the fastest.

No, I am the fastest!

Let's race.

Fine!

Malo's Grelik suddenly ran much faster. He looked back to see Athena and her Grelik but they were very far behind.

'Why aren't you going faster?' Athena asked.

Don't worry. He has a very short stamina. I have a long one. As soon as I sense that he is slowing down, I will run past him!

'Devious plan!' Athena said.

Thanks!

I heard what you said.

Sorry mate but it's true!

We'll see about that!

Athena's Grelik saw his friend slow down so he ran at his fastest. Athena waved at Malo as she passed him in a second.

'Why are they faster than us? Run faster!' Malo told his Grelik.

Hey, buddy! If I could go any faster, I would. You know what? Because you pressurized me, I'm stopping. I'm stopping!

'Why aren't you moving at all? They are almost at the top!' Malo exclaimed.

The Grelik waited till Malo loosened his grip on its fur and then it suddenly ran very fast again, hoping that Malo would fall off.

Fine, you win! We will race back down the Grelik told Athena's Grelik.

'I can't believe you got to the top of the mountain so fast. You were going so quick, I could barely breathe!' Athena told the Grelik as she climbed down from its back.

Same! Although, I have to tell you a secret. He and I are both as fast as each other. If anything, he is faster than me, but I was carrying you. You are very light where as he was carrying Malo and from the sounds of it, he weighs a great deal more than you.

'When are they coming? I can't see them.' she said as she looked down.

Suddenly Malo's Grelik ran right in front of her, making Athena scream.

I'm sorry, did I scare you? I don't know what came over me.

Malo climbed down his Grelik, almost falling off. He walked towards Athena as though he had seen something absolutely horrific.

'Malo... Malo are you alright?' Athena asked, holding his shoulder, looking into his eyes.

Malo looked at her and smiled awkwardly.

'I'm fine. Just give me a moment,' he said as he walked over to the small bushes nearby.

Look what you did! You made him vomit. I told you this morning you really stunk and that you should have gone to the river, but did you listen?

No...

What are you going to do when we arrive home?

Wash myself!

Exactly, now I want you to go and apologise to Malo!

But he can't even hear me.

GO!

The Grelik unwillingly walked to Malo with its tail between its hind legs.

I love playing with him.

Athena grinned, feeling slightly sorry for the Grelik.

Don't feel sorry for him. He doesn't mind, really.

'Thanks for the ride! I won't be doing that again.' Malo yelled as he watched both Greliks race down the mountain.

He turned to Athena.

'The castle is right in front of us! Are you ready?'

Athena gave him the biggest smile with so much light in her eyes.

XVIII

'Please, let us through! We have an urgent message for the King,' Athena begged the guards.

The guards looked at one another, then looked back at her.

'The King is the most important person in the lands. Especially at these critical times, our security is extremely tight. I'm sorry but you are not to see the King. Is there anything else you could show to prove that you're—?'

'Oh for the love of the Gods!' Malo said, his hands raised to the sky. 'Athena is an Agalit! Can't you see? Her being an Agalit is a good enough reason to go and see the King. I'm sure he will appreciate any help, especially at these... critical times.'

'We do not usually respond to such insolence, young man. I would watch your attitude. However, you're right. Her being an Agalit puts you both in a more favourable position.'

The guard moved closer to Athena and examined her. She remained completely still but started to breathe heavily as he looked at her right in the eyes.

'What is your gift?'

'Hearing thoughts.'

'Interesting. What am I thinking right now?'

Athena concentrated very hard.

'You want to move to Clandon with your family. You want to live by the seaside. You want to go fishing by the crescent bay with your son. You want to build a small boat and travel to the East on it.'

The guard walked back to his assigned place and conversed with the other guard.

'The King would want to see her straight away.' he whispered.

The guards turned back to Athena and Malo and signalled for them to come forward.

Athena looked at Malo who was already walking towards the two huge oak doors which slowly opened up.

Athena and Malo looked at each and neither of them could stop smiling. Malo took Athena's hand and kissed it.

'This is it. We finally made it!' he said, trying to contain his excitement. They held hands and followed the guards down the long red carpet which ran all the way down the huge hall. It ended directly at the Kings feet.

Athena quickly looked around. There were four huge pillars on either side of the hall with the walls painted white and the ceiling, covered with mosaics in a familiar pattern.

'My King, you have visitors!' the guard announced.

The King's beaming, kind blue eyes turned towards Athena. He nodded and kept his smile to a minimum.

'What is your business here?' he asked, in a loud voice.

Malo stepped forward and bent down on his good leg.

'Your Majesty, we are both extremely poor peasants. The only way we wash ourselves is in the manure of our animals. We were walking along a pathway a few days ago and two Blucks came towards us. They gave us a horse and a letter to deliver to you. We have just arrived here.'

Athena rolled her eyes. Even for Malo, that was a bit too dramatic.

'I see.' the King said, playing along with Malo's pathetic little story. He stroked his chin.

'So, where is this letter you speak of?'

Malo's eyes widened. He hadn't thought about that part.

'Your majesty, I lost it. I found a woman on the path and she was giving birth. I gave her the letter to use as a cloth. To clean up the child!'

Athena looked up at the ceiling with her eyes closed, biting her lip, trying her very best not to laugh.

The King nodded and grinned.

'What did the letter say?'

Malo turned to Athena.

'Say something,' he whispered.

Athena walked a few paces closer to the King.

'Your majesty. Everything my friend has just said is a complete load of nonsense.'

'Yes, I didn't find it very convincing. Did you, Malo?' the King asked, looking directly at him.

Malo turned away but then suddenly looked up at the King.

'How did you know my name?' he asked.

'How would I *not* know your name? Malo the unbeatable, Malo the invincible. Ever since the duel competition a few years ago, everyone remembers you, including one of my daughters who just won't hush about you. The Chamcoks were especially livid, so every few months they write to me and ask when you would be returning to the Four Flames in order to have another duel. From what I hear though, you already won that duel a few hours ago! Even more impressive considering all your injuries.' he said with such admiration in his voice.

Malo bowed again to show his respect but also to hide the fact that he was turning slightly red from embarrassment.

'You may stay here for the time being to recover from your wounds. We have doctors who will offer you their assistance should you want it.'

The King turned towards Athena and their blue eyes met.

'And what about you... Athena? Does any of this seem familiar?' the King asked, looking around the hall.

However, Athena continued staring at the king.

'Mildly. You seem extremely familiar, however. Have we met before?' Athena asked, certain that they had. Perhaps in a dream.

I wonder if I should just tell her. Hmm.

'Of course we have. I knew your father.'

'You don't know him, you *are* him! You are my father!' Athena blurted out in a high voice, suddenly recognising him.

Malo couldn't help but make a high pitched sound. 'No way!'

The King beamed at her with tears and love in his eyes. 'Athena, these past thirteen years have felt like five centuries to me. Believe me, I would know!' the King chuckled as he stood up from his huge throne.

He walked down to Athena and embraced her.

'Welcome home, Atheneglary,' he whispered.

This gave Athena a sudden shock. She felt her heart skip a beat. That name was buried far back in her memory, but she suddenly remembered it. Her father used to call her that when he came to kiss her goodnight each evening.

A tear fell down Athena's cheek and she discreetly wiped it away. The

King moved back a few paces and continued looking at Athena.

'You look so much like your mother.'

Athena frowned and took a deep breath, knowing that she would never meet her mother.

He knew what his daughter was thinking. He could read it on her face.

'Your mother was in the forest that day because she was determined to find both you and your brother. She knew where your brother was located and she was willing to give up her life just to see him one more time. She couldn't live without all her children close to her. She loved you dearly, Athena.'

Athena looked down.

'I don't remember her. I don't remember what she looked like!' she said as she burst into tears, burying her head into her hands.

Malo put his arm around her shoulder and gently swayed her.

Don't cry, dear Athena. You may not have your mother, but at least you have your father. You found him! He's the King, Athena. The King! This is madness. I can't believe it. It's amazing!

'It's alright, Malo. I will comfort her.' her father responded. 'You must be hungry! There is a buffet on the other side of the door.' he said, pointing at the huge door to the left of his throne.

Malo understood that the King didn't feel comfortable with the whole idea of him touching his precious Atheneglary and realised that there was no point arguing. So, he dragged himself to the huge door.

He took one last glance at Athena who was still crying but was being looked after by her father.

Malo gave her a little wave as she glanced at him and then went through the doors.

'Scarlet, come here you little pest!' a girl was screaming after another girl, who was giggling and crawling under the huge table where all the food was laid out.

'You have to first catch me, Gemma,' the girl squeaked in a high pitched voice.

'Why are you so irritating? I'm going to find Juliet to set you straight,' the frustrated girl groaned, walking out through another set of huge doors.

The girl rose from under the buffet table that ran from one side of the room to the other, pushed against the white wall.

As she got up, she caught sight of Malo. Her eyes widened.

'Hello there!' Malo said.

The girl walked straight up to him and stopped, studying him intently.

'You must be Malo, I presume!' she said, suddenly skipping back to the part of the table which was full of wild berries.

Malo wasn't able to speak, he was so entranced by the girl. All he could do was merely gaze, wondrously, at her.

'So, a little bird tells me you were the champion here four years ago. You then went to serve in the evil army and now you plan to serve in the good army,' the girl continued, looking at Malo from the other side of the room.

'That bird sure knows a lot about me!' Malo replied truthfully, scratching the back of his head and clearing his throat.

The girl smiled. The sunlight suddenly came across her face and Malo gawked at her.

She had soft brown hair with natural blonde highlights on the first few strands of her hair, her light blue eyes which showed intelligence, yet her smile and high pitched giggle revealed her immaturity.

'How old are you?' Malo asked.

The girl frowned.

'You're not going to ask for my name?' she asked, slightly disappointed.

'I'm sorry. What is your-'

Suddenly, two girls came in.

'Gemma has told me that you have been misbehaving again!' the unfamiliar girl sighed.

'Gemma over reacts. Besides, these berries have a tendency to make me happy. I am allowed to be happy once in a while. Well, right now, I am *very* happy.'

The girl sighed but then saw Malo.

She looked at Scarlet and nodded her head towards Malo. 'Who is this?'

Scarlet turned around and smiled at him. 'This is Malo.'

'Well, Malo, help yourself to the food on the table. I apologise, but my sisters and I have some business to attend to,' the girl explained, smiling at Malo.

'Of course, don't mind me.' he said, turning towards the food. 'I'm sure I will find a way to pass the time.'

The two girls walked out with Scarlet right behind them. She turned around to see Malo help himself to various types of meat. She smiled and then quietly shut the doors behind her.

Malo stayed still for a few moments and then slowly walked towards the berry section and chucked a few in his mouth.

He had finally met her. After four, long years. He had finally met the girl who had brought him so much light when he was being tortured in the dark dungeons.

'Do you mind if I can read your mind and find out what really happened the day you were taken away?' the King asked Athena, in a small private chamber which now belonged to her. They were sitting by the windowsill with the great view of the Forest Tatila and the riverbank close by. In the very far distance the volcano could be seen.

'How would you do that?' Athena asked out of curiosity.

'Well, you close your eyes,' the King said, gently shutting her eyelids, 'and you think of nothing.'

'Nothing?' Athena repeated, immediately opening her eyes.

He chuckled and once again softly closed her eyelids with his fingers.

'Think of nothing. Clear your mind. Just think of blackness. Nothing. Absolutely nothing,' the King said, gradually lowering his voice.

Athena did as she was told. Her father also shut his eyes and held Athena's arm with one hand and with the other, placed his thumb on her forehead.

He started drifting away in her mind as a small person in a room with all four walls, the ground and ceiling covered in moving images. He suddenly saw one of Athena as a six-year-old being held by Tomas in his arms. She was laughing and Tomas kissed her on the cheek. He let her go and he watched her run in the fields.

The King took a deep breath and her arm a bit tighter.

He wanted to go all the way back to when Athena was taken. He saw himself walking through many images but he couldn't find one that matched the date. As he was about to give up to take a break, he saw one that resembled the river bank near the Naran Flame.

Athena and Nicolas were encircled by a line of green electricity. Gemma ran by. A man called her and threatened to kill Nicolas if she wasn't able to get Nicolas to him. However, Gemma joined her siblings in the protected circle and ignored the man.

It was Juliet who fell for the lies.

The King saw how Nicolas was taken. He had seen it in Juliet and Gemma's memories. Now, it was time to see what happened to Athena. He finally found an image of her and Tomas.

They had passed the bridges and were on their way towards the volcano. Tomas was holding her hand and listening to Athena tell her stories in a very animated way. Tomas suddenly noticed a man walking towards them. Behind him were two horses walking, side by side, at a slow pace. As they approached each other, the man started speaking to Tomas. Tomas explained how the Naran Flame was up in flames and how he found Athena. The man looked down at little Athena and studied her.

He turned back to Tomas.

'This girl is our future queen. There is no better place for her than to be here with you, safe from Tatila. Teach her everything you know, how to be kind but how to also make her own decisions. Tell her nothing of this before her sixteenth birthday. Fate will protect her the day she chooses to leave. Tell no one of who she is. Even your wife. Keep this to yourself. Love her. Protect her. Then, let her go.'

Tomas looked at the man in shock, his mouth hanging open. 'How do you know this? Who are you?'

'I am a Wueltin.'

The man bent down and looked at Athena. Her big, innocent eyes were beginning to get tired. Soon, she would fall fast asleep.

Perfect.

'What's perfect?' she asked, yawning.

'I'm going to make you forget everything, Athena. One day it will come to you and all this will make sense. For now, you will be an ordinary girl, living an ordinary life with ordinary parents in Oakrose.'

He rested his forehead against hers, held her hands and whispered a spell in Dertiym. After a few minutes, Athena fell asleep and the Wueltin picked her up. He slowly stood up and brought her to Tomas, who was still in shock, and placed her in his arms.

'She is your responsibility now. Don't worry. I know this must overwhelm you, but remember, you will be guided and protected by Fate. Now, go home to your wife. She is in distress and will need you by her side.'

'Forgive me… how can I trust you?'

'Why did you go to the Four Flames, Tomas?'

'I was asked to deliver the King a message.'

'Did you deliver it? Did you even see the King? No! You were sent there because you were meant to save this child. Your child now. You are already attached to her. When I came your way, you held her hand tighter.'

The Wueltin walked over to his two horses and led one over to Tomas. 'This is your horse now. Hurry home. Your wife is in distress.'

'You keep saying that. What happened?' Tomas asked in a quiet yet aggressive tone.

The Wueltin walked back to the other horse and brought down a wrapped blanket. He walked back to Tomas and revealed the baby. 'This is your son, Tomas. He was born a few hours ago.'

'You took my son?'

'Yes. You need to give all your energy and love to this little one here.' he replied, looking over at Athena.

'We can do both! Give my son back!' Tomas demanded, his voice trembling.

The Wueltin shook his head. 'I am sorry but this is how it's meant to be. When Athena leaves you to return back to the Four Flames, he will return to you. I can promise you that. You do believe me. I know you do.'

'STOP! I want my son! We can raise both of them.' Tomas started to cry and shout. The Wueltin could see that Athena was waking up from the noise.

'Stop crying, Tomas. You achieve nothing. It is out of your control. Tell me, what should I call your son?'

'We can raise them both!' Tomas kept repeating, tears flooding down his cheeks.

He fell to the ground on his knees and sobbed. He continued holding Athena in his arms. He knew there was nothing he could do. The power of this Wueltin was more than he could imagine.

'You promise me that he will come back one day?'

'You have my word.'

'Yan. That's the name my wife wanted if it was a boy.'

'He will be called Yan. He will live in the Four Flames and he will be safe and loved. This is what I promise you. Now, I am afraid this will affect Athena in some way. The fact that you know she is taking the place of your son. She didn't ask for this. Neither did you. It's just how it is. I will have to wipe this memory from your mind. I can see it's too painful for you. You never saw your son. According to you, your wife is in labour.'

The Wueltin lifted Tomas back up and performed a spell on him.

He walked away with one horse and Yan, leaving Tomas in shock from the news he was told about Athena. He looked down at Athena who was fast asleep.

'I'm holding the future queen in my hands. I have to raise her. I have to teach her everything I know. I can't tell Agatha a word even though she can sniff information out of me like a hound. Hhmm. I don't know which of these give me more anxiety.'

Tomas cracked his neck in order to feel relief but he suddenly remembered what the Wueltin had said about his wife.

'Agatha! She must be in distress because she's in labour! Our little child might be born by the time we get there.'

He looked down at young Athena and smiled. 'Our other child.'

He gave her a kiss on the forehead and then mounted the horse, keeping Athena safe in his arms.

The King slowly opened his eyes and wiped a tear away.

'You were enchanted by a Wueltin. That's why you have never been able to remember your past. Don't worry. It will take some work, but we will be able to retrieve your memories. Some will come in their own with time while others can be encouraged to come out with reminders. For example, the mosaics in the hall and the little doll you found. It triggered something.'

However, Athena was still trapped in her own mind. She, too, saw the memories he saw. A small figure herself in a room covered in memories.

She suddenly fell in one.

She was called to the river bank by the Greliks. They told her to stay still and call for Nicolas. She obeyed them, sat down and started calling for her brother.

We can't protect you, Athena, because you haven't been accepted. You are too young but we love you like our own, so we will try our very best!

'Father, I can't open my eyes!' Athena whispered, beginning to panic.

'That means that your mind wants you to see something that you haven't seen before. Something of great importance.'

Athena gulped and started looking around the room in her mind. She suddenly came across one where she was being held by Tomas near the river bank.

'Are you lost little girl?' he asked.

Athena watched her younger self look up at Tomas, with watering eyes.

'I can't find anyone. My brother was kidnapped, and now I will never see him again!' she cried, breaking off into a deep sob.

Athena held back her tears. She really did care so much for her brother when she was younger.

Tomas picked her up and young Athena trusted him.

'Which Flame do you live in?' he asked her.

Young Athena pointed towards the Naran Flame which was burning up to the sky in a blood orange colour.

Tomas groaned.

'Don't worry. I think it is a good idea that I come and live with you and your wife as well!' Athena said, looking deep in Tomas's eyes.

'How did you know that I was thinking that?' Tomas asked slowly, realising he wasn't dealing with a normal child.

Young Athena looked away. Athena walked to her younger self and saw that she was smiling.

Why was I smiling? Athena asked herself. The young Athena suddenly looked up at her. Athena froze. *Can you see me?*

The young Athena nodded and gave the warmest of smiles.

'What are you looking at?' Tomas asked Athena who was looking at another direction and nodding.

The young Athena turned back to him.

'Just myself. Let's go home, Tomas! I am an Agalit. I can read minds.' Young Athena said, smiling at him.

Tomas realised that he had never mentioned his name to her, but decided there was no point in asking. As she said, she was a special girl.

With Athena in his arms, Tomas quickly walked away.

Athena suddenly opened her eyes and looked at her father sitting in front of her.

'Why was that particular memory important?' she asked impatiently.

'That is for you to figure out. I didn't see that memory. I wasn't touching either your hand or forehead. It is presumably a memory that is only for your eyes alone.'

The King stood up and held Athena's hand, lifting her up from the bench. He held her chin and looked into her worried eyes.

'You will figure it out, my dear Atheneglary,' he whispered.

'My gift...' she started.

The King nodded.

'One moment it's there, the next moment it is gone! Why?'

'That is because you have never been able to master it. I taught your sisters how to master their gift. It is a shame that you have never been able to do so. However, that will change. From now on, I will help you perfect it. We can do it every afternoon, right here!'

Athena smiled, 'I would like that.'

He kissed her cheek and looked at her face, 'I am so happy that you are here, you have no idea.'

Athena followed him with her eyes, until he shut the door of her room behind him. After a few minutes, she walked out onto her balcony and looked down at the whole Flame.

She saw children in groups all licking their huge lollipops, the size of their heads. There were young couples, sitting on the benches close to the huge fountain in the centre of the big green park. Athena realised that Malo was right: one couldn't see the purple force shield from within.

She closed her eyes and took a deep breath and allowed herself to smell the sweet air. She opened her eyes and decided to go and find Malo. At that exact moment, somebody knocked on her door.

She quickly left the balcony and ran to the door and opened it, only to see him standing in front of her. He didn't say anything. He just looked deep into her eyes and then hugged her. Athena almost fell backwards but he caught her just before she hurt herself.

'Dear Athena,' Malo whispered with a croak in his voice, 'I saw her. She's here!'

XIX

Scarlet was reading her favourite book out loud in her private chambers. She was on her big bed with her legs lined up against the wall. Her little blue bird suddenly flew into her chambers from the keyhole at full speed, heading towards her bed.

Scarlet held out her hand just before the bird slammed straight into the wall.

'Thanks, Scarlet!' the bird gasped as it picked itself up from the bed.

Scarlet nodded as she continued reading. The little bird hopped onto Scarlet's shoulder and only read a few lines until he realised that it was her favourite book.

'For your birthday, I'm going to buy you a new book.'

Scarlet shook her head but continued to read. The little bird flew in front of the pages, blocking her view from the words.

However, Scarlet knowing the book so well, continued reciting from memory. The bird flapped its wings, trying to gain her attention but failed.

'Okay, I won't tell you what I saw Malo doing a few minutes ago,' the little bird said, slowly hopping away from her.

Scarlet slammed her book and rolled around.

'What did he do? Please tell me!' she pleaded. The bird held up its wing and paused.

'No, no. I don't want to interrupt you from reading that book. I will leave you in peace!' the bird said.

Scarlet jumped out of the bed, knelt on the floor and looked at her little bird straight in the eye.

'Please, Todd! Tell me what you wanted to say!' Scarlet begged in a sweet voice.

Todd looked away.

'Please?' Scarlet quietly asked, giggling and also tickling Todd. He was a beautiful bird with a white tummy that gradually turned to light blue around the rest of his small body. He was so small, he was the size of Scarlet's palm.

Todd giggled and then looked at Scarlet. He could never resist his best friend's laugh.

'Oh, alright! A few minutes ago,' Todd slowly began, watching Scarlet nod along, 'I saw Malo...'

Scarlet's eyes widened as she waited in anticipation for him to continue. 'You saw Malo doing what?' she asked.

Todd giggled but wasn't able to keep it in anymore.

'I saw Malo walk around the castle with Athena, and now he is alone on this floor, looking in every room. He'll be at your door soon.' he burst out.

Scarlet's eyes widened even more. 'How soon?'

All of a sudden, they heard a knock. Both Scarlet and Todd immediately turned to the door.

'Now!' Todd whispered and flew behind her large wardrobe.

'Todd, come back here!' Scarlet hissed after him.

Malo walked in and heard Scarlet.

'Anything wrong?' he asked, unable to figure out why Scarlet was talking to a piece of furniture.

She suddenly turned around with a huge grin on her face.

For a brief moment, which felt like hours to them both, there was an awkward silence, but it was quickly broken by both of them laughing.

'What brings you to my chambers?' she asked.

'Well, I was looking around the castle and-'

'What do you think?' Scarlet asked enthusiastically.

'It's great! Much bigger than I thought it would be,' he commented, subtly looking around. There was a huge bed on the right hand side of the room. The wall facing the door was in fact, a floor-to-ceiling window with a great view of the Forest Tatila. A huge wardrobe and a desk were on the left of the room. The ground was covered with a soft white carpet and finally, on the corner to the right of the door, were two huge cushions by a small fireplace.

'Nice room.' Malo commented.

Scarlet smiled and returned to her bed, assuming Malo would follow her.

'So, from what I have heard, you and Athena came a long way.' she said, staring hard at her book.

'Yes! We had a few problems along the way too!' Malo replied truthfully.

'Did she tell you her biggest secret?' Scarlet asked.

'That she was part of the Royal Family? No! Though, I doubt dear Athena knew herself.'

Scarlet closed her eyes. It hurt her to know how fond both Athena and Malo were of each other.

Malo, seeing that Scarlet hadn't replied thought it would be best to leave as she probably wanted to read her book in peace.

He was making his way to the door, but then turned around.

'You never told me what your name was?' Malo said, trying to make conversation with her.

Scarlet immediately smiled and turned to him.

'It's Scarlet.'

'I like it. I like the flower too!'

Scarlet blushed but didn't hide it as she wanted to show Malo her feelings for him.

'But you already knew my name! When Gemma was chasing me, remember?'

This time, it was Malo's turn to blush. 'We never officially introduced ourselves is what I meant.'

He held out his hand. 'I'm Malo.'

'I'm Scarlet,' she said as she walked over to shake it.

She took his hand and led him to the bed. Now, Malo could *really* feel the blood rushing from his head. They sat down and Scarlet kept her hand on his.

'So, aren't you going to ask me what *my* gift is?' she asked, her face only a few inches away from his.

'What is your gift?' Malo whispered, taking deep breaths to calm himself down.

'Well, I thought you'd never ask!' Scarlet shrieked, jumping off the bed.

And I thought Athena gave me anxiety? This girl will actually kill me!

'I can communicate with animals. I talk to them. I discuss with them and my best friend is a bird called Todd.'

Malo smiled.

'So, that's who you were talking to when I came in?' Malo asked, hoping it was.

'Yes! Todd, come here,' Scarlet said.

Todd slowly flew onto Scarlet's shoulder. He held out his right wing and waved at Malo.

Malo, completely stunned, slowly waved back.

'Wait, so when you said "a little bird told me", you meant that quite literally!'

Scarlet smiled. Malo turned to Todd.

'How long have you been spying on me?' he asked.

Todd replied in a language Malo couldn't understand, so he turned to Scarlet for a translation.

'Last time you came to the Four Flames, I really liked you. I told Todd and he has been watching over you ever since you were thrown out of the Seven Hundred Army, because I..'

'Because you?'

'I wanted to make sure that you didn't meet anyone. I wanted to know how you were, to make sure you were alright. I'm sorry!'

Malo didn't know what to say.

'Please say something. Tell me that you like me back. Please. There is nothing worse in the entire world than loving someone and not have them love you back,' Scarlet exasperated, tears coming to her eyes.

Malo cleared his throat and made an uncomfortable laugh. Was this really happening? The best possible scenario. The girl he loved so much was confessing her own love.

'I don't know.'

This was all he managed to say.

I don't know? That's all I can come up with?

He was at a loss for words.

He stood up and almost ran out the door. He dreamt of this moment but he never imagined what he'd say in return. And he wanted it to be perfect.

He quietly shut the door, leaving Scarlet in tears.

Todd gently stroked her nose.

'I know he loves you, Scarlet! I can feel the attraction between you both,' he whispered.

'No, you don't! You know nothing. Leave me alone! You ruined EVERYTHING! He thinks I'm weird because I make friends with animals,' Scarlet sobbed into her pillow.

'Fine, I was trying to comfort you but obviously you don't need me. I will leave. Goodbye, Scarlet!' Todd replied back and flew out of her room.

She immediately regretted her actions.

'Finally. The passes have arrived!' Oliver said as he snatched the two small pieces of parchment from the young messenger.

'That will be one hundred rubies and-'

Oliver slammed the door in the boy's face and walked over to Mark who was reading a book on the ground.

'Would you please get up, Mark! We aren't poor scavengers. We are important men who deserve better than this *stupid* makeshift house!' he spat out.

Mark widened his eyes but continued to read the book.

'Would you *please* stop reading that book?' Oliver shouted as he kicked the book out of Mark's hand. Mark immediately picked it up and continued to read it, ignoring Oliver.

'What's wrong with you?'

Mark rolled his eyes and slowly turned to Oliver.

'Are you really asking me that question? *What's wrong?* You have pushed Nicolas too far by chasing his own sister! You've gone too far this time, Head of Council! Look around you! Is this where you pictured us to be? Stuck in a makeshift house somewhere that is of no significance? Is it? Because it certainly isn't how I pictured it! I have one hand and I'm stuck with you who hasn't stopped *whining* since we abandoned the Council's headquarters!'

Oliver stared at Mark straight in the eyes for a while as if he had been hypnotized. He looked away and whispered, 'You're right, Mark!'

He grabbed hold of Mark's shoulder and looked back at him straight in the eye and said, 'We have pushed Nicolas over the edge! Perhaps we should...comfort him. Let's go back to him and say we are sorry! He will forgive us. However, since he has humiliated us and chopped off your hand, I will kill him in front of the entire army. Yes, I like this idea. I'll do it on the day of the war and I shall lead the greatest army the world has ever known to victory. I shall be known until the end of time and it will all be thanks to you, Mark, for opening my eyes!'

Mark snatched the two pieces of parchment from Oliver's hand and whispered, 'Well then! I pray that you kill him in a dignified way.'

Mark spat on Oliver's face as he walked out. His hatred for that man was becoming unbearable and it took every inch of his being not to kill him right there and then.

'Athena, please come here!' the King said as he saw her walking past the door.

Athena took three steps back and looked into a room. She saw her father with three girls.

'Athena, these are your sisters: Juliet, Gemma and Scarlet,' the King proudly announced.

Athena hurried towards them and gave them all individual hugs.

'I saw you! In my memory!' Athena gasped as she hugged all of them.

'Except for you.' she said as she came across Scarlet. She studied the young girl. She had beautiful piercing blue eyes, but they were swollen as though she had been crying.

'Are you alright?' Athena asked.

'No, she isn't. She is madly in love and she knows that she isn't loved back,' Gemma replied back for her while fiddling with her hair.

Scarlet suddenly burst into tears and left the room in a rush. The King turned towards Gemma.

'Was that really necessary? She is fragile at the moment.'

'Please, she's always fragile. The smallest thing makes her cry. She needs to grow up.' Gemma snapped back.

The King ignored her comment. 'Everything that is happening at the moment is overwhelming her. With the war, her sister's return and her bruised heart. You could at least be supportive!'

He sighed as he left the room to comfort his daughter.

'Anyway,' Juliet said, cutting the silence, 'I suppose you have had quite the journey of your life!'

Athena nodded. 'Yes. We ended up getting thrown into the Seven Hundred Army dungeons.'

Both Juliet and Gemma suddenly looked at each other and then turned to Athena.

'You saw Nicolas?' Gemma asked.

'Yes, I-'

'How is he? Any signs of him returning to normal?' Juliet demanded to know.

Athena shrugged her shoulders. 'I think he is alright. He does have something inside of him which shows that he can be a decent person. However, it's buried deep, deep down. Being in that place for such a long time has clearly done some damage to him. I think if he gets to a safe environment where he feels in control, it would do him a great deal of good.'

Both Gemma and Juliet looked down in disappointment.
They always believed that their only brother would one day return to them.
'At the end of the day, he just grew up too fast in a terrible place. The fact that he still has some compassion in him proves that he is strong. Don't worry, he will come back!'

Athena could see they were sad, so she decided to change the subject.

'What are your powers?' Athena asked them both.

Gemma and Juliet both looked at each other with a grin on their face and skipped over to the bench by the window sill.

Athena sat in between them and looked at Juliet.

'Well, I can control all four elements: Fire, Earth, Water and Air,' she began. She then turned to a vase filled with water. With just the power of her mind, she made the water float from the vase into mid-air. Suddenly, a gush of wind swept through the room, starting a small whirlpool in the middle of the floating water. Fire then appeared from the bottom, quickly evaporating the water until there was none left.

'That was amazing.' Athena smiled.

'I know.' Juliet replied, gleaming.

'How long have you been able to do that?'

'When I was four years old. We all got our power at that age.'

Athena remained silent for a moment. The moment Juliet spoke about her gift, she couldn't stop thinking about the night before. She knew something was controlling her.

'Juliet, something incredible happened. I was with Malo in the forest and we were being chased, so-'

'Are you getting to the point where you were flying in the air?'

'Yes! Was that you?' she asked, her eyes gleaming with admiration. She already knew the answer.

Juliet gave her a kind smile. 'It was a joint effort. Scarlet, whose gift is to communicate with animals, had her little bluebird follow you two. When you were both so close to the Four Flames, father sent out one of the Royal cats. All three of us were on the balcony watching over you and helping you both as much as we could.'

'Thank you,' Athena whispered. She then kissed Juliet on the cheek and turned towards Gemma.

'What about you Gemma? What is your gift?'

'I control the speed things grow at.' Gemma replied.

Athena waited in silence for a demonstration.

Gemma stood up, went over to the corner of the grand room and picked up a small tree that came up to her knee. She came back and placed it in front of them.

She sat back down and whispered, 'Watch this.'

Gemma stared at the small green tree and, after a few seconds, saw it grow a few inches every second. It kept on growing until it touched the very high, white ceiling.

'That is incredible!' Athena whispered.

Gemma smirked and Athena watched the plant return to its original size.

'So, you can make things grow and shrink. Does that mean you can make things live and die?' Athena asked.

'Yes. I can make plants, trees, small insects live or die but not humans. The human body or, in our case, Agalit body is too complex. There are far too many components to take into consideration. It's a big step up from trees and insects, you know? Besides, father forbids it.'

'That's amazing! I suppose you have been able to do this since you were four as well?'

'We all gained our power at that age. Even you gained your powers at that age. Did you not just tell her that?' Gemma asked Juliet, looking past Athena's shoulder. 'Did she hit her head one too many times when she was younger or what?'

Athena knew she was strong and usually brushed off criticism. However, the way Gemma spoke was certainly testing. Athena could understand why Scarlet was so quick to get upset.

'Now, now, Gemma. Let's not be mean to our dear sister. She just arrived! What sort of impression are you trying to give her?'

Athena felt her heart race. She decided to quickly go back to the subject at hand.

'You said I had powers? I thought we all had one power. Mine is to read minds.'

Gemma shook her head. 'Not from what I can remember! Do you remember, Juliet? When young Athena used to tell us she could see people in the future?'

Juliet laughed. 'We all could when we were one-year olds, but it usually left us when our new power came intact. Not with you, Athena. You seemed to be able to have two powers.'

'Did our father know about this?' Athena asked, suddenly realising what her memory was about.

'I'm not sure. Remember there was a revolt at that time.' Juliet sighed. 'Father is always modest when it comes to speaking of gifts. He only ever says that his gift is immortality but he can also see the memories in someone's mind.'

'Only in pictures though!' Gemma added.

Athena suddenly stood up and ran out of the room.

Athena suddenly burst into her father's chambers.

'Father... memory... sense... make... really...' she said as she was catching her breath.

The King chuckled. 'Take deep breaths and think of what you are going to say and perhaps this time, in order.'

Athena smiled, taking deep breaths.

'Alright! In my memory I saw myself when I was being taken by Tomas. When my present-self walked over to my younger self I could see myself... if that makes sense!'

The King made a face. 'So, you are telling me that when you were younger at the very moment you were being picked up by Tomas you saw yourself in the future look at yo—'

'Yes! That's what I mean!'

He nodded. 'That means that you have two gifts. When was the last time you saw someone in the future?' the King asked.

Athena shrugged her shoulders and tried to remember. How could she know that she was meeting someone from the future?

Suddenly a man walked into the chambers. 'My King, there is a messenger for you in the main hall. He says it is of great importance.'

'I will be right with him!' the King replied as he quickly walked out of the room.

Before he left, he turned to Athena and said, 'Having two gifts in this family means that you are the most powerful child. This means when I choose to step down from the throne, you will take my place.'

Nicolas returned to his makeshift house. He threw his sword to the ground and screamed, gripping onto his thick dark blond hair.

He tried to hold back the tears coming to his eyes, but had great difficulty. He could feel a lump at the back of this throat grow bigger.

He took deep breaths and threw himself onto his bed, shutting his eyes tight.

So many thoughts were rushing through his mind. He felt as though they were tearing out of his forehead.

How dare he question my authority?

'I want to kill him. I want to kill Sedty,' Nicolas kept repeating to himself until a guard walked into his room.

'General Avran, you have been in here for a few hours now. Is everything alright?'

'Is everything alright? Remind me to run an intelligence test when men want to join the army! Of course everything's not alright! The big war, which apparently everybody in the entire world has known about for hundreds and hundreds of years, is happening incredibly soon. I fired my Council which has held this army together ever since I became the commander and now, half my army belongs to Sedty, that big great Agalit which I created. How could I be so ignorant of the fact that all he really wanted was power!? He doesn't care about the war, he just cares about his personal pride!'

The guard looked down, not knowing what to respond.

'Go! Assemble the soldiers in the courtroom.'

'That is already done, Nicolas!' Sedty said as he walked into the room.

Nicolas immediately stood up and drew his sword out.

He pointed it to Sedty's neck, hoping Sedty would feel vulnerable but he simply remained calm. They both knew that metal could no longer hurt him.

'I came in here to tell you that all the men are assembled in the courtroom at this very moment.'

'Why?'

'I wanted to make a formal apology to you in front of all of them.'

Nicolas tightened his grip.

'What game are you playing at, Sedty? You presumably don't understand that the war that has been written in the Prophecy is happening. The day that the whole world has been waiting for, for centuries is *finally* arriving and it is not written that this army – The Seven Hundred Army – will be able to take over the throne. So, we take our precautions; we train our soldiers to their fullest potential, we have spies with information from the other side. We do *all* this yet it has never occurred to me that we could fail because of an imbecile called Sedty who wanted personal glory. An imbecile ignorant from the fact that he would be key in leading the army to great victory.'

'I know the way I acted in the forest was disrespectful and I apologise profoundly. I will give a formal apology in front of the army in a few minutes.'

Nicolas loosened his grip and after staring hard in Sedty's blue eyes, he dropped the sword onto the ground. He could feel the vibrations run up his body.

'Do you remember what happened to me when I started out as a soldier in the army, general?'

Nicolas shook his head.

'All the soldiers looked at me as though I was different because I was a different colour to them all. They ignored the fact that I was twice their size. All they could see was my dark skin and they judged me for it. It wasn't till you came up to me one day in front of them all that they started to acknowledge me and include me in their games and daily routine.

You told me that you thought I deserved my place more than anyone else in the army, and that because I was different and therefore treated differently, I was the strongest soldier in every way. Since then, I have been treated like the others-sometimes better- because they respect me and I got that from you. For that, I respect *you*!'

Nicolas nodded.

'Do you promise to never betray me again?' he asked.

Sedty nodded. 'Now, general, your army awaits you.'

Malo was walking around the gardens, thinking about what he should do next.

He sat on the circular marble bench that surrounded the clear blue water. He leant on the fountain edge and skimmed his fingers along the water, over and over again.

Athena saw him from the balcony and quickly made her way to him.

She decided to creep up behind him and give him a scare and, sure enough, she did.

'Athena, that isn't funny.' he groaned.

She frowned and sat down next to him.

'That wasn't the response I thought I would get from you! What's wrong?' Athena asked, patting his back.

'It's nothing…' Malo said as he quickly leapt up. He started to walk away slowly, hoping Athena would beg him to tell her what was wrong, but she remained quiet with a smirk on her face. She knew Malo was seeking attention.

He suddenly turned around, 'It's your sister Scarlet. She told me she liked me!'

Athena smiled, 'That's what you've wanted all this time, no? What did you say?'

'I don't even remember, I just left in a rush. She caught me off-guard.'

'That's why she was upset.'

Malo took a deep breath. 'I don't know how to approach her, dear Athena, I really don't! I care too much that I can't say anything in case they're not the perfect words.'

Athena stood up and walked over to him.

'You're scared, Malo. It's okay! Look, she cares for you. All she wants is to have you at least *show* that you care for her. Hold her hand or ask her to go on a stroll with you by the river bank. These sort of gestures will go a very long way.'

They remained in silence as they sat back down. Athena could see he was thinking hard about what she had just said.

'Whenever I have problems, dear Athena, you are the one I will go to because you just give the most useful advice. Thank you!' he said as he kissed her on the cheek.

He quickly sat back down and asked, 'have you spoken to your father yet?'

Athena nodded and told him about her conversations with her father.

'Wow!' Malo said, scratching his head when Athena had finally finished.

'So, you are the heir to the throne?' he asked, making sure he heard it right the first time. He gave her the biggest smile and hugged her.

'Little Athena who was only a simple country girl a few weeks ago will now be queen. And now, I have got the love of my life who loves me. It's safe to say that it's a great day for us both, don't you think? I'd say this is a nice reward for our last few days of hard work on surviving.'

At that particular moment, Scarlet walked into the gardens, but as soon as she saw Athena and Malo embracing, she quickly hid around the corner.

Her heart was pounding so fast, she was afraid that Athena would hear it. At that moment, Athena heard that exact thought and quickly crept to where Scarlet was hiding.

Scarlet suddenly turned around only to see Athena. She screamed and fell into a small pond behind her.

'Oh Scarlet, I'm so sorry!' Athena said, as she offered her hand.

However, Malo quickly interfered and pushed Athena out of the way as he held out his hand.

This is my gesture to show Scarlet how I feel.

Athena nodded and discreetly left the gardens. Scarlet took hold of Malo's hand and stepped out of the pond carefully.

She continued to look down at the ground but whispered "thanks" to

Malo.

'You're welcome.' he whispered as he gently stroked her neck. Scarlet looked at him for a brief moment but then quickly turned another direction to hide her smile before he could see her.

Once she finished soaking all the water out of her hair, she looked into his eyes.

'Does this mean that you like me?' she asked in a high pitch.

Malo laughed, scratched the back of his head and walked back to the circular bench by the fountain.

Scarlet quickly followed him.

'You have liked me since I last came here?' Malo asked.

'Yes.'

'That's a long time! You've been waiting all this time for me to come back?'

Scarlet nodded.

Malo felt as though he was about to cry and that his heart was about to burst. He realised he'd have to say something now as it was the right time. All he had to do was find the right words. Malo had never cared what people thought of him. So, people either loved him or hated him. However, all the care he dismissed over the last years now came back in a form of a cloud within his mind. He cared so much that he didn't want to say anything. That cloud was slowly suffocating him along with anxiety from the whole situation.

'You are my light in shining armour.' he began.

Scarlet immediately shook her head. 'No. Absolutely not. This is *not* how you are going to start the most romantic thing I'm ever going to hear. It's too corny. Try again.'

Malo felt his ears turn red and every inch of his body sweat.

I think this is the most painful type of torture I've ever had to endure!

He cleared his throat and let the words slowly come out.

'I have also been waiting all this time for you, Scarlet. I didn't know your name back then, so in my mind, I called you "future wife". I have loved you since that moment we met. I dreamt that one day I'd be lucky enough to meet you again and now, I have! I don't know how to express just how much I love you because this all feels too surreal. It's too good to be true.'

Scarlet put her hands on his knee and gently pushed his head towards hers with the other hand. She placed her forehead against his and closed her eyes.

She whispered, 'It does feel surreal. However, you're wrong. It's not too good to be true. It's exactly how it's meant to be, Malo. You dreamt of me and I, you. We must have met in some of them. I've had many men proposition me.'

Scarlet paused for a moment and then looked Malo in the eyes. 'But I said no to them all because I knew that I would see you again. And when that day would come, I'd...'

She couldn't talk anymore because her lips were trembling and she was trying her absolute hardest not to cry.

However, Malo couldn't restrain himself and tears were rolling down his cheeks. 'Scarlet, I have had to fight my entire life. And many times, I could have died. Still, I was never afraid. I never felt vulnerable because it's what I have had to do in order to survive. With you, however, I am afraid. And I am vulnerable. Because I have never loved anything so much and having you right here where I can feel you and smell you, it's divine. That's why it's too good to be true. Nothing should be so sweet.'

He kissed the palm of her hand. She looked into his eyes and whispered, 'Close your eyes.'

Malo was so sure she would kiss him but after a few moments, he opened his eyes and she was no longer in front of him.

'To prove to you that this isn't too good to be true. You have to chase me, Malo! As you have done in your dreams. Except this time, when you catch me, you will feel just how real this is,' he heard a little voice call out from the other side of the pond. He smiled and started running after her, the adrenaline rush he needed.

She is right! This is exactly how it's meant to be.

He soon caught her and she happily surrendered in his arms. Before they passionately kissed, he whispered, 'my light in shining armour.'

Scarlet pretended like she was going to be sick. 'No, Malo! I don't like that!'

Malo laughed evilly. 'Now I know how to torture you for the rest of your life.'

'The rest of my life? Is there something you would like to ask me, Malo?' she asked with the cheekiest of smiles. Malo gave such a big grin because he didn't exactly know what to respond. He just held her even tighter and eventually groaned, 'you know how to drive me crazy.'

Scarlet stroked his cheek. 'That's how we know we're perfect for each other.'

And after four years of waiting, they finally kissed each other.

XX

It was late in the evening and Athena, once again, walked around the gardens. This time, nobody was around. Scarlet and Malo had left hours beforehand and the gardeners had already retired for the evening. She sat on a white marble bench overlooking the Forest Tatila with the red sky overhead and the pond with a small statue of a beautiful nymph surrounded by the clear blue water. She smiled and closed her eyes and listened to the nature surrounding her.

She heard the little birds tweeting close by and the sound of water flowing down the fountains. It was, indeed, a very tranquil moment.

Athena opened her eyes only to see that it was now much darker. The sky was gradually changing from red to navy and the stars were beginning to come out.

She stood up and slowly walked over to the swing hanging down from a very tall oak tree.

She gently sat down on the swing and leant her head against the coarse rope. She looked up and saw the branches of the tree, overlapping one another.

Athena felt like crying as it reminded her of the oak tree near her home back in Oakrose.

But she *was* home. Her original home. Although she had only left her house a few weeks ago, it seemed as though she had been away for a whole lot longer.

What happened to Tomas? Was he still alive and how was Agatha coping? Athena felt a sudden wave of guilt overcome her. How could she do such a thing to the people who had raised her since she was an infant?

Athena took a deep breath and decided to not worry about it. One day, she would return to them and when she did, Yan would be there looking after his mother.

She looked ahead. The fountain with the nymph had suddenly lit up with underwater lights that shone the colour of the sun. Only a few moments later did the rest of the garden light up, with lights in the shape of candles lighting up every path. The garden was shaped as a maze. It was hard for her to see any other part of the garden apart from the small sector she was in.

Athena, however, caught sight of a small beige harpsichord, behind another part of the maze.

She slowly got up from the swing and walked over to it. She slid her fingers along the ivory keys and noticed pictures painted around the main body of the instrument. On one side, there was the Forest Tatila with the view of the Four Flames in the distance. On the other side, there were five little children lined up in a row in front of the castle. Behind the children were their parents. Athena looked away. She knew without looking into great detail that it was a portrait of her family before the revolt. She could tell from far that it was her mother holding her shoulder in the picture. Athena took a deep breath and looked at the picture of her mother. She had long, beautiful, dark blonde hair and a captivating smile with dimples on either side.

Her smile must have been even more enchanting in real-life.

There was so much life and happiness in her eyes. Athena then looked down at her younger self. She looked about two years old. At that age, Athena still had her blonde curls. She was touching her mother's hand with a few fingers. At the same time, she was sucking her thumb with her other hand. Athena could see how happy she was then because she could see she was, in fact, smiling so much that her eyes were squinting. Athena smiled at that. She could feel the love and happiness radiate from the painting onto herself. Her attention slowly headed towards the soft, calming sounds she could hear.

She looked up and saw the most beautiful fountain only a few yards away from harpsichord. It stood firmly against the very tall bush behind it. Athena gazed up at the magnificent fountain as she walked towards it.

It was shaped in the form of a goblet cut in half. There was a bird shaped in light grey marble with water gently pouring out of its open beak. The water landed below, past other marble birds, placed on different levels of transparent platforms.

Athena walked towards the fountain, holding her breath as she admired its beauty. She felt as though she was walking into another world. She could really feel the magic.

She looked at the pool of water which was at the level of her waist. The underwater lights shone up against each bird, allowing each of them to stand out.

Athena gazed up at the beautifully carved birds and almost felt obliged to touch them, when she suddenly felt a warmth from behind her.

'Beautiful, isn't it?'

Athena, usually hearing a voice from so close, would have jumped, but there was something about this particular voice. Something comforting.

She slowly nodded and turned around slowly only to see the most attractive man she had ever seen.

He was much taller than her and had light brown hair. She studied his eyes and noticed they weren't just hazel brown. They also had a light green circle around his, now dilated, pupils. He wasn't pale, nor was he dark. He was olive-skinned and very built.

Athena suddenly looked away after realising that she was staring at him with her mouth open.

She drummed her fingers against her forehead and then looked back up at him.

'Sorry. My... my name is Athena.' she stumbled out.

The man smiled. 'I'm Nathan.'

Athena nodded her head as she also smiled.

'You have to be part of the Royal Family!' Nathan stated.

Athena continued to nod, not knowing what else to do.

'You have really nice blue eyes. If you don't me saying, they are much nicer than all your other sisters.'

Athena stopped nodding and asked, 'You know my sisters?'

'Yes, I do! I spend the majority of my time in the castle, discussing matters with your father.'

'You and my father are close friends?'

'I am the general of his army.'

'Really?'

'Why do you look so surprised?' he asked, grinning.

'No... I'm not... I mean, you *do* seem a bit young to be a general!' Athena said, slightly embarrassed.

'Well, I'm twenty-one! That isn't as young as General Avran.'

Athena smiled but didn't know what to say. Nathan could see her embarrassment so decided to change the subject.

'You haven't changed a bit!' Nathan said as he gently held Athena's chin, lifting her face up.

'What do you mean?'

'Do you not remember? We used to be the best of friends when we were very small,' Nathan said, a bit disappointed.

'Sorry. I have no recollection of what happened to me before I was four years old.'

Nathan sighed.

'Let me finish,' Athena said, sensing his disappointment. 'I was met by a Wueltin. My memory was somewhat erased.'

Nathan straightened his back.

'But if you weren't enchanted by a Wueltin, you would have remembered me?' he asked with some hope.

'As mundane as it sounds, which I apologise for, I wouldn't be able to forget a face like yours!' Athena whispered, feeling her cheeks burn.

Nathan didn't say anything. He simply gazed at her beautiful face.

She decided to ask him more questions.

'So, what did we used to do together?'

Nathan looked down at her.

'Well, we used to play together, along with your brother and sisters and other children living close by the castle,' he began. He suddenly laughed.

'One day, there was a place we discovered together while hiding from the others. It was actually right here!' he said, looking around, eyeing the grass between the harpsichord and themselves.

Athena followed his eyes.

'Tell me another story,' she whispered.

'Well, one day, we were playing outside and it began to pour down with rain. It was you, me, Gemma and her friend, William. We found a cave close to the waterfall in the Forest Tatila. Only, it wasn't an ordinary cave. A group of baby Greliks came towards us and Gemma was sitting in a position that blocked the entrance to a small passageway to go deeper into the cave. That's where these little guys wanted to go. So, they kept running into her, trying to make her move.

She screamed and to help her, you walked over to the little Greliks to hug them and soon enough, they were all over *you*.'

Athena smiled and looked up. A drop of rain fell on her cheek. Then several drops fell down and soon, it started to rain down hard.

'Look at that! You talk of rain and it starts to pour down like in the story.'

'I know where we can go.' Nathan said, holding Athena's hand and leading her somewhere.

They ran to the other side of the enormous garden, making their way through the maze.

'If you stick to the left wall of the maze, you will always find your way out.'

Athena smiled at him and asked 'How do you know that?'

'I like to read books and learn.'

That was the most charming thing Athena had ever heard.

Finally, Nathan found the place where he wanted to go. It was a small bandstand, surrounded by a small pond. There was a small wooden bridge, decorated with red and white flowers, which they both ran over to reach their shelter.

Athena and Nathan let go of each other and they were both panting and laughing.

She quickly looked around. The bandstand had a white-marbled roof that was completely flat. The roof was supported by four pillars made of white shiny marble on each corner. There were vines engraved from the top to the bottom and when it reached the marble floor of the bandstand, the vines continued on until they met the next pillar.

There was one long bench made of white marble that was so shiny, she could vaguely make out her petite figure compared to the very tall man next to her.

Nathan sat down on the bench and took a deep breath.

'I forgot how good it feels to be under rain. It's so refreshing and I love the smell. Is that a strange thing to say? To love the smell of rain?' he asked.

'Not at all.' she whispered.

Athena sat down next to him and leant against his chest and closed her eyes. This was the closest she had ever been to a man and she knew it felt right. She knew he wanted her to be there. For the first time since she left Oakrose, she was able to fully relax.

Nathan cleared his throat.

'What are you thinking of?' he asked.

'I know what *you* are thinking,' Athena said with a smirk on her wet face, her eyes still closed.

Nathan laughed. 'Can you control it?'

'Control myself?'

Nathan tried hard not to turn red himself. 'I mean... I mean, I meant your gift.'

'Oh.'

Athena wiped a wet piece of hair from her mouth and continued.

'Well, I don't know! If I concentrate very hard, I can control it. But I'm not at ease with it yet. I feel like a gift should be a part of you and should be easy. It shouldn't require you to think hard. At least, that's my opinion.'

Continue.

'I only realised that I had a gift when I left Oakrose.'

He put his hand around her shoulder.

'What are you doing?' she immediately asked.

'We used to be like this when we were younger. We'd cuddle while I listened to your interesting stories for hours on end. You haven't changed that much.' Nathan said, winking.

Athena sighed. She hated that she had no re-collection of her earliest memories.

'Wait a minute!' she said as she turned to him.

'I think I can remember those memories you told me. My father was able to show me how to find my memories.'

Nathan smiled and stood up. He nodded towards the castle.

'Well, what are we waiting for?' he asked, offering his hand to Athena.

'Brace yourself!' she said as they ran out into the pouring rain.

Scarlet and Malo were sitting down on cushions near the fireplace in her chambers.

Malo subtly took some nuts from dinner, which he hid in his pockets, and stuck them onto three sticks. He handed one over to Scarlet and together, they were roasting them above the fire.

Todd and Scarlet had made up after their little dispute earlier on and the three of them were sitting down.

Todd was positioned a lot closer to the fire that way the nuts on his stick could reach.

Scarlet laughed as she removed the nuts from her stick and she fed them to Malo.

'How are you able to laugh every minute? Do you laugh in your sleep? That would be quite impressive!' Malo said as he chewed his roasted nuts.

Scarlet started to giggle slightly louder. 'I don't laugh in my sleep, thank you very much! However, as soon as I wake up I do start to giggle!'

'Like you are now… when it's nearly time to go to sleep.'

Todd yawned when he heard the word "sleep". 'I'm going to go fly outside one more time before I come back to sleep.'

Malo watched Todd fly away. 'Where's he going?'

'He wanted to give us some privacy, that's all. I don't think it's time to sleep yet. I am happy how we are now,' she said, looking deep into his eyes.

Malo leant in to kiss her but as soon as he moved his hand, the stick dropped and landed in the fire, setting off a series of loud crackling noises.

Malo's eyes widened. 'Um, shouldn't we do something?'

Scarlet held Malo's shoulder.

'Don't worry! When I was six years old, I accidentally caused a huge fire. A Wueltin then came and put a spell on the fireplace. It's impossible for there to be an accident.'

Malo gave a defeated laugh. 'Magic. Logic I can never understand.'

'Sometimes, it's nicer when things cannot be understood. It leaves things to the… imagination.'

She looked up at him and gave him a cheeky smile.

'Your eyes are lit up with so much happiness and love,' Malo remarked as he fluttered his eyelashes.

Scarlet moved in closer. 'Why do you think that is?'

Malo was about to respond when somebody entered.

'Malo, you are needed elsewhere! My general would like to see you immediately!' the King ordered in a hoarse voice.

Malo nodded as he reluctantly left Scarlet.

The King watched Malo leave until he was out of sight. He then walked towards Scarlet.

'You know what? Life is too short!' Malo said as he quickly came back in. He walked up to Scarlet and gave her a kiss on the lips. Malo didn't care he did this in front of her father. He loved this girl and nobody, not even the King, could keep him away for too long.

'Okay.' he said as he walked back out. He blew Scarlet a kiss and bowed down to the King. 'Now, I will see the general.'

Scarlet touched her lips and then slowly looked over at her father. She raised her eyebrow and laughed. She didn't know what else to do.

'Well, what can I say? He is quite a character! He definitely matches you in that regard. I am happy for you, my sweet Scarlet!' the King said in a gentle whisper, kissing her on the forehead. 'However, I want you to be careful. Please do not get too attached to him. Remember, there is a war in a few weeks and Malo will be playing a vital role on our side. He could... as you are well aware... he could—'

'Please, don't even think that. I know he won't die. If the power of love is as powerful as it is told in the books, then he will not die.'

The King sighed and looked down.

'I know, my sweet child, that you love him so very dearly. However, there are always tragedies in war. I know how much the death of your mother has affected you.'

Scarlet looked away. 'I will be just fine.'

'You loved her as much as you love Malo and I'm afraid of the consequences. You barely made it through when your mother died. Tell me, how you will be "just fine" if Malo dies?'

Scarlet looked up at her father. By now, her face was red and her eyes were swelling up with tears. She hesitated for a moment.

'Why are you doing this to me?' she asked, breaking into a sob.

'I want to protect you, my sweet Scarlet. I want to protect you because I love you! You will always be my darling, charming, cheeky Scarlet.'

Scarlet made a muffled sound.

'Is that you trying to laugh?' the King asked with a smile.

Scarlet looked up at him and nodded.

'You have always been the most cheerful child. You were just like your mother on that subject,' he said as he embraced her.

'But I want to tell you that I know Malo won't die. He wouldn't do that to me! He knows how much I love him. He wouldn't do that to me.'

'You love him so much that you would risk getting in your chambers into flames... again?' the King asked, pointing towards the fireplace.

'That wasn't me.'

'Well, whoever it was, thank the Gods I got a Wueltin to cast a spell over that wretched fireplace.'

Scarlet laughed, wiping the hair away from her wet cheeks.

The King smiled and held her hand. 'I just love you so much, I don't want to see you in pain.'

'I won't be! Nothing will happen to him. I promise.'

Malo walked down the hallway until he reached a man broader and taller than himself.

'Malo! At long last we meet!' General Lamber said as he held out his hand.

They firmly shook hands.

'You asked to see me?' Malo asked with a smile on his face, yet he spoke with a tone of impatience.

'I want you to talk to me about the Seven Hundred Army. How strong is it?'

Malo started to laugh but when he saw the seriousness on the general's face, he immediately stopped.

'The Seven Hundred Army is incredibly strong and powerful. To get a secure place in the army alone, you have to endure months of training and if you *still* aren't up to their standards, they won't give you a place as one of their precious soldiers.'

The general nodded.

'How long have you been in the army?' he asked, stroking his chin.

'Four years. I started quite young. I know how the army works. I know their weaknesses!'

'What about their strengths? What is it about them that makes everyone else frightened?'

Malo sighed.

'In previous wars, they simply had great tactics, weapons and they knew what they were doing, but for this war... it is slightly different.'

'How? Are there more men?'

'There will always be seven hundred men. It kind of defeats the point otherwise...'

The general smacked his head, 'Of course!'

'They have Agalits. I have seen them change a man into an Agalit myself. It is rather frightful! The advanced scientists who work for the army have found a code in our genetic material that changes the power in the Agalit's blood to another. They change it to whatever power General Avran wants. They changed a human soldier into an Agalit and gave him the power of immense strength.'

Malo paused and looked down. 'He would even be able to destroy a force-shield.'

The general took a deep breath. 'So when the war comes, the force shield will be completely useless.'

Malo nodded.

The general scratched the back of his head, 'Malo, you and I are going to have a long talk about how we can defeat this army!'

'Absolutely! Nothing would make me happier than to see the Blucks and Chamcoks lose, but perhaps another time. It is getting late and I would like to wish Scarlet a good night,' Malo said, turning around.

'Of course! And I must go and say good night to Athena!' the general said.

Malo turned back to him.

'A... Athena, *dear* Athena?' he asked, completely shocked.

'Yes. Athena. I heard you accompanied her here.'

Malo nodded.

'Well, I must thank you so much for keeping her safe. I have waited for her for what seems an eternity to me.'

'You knew her?'

'As a child, yes. I was eight years old when I last saw her. The late queen told me of Athena's disappearance the day after the revolt. It was one of the most striking days of my life. I knew I would probably never meet anyone as intelligent and humble as her.'

Malo smiled as he took those words in.

He gave the general a firm handshake and slowly let him go to Athena.

I would have thought she would have chosen someone a bit smarter. Someone who would know the Seven Hundred Army would only have seven hundred soldiers, not more.

Nathan walked away. He was glad he could get that information out of Malo. However, he already knew everything that was said. The information had reached the King already who passed it onto him. They had been preparing for years as well. Even though the Four Flames had always been regarded a peaceful place, since the revolt thirteen years ago, the men of Tatila knew that one day they would have to fight in the upcoming war. It had always been known that this war would change Fairoses. For better or for worse. So, the Kings army was a lot bigger than what Malo or the Seven Hundred Army could ever imagine it to be.

XXI

Gemma walked into the huge dining room and greedily looked over at the long table covered with a variety of food.

She was about to grab a plate but realised that nobody else was there.

'Nathan, Athena, Malo and Scarlet all went down to the market early this morning and father is talking to some noble families. So, it's just you and me.' Juliet said as she was concentrating on a vase of water, floating in mid-air.

She took a deep breath and allowed the glass to fall down and shatter on the ground.

Gemma shook her head.

'I wonder who is going to clean that up?' she asked as she grabbed a plate violently.

'You have no faith in my gift,' Juliet said. The doors suddenly flew open and a gush of cold wind suddenly whipped through the room.

Juliet continued to keep the water in mid-air but she turned her attention towards the wind.

Gemma grunted.

'I *hate* it when you do that! Now, I'm very cold!'

Juliet rolled her eyes. She shut the doors with the wind returning outside. Then, fire appeared under the water to rapidly evaporate it. The room soon turned hot.

'Is *that* better?' Juliet asked with a smirk on her face.

Gemma looked at Juliet with disgust, grabbed a handful of red berries and left the room, slamming the door on her way out.

Juliet laughed. She then controlled the fire, making it smaller until it was the size of palm. She lowered her palm down to the shattered glass and watched it slowly melt away.

'My dear friend. How good it is to see you again,' a nobleman said as the

King entered a large room, filled with men from noble families.

'Tibuy, it is only a pleasure to be in your presence. Tell me, how is your family?' he asked sincerely.

Tibuy frowned. 'My wife has just given birth to a daughter.'

'Then why do you frown? Daughters are such a blessing.'

'It's not that. I am thrilled to have a little girl. It just *isn't* the right time. The war is so close. I am afraid that the enemy will slaughter her without any mercy.'

'What is her name?'

'We call her Florence.'

The King gently held Tibuy's shoulder and promised, 'Florence will survive the war. I give you my own word and if anything were to happen to you or your wife, I will personally take her in and raise her like my own.'

Tibuy nodded. 'Nothing has ever sounded so sweet to the ears! Thank you for your kindness, my King!'

King Agalaya smiled and continued to walk through the chamber. He could never admire the beauty of this place enough. It was a huge circular room with windowed walls and it was able to hold at least one hundred men. The very end of the room had no windows and exposed everyone to the soft breeze. The ceiling was supported by five white pillars, placed evenly around the chamber.

A man sounded his horn and silence followed. The King walked up a few stairs and was just inches away from the edge of the chamber when he turned around.

'My noble friends,' he said, as he made a kind gesture, 'this will be the last time we meet before the war.'

There were several grunts and sighs of dismay among the crowd. The King held his hand out and ordered for silence.

'However, as I am immortal, I offer help to the families of all those who do not survive. I have promised Tibuy that if anything were to happen to him, I would take his daughter Florence in and treat her like my own. Now, if any of you have children, I promise to treat them like my own.'

There was a cheer amongst the crowd.

'As most of you know, Athena is finally back home. With her on our side now, we come closer to defeating the enemy. The more Agalits we have, the better. The enemy also has Agalits. Powerful Agalits that are man-made. These Agalits are made for one purpose – to destroy.

We have well over seven hundred soldiers in the army and over the past week alone, we have had another hundred men step forward! Since Athena has returned, the people feel like there is hope. She has given them hope in Fate. My friends, the fate of Fairoses has been written in the Prophecy. If things are going as well as they have so far, we are surely on the path to victory!'

The men cheered and for the first time in seven years, since his wife's death, the King could feel an electric impulse travel around his body. He felt so confident that they would win. His daughter returning really helped him believe that there was hope, after all.

Athena and Nathan were walking along the markets, holding hands and glancing at every stall. The entire morning, they were playfully teasing one another, making the other try disgusting sweets and foods. They had finally come a truce and decided no more tricks for the day.

Athena suddenly caught sight of a beautiful purple necklace. The necklace was structured together by small purple leaves made from a beautiful glimmering crystal. The two ends of the necklace joined together with a flower, and then came down a few inches with the same purple leaves.

She walked over to the counter with Nathan right behind her, and asked, 'What crystal is that? It's the most beautiful piece of jewellery, I have to say!'

The man standing behind the stall looked up at Athena.

'You have excellent taste! The crystal is called Alexandrite. It is unique in the way that its colour changes throughout the day. Most commonly they change from a light green in the day to a dark red in the evening. This one, however, has settled more on a purple during the day and changes to a dark orange at night. The wonderful thing about Alexandrite is that each crystal has a personality of its own. It is the most beautiful necklace here, but also the most expensive at six hundred rubies.' the kind stall owner explained as he delicately picked up the necklace and handed it over to Athena.

Athena smiled as she carefully picked up the intriguing necklace. She was about to try it on but Nathan quickly intervened and put the necklace around her neck. He looked at her reflection in the small mirror the stall owner was holding up.

'It's beautiful.' he whispered as he kissed her neck.

He subtly reached for his pocket and silently groaned as he realised he didn't have enough money on him.

'Six hundred rubies you said?' Athena asked the stall owner once again.

'Precisely!'

Athena looked through her bag and saw that she didn't have enough rubies as both she and Malo shared their rubies among themselves.

'I'll come back another time.' Athena said as she gave the necklace back.

She began to walk away and Nathan whispered, 'Put the necklace away. I will come back later today to collect it.'

The stall owner winked at him and obeyed. 'I'm glad for you Nathan, I really am. It's nice to see you together again. Like it should have always been.' he said as he leant over and patted his friend on the shoulder.

'Thanks, William.' Nathan whispered as he strode away to catch up with Athena.

Meanwhile, Scarlet and Malo, were on the other side of the market. They were looking at the stalls with animals, having just visited an old man who had translated the mark on Malo's back.

'I can't believe it means "you shall die before your time". It's absolutely absurd!' Scarlet said, looking at the animals.

'I know! Probably the army trying to scare me away.'

Malo's eye suddenly caught sight of a huge bird in a cage.

'Why, hello there.' Malo said as the bird leant against the other side of the cage.

Scarlet giggled. 'He thinks that your teeth are a bit too white and that you have really fat fingers!'

Malo cleared his throat and quickly removed his fat finger from the cage, hoping to stroke its forehead.

Scarlet grabbed Malo's hand and brought him to another stall which was selling kittens.

'How old is this one?' Scarlet asked the stall owner as she picked up a small ginger cat, only the size of her palm.

'That one was born only last month and because it was thundering that night, I decided to give him the name Thunder!' the stall owner announced.

Scarlet smiled as she stroked the chin of the tiny kitten.

'Oh my, I love him!' Scarlet said as she turned towards Malo.

'He is very cute,' Malo said as he put his finger out, hoping that Thunder would lick it.

Scarlet smiled.

'Let me guess! What is my fat finger doing in his face?' Malo asked as he saw Scarlet's facial expression. Scarlet nodded as she lifted the kitten towards her face. She closed her eyes, listening to its little thoughts. Malo took the opportunity to secretly buy it for her.

He gave the stall owner fifty rubies and then quickly removed the cat from Scarlet's hand.

Scarlet immediately opened her eyes.

'Why did you do that? Thunder was telling me what it just had to eat this morning.' she said in a disappointed voice.

'Well, I took Thunder away because I want to give him back to you as a gift!'

Scarlet beamed and screeched, 'You did?'

Malo nodded as he handed Thunder back down to Scarlet. Scarlet gave him the biggest smile as she stroked the unimpressed-looking kitten.

'Come on, Todd. Please come down!'

Scarlet was alone in her room with Thunder and Todd. Thunder was lying on Scarlet's bed with its irresistible white, fluffy tummy in view. He was wanting a cuddle.

'Todd, please! Just because Thunder lives here now, it doesn't mean I don't like you any less. I love you, so please come down!' Scarlet begged as she was looking up at Todd who was standing on top of her wardrobe.

Todd folded his wings and looked away, pouting.

Scarlet rolled her eyes and decided talking was of no use, so she walked over to her armchair and dragged it towards the wardrobe. She climbed on it to reach Todd.

She rested her arms on the top of the wardrobe and stared directly at him.

'Hi!' she said as she took a deep breath.

Todd looked away, still folding his wings.

'Please talk to me, Todd! You have no idea how much it hurts me seeing you like this.'

Todd slowly unfolded his wings.

'And you know how much I love you and need you! You are my best friend. I would never ever try to replace you!' Scarlet continued.

Todd slowly turned towards Scarlet, looking down.

'And you know that,' Scarlet said as she softly poked his stomach. Todd flew over to her and gave her a peck on the cheek.

Scarlet smiled as he did so and whispered, 'you will always be my favourite.'

'I hope so,' Todd replied as he flew outside.

Scarlet slowly climbed down from the chair and walked onto her balcony. She ran her fingers along the dark green ivy which covered the marble railing.

She took a deep breath and looked at the beautiful view ahead. The mountains, the forest, the countryside. She closed her eyes to hear the water from the waterfall splash against the rocks.

She imagined herself laughing and hopping from rock to rock on the water close by the waterfall with Malo hopping after her. He finally caught her by grabbing her waist. He then turned her around to kiss her on the lips. They finally rested on the biggest rock of all, which was in front of the waterfall itself. They both sat down and Malo put his hand around Scarlet's shoulders. They were both so close to where the water silently and softly hit the rocks, that the humidity resulted in them both being completely soaked.

She stood up, bringing Malo up as well, and together they jumped into the warm water.

After they spent a few minutes in the steaming pool of water, they jumped out and laid on the ground whilst looking at each other.

Suddenly Scarlet felt Malo hugging her from behind and awoke from her reverie. She smiled as she held his hand and giggled as he kissed her on the neck.

'I love you, my light in shining armour,' he whispered as he then kissed her forehead.

Scarlet closed her eyes as he did and whispered back, 'I love you more than you can imagine. And I hate it when you say that!'

Malo laughed evilly as he led her back inside.

'General Avran, wait, General Avran!' a low-ranking soldier was calling out as he ran after Nicolas.

Nicolas turned around with a look of disgust. How dare a low-ranking soldier come and talk to him!

'Me and the other soldiers-'

'The other soldiers and I,' Nicolas corrected him.

'Yes. Right. The other soldiers and I were hoping that you would join us for our training session?'

Nicolas laughed at the idea, but after stroking his chin he nodded.

'I have never trained with low-ranking soldiers. Only my professional trainers.'

The soldier nodded and led Nicolas to where all the other soldiers were — the arena.

'Look, General Avran has decided to join us!'

All the soldiers looked at each other and then greeted the general into their private yet huge circle.

'We thought it was about time we got to know each other,' one soldier said as he stood up.

The general straightened his back, 'I already know each and every one of you! It was I who gave you all a place in this army.'

'That may be so, but how well you do *really* know us?' another soldier asked.

'What is my daughter's name?'

'Which part of Fairoses do I come from?'

They all bombarded General Avran with questions which he admitted, he could not answer.

'We shall change this! After tonight, we will all know each other much better,' a soldier said as he patted General Avran on the back.

Nicolas smiled as two soldiers brought in a huge chest filled with beer bottles.

After talking and drinking for many hours, Nicolas fell into a heavy sleep. A few soldiers, who were still conscious looked down at his young face.

'We can kill him right now. Nobody would know. We could just say it was the alcohol that killed him.'

'Except alcohol doesn't leave blood wounds, you nugget!'

The soldier who spoke first bent down and moved General Avran's hair away from his face.

All his anger he had towards the general had suddenly vanished. It was he who plotted to kill Nicolas, but in the end, seeing his face just made the soldier realise that the general was only a child. He was, after all, the youngest person there.

'Let's leave him to rest.'

'But what about your plan, Benny?'

Benny looked down, sighed heavily and shook his head. 'Let's not kill him just yet.'

King Agalaya entered his chambers and threw his shoes to one side. He fell back on his bed and took continuous deep breaths.

After a while, he slowly slid off the bed and walked over to the large, light blue leather armchair, next to the fireplace, and collapsed into it.

He looked directly at the chair opposite to him, a leather rock chair.

He smiled as he had a flash back from years ago.

'Mama, when can we go out in the gardens? It's thundering and pouring down rain. I love it when it's thundering and pouring down with rain!' Scarlet said in her demanding voice, tugging at her mother's dress.

King Agalaya continued to smile.

'In a minute, darling!' his wife replied as she smiled and picked Scarlet up.

Scarlet snuggled in, grabbing hold of her mother's arm with one hand and sucking her thumb with her other.

The queen looked directly at the King and softly laughed. 'It's getting easier to make this one fall asleep.' she said as she caressed Scarlet's long brown hair and kissed the top of her head.

Suddenly the queen jerked, making Scarlet immediately wake up.

She removed her thumb from her mouth and screamed, 'is it time to go outside? Yay!'

Scarlet ran out of the room.

'What is it, Amber? What is it, my love?' asked both the young King in the past and the King in the present at exactly the same time, shifting their position in the chair slightly.

'I don't know! This child is kicking very aggressively!' she replied, looking down at her enormous stomach.

Both Kings, old and young looked down and sighed.

'It feels...different! Perhaps it is a boy. After three girls, it would be pleasant to have a boy.'

'My King, there is someone for you at the door,' a guard suddenly announced as he entered the Kings chamber.

The King shook his head, returning to the present.

'Who is it?' he asked in a hoarse voice.

'A young man named Malo,' the guard answered.

The King cleared his throat and signalled the guard to bring Malo in. Malo quickly entered and walked straight up to Scarlet's father.

'Your Highness, I need to ask you something,' he said, raising his voice slightly.

The King nodded and covered his mouth with his fingers to conceal his amusement.

'I am in love with your daughter... Scarlet!' he blurted out.

The King laughed and replied, 'I know! I am not blinded from such things. I may be a busy person but I am also her father.'

The King had known for a long time that his Scarlet was in love with Malo since the duel challenge a few years ago.

'Well, I came here to ask for your permission to ask Scarlet for her hand in marriage.'

The King smiled and got up from his huge armchair and patted Malo on the back.

'I accept. Of course. Scarlet has always loved you and from what I have seen from the past few weeks, you make her very happy indeed!'

Malo smiled, his heart still pounding.

Juliet entered Gemma's chambers in the middle of the night.

'Gemma! Gemma, wake up!' Juliet whispered as she sat down on her sister's bed.

Gemma groaned as she slowly opened her eyes.

'What do you want, Juliet?' she whined.

'Well, the war, if the Prophecy is correct, should be in a few days. I don't believe that we have a chance to win! They have many Agalits now! We have no chance what so ever.'

Gemma rolled her eyes.

'If that is the only reason you came in, then I don't want to hear it! A few weeks ago, yes, I agree we would have been heavily disadvantaged, but now our sister has returned and both she and General Lamber have had many men offer their service. We have the same chance of winning as O... the enemy has now!'

'Thirteen years ago, I would have never imagined that Nicolas would be able to be the very reason why we are recruiting people to fight to their death.'

Gemma looked down and suddenly heard Juliet cry.

'Go back to your chambers, Juliet!' she said coldly.

Juliet looked at her.

'I would have thought you would have been nice to me, considering I know your little secret!'

Gemma's eyes widened but then she immediately calmed herself.

'You don't have it in yourself to tell father.'

Juliet walked out. 'We shall see!'

'Come in!' Athena said as she heard someone knock on her door.

Nathan entered, with a bouquet of wild flowers in his hand.

Athena walked up to him and looked at the flowers.

'Are those for me?' she asked.

Nathan suddenly looked at the flowers and looked back up with his heart-warming smile.

'Yes! Well, I thought since I was coming up, I couldn't possibly come to my love empty-handed.'

Athena smiled and took the flowers from his hand.

'Well, that was very sweet!' she whispered as she kissed him on the cheek.

She walked back to her bed and placed them on her nightstand.

She slowly turned around and for a moment, neither of them said anything, but just stared at each other from across the room.

Nathan suddenly walked over to her, picked her up and slowly laid her onto the bed and laid beside her.

She leant against his shoulder and closed her eyes.

This is exactly how I imagined it!

Athena smiled.

'You imagined this for thirteen years?'

Yes. Every day.

She put her hand on top of his and saw his fingertips were almost three inches longer than hers.

'Your hands are really small. Like baby fingers. Have they even grown?' he asked, jokingly, as he gently prodded each one.

Athena laughed.

'I remember what I wanted to do! You told me the other day that your memory could be somewhat jolted? And would break the spell the Wueltin cast on you if you saw something that helped you remember? Well, I know we re-discovered many of them over the past few weeks-'

'And we were two cheeky little children!' Athena commented.

Nathan smiled before he continued. 'I came across this picture. This isn't a memory you have seen yet. I think it's one you will really enjoy!'

He took out a tattered picture from his pocket and handed it over to her. There was little Athena, on Nathan's back, with the biggest smile on her face and her hands reaching up to the sky. They were by the oak tree with the swing in the gardens.

'Does it trigger anything in here?' he whispered as he kissed her head.

Athena stared at the picture for a while but nothing happened. 'Could you tell me a little something that happened?'

Nathan took her hand and held it up to the ceiling. 'Well, my love, your hands were reaching for the skies because you were saying you were so happy that you could touch the heavens! You did that a lot, actually. You were always so happy. Different to Scarlet in the way that she runs around wild. She shows her happiness in a very extrovert way. You, on the other hand, keep it on the inside. When you are happy it shows through your eyes. Those beautiful, blue eyes.'

Athena smiled as he kissed her eyelids. She asked him to tell her more.

Nathan kissed her head once more with tears in his eyes. It hurt him that she couldn't remember these memories.

'You loved to learn. Your parents used to say that you had an intelligence far superior to anyone else of your age. I would remember finding you in the library many times. You would love to learn about the history and geography of the world. You always knew where all the lands were and always talked about how you wanted to explore them all! When we would meet, you would always want to go to a different place and explore different parts of the forest. You were very ambitious for a four year old.'

'What did my mother say about that? Did she help me learn?'

'Your mother was an amazing woman. She could see you held such interest in geography. So, every couple of weeks, you two would explore a new land from around the world. You would learn about their history, their type of cuisine and their traditional costumes. Every few weeks, you would hold a feast. You and your mother would go to the kitchens and help make these traditional dishes. Your father loved those evenings. Family friends would be invited. The main hall would be decorated with the colours of that particular country. It was just so much fun. I always looked forward to those evenings. Everyone did. However, after you left, your mother couldn't continue without you.'

Athena closed her eyes as she imagined those huge feasts taking place in the hall filled with bright colours, and everyone enjoying themselves and having interesting conversations about the culture they were experiencing.

'It was always in me to be like that. I always asked Agatha and Tomas if I could walk past the volcano or if I could walk towards the sea. They never allowed me. They said it was too dangerous for me. I never asked why, but I figured it out the moment I left. I was in danger because I am an Agalit.'

Nathan just held her tighter to comfort her.

'What do you think would have happened if I was never taken to the countryside? Where do you think we would be?'

Nathan thought about it for a little while but then whispered, 'Honestly, I think we would be right here.'

Athena slid her fingers into his. 'Can I ask you a question, Nathan?'

'Of course, my love!'

Athena sat up. 'Why did nobody ever go and look for me? My father could have sent his soldiers out to find me. Why didn't he?'

Nathan gulped and Athena noticed his jaw clench.

'That was the first thing I asked your mother after I cried in her arms. She brought me to your father and left us both together. Your father was in such a state. Losing his two youngest children was devastating!

He told me he had already sent his soldiers to search the Four Flames for you and your brother. When they came back without any success, your father then sent out his spies. He knew where Nicolas was. He knew he was taken to the Seven Hundred Army. So, he sent out his own spies to pose as soldiers so they could keep an eye on him.

However, there was still no sign of you. Nobody had seen you, nobody had asked for a ransom. So, your father didn't think that was bad news. He knew you must have been some place far, but he could feel that you were safe.

He told me, every time I asked about you, the same words, "She will return when Fate allows it." He knew you'd return one day and he knew you were safe. That was enough for him.'

Athena nodded. Nathan didn't have to read minds to tell what she was thinking.

'None of us forgot about you, Athena! Not even for one moment. Your mother couldn't wait any longer. Your father kept telling her to the same as me. "She will return when Fate allows it." But she just needed to see you again. She needed to see her Atheneglary again.'

Athena let a tear roll down her cheek as she took deep breaths. What she would do to see her mother.

After talking a long time about her family, and then other topics, Athena began to laugh again and fall more in love with him. The more time she spent with him, the more she remembered how she felt towards him when she was younger.

When the sun began to rise, Nathan knew he had to leave in order to get a few hours of sleep before he started his busy day.

Athena held his hand as she led him to the door. 'Before you leave, tell me why I was so happy in that picture. What happened just before it was taken?'

Nathan stroked the side of her face. 'You were on the swing going as high as you could, when your dress flew upwards. You were embarrassed, so you quickly used one hand to push it back down, but then you lost balance and fell off. I caught you and saved you from hitting your head against the thick roots of the tree.'

Athena smiled and gave him loving eyes as she leant against the door. 'You saved me. I think it's only fitting to give my saviour a kiss before he goes off to save his next maiden.'

She kissed him on the cheek.

'It's only ever been you, Athena,' he whispered. He kissed her hand and wished her a good sleep, and then retired to his chambers.

XXII

'The war is in a few days' time. We have hundreds of men who have offered to join the Kings Army. Even with the increase in men coming forward, we have a weapon for every individual. We also have three Agalits as well as your four daughters. The caves deep in the Flame are all ready for the women, children and the old. We also have the Greliks on our side.'

General Lamber nodded in a formal manner to the King to confirm that everything was true.

The King smiled and patted Nathan on the cheek.

'You have done well and I am very proud of your efforts, Nathan!' the King said.

Nathan cleared his throat and said, 'The only downside is that some of the men who are fighting for us have no idea how to fight and have never used weapons. One of the Agalits, whose gift is to lift the lava from the inner core of the earth up to the surface in seconds, has not yet mastered his gift. He seems to be unable to bring the lava up in the particular place he wants it to be, so there is a small chance that he could be killing some of our men without meaning to. He was too embarrassed to reveal that little fact earlier.'

'I will teach him how to control his power. I haven't been living for so long for no reason!'

Nathan laughed, feeling a bit uncomfortable at the very thought.

'My boy, I feel as though I haven't given you enough praise over the last few weeks. My mind has been occupied elsewhere.'

The King took out a small, velvet bag of money. Nathan gasped as the he handed it over to him.

'There must be over a few thousand rubies in here!' Nathan exclaimed as he opened up the bag.

He returned the bag and said, 'I don't deserve all this money!'

The King put the bag back into his hand and patted Nathan's

shoulder.

'You have given me the best gift of all: My daughter's happiness! I'm not giving you these rubies because of that. I am giving them to you because you are a great general. You never gave up and kept persisting with a humble and positive attitude.'

'You offer me too much praise, my King.'

'You always underplay your efforts. Give yourself credit for once, dear boy.' he whispered.

Nathan smiled and swiftly left the room.

The King remained where he was for a few minutes before he turned around to look out from his balcony.

He looked at the park from above. He saw Malo and Scarlet all over each other.

The King grinned while he shook his head. He looked at the other side of the park and he saw Tibuy and his wife, holding Florence.

These kind of moments made him realise that he couldn't lose the Schumy War. The results would be catastrophic. All the people he knew in the Azul Flame were kind-hearted people. He couldn't let them die. It was unthinkable.

As Scarlet made her way to her father's chambers, she found Malo waiting for her across the hallway from her chambers.

'Scarlet, is it?' he asked as he walked towards her.

'Why, yes it is! And you are?'

'My name is Malo. We may have met once or twice before. I don't know if you remember me?'

Scarlet laughed and put her hands around his neck.

'Your face does seem, somewhat familiar, but please refreshen my memory.'

With that, they kissed.

Malo then presented a flower he was hiding behind his back. It was a red flower. It was a Scarlet flower.

'I saw this and thought of you,' he said as he placed it behind her right ear.

'How do I look?' Scarlet asked as she winked at him and tilted her waist upwards.

Malo laughed and then gazed at her.

'Truly the most beautiful girl I have ever set my eyes on.'

Scarlet gave him her loving eyes and fluttered her eyelashes. 'What a line.'

'It's true. When I wake up next to you in the morning and just watch you sleep with your little mouth slightly open, I just can't imagine seeing anything else. Even if your snoring is not the most pleasant thing to listen to.'

Scarlet hit his arm. 'I do *not* snore! You snore!! Thank you very much!'

Malo laughed and shook his head. 'You don't, but you're asleep so how would you know what you do or do not do?'

'Well, what other things might I do or not do?'

Malo scratched his chin and looked into the distance with a cheeky smile. 'You may have said I love you Malo last night in your sleep?'

Scarlet leant in and stroked his hair. 'Now, that sounds much more likely!'

Oliver and Mark had finally arrived at the Seven Hundred Army Headquarters where they saw Nicolas.

'Nicolas, we are here to beg for your pardon! Our actions were repulsive, incomprehensible and we only pray for you to let us back in the army. Whatever position you give us, we will only be so grateful!' Oliver said, on one leg, looking down at the ground.

Nicolas, having just finished his training practice with other soldiers, drew out his sword, still panting from the tiresome exercises.

He placed his sword to Oliver's throat as he made him kneel to the ground. Oliver relaxed. He knew that no good would come from panicking.

'You tried to kill my sister. You humiliated me, turned the Greliks in the forest against me, plotted against me and you dare ask for my forgiveness? My time away from you has truly helped me clear my mind. Thanks to your absence, my army and I are closer. I don't have to live by your rules. I can do my daily training with the soldiers here. We learn skills from each other – help each other improve our faults. We all act as though we are all friends – we even have informal discussions! I feel like I am one of them. They like it, I like it! I haven't felt this happy and free since I can last remember!'

'You only feel happy because you feel equal to the others. You just want friends. However, for that, you must pay with your authority. Is that what you want? Jeopardize your authority just to experience having... friends?'

'Do *not* question my authority, Oliver! You can't stand the thought of me being happy. Admit it, you hate me, you despise me!' he said as he dug the sword deeper into Oliver's neck.

Oliver smiled. 'I don't hate you, Nicolas. I just sometimes think that your judgment or opinion isn't the best. I just want to help you.'

Mark, who was leaning against one of the pillars in the arena, shook his head as he was hearing Oliver's false words.

'I know where you'll be needed – in the stables! You will be a horse cleaner if you want to stay in the Army's headquarters. Every day you will have to clean the stables. We have eight hundred horses and twenty part-time horse cleaners. You can be the only one full-time!'

Oliver restrained himself from getting up and strangling Nicolas with his own bare hands. Instead, he looked up at General Avran's smug face. He forced a smile upon his own and nodded.

Nicolas drew away his sword and walked over towards Mark.

He looked down at his arm and saw the missing hand. He sighed.

'I am truly sorry about that. You didn't deserve it – he did!' Nicolas said, turning back towards Oliver who, by now, was standing up.

Mark smiled at the thought that, for once, Nicolas's stubbornness didn't get in the way of seeing what was right.

'You can be my partner, Mark. We will be equals. We will both sit next to each other, discuss matters, talk about irrelevant and relevant matters concerning the Schumy War and we will both snigger at Oliver while he cleans the horses!' General Avran said, patting Mark on the back as he walked out of the arena.

Oliver waited till everyone, including the guards, had left and walked over to Mark and whispered, 'Our plan is working. Get close to him, Mark. Find out more things about him. Find out the particular soldiers he is close to and when the time is right, we will kill them in front of him and his army. In this way, we make him so angry, he will try to kill us but we will kill him first and then it shall be *us* leading the army to the victory!'

Oliver began to walk away but then turned back to Mark. His facial expression had completely changed.

He explained, 'If I find out that you are not going along with my plan, then I shall personally kill you. Nobody will even know it was me because we are supposed to be best friends. We were practically equal in the Council, so your death would be nothing but a tragedy. Besides, I have a few more tricks up my sleeve.'

As he walked away, Mark heard his footsteps grow weaker and weaker until he no longer heard them. He closed his eyes, leant his head against the stone wall and took a deep breath. His heart was still pounding.

Athena was walking back from the main hall when she noticed Nathan was walking up from the gardens. He walked up to her, took her hand and kissed it.

'My love,' he said as he looked into her eyes. She could tell he was up to something, but since she had learnt to control her gift with the help of her father, she left his thoughts alone. She decided she would never listen to his thoughts as he deserved his own privacy.

'I want to take you somewhere.' he whispered as he kissed her on the cheek.

Athena beamed at him and let herself be taken to the terrace. He walked behind her, covering her eyes with his hands and guided her through the maze.

He was going to lead her to where they were in the picture he had shown her – the oak tree with the swing.

As he reached the swing and carefully placed her on it, he slowly took his hands away from her eyes.

'Open your eyes,' he whispered.

Athena quickly opened her eyes and gasped. The entire place was lit with the candles.

'Nathan!' she whispered as she turned to him. 'When did you do all of this?'

'Whilst you were at dinner.'

She turned back to gaze at the view. She looked up at the sky and saw the sunset.

'In the books I always used to read, there were always passages where everything was just so perfect. This is definitely one of them.'

She leant against the rope of the swing and just took a deep breath. Her heart was racing. She was overwhelmed from the fact that Nathan would surprise her like this.

Nathan walked in front of her and leant down on one knee on the grass. 'Athena, my love, will you marry me?' he whispered as he took out her hand to kiss it.

Athena swung her arms around his neck and hugged him. She caught Nathan off-guard so that they both fell backwards, her on top of him. They simply laughed.

'Yes,' she whispered back as she showered him with kisses.

Nathan stroked her back and this time, it was his turn to take a deep breath. Just like Athena, he could not be happier. He had planned this very moment over and over again in his mind. This is what helped him believe that Athena was alive and that she would one day come back. And now that she was back, it was better than he could have ever imagined.

'My love, do you know why I chose this place?'

She nodded and whispered in his ear, 'Because it's where the picture was taken.'

Nathan smiled, 'Exactly! I thought this place was perfect. In the picture, your happiness reached the heavens...figuratively speaking. I wanted to make you that happy again. And that's how happy I want to make you for the rest of your life.'

Athena sat up and lifted her hands up to the air and shouted out, 'To the Gods, I want to tell you I am the happiest I have *ever* been in my entire life. Right here, right now!'

Athena then lent down and kissed her future husband. At that moment, a soft breeze made some of the leaves from the oak tree circle around them.

'This is incredible. I feel as though this is a sign that the Gods are giving us their blessing,' Athena said with such light in her eyes. Before Nathan could even reply, the leaves that encircled them began to form a distinct trail towards the bandstand.

'I think we should go there,' Nathan said, thinking it was indeed a sign from the Gods.

He was right!

Within the next few minutes it started to pour down with rain and soon it began to thunder. Nathan picked Athena up and carried her all the way to the bandstand, running through the rain.

Once they got there, Athena, for once, had nothing to say. She just looked up at him, beaming. He smiled down at her as he wiped all the wet strands of her hair from her face. He then took something from his pocket and presented it to Athena.

'Nathan...' she began as she suddenly sat up straight.

'The usual engagement gift here from a man to a woman is a bracelet. However, I saw you at the market and I knew you would much prefer this than a bracelet, so I offer this to you as an engagement gift.'

Athena lifted her hair up and let him tie up the necklace, with all the formidable Alexandrite crystals, around her neck.

She looked back at him and leant her forehead against his and whispered, 'I love you!'

'I love you more.'

Juliet ran into her father's chambers and burst out, 'There is going to be a storm tonight, father.'

'I know,' the King said, standing on his balcony, feeling the strong breeze whip against his ageless face.

'You do know what this means?'

The King nodded, looking deep into the woods.

'Who should I send to go after him then?' she asked, desperately.

'I shall go! After all, I was the one who told him to go to the woods tonight.'

'Alone? That's ridiculous! It is getting dangerous out there father. I can protect you!'

The King turned around and smiled at his eldest daughter.

'No, my dear Juliet! You stay here and look after your sisters.'

He left his daughter and walked out of his chambers.

Juliet remained stationary. It had suddenly hit her that the war was, indeed, upon them.

'How does time go by so fast?' she whispered with a single tear running down her right cheek.

King Agalaya made his way to the Forest Tatila. The wind was picking up speed by the minute, and by the time he got to the forest, he could no longer see anything clearly.

He would have naturally panicked, but from previous experience thirteen years ago, he knew that the wind would have to eventually die out.

He suddenly had a flashback.

He and his eight-year-old daughter were near the waterfall as the storm was brewing up. It was in the middle of the night and nothing could be seen, apart from the few lights from the castle far away.

'Father, I'm terrified!' the child screamed, clinging on to her father's robe.

He patted her head.

'Do not worry, my darling, it will blow over soon,' he said, comforting her, even though he himself was absolutely terrified.

'Why is it windy? Why can't I see clearly? I think I'm turning blind!' the girl wailed, forcing her big, blue eyes wide open.

'Nature is telling us something bad is going to happen my dear Juliet! We have been given a warning. We must not ignore it. Do you understand? Do not be afraid. Nature's purpose is to help us – not frighten us.'

Juliet nodded, closed her eyes and took a deep breath. Her heart gradually stopped racing.

The wind began to die out until a small cluster of dust surrounded Juliet's knees.

The King moved back a few steps, smiling.

Juliet's eyes were still closed but she was muttering words only understood by her and her surroundings.

When she finished muttering the words, the dust stayed still in the air for a few seconds and then fell to the ground.

She slowly opened her eyes.

Her father smiled down to her. 'You have finally mastered your gift, Juliet.'

The King came back to reality as he heard explosions close by on his left.

He slowly walked towards to the explosions. Although he could not see through the mist of brown dust, there was dark-red lava emerging from the ground nearby.

He suddenly caught sight of a figure in the distant. A man in the centre of all these huge holes, with spurts of lava shooting upwards, was standing on the brown ground with his hands reaching up to the sky.

All of a sudden, lava emerged from the ground and right in front of the King. His heart began to beat faster. This Agalit was clearly out of control and Nature was not happy with the way it was being controlled.

As the King walked forwards very slowly, to make sure he wouldn't accidentally step into a hole, more and more lava burst from the ground randomly. The heat was becoming unbearable.

He closed his eyes, trying to connect with the Agalit, but the Agalit was completely out of control. He was almost in a frenzy.

'Damon, you must stop and relax. If you are in a frustrated mood, no good will come out of it!' the King yelled out, trying to be heard through all the chaos. The Agalit turned around. He was all red in the face and his piercing blue eyes were wet with tears.

'I can't stop it. I can't control it.' he yelled out.

The King continued to walk towards him with more and more lava erupting from the ground, making it almost impossible to move without being blown up.

'Get away!' the young man screamed, grabbing hold of his black hair.

The King ignored his warning and continued to proceed towards him.

'STOP!'

There were multiple explosions suddenly going off at once. The King fell to the ground as lava had erupted from the ground, left from where he was standing.

The Agalit ran towards him and knelt down. 'My King, I'm so sorry, I didn't mean to.'

The King patted Damon's hot face.

'I am immortal, I cannot die...not this way anyway.' he said as he coughed abruptly.

Damon helped him up.

'Come! I should bring you back to the castle immediately!' he said, putting the King's right shoulder around his neck.

'I am here to help you control your gift, Damon, and I am afraid neither of us *can* leave until you learn how to manage it,' he said as he pointed around them. There were huge craters surrounding them.

'Close your eyes, Damon, and think of a safe place. No worries, no fear.' the King began in a soothing voice.

Amidst his chaotic surroundings, Damon took continuous deep breaths and tried to relax.

The King put the palm of his hand on Damon's forehead and held his other hand to see what Damon was seeing.

They were both in a green meadow surrounded by orange flowers, far away from the rest of the world. Damon was barefoot and lying down. The King was standing directly above him, shading Damon's face from the brightness of the sun.

Damon closed his eyes and gentle gripped the grass. His breathing began to slow down. He was aware of all the insects on the flowers, the grass, the thin trees and the little grains of pollen in the orange flowers.

He kept inhaling and exhaling until he was completely calm. A crater slowly formed between two trees and soon enough, lava was erupting from it.

'Well done, Damon! Now, make a crater right behind me.'

Damon's heart beat suddenly began to race again.

'Do not worry. I have complete faith in you.'

Damon took one last deep breath, breathing in the smell of the sweet grass and created a crater directly behind King Agalaya. As he inhaled, lava came up from the inner core and right up to the tree tops in a perfectly straight line, ascending and descending in reaction to Damon's breathing.

'That was perfect! Try one more time and then we shall get back to reality if that's alright with you.'

Damon nodded and tried to remember the sweet smell of the orange flowers. A crater formed and he inhaled at the exact same time as the lava spurted out towards the surface. As he exhaled, the lava returned to the ground. With his last inhale, the crater disappeared completely from the ground. It was as if nothing had ever happened.

The King smiled.

Damon had finally mastered his gift.

XXIII

Scarlet suddenly woke up. She got out of bed, panting. She looked back at the bed to see Malo fast asleep with his hands behind his head.

She looked away, taking a deep breath. She then walked out onto her balcony to find Thunder on the rail of the marble balcony. She smiled as it came towards her and laughed under her breath as it licked her hand.

Something will happen.

She could sense it.

Scarlet slowly raised the palm of her hand to her forehead and rested her elbow on the marble top of the balcony. She closed her eyes peacefully. For some reason, she was shaking. She didn't feel well.

All of a sudden she threw up, followed by a coughing fit.

'What's wrong?' Malo whispered into her ear, giving Scarlet a fright.

'I... I don't know!' she cried out, finding herself in Malo's arms. 'I don't feel well and I feel as though something bad is going to happen!'

Malo kissed the top of her head and hugged her even tighter.

'What do you mean you don't feel well? Are you coming down with a fever?' he asked, touching her forehead.

Scarlet pulled back with a smile on her face. 'Scarlet fever.'

They both started laughing.

'I don't think it's a fever. Perhaps it was something you ate last night? Or nerves?' Malo suggested.

Scarlet looked away and then nodded. 'Most probably my nerves.'

'Come on, my light in shining armour. Let's go back to bed! I'll make you feel better.' Malo said, stroking her arm.

Scarlet made a feeble laugh. 'Oh no, I'm *really* going to be sick now!'

'You missed a spot!'

'Sorry.'

'You missed another spot!'

'Sorry.'

'Oh look... you missed *another* spot!'

Oliver gritted his teeth.

'I'm sorry, Nicolas.' he said, forcing a smile upon his face.

'I certainly hope so. These horses aren't going to clean themselves!'

'No, they will not.'

'Well, then, hurry up!'

'Yes, Nicolas!'

Nicolas walked away with a huge grin on his face. Nothing pleased him more than humiliating Oliver.

Oliver watched Nicolas leave and as soon as he was out of sight, he threw the wet brush onto the stone floor.

'I hate this.' he whispered to himself.

'Hate what?' Mark asked, walking towards him, smiling.

'*This*!' Oliver snapped, pointing towards all his cleaning materials, including the apron he was forced to wear.

'Wait, this *wasn't* part of your diabolic plan?' Mark asked, trying not to laugh.

'Well... yes it is, but-'

'Then why are you complaining? As far as I'm concerned, Nicolas doesn't suspect a thing!'

He lowered his voice and crouched down to Oliver. 'The army leaves tomorrow for the Four Flames. You only have to put up with this for just a few more hours. I am sure you can cope, so stop complaining!'

Oliver sighed and picked up the brush.

'You're right. You are always right!' he muttered to himself.

'By the way...' Mark started.

Oliver turned to him.

'You missed a spot.' Mark said, grinning and pointing at a particular place.

Oliver's face remained motionless while Mark was laughing away. After a few seconds, Mark handed over a piece of paper.

'I wrote this down for you. It explains where and when we meet. If our plan is going to work, then you better do every last thing on that list!' Mark said, now serious. Oliver looked up at him with an evil smile and nodded.

'Nicolas, the pretty young lady is to see you,' a soldier said as he walked into Nicolas's room.

'She is late. Well, send her in!' he said.

'Of course,' the guard replied after they had a knuckle shake.

A young woman walked into his room with a dark hood covering her face.

'Hello.' he began.

The young woman looked somewhere else as though he wasn't there.

Nicolas, said in a rather frustrated voice, 'You are late!'

'You should know by now, Nicolas, that time has never been on my side. We have been working together for seven years, have we not?'

'And finally the day we have been waiting for has arrived!' he finished.

She removed her hood and smiled.

'The day we've both been waiting for, brother!'

'Gemma, have you seen Juliet today? I was supposed to have a little talk with her before dinner!' the King asked.

Gemma could sense the worry in his voice.

'No, father! In fact, I have noticed that Juliet has been acting differently ever since Athena arrived.'

The King laughed. 'How do you mean? Athena and Juliet have been getting along very well!'

'Yes, I know, but don't you find it bizarre how ever since Athena has arrived, Juliet has... never mind.'

She started to walk off and stopped when she heard her father say her name. She smiled before she turned around to him.

'Wait! Ju – Gemma, I mean. Tell me what you want to say.'

Gemma took her time to answer. 'Well, it's just that Juliet has always liked Nathan.'

'What? General Lamber?' the King asked, slightly confused.

'Yes.'

'Are you sure? She has never mentioned this to me before. I really have difficulty believing that actually, Gemma.'

'You are our father! Of course she won't talk to *you* about it! She only talks to me about this subject.'

The King stroked his chin. 'Continue.'

'Well, ever since Athena and Nathan have gotten intimate, Juliet has been mentally and emotionally wounded. I notice she talks to herself nowadays and it's not natural father. Also, she... she has many secrets!'

'Are they serious?'

'Would you like me to tell them to you?' Gemma asked, wanting him eagerly to say yes.

'No!' he firmly said after a minute or so.

'If she wanted to tell me, then she would have done so by now. However, she has not. I shall respect her decision.'

For a moment, Gemma had a look of hatred on her face but then immediately changed it to her sweet, naive look.

'Listen, Ju – Gemma, I must go now but I am glad we had this little talk.' he said as he quickly kissed her on the cheek.

She remained still as he left her in the corridor.

'So am I, father. So am I!'

'Where is it?' Juliet repeated to herself, throwing all the books off her shelf.

'Where are you?' she repeated over and over again.

'Looking for this?'

Juliet turned to the figure who had suddenly appeared at her door, holding the very object she had been searching for.

'Why did you take it?' Juliet hissed, striding towards her.

'I walked into your room the other day and found it under your bed.' Gemma replied blankly.

Juliet's eyes widened. 'You looked under my bed? Why? You aren't even allowed in my chambers without my permission!'

'So?'

'So, you are going to get into a lot of trouble! Wait till I tell father!' Juliet said, snatching the book off Gemma's hand, starting to walk out.

'I wouldn't do that, Juliet! That journal has very interesting facts... theories... secrets...' Gemma said, smiling as she played with her hair.

'You read the *entire* journal? You didn't just take it to be annoying?' Juliet asked, slowly turning around, shaking as she held the huge book in her hands.

'Oh yes! I have plenty of time these days and if you tell father about me going into your room, well let's just say I think I can come up with things much worse from *that*!' she said pointing to the journal.

'You wouldn't!' Juliet gasped, dropping the book to the ground.

'Well, actually, I already have! I had a little talk with father this morning – oh, he's looking for you by the way. Anyway, I told him about your secrets.'

Juliet laughed, fighting back the tears.

'You are cruel but you are not that cruel. We have never been close and since that revolt thirteen years ago...'

Juliet broke off into a sob. 'You hate me!'

Gemma looked down at the floor. She hated being in awkward situations and this was certainly one of them.

'How did father react when you told him my secrets which I have *never* told *anybody*? Tell me! HOW DID HE REACT?' Juliet screamed, falling to her knees.

Gemma sighed.

'He didn't! Even if *all* your secrets were exposed at the same time, he wouldn't react at all! You're his favourite. You always have been.' Gemma said as she walked out.

'Gemma!' Juliet began as she ran after her sister but she could no longer see her.

Gemma hid behind the stairway. Her heart was still pounding and she could feel tears coming to her eyes. She knew about Juliet's biggest secret. For years now. The only reason why she wanted to tell her father about it now was because very soon, her own secret would be revealed.

'I am no better than her,' she whispered to herself.

'Are you alright, Lady Gemma?' an old servant suddenly asked.

Gemma quickly turned around to wipe the tears from her face and turned back again.

'Of course I'm alright! Don't you have floorboards to scrub?' Gemma snapped as she walked back to her chambers.

'Are you sure you are alright?' Athena asked Scarlet as they were walking along the gardens.

Scarlet nodded and made a weak smile. 'I think I was just sick this morning because I woke up with the worst feeling. In my mind, I heard a voice say *something will happen* and from the tone, I know it has to be something bad. I'm just afraid that someone close to us will die. I'm terrified, Athena.'

Athena didn't know what to reply. Of course, it would be inevitable that someone close to Scarlet would die. The question was who?

'I know for one thing that it won't be father,' Scarlet said in a positive way. Athena smiled.

'I think that this voice in your head is one that is trying to cause harm and malice. Probably an Agalit from the Seven Hundred Army. I'm not sure, but what I do know is that you can't let it get to you. If you feel defeated or even worried, then something bad *will* happen. You just need to believe that everything will be okay.'

Scarlet hugged Athena as they sat down by the water fountain with the statue of the nymph.

'A little bird told me that someone got engaged last night?' Scarlet asked, winking repeatedly at her little sister.

Athena gave the biggest of smiles and pushed her long hair behind her shoulders to show her necklace, 'It was perfect, Scarlet. I felt as if my heart was going to burst out of my chest. I feel like since I've spent a lot of time with him the last few weeks, my happiness has reached another level.'

Scarlet just looked at her little sister with such a brightness in her eyes.

'It warms my heart so much knowing this has happened. I always *knew* it, Athena, from the beginning. I knew you were the right one for Nathan. Over the past few years, girls have tried to catch Nathan's eye. None interested him. He became a brother to us. We all missed you and Nicolas. We grieved together and grew up together. We managed to be happy through all that misery because father convinced us that you would return. We just had to be patient.'

Scarlet then stroked Athena's face. 'Even though you are much older now, your face hasn't changed. You still have your beautiful eyes and smile.'

Athena felt her heart beat faster. How different her entire life would have been if she had stayed.

Scarlet could see that Athena was deep in her thoughts, so said something she knew would lift her sister's spirit.

'Do you remember the night you met Nathan… again?'

'Yes. It was by the waterfall with the little birds.'

'Do you know why Nathan happened to be in that secluded area of the gardens? Because I sent him there. Todd flew into my room that evening and told me you were on the swing. I ran to Nathan's chambers and told him.

He wanted to see you so desperately, but he could never find the right time. He was also incredibly excited and nervous to see you again. Can you imagine? Thirteen years of waiting for you and finally the day arrives. It is bound to feel surreal.

Anyway, I told him you were on the swing and immediately, his eyes widened. I could see, after telling him many times where you were and many times him replying it wasn't the perfect time, this was it!

He came up to me and hugged me and told me he was going to see his little Athena. I could feel his heart beating very fast. He was so anxious to meet you. I had to slap him in the face to calm him down!'

Athena laughed.

Scarlet was going to continue but she saw Malo walk up to them.

'My sweetheart,' he said as he kissed Scarlet's head. Scarlet beamed up at him but then felt that sudden tightness in her stomach.

'I think I am going to be sick again. I need a lie down,' Scarlet said as she held her stomach. She slowly stood up. Malo was about to get up as well.

'Please, Malo, stay here! I don't want you to witness what I am about to do.'

With that, she turned to Athena and gave her a fragile smile and then slowly walked away, thinking of her big, comfortable bed.

Malo turned to Athena with a worried face. 'I'm afraid for her, dear Athena. Why is she feeling like this?'

Athena shrugged her shoulders, 'I don't know. All I know is that Scarlet is the most sensitive person I have met. She is physically sick because of the war. I know she is terrified by the thought of losing you.'

Malo sighed. His eyes were immediately distracted by the necklace around Athena's neck.

'That is the most beautiful necklace I have ever seen,' he said as he touched it and had a closer look at the unique gemstone.

'It changes colour, Malo! Isn't that incredible? Nathan gave it to me when he asked me to marry him.'

Malo didn't move. He just simply stared at Athena for a few moments. Athena looked at him with a mysterious smile and asked, 'what are you thinking, Malo?'

'You tell me!'

'I have controlled my gift now. I don't want to go into your mind because you deserve your own privacy.'

Malo continued to look at her. Suddenly, he smiled and hugged her very tightly.

'My dear, little Athena is growing up. I feel like I have something to do with this engagement. You're welcome!'

Athena laughed. 'Why?'

'Well, I showed you the way here. If it weren't for me, you would have ended up in the headquarters of the army because of Olimm. Or if that didn't happen, you would have been caught by the Striberosse. I helped you through all those dangers.'

'You have certainly saved my life more than once, that is for sure!' Athena said as she looked him in the eyes. 'I love you, Malo, like a very dear friend. You have done so much for me and I only hope that you are as happy as I am at this moment.'

Malo took her hand and kissed it. 'We have both come here and found what we were looking and were destined for. I can see from that look in your eyes that you are in love. I have never seen that yet in you. I feel like I am your father, seeing you grow up like this. And I couldn't be more proud!' he said as he pretended to cry.

They sat there for a few moments in silence, thinking of how far they had to come to get to that bench they were now sitting on. It almost felt surreal to them both. Was it possible to be this happy?

Malo laughed to himself.

'What?' Athena asked, grinning.

Malo shook his head. 'It's just... I had an interesting conversation with a few soldiers from your father's army the other day, and one of them asked me why you and I never fell in love.'

Athena felt her ears burn up. 'What did you respond?'

'I told them,' Malo began as he held her hand, 'that I loved you and felt very protective over you, but I always saw you as a sister. A daughter at other times, especially when you told me you couldn't swim, but a sister most of the time. And would you look at that? Soon, we will be related! All this to say, I adore you my dear Athena! I wouldn't have changed a moment of our hectic journey. Everything happens for a reason, you know?'

Athena gave him an endearing look and lunged on him to give the biggest of hugs.

'Now, tell me how he asked you then!' Malo said as he beamed down at her.

Athena gladly began to tell him the story.

'Todd?'

Todd peeped through his peep-hole in the beautifully carved cage Malo had made him.

'I know I don't understand you but I know that you understand me, so can you please come out here?'

Todd willingly flew out of the cage and looked Malo straight between the eyes.

'I am going to ask Scarlet to marry me.'

Todd chirped a wedding tune and flapped his wings in delight.

Malo chuckled, 'Exactly! I have a little problem though. I haven't made enough preparations. You see, I want it to be perfect for her. She only deserves the best! In case I don't have a chance to see you again, and also I don't want to mention anything to Scarlet as it's a surprise, can you tell her to come to the waterfall tomorrow evening? I will wait for her there. I know she doesn't like things done the conventional way so I bought her a ring instead of a bracelet. Do you think she will that?'

Todd nodded.

Malo smiled and began to walk away, but Todd quickly flew in front of him and placed his wing onto Malo's cheek.

'Thank you.' Malo whispered.

'Mark! Mark come here!' Oliver hissed, gesturing Mark to go over to him.

Mark casually walked over to him. 'Our secret weapon is here!'

Mark's eyes widened. 'Here? In the headquarters?'

'Well, not anymore. She was talking with Nicolas this morning.'

'But... she...' Mark began but was too confused.

Oliver rolled his eyes, 'I told her that Nicolas and I were no longer on good terms. Besides, months ago, I knew something like this was going to happen so I warned her in advance. She promised me that no matter what, she would always be on my side. I spoke to her privately last night and she is up-to-date with our...diabolical plan as you call it.'

Mark shook his head. 'So everyone is against Nicolas now! His sister, you, me.'

'Come on, Mark. Don't feel bad. He has the army and besides,' Oliver said, patting Mark's shoulder, 'he brought it upon himself! He has no one to blame but himself for his own downfall.'

Oliver returned back to the stables. He only had an hour left of his scrubbing. After that, he would prepare everything for the night ahead.

The war was going to start as soon as the sun raised itself from under the horizon. In the Prophecy, it was written:

And the soldiers who shall rise from the darkness of the Earth
Will ride to the Flames before dawn
And will be seen on the top of the hill
As the sun will be directly behind them
Slowly raising itself as the army descends

Only one day this war shall last
But the day that will decide the
Rule and Fate of
Fairoses

Mark shuddered. How could he let this happen to Nicolas? He was, after all, only a child.

The Greliks assembled together near the river bank. This was the first time they were doing so and indeed, the last time. The leader of the Greliks looked out to his family.

We all stand here side by side tonight. Tomorrow, we are going to fight with our King. He has given us our space and freedom for the last few centuries. I am sure our ancestors would agree with us that he is the right man to follow.

The Greliks looked among themselves and nodded with agreement.

We, Greliks, do not like being involved in wars and conflicts. We like to be left alone and being independent. However, whenever trouble strikes one of us, we all come to the rescue.

This war has been written centuries ago. It has been known through all the ages that this day would come and to our dismay, we are the ones who are going to have to endure it, but we cannot fail our ancestors by simply walking away without helping. We must fight and sadly, fight to the death. We all hear each other and feel each other's emotions, happiness, pain and grief. We will be there for one another tomorrow.

This is what we will do…

The Grelik continued and shared his ideas to the hundreds of Greliks standing before him.

'Father, you wanted to see me?' Juliet asked as she shyly walked into her father's chambers.

'My dear! Yes, I want to see you. Where have you been all day? I looked for you everywhere this afternoon!' the King replied in his usual gentle voice, sitting in his armchair close to the fireplace.

Juliet walked over to the armchair opposite his and sat down, fidgeting with her fingers.

The King leant over and touched her hand.

'What is wrong?'

'Gemma told me she had a little talk with you today.'

The King slowly nodded, looking deep into her eyes.

'I was wondering what she might have told you?' Juliet asked, in a very soft voice.

'She told me that you have not been yourself lately. She fears that you are hurting because of your love for Nathan!'

Juliet remained completely still for a moment and then sighed with relief.

'That's all she said? Are you sure?' Juliet said, smiling.

The King, too, smiled.

'Yes! That is all she said, my dear. Is there anything you would like to tell me? Anything at all?'

Juliet hesitated for a moment. Should she risk the relationship she had with her father just to get the guilt off her shoulders? Or should she just suffer in silence like she had done all these years?

'No, father. Everything is fine apart from the war tomorrow and a risk that people close to me might die...'

The King kissed Juliet on the forehead.

'You have always been brave, my dear...just like your mother,' the King whispered.

Juliet looked away and before the King could say anything, she reached for the door handle. As she left, she closed her eyes and lit a fire in the fireplace. She then walked out.

The King sat down in his armchair and stared at the fireplace. He looked deep in the flames and had a flashback from the time he used to go down to the markets to keep a good relation with the community.

'I'm sorry, sir, you dropped your oranges! Sorry about the colour but the skin is brown because they were left on the ground,' a teenage girl said as she brought the oranges she had picked up to the man. She wiped the dirt off them with her hands and revealed their bright orange colour. However, the last orange she wiped was actually a red-blood one.

He suddenly turned around and immediately knew: it was her.

'Thank you, my dear. I love red oranges and their taste, though they are quite rare to come across. Sorry about me talking on and on. Tell me, what is your name?'

'Amber, sir! I am a daughter of the stall owner. I work here and hold the stall for him while he is away.'

'Where is he now?'

'I do not know! I know he is with my mother. That is all. I do this regularly, you see. They leave a note on my pillow on the morning of their unexpected departure, telling me when they will be back and for me to behave and to look after the stall properly.'

'Well, then, you better go back to your stall, otherwise, I should have to tell on you!' he said, grinning.

The girl smiled as well and then rushed back to her stall.

He looked at her. She was probably around sixteen, no younger. As he walked away, the girl stopped running and turned back to look at him.

The next day it was pouring down with rain, but he still came back to buy more oranges. However, Amber was not there. In fact, the wooden stall was completely closed off. He looked everywhere but she was nowhere in sight.

'I'm sorry, my King, are you looking for someone?' an old woman asked, tugging at his cloak.

'As a matter of fact, I am! That stall over there,' he said pointing towards Amber's stall. 'Where are the owners or that young lady who ran it yesterday?'

'I am sorry, my King, but the owners died years ago. The young girl, Amber, left the stall yesterday. In fact, almost immediately after you left! Haven't seen her since.'

He looked down, feeling the heavy rain fall harshly on the top of his neck.

'I am sorry, my King. If I had known she was of some importance to you, I would have stopped her myself!'

The King remained silent.

'What is a poor orphan girl like her to you anyway?' the old woman continued.

The King smiled at the woman, thanked her for the information and returned to the castle straightaway.

He threw his cloak on his bed and fell back into his armchair – the very one he was sitting on right now.

'Where is she?' he murmured to himself.

For the next few days, the King disguised himself so that no one would recognise him and casually passed Amber's stall. It was almost a week until she returned.

As he anxiously waited in line to buy fruit, he popped his head out of the straight line and met her eyes.

She quickly looked away, smiling. It was finally his turn to buy fruit.

At first they just stared at each other. Him into her blue eyes and her, into his deep blue eyes. They were then interrupted by a grumpy old man in the queue telling them to get a move on.

'What can I get you, sir?' she suddenly asked, still smiling and looking into his eyes.

'Sixteen oranges, please!'

'Just like my age,' Amber muttered to herself. She bent down and looked under the counter to find the bag with the many red oranges she had spent so long finding over the last couple of days.

'Here you go. Sixteen red oranges,' she said, handing the bag over to him.

'Red oranges. But these are so rare! Wait... that's what you were doing, wasn't it? Finding them?'

Amber shrugged her shoulders.

'Hurry up!' a man from the accumulating queue yelled out.

'I... I don't have any money on me,' he said, realising he left all of it in his chambers as he wasn't sure he'd see her.

'It's fine. It is a gift.' Amber said in her low, soothing voice.

'No, it's not fine! Come to my home and have dinner with me. Tonight at six o'clock?'

Amber nodded and waved as he left.

'Wait... I don't know where you live!' she called out, but it was too late. He was too far away to hear her.

'I will have the same oranges please!' an old man said, as he slapped some rubies onto the wooden counter.

'Sorry. They are all gone.' Amber truthfully replied.

'Oh, I forgot! The King gets everything he wants and not us commoners.' the old man snapped.

'Wait... that man was the King?' Amber gasped. She genuinely had no idea.

'At least I know where he lives.' she muttered to herself.

'What was that, girl?' the old man asked.

'Nothing, here are some ordinary oranges. Free of charge!'

'My King, the young lady is here to dine with you,' the King's advisor said, grinning as he entered the King's chambers.

'Excellent! Thank you, Mark.' he said as he stood up. He took a deep breath as Amber walked in.

She had washed her face and brushed her long beautiful blonde hair. She wore a light blue dress to match her eyes and she smiled as he kissed her hand.

They dined in his chambers and had the most enjoyable time. After the fifth dish went out, they both laid back on their big chairs, both feeling full.

'I don't remember ever eating that much!' she said as she put her hands on her big stomach. 'In fact, I don't think I've ever eaten that much!'

The King leant back and gradually a frown crossed his face.

'Why did you lie to me? About your parents? I know they passed away many years ago.'

'Why ask me if you already know the truth?'

'I didn't know at the beginning. It was only the next day that somebody told me.'

Amber smiled. He had come back to see her.

'Why did you lie?' he whispered.

'I didn't want you to feel sorry for me. I don't want pity just because my parents are dead! I want to be treated like everyone else and when that man in the queue behind told me who you were, I felt-'

'You didn't know who I was?' he asked quickly.

She shook her head, 'I had absolutely no idea! When you told me to come to your home tonight, I didn't know where to go until a man told me you were the King.'

He smiled inside. She didn't agree to come here because he was King but because...because she wanted to!

'How old are you?' she suddenly asked, breaking the silence.

'Well, you see, I'm an Agalit so I have-'

'If you don't mind me asking, what's an Agalit?'

'You don't know what an Agalit is? You have blue eyes though. You are an Agalit yourself.'

Amber looked at him with a bit of shame. 'People have told me I am an Agalit but have never told me what it actually means. They seemed rather angry about it so I never pressed on with the subject.'

'Well, Agalits are slightly different to humans. We look the same and we act the same and we do everything the same except that Agalits have blue eyes and green blood. Each Agalit has their own, unique power.'

'What's your power?'

'It's not really a power. It's immortality, but I won't live forever. In my case, it means just living for a millennium –a thousand years.'

Amber's heart missed a beat. He would continue living while she would die. She was suddenly upset.

'How old are you?' she asked once again, fighting the tears back.

'Six hundred and forty seven years old.'

She nodded and then made a laugh, unable to hide how uncomfortable she felt.

'You look no older than forty though!'

He looked down and sighed.

'What's your name?'

'Kendin.'

Amber smiled, raising her rosy cheeks, exposing her dimples.

She began to tell him the most important story of her life. A few days before her parents died, she had her fortune read by a fortune teller who needed a place to stay for the night. Her parents allowed her to spend the night in their house which was in the middle of nowhere, deep inside the county of Clandon. Instead of paying money, she promised to tell them their fortune.

After both her parents came out of her room with very worried faces, she went in and closed the door.

'Amber, darling! What would you like me to tell you?' she asked, wiping tears away from her black cheeks.

'I want to know if I will get married and have children and what the name of my husband will be and what–'

'Alright, alright! Let me see,' she began. Out of her small brown leather bag, she took out many pieces of small, smooth pebbles. On some pebbles, a letter was engraved in capitals and on others, numbers.

'You would like to know if you will get married?'

Amber nodded with enthusiasm.

'Very well.'

She drew all the pebbles into both her hands and threw them onto the table. Amber watched them fall with amazement and when they touched the table, all the pebbles were facing downwards, apart from three – YES

Amber smiled as she read the word over and over again.

'Now, darling, you want to know how many children you will have?'

Amber smiled and nodded, greedily awaiting the answer.

Once again, the black woman drew all the pebbles into her hands and once again, Amber watched them drop on the table in awe.

All the pebbles faced downwards, apart from one – 5

'Five children? That's an awful lot, isn't it?' Amber asked.

'It depends on how much you love your husband.' the woman replied with a cheeky smile, drawing the pebbles back to her.

'Okay, darling, one more and then time for bed!' she said with a kind smile and all the pebbles in her hands, ready to be thrown once more.

Amber paused for a moment and then asked her question.

'What will the name of my husband be?' she asked seriously.

The black woman threw the pebbles into the air and the pebbles flew for the last time.

KENDIN.

'Kendin! That's a nice name,' Amber beamed.

'Come on, darling. Time for bed.' the fortune teller said as she got up from her chair.

'No! Can't I have one more go? Please!' Amber begged, fluttering her long eyelashes and showing off her big blue eyes.

'No, darling! Come on, let's go to sleep!'

Amber unwillingly got up from her chair and dragged her feet to the door.

The woman walked Amber to the door. She hesitated for one moment but then quickly kissed Amber on the cheek.

'You will be happy one day, my darling. Trust me!' she whispered.

Amber only understood what she meant a few days later. Losing both her parents was devastating. The only thing that kept her going on with her life was knowing that she would one day be happy again.

One day.

And here she was – facing her future husband, who was the King of Fairoses, and together they would have five children.

Amber told him all of this and he listened intently, now certain that she was the one he had been waiting for.

She suddenly got up and tucked her chair behind her. He, too, stood up.

For a moment, they just gazed at each other and then moments later, Amber hugged him tightly. For a moment, he thought she would never let him go. That was how tight her grasp was.

The next few weeks, he went to her stall twice a day and they would talk until some angry person in the queue would tell them to hurry up.

He invited her to dinner every night during those two weeks of talking, laughing and telling each other stories. He had many, many stories to tell!

Finally, he plucked up the courage and asked her to marry him with the most beautiful bracelet he found.

She, of course, said yes.

After the wedding they would spend their evenings talking, their hands intertwined.

'So, tell me about the Schumy War!' she whispered, kissing his neck.

'How do you know about the Schumy War?'

'Well, seeing that I am now married to the King, I must know a bit about history.'

He laughed.

'It's supposed to take place a thousand years after the prophecy was written so... it's in twenty five years! Wow, it's so soon,' he said, scratching his head.

'Kendin, I promise you, I will be right there,' she said as she pointed to her armchair that was opposite his by the fireplace. 'I will be there the night before that war, and we will talk about this very moment! I promise you, I will be right there with you, sweetheart.'

She leant in and kissed him.

'I love you!' he whispered.

'And I love you more than you can ever imagine!' she said, smiling, her heart aching.

The King suddenly awoke from his flashback and was about to talk to his Amber opposite him, but his smile went away as quickly as it came.

The armchair was empty and unstoppable tears fell from his ageless cheeks.

No one had ever understood why he waited so long to marry someone. However, he knew that she was going to be the only one for him.

He knew Scarlet had the same heart and passion and love for Malo as he did for Amber. For her to finally be with her soulmate gave Kendin the energy he needed to rise from his armchair.

Oliver and Mark spoke to each other after the 'Last dinner', as Nicolas wanted to call it.

'Oliver, you can stop avoiding Nicolas. It was part of the deal – you clean and then you will be part of the invasion!'

'That *wasn't* the plan, Mark.'

'I changed his mind. I made him believe that you were really good and everything you did in the past was because you loved him like your own son!'

Oliver stared at Mark and groaned deeply.

'Come on, Nicolas is holding the 'Last council' before the soldiers leave in a few hours.'

'I don't understand where that boy comes up with all these names. Last dinner. Last training. Last rest. It's not like we are all going to die!'

'They are going to be exhausted. Dawn is only in a few short hours. They will only have a maximum of an hours sleep!' Mark continued, ignoring Oliver.

Oliver leant on Mark's shoulder and said, 'It's what they've expected ever since they joined the army. It's their problem.'

He walked off.

The 'Last council' was held in the arena. All seven hundred soldiers were either standing or sitting on some of the marble pillars which had been deliberately knocked onto the ground.

Nicolas was standing on top of the mosaic where the tips of the two swords met. The palms of his hands were sweating. He looked around and saw he was completely surrounded. The important people he had assigned, including Oliver, were all sitting on a circular marble bench in front of all the soldiers.

'Thank you all for coming. We should get right down to business. We all leave in a few hours, three to be precise, and we ride to that hill. I have done some research and it turns out that "that hill", the one written in the Prophecy, is actually the river bank close to the Naran Flame. It's very steep and we have to cross a river, so I know that is definitely the place we are destined to reach.

Anyway, we will get Sedty to go to the Naran Flame. He will break the force shield once and for all. I have already informed the Chamcoks in the Naran Flame when we will be arriving there. They have agreed to help us. Of course they would. They're nothing without us!'

The laughing and cheering of the soldiers made the ground shake.

Mark was rather puzzled at how Nicolas was talking. He was usually strong and assertive and always knew *exactly* what he was going to say, but for some reason he seemed somewhat relaxed.

'I will then give a speech to all the soldiers and tell them that we need to win this... this war.'

Oliver smiled and nudged Mark.

'No, little Nicolas, I will be giving the speech, with your head in my right hand,' Oliver murmured as he sniggered.

'All the practice you have done over the last few years? Well, it all comes down to this. This is what you have been training hard for, every single day.

After this victory, if you choose to come back to the army, you will be assigned a place in one of the Four Flames. I, personally, will take charge of the castle in the Azul Flame.

From tomorrow forth, the whole of Fairoses will live under *our* rule!'

There was a loud uproar in the crowd and everyone, including the few remaining members from the Council, stood up and applauded.

Oliver, however, remained seated and watched everybody around him, to his horror, support Nicolas.

'Perhaps not all of them will stand him being killed tomorrow!' he said quietly.

'All the women, children and men who aren't fighting are safely and comfortably sleeping in the underground cave of the Azul Flame.'

Nathan lowered his voice, 'the only way into the cave is through a secret passageway in the gardens. There are five loose rocks, surrounding one of the many big fountains. It is big enough for five people to go in at once. Nobody else knows about this – apart from your family and Malo. I hope we can keep it this way because if the enemy were to ever find out that particular opening, everyone in the caves will be killed without mercy.'

The King nodded and patted Nathan on the shoulder.

'Tomorrow is going to be a long day,' he murmured to himself.

The King nodded. He didn't speak yet as Nathan wasn't finished.

'It's strange, isn't it? The biggest war that these lands have ever witnessed is going to last only one day? It seems too short for there to be a drastic change.'

The King went to sit on his throne and took a deep breath, 'I have sat on this very throne for over half a millennia. One would think that during that time there have been many wars in these lands but the truth is, there has never been unrest in Fairoses. We are known to be one of the most peaceful lands in this world. The first outbreak came thirteen years ago when the Chamcoks decided to revolt. They didn't have a purpose though. They just wanted to destroy where they could get the most wealth – the castle. They caused a lot of devastation and many people lost their lives that day. It was neither a battle nor a war. It was a massacre.

There has been tension in the air since that day though, and now the Seven Hundred Army has declared war. For two reasons: it is destined and because they want to destroy the Agalits. That is their purpose. They want to take the throne, rule the lands and eliminate all the Agalits. Even though they create their own to make the army stronger for tomorrow, they will be returned to their normal human state after all this. Truthfully, dear boy, that is what gives me the most anxiety. All my children have a key role tomorrow. My daughters, especially, will be prime targets.'

XXIV

Nathan kissed Athena's shoulder as he slipped out of bed. He took one last glance at her before he left.

'Please don't wake up, please don't wake up!' he kept thinking to himself as he quietly crept to the door.

Athena turned around and looked at him and said, 'too late!'

He smiled and jumped back into bed. She leant her head against his shoulder.

'I want today to happen so fast.' she whispered.

'I know!' he whispered back as he kissed her head. 'We are going to have to face it though.'

He kissed his biceps which made Athena laugh.

She looked him deep in the eyes. 'Both of us will be fine. I know it!'

Nathan leant in to kiss her.

'I know it too,' he whispered.

The King had slept in his armchair all night and woke up as the last flame burnt out.

He stared at the armchair opposite him, imagining that both he and his Amber were talking, when a guard came into his chambers.

'My King! They have arrived at the river bank! They are now heading towards the Naran Flame.'

'To collect the Chamcoks!' the King muttered to himself.

The guard remained silent.

'Get the general and order him to assemble the soldiers in the training arena.'

'Yes, my King!' the guard said and with that, he set off straight away to Athena's chambers.

'I don't want you to go!' Scarlet cried, grabbing Malo so tightly, he actually had difficulty putting her back on the bed.

'Listen, Scarlet, I *have* to go! And so do you. You, Athena, Gemma and Juliet have to all get together. If you are all together, you then have a better chance of helping everyone.'

'You don't understand, I have a bad feeling. A really bad feeling. I will never forgive myself if I let you go and you die!'

Scarlet was about to continue, but then quickly rushed to the bathroom to throw up.

She came back out with her eyes all wet and her hair all tangled.

'I am so scared of losing you Malo, it's actually making me sick!' she said, with tears streaming down her cheeks.

Malo walked towards her and looked her deep in the eyes.

'Stop it, Scarlet. You have to be brave!'

He kissed her on the forehead and then headed to the door.

Scarlet, however reached it first and blocked his way.

'I don't want you to go!' she wailed as she hugged him.

Malo sighed. He tried to fight back the tears that were beginning to form. Seeing Scarlet this upset broke his whole being. If she was unhappy, then he was unhappy. He had to make sure she was on top form that way he could fight his best.

He took her hand and led her to the bed. He sat her down on his lap and held her hand.

'Listen! Tomorrow morning, you are going to wake up with me right beside you. Everything will be over – the war, the evil and you being sick. We're going to spend the rest of our lives together and I wouldn't have it any other way. I love you! And then we will live somewhere far away, just you and me and our children. I always wanted to call my boy Jack and my girl Rebecca.

I have always kept this to myself. I will tell you now though, so you understand how serious I am about us. I have always envisaged the next chapter of my life with you and our cheeky children living in a big house, surrounded by vineyards and hundreds of acres of green land. I wish for nothing more. And I am going to fight today so you can have that vision as well and live it out with me,' he said as he kissed her.

'Jack and Rebecca. Scarlet, Malo, Jack and Rebecca, all living in a small castle where we, the adults will try out the wine whilst the children play and chase pigs. It sounds perfect!' Scarlet whispered, laughing.

Malo wiped the tears from her eyes, trying his hardest not to cry as well. He had to be strong for her.

Sedty, along with Nicolas, Mark and Oliver all proceeded towards the Naran Flame exactly on time.

All the Chamcoks were assembled in single file, in many rows, forming an exact square.

'Very organised,' Mark said, rather impressed.

'We have not slept this night! All the soldiers are keen to fight. The ones who were... less keen than the others have been killed.' the general of the Chamcoks said with no emotion in his voice.

Oliver gulped. The way the Chamcoks dealt with traitors was known throughout the land. Nobody dared speak of it but everyone knew. They would take out all the organs of their traitors without any form of anaesthesia. That was one of many methods. Oliver couldn't even bring himself to think of the others.

'They are each fully equipped with at least two years training. To get this far, to be standing here right now, each and every one of them have had to kill one man in their duels fought to the death. Our army would have been doubled if they were not killed in single combat, but we want the best, so we have the best.' the general concluded.

Nicolas nodded. He was mildly impressed but didn't dare show it. The general gave the impression he was superior to everyone else. Why add to his ego?

'I am sure that will suffice.' he said.

The general of the Chamcoks nodded in satisfaction and whistled loudly, signalling the soldiers to assemble by the entrance of the mountain.

Mark smiled smugly at Oliver as he followed the soldiers. *Oliver is going to get into so much trouble, he has no idea.*

'Listen up, soldiers! These are the Blucks! All of them have trained incredibly hard for this day, so you are all going to get along!

We all have one aim: to destroy the people of the Flames. We hate them, despise them. For years, we have been living close to each other yet we have not exchanged one kind word to one another. They think they are above us.

They are *wrong*. We are above *them*! And when we win this war, we will show that clearly. They will be begging for our mercy as our swords touch their neck, and they will be regretting the fact that they have ignored our very existence for the past thirteen years. It is time for payback!'

There was a huge uproar from the one thousand soldiers, both from the Blucks and the Chamcoks.

The general grimaced as he saw his speech was a success. He knew he was the dominant one and knew that when they were to win, Nicolas was going to want all the glory to himself.

'But I'm not going to let that happen!' the general said to himself.

Nicolas knew what the general of the Chamcoks was thinking.

'Not a chance, you barbarian! I lived here. This was *my* home before you took it!' he said, snarling, but due to the loud uproar still continuing, his words were not heard.

Nicolas waved his hands to make the army stop and listen to his speech.

'Too long have we waited for this day. For centuries we have all known what is going to hit us today. For centuries, everyone has known about this day, but no one knows how it will be tomorrow. Today, we re-write history and tomorrow we write the future. It is up to us, right now and right here, to decide the country's fate. It is up to *all* of us!'

Nicolas spoke with such passion in his words, not a single soldier dared breathe.

Even Oliver was mesmerized, but as soon as Nicolas stopped speaking, he shook his head and returned to reality.

Oliver suddenly walked over and stood beside Nicolas, putting his hand around Nicolas's shoulders.

'Yes, soldiers! We will be led by this man and this man only. However, we must not forget we have our own weapons which will help us win this war. Gentlemen, I give you our very own Agalits!'

He pointed towards the Agalits, with Sedty in front of them all with a huge grin on his face.

'Our scientists have the technology and talent to change the power of the Agalit we kill to whatever power we desire. Sedty is the strongest man in the world. He can break the unbreakable with a simple punch. This man will be the one to break the force shield!'

There were murmurs going through the crowd of Chamcoks.

A Chamcok soldier called out, 'If we want to destroy the Agalits, why make our own?'

Oliver held out his hand and ordered silence.

'We want to match them on every level. We want to fight them with the very thing that has kept them ruling for hundreds of years- Power. Magic. Agalits. Now, with Sedty's unmatchable strength, it will certainly be a match against all their powers combined. Does that answer your question?'

The soldier nodded and those around him sniggered slightly.

Oliver continued.

'To win this war, not only do we need help from the outside, but also from the inside. This is General Avran's beloved sister. No one knows about her helping us which will make it even easier for us to get into the caves where all the children and women are. King Agalaya would never suspect his darling daughter to help the enemy, would he now?' Oliver said, now with his other arm around her shoulder.

She shook her head with her hood covering her face.

'Remember, gentlemen, we all have our own vials around our necks. Each with different substances. I can tell you, I remember the day I handed these vials out to each and every one of you!' he said, looking at his soldiers – the Blucks.

'All different but served for the same purpose – to torture and even kill.'

Every soldier from the Seven Hundred Army looked down at their vial and then looked at the Bluck next to them and chuckled.

'You all have more protection in you than you think.' Oliver finished off.

The Chamcoks, who didn't have vials around their necks, looked at the Blucks with jealousy.

'Let's go! We have a war to win!' the general of the Chamcoks screamed out. The two armies matched his enthusiasm and together, they all marched towards the Azul Flame.

'Where's Gemma? And Juliet?' Athena asked Scarlet as she walked into the main hall, looking around.

'I don't know.' Scarlet said, wiping tears away from her eyes.

'Scarlet, what's wrong?' Athena said as she walked over to her sister, caressing her face.

Scarlet broke out into tears and allowed Athena to listen to her thoughts.

'You can't be afraid of losing Malo, Scarlet! We talked about this yesterday.'

Scarlet looked away.

'Scarlet, listen to me. It's alright to be afraid. Please don't hide it from me! Let me help you by...'

Suddenly, the King walked in the main hall and smiled at his daughters.

'Scarlet and Athena,' he said as he kissed them both on the forehead.

'But where are you dear sisters?' he asked looking around.

'Here!' Juliet said, out of breath, with Gemma behind her. They both hurried towards their siblings and father.

'Now, it is up to you, my four children to defend this kingdom. Yes, we have soldiers and yes, the women and children are safe but really, we all know that without your powers, the kingdom doesn't stand a chance. I need all of you to stick together!'

Juliet gulped. She shouldn't have written down in her journal where the women and children were being kept.

Suddenly, a few figures emerged from the door and walked over to the King.

'Ah! These are your fellow Agalits! We have Max, he is able to control metal. Then we have Subo, she is able to move things with her mind and finally this is Damon. He can control the lava from inside the earth to the surface.'

Damon smiled as his name was mentioned. He suddenly glanced at Scarlet who quickly looked away.

'Between the seven of you, you are undefeatable. But only if you all get along!'

Juliet looked away.

'I need you to all be faithful.' the King whispered.

This time, Gemma looked away as her heart beat faster.

'I will leave you all now! I shall join the soldiers in the caves and fight. I expect you to all go on the terrace at the very top of the castle. There, it will be easier to control your powers as you can see everything that is going on.'

Athena walked her father to the door and hugged him.

'Out of all of them, my dear, I know you will do me the most proud.'

Athena looked down and smiled.

The King was about to leave but then turned back to her.

'I forgot to tell you but that's the most beautiful necklace I have ever seen and trust me, how long I have been living for, I have come across a fair few.'

Athena smiled and then walked back to the crowd of Agalits.

'So, I'm in charge everybody. You must all listen to me,' Athena heard Juliet say. 'Everyone has to do what I tell them. Understood?'

Athena gently grabbed Juliet's arm and smiled to the others as she pulled her away.

'What are you doing, Juliet?' Athena asked, still smiling.

'Someone has to be in charge! Besides, I am the oldest. It only makes sense!'

Athena turned to look at the Agalits and then turned back to Juliet.

'Actually, Damon is the oldest.'

Juliet leant slightly to the left to take a closer look at Damon.

'Well, he is handsome I must say!' she said to herself.

'Ju... Juliet!' Athena said, clicking her fingers to get her attention.

'No. Not now Juliet! We have to first win this war that way you can be with Damon. Right now, I need you to focus.'

Juliet suddenly looked at Athena and smiled.

'You're right, you are! First win, then... Damon...' she trailed off, walking back towards the group of Agalits and stood right next to Damon who was staring at Scarlet.

Athena took a deep breath and then walked back to the group as well.

'Alright! Now that we are all back here, let's go through today's agenda,' Damon started.

'The King said that we should all be at the top of the castle. I completely agree with him. However, I don't think it would be the wisest idea for all of us to be in the same place. If there are spies, then they may be able to sneak up on us!'

Scarlet suddenly intervened.

'Yes, but do remember that Athena's gift is to be able to *hear* voices. She will have no problem of hearing them.'

Damon looked at her and then nodded.

'You are absolutely correct, Scarlet, but I still think a few of us should go somewhere else. For example, I think it would be right in saying that you and I should go because you can communicate with animals and I can control the lava from inside the earth. What better place than to be on the actual earth?'

'Yes, Damon, I think you are right. However, Scarlet? She can communicate with animals up here just fine! My gift is to be able to control the four elements. I think I should go with you!' Juliet burst out.

Damon laughed uneasily.

'No, she's right Damon. I don't see how it could help me going down while I am fine right up here. Besides, I feel safer up here,' Scarlet said, looking up at him for the last few words.

Oh no! She caught me! But I don't want to go outside with Juliet. I want Scarlet! Oh well, it doesn't matter. I don't want to seem forward by insisting.

Athena suddenly looked at Damon as she heard him. Her eyes studied him intensely.

'Well, what are we waiting for? Let's go!' Juliet said, grabbing hold of Damon's wrist.

Damon sighed heavily as he let Juliet drag him away. He looked over at Scarlet before he left just to see her hugging Athena.

'Everything is going so *slowly*! I want today to be over!' Scarlet whined.

'I know, I know!' Athena whispered, as she stroked Scarlet's long, fine hair.

Juliet seems to like that Damon.

Athena laughed and nodded.

'Yes, I really think she does.'

'I have never seen her like that before! She always behaves as the dominant one and doesn't care what people think of her, but with him, it seems as though she is dying for him to like her. I don't think he likes her though!' Scarlet concluded.

Athena shook her head and finally let Scarlet go.

'Everyone, to the terrace.' Gemma said as she clapped her hands to get everyone's attention.

'I really don't like *that* sister.' Subo muttered to herself.

Athena smiled to herself.

'Hello! I'm Subo!' Subo said to Gemma in a rather high voice.

'The poor thing is scared of Gemma,' Athena thought to herself.

'Yes, we are both Agalits and yes, we have to work together but no, we don't have to be friends and no, we *won't* be friends!' Gemma snapped and walked away.

'Don't worry about her, Subo. She's on edge today but we can't blame her.' Athena said as she patted Subo's back.

'No, I suppose we can't,' Subo replied as she smiled.

'So, you can move things with your mind?' Athena quickly asked.

'Yes. I can move anything I want!'

Scarlet and Max joined them. Scarlet whispered something into Subo's ear, while she was trying to restrain her laughter.

Subo grinned and nodded.

'Come on, Agalits! We don't have time. Hurry up!' Gemma screamed down the long, wide spiral staircase. She turned around only to trip over a chair.

Gemma clenched her fists and groaned. Scarlet, Athena, Subo and Max had suddenly appeared with guilty smiles on their faces.

'What's wrong, Gemma?' they asked in unison.

'Very funny, Subo! I suppose that's what I deserve for what I said earlier, isn't it?'

Subo wanted to reply but Scarlet's laughter was so contagious that she couldn't stop laughing.

Gemma stood up, kicked the chair to the side and slapped Scarlet on the face aggressively.

Everyone stopped giggling immediately. Tears were flooding down Scarlet's cheeks.

'Why did you do that?' Athena hissed, in a low voice.

'I bet it was *her* who put Subo up to it!' Gemma said, as she walked back to the terrace and leaned on the balcony.

Athena stomped after her, while Subo and Max comforted Scarlet.

'Why did you do that?' Athena demanded, as she leant her back against the balcony in order to see Gemma's face, but Gemma seemed to be somewhere else as she was gazing at the forest.

'Gemma!'

Gemma didn't reply nor did she look at Athena. She continued staring into the forest.

'Gemma, are you alright?' she asked sympathetically. Her rage for her sister had suddenly vanished. Something was wrong.

'Do you ever feel unloved, Athena?' she whispered, as she wiped her hair away from her face. The wind was picking up speed by the minute.

'Why do you ask that?' Athena asked, as she touched her sister's hand.

'You don't know how it feels! No matter how hard you try to earn someone's love, somebody always beats you to it, even though they never even tried in the first place!'

A tear fell down her cheek. She suddenly turned to Athena with a look in her eyes that Athena had never seen before. Vulnerability.

'I have done terrible things, but there is this one thing that outweighs the others put together.'

'And what is that?'

Gemma suddenly started sobbing and brought her hands to her cheeks, 'Oh, what have I done?'

'Gemma, tell me! Tell me and I promise I will help you. Just tell me!'

'The things I have done to earn father's love. I realised that I would never get it. His precious Juliet would always be more loved so, I turned to a different path. We both have secrets. Both are as bad as the other. He doesn't see that though.

I thought, if father understood how much I needed his love, he would have given it! Instead, I did the very opposite. I just wanted him to love...'

Scarlet was standing right behind her, with tears. Not from the pain but for the pity she had for her sister.

She suddenly embraced Gemma from behind and whispered, '*I love you Gemma. I love you so much!* And so does Athena... and Juliet...and father. Especially father. He loves you more than you can imagine!'

Gemma held Scarlet's arm and smiled for a brief second, but then she ran to the staircase.

'I have to stop this right now!'

'Stop what?' Scarlet wondered to herself.

'What did you say?' Max shouted, coming onto the terrace as the wind started to get stronger. It was almost impossible to hear anything.

'Did you say we have go back inside?' Scarlet screamed.

'We have to stay here!' Athena screamed back.

She turned around and looked out into the clearing.

The wind was so strong, a tornado was bound to happen any minute. The sky was turning darker. Dust was now combined with wind and it made it almost unbearable for them to open their eyes.

They all brought their hands to their eyes and left small gaps between their fingers to be able to have a glimpse of what was happening.

Suddenly, they all saw lava emerge from nowhere and followed it as it went up, higher than where they were standing.

'What a sight!' Max said.

Athena agreed.

'I wonder where they are exactly.' Scarlet wondered to herself.

'Your power is such an interesting one,' Juliet screamed.

Damon didn't reply, because he knew that if he lost concentration, then he would have no control over the lava once it reached the surface of the Earth.

Juliet was standing on the top of a small hill close to the Azul Flame.

They had reached the bottom of the mountain so fast because they had practically jumped off! The King had Juliet perfect her gift from a very young age. So, she was able to control the descent of their fall. They had fallen on thick air she had created, just a few inches off the ground.

The only word Damon had said since that fall was, "No", when Juliet had wanted to break the awkward silence and asked if he was hungry.

Damon couldn't stand Juliet. He found her proud and arrogant. He genuinely hated her. Scarlet, on the other hand, was fragile and vulnerable and he wanted to be with her.

'Your sister.' Damon began.

'Which one?' Juliet asked almost immediately, unhappy about the topic but delighted that, for once, he started the conversation.

'Scarlet.'

'What about her?'

'Tell me about her! What's her gift?' Damon asked. He knew perfectly well that she could communicate with animals. He just wanted to ease his way into the conversation.

'She communicates with animals! Boring, isn't it?'

'Well, I would love to be able to speak to animals.'

'Yes, me too. You would know what they killed for breakfast and where they left their droppings. Animals are *really* fascinating!'

Damon didn't reply. He disliked her *so* much. He was afraid those personal feelings for her would affect the lava.

Juliet sighed but continued.

'She's soon to be engaged to a soldier called Malo.'

Lava suddenly emerged right besides Damon, burning his arm.

Damon screamed in agony.

Juliet stopped controlling the wind and ran over to Damon and fell on the ground besides him.

'Oh, Damon, are you alright?' Juliet asked in a high voice.

'You said Scarlet is getting married?'

'Well, one day, yes! She and Malo are madly in love. They are practically inseparable but, are you alright?'

Damon wasn't sure whether it was the heat or the pain but his eyes watered.

'No.'

'Everyone down here is safe. There is only one entrance to these caves. No one else apart from the King's family know where the entrance is as well as Malo and me. The King has ordered plenty of good food and water and juice for you all. There are also toilet facilities.'

'Very important!' Malo murmured.

'And there are also blankets. Everyone should be alright and comfortable.' Nathan finished.

He turned to Malo who gave him the thumbs up as he winked.

Malo walked forward and looked at all the children and women before his eyes.

'I used to be on the enemy's side. I know them. I have lived with them, eaten with them, fought with and against them. I have even been one of them and if I have learnt only one thing, it is that they are ruthless. They wouldn't care if you were one or one *hundred* years old, they get the same satisfaction nonetheless. If they do manage to get in these caves, do not ask for mercy. They shall not give you any. Quite the opposite, they will kill you even more cruelly and painfully.

However, just in case they do manage to find the entrance, I have placed hundreds of weapons and shields in the dark corners of the caves. They won't necessarily stop you from being killed but they will certainly help. All I can say, is that the King cares for every single one of you and so does General Lamber and I! I will protect you all as best as I can, that I promise!' Malo said in a strong voice.

He bowed as he turned away and walked off with Nathan.

'You could have told me about the weapons. The children are young. They will not know how to use metal swords properly!'

'I know, I know. For the kids, there are two hundred wooden swords.' Malo said as he grinned.

Nathan laughed to himself. 'You knew this all along! You were going to give them weapons and you weren't going to tell me? I can see why Scarlet likes you. You are a devious one.'

'That's only the beginning.' Malo said in an accent.

Both he and Nathan took one last look around the caves before they left. To Malo, it very much resembled to the entrance of the Seven Hundred Soldiers Army. There were many steps going down and the cave was circular in shape. However, the place was more magical than the arena. There were blue crystals on every angle of the cave walls, making the whole place gleam with blue light. There were also crystal icicles on the ceiling, pointing downwards.

'I wonder if this Flame was named the Azul Flame because the inside of the mountain is full of blue crystals.' Nathan said.

'I'm not sure, but it's a certainly, isn't it!' Malo replied, looking down to see all the adults forming a small circle and all the children playing with the wooden swords.

'Would you look at that? They found the swords!' Malo said to Nathan, smiling.

The soldiers were now right in front of the Azul Flame and Sedty was called up to the front.

Suddenly a figure emerged from the dusty air.

'I need to speak with you!' she said to Oliver.

Oliver got down from his horse and grabbed the girl from the wrist.

'What do you want?' he hissed.

'Stop it! Stop everything.'

Oliver suddenly laughed.

'This war can't be stopped whether you like it or not! So, get out of the way and stop being a nuisance.'

'I should have never told you about the cave opening. Please don't go in there. For me?'

'That cave opening will be the very reason why your petty brother will trust me again. That will be the perfect time to kill him.'

'Keep Nicolas out of this. Don't touch him otherwise I will kill you myself...with my bare hands if I have to!'

'Oh, my dear darling. You will never do that. You love me and I love you. After this war is over, you and I will be together. You do love me, don't you?'

'I... I don't know...'

Oliver leant in and aggressively kissed her.

'You *do* love me!' he answered for her and walked back to the army, who were staring at them.

'Sedty! Break the force shield now!' Oliver demanded.

Nathan looked at some of the worried faces behind him. There were a little under a thousand of them which meant that they were just outnumbered by the Blucks and Chamcoks combined together.

'We have no chance of winning!'

'Why are we here?'

Nathan and Malo heard other comments too, from the unenthusiastic soldiers.

They turned to one another and Malo nodded his head to show Nathan that he should say something.

Nathan turned around to face them.

'Listen! All of you! We all know that today is a very dark day indeed but we have to try. We *need* to try. We have elements on our side which the enemy don't!'

'Really? Like what?' a middle-aged man asked.

'We have Greliks! All of them. Here. On our side!' Nathan replied.

The man looked away.

'We also have Agalits. Seven of them!'

'I heard the enemy have Agalits too!' another soldier called out.

'You're right, they do, but they haven't mastered their gifts like our Agalits have. Ours have known this day for many years. This day is their chance to save Fairoses! To save *our* kingdom. We control almost every element in the world between our seven Agalits! From the inner mantle to the sky. We can control it. We can win. We will win! And then all of you can go home to your family and never be asked to fight in battle again because this is the war that has been known throughout centuries! It has even been written. It is, however, also told that nothing is ever certain. We cannot sit back and allow fortune to win this war for us. Our victory, that is up to us! So, let's go and win the war that is ours to win!'

Sedty moved forwards. He had already broken down the gate that surrounded the Azul Flame. Now, he was inches away from the force shield.

At first, he put his fist forward. He pointed out his second finger to delicately touch the faint, purple force shield. He cleared his throat and stepped back. With a deep breath, he delivered his most powerful punch.

For a moment nothing happened.

'Oh no.' the General of the Chamcoks said. He tutted and shook his head.

Sedty, after a moment, thought his powers weren't strong enough to destruct such a strong force shield.

He walked back to Nicolas.

'I'm sorry, General Avran! I don't know...'

He was lost for words and kept his head down as he took his place in the front row of the army.

For a moment, silence fell through the entire army. The Chamcoks had never even thought of what should be done if Sedty was ever to fail. The Chamcoks relied on the Blucks and the Blucks relied on Sedty.

General Avran got down from his horse and walked over to Sedty.

'Can't you try again?' he asked desperately.

Sedty was about to answer but suddenly saw something happen at the top of the force shield. It slowly disintegrated downwards into thin air.

The entire army watched the shield destroy itself until the very bottom was no longer visible.

Sedty walked up to where the force shield previously stood. Once again, he reached out with his second finger and almost fell forward as he put all his weight forward.

He had successfully destroyed the greatest force shield in the world.

Another moment passed in complete silence but then a cheer among the soldiers gradually became louder. Just as Nicolas looked over to his soldiers and smiled, he felt the ground tremble.

All of a sudden, lava erupted from the ground, injuring several soldiers at a time. They howled out in pain and ran around, trying to find some sort of relief for their burns.

Lava erupted once again, and this time it was near Nicolas and the General of the Chamcoks. Another handful of soldiers were either killed or severely injured.

Nicolas galloped forward and everyone followed him to get out of the heat and to safety-up the Azul Flame.

The Agalits just watched their greatest protection disintegrate before their very own eyes.

'Oh, the dear Gods, help us!' Subo gasped.

Scarlet remained silent as a tear fell down her cheek.

'Where's Juliet and Damon? Where's Gemma?' Athena suddenly asked, looking around the terrace.

Scarlet suddenly shook her head, as though she was in the middle of a dream.

'Juliet and Damon. They must be on their way up by now! I can't see any more lava and I can't see any weather that would distract the army.' Athena said as she looked up at the grey sky.

Suddenly Gemma arrived, in tears.

'Gemma, what's wrong?' Max asked.

'Well, I...'

She was cut off by Juliet who suddenly appeared from the grey-stoned stairway. She pushed Gemma out of the way and yelled out, 'Damon is downstairs. He tried his best to stop the army but he is too badly wounded!'

They all remained silent, thinking Juliet hadn't quite finished.

Her eyes widened.

'Help him!' she shrieked.

Max and Subo rushed down the stairs to help.

'Well, come on everyone, Damon needs help! Why are you on the ground, Gemma? Get up!' Juliet said, with no sympathy or kindness in her voice.

'You pushed me.' Gemma hissed as she slowly got up.

Juliet ignored her.

'Well, all of you have to help him! What is taking you so *long*?'

'I am sure Damon will survive. Besides, he has Max and Subo,' Gemma replied on Athena's and Scarlet's part.

'You three are completely useless!' Juliet said as she ran back downstairs.

Athena rolled her eyes and Scarlet clenched her fists.

'Sometimes...' Scarlet began, cracking her neck.

'Yes. Yes, I know. We feel like strangling her,' Gemma said, joining her sisters.

'We shouldn't think like that though! She's our sister and we love her very much. Even if she does have many secrets,' Gemma continued, hoping someone would ask more about that.

'Oh no.' Athena said, as she leant over the balcony.

'What? What is it?' Scarlet and Gemma asked in unison.

'The Chamcoks and the Blucks have passed the gate. They are going to be up here sooner than we thought!'

'We have to warn Malo and Nathan!' Scarlet said, making her way down the stairs.

'Oh, no you don't! Scarlet, we need you up here to summon the Greliks!' Athena said, holding Scarlet's shoulder.

'But-'

'No, Athena's right! You need to be here. I will go. I will tell Malo and Nathan. Just stay put, alright? You won't leave this terrace no matter what!' Gemma said in a firm voice.

She ran down the spiral stairway before either Athena or Scarlet could say anything.

'That sounded like a demand to me.' Athena pointed out.

Scarlet turned to her.

'Do you think she knows something we don't?' Scarlet asked.

Athena shrugged her shoulders and sighed, 'I don't know. Lately, I can't hear her thoughts at all. I can control when I do and do not want to hear thoughts but with her, I hear nothing even when I try! The same goes for Juliet. What is going on? Is it my gift I can't control? No, it has to be something else.'

The Chamcoks and the Blucks swiftly made their way up the mountain. As they looked on either side, every shop was deserted.

Not a person was in sight.

The general of the Chamcoks rode between Oliver and Nicolas.

'So, where do you think everybody is?' he asked.

Oliver smiled as he pointed towards the gardens of the castle.

'The gardens? Why would they choose such an exposed area?'

Oliver rolled his eyes and said impatiently, 'No! Not *on* the gardens, *in* the gardens!'

'I don't follow you…'

'I'm not surprised. You are the very definition of stupid.' Oliver mumbled to himself but it was loud enough for the general of the Chamcoks to hear.

'*I* am the definition of stupid? How about you being in love with a girl over half your age! Not only is she any girl — she's an Agalit. A daughter of the King and you plan to dispose of her when you get the chance even though you say you "love her"!'

'Have you been listening to my conversations, general?'

'Some of them. Certainly the ones you have with the Agalit!'

'Where did you hear that I was planning to dispose of her?'

'Not everyone thinks good of you, you know? You should try and listen carefully to what your army says about you. Yet again, if you kill or mutilate,' he said looking over at Mark, 'anyone who says anything about you, very few of your men would be fighting today.'

He rode on.

Oliver gasped. No one had ever spoken to him that bluntly in his life. Nicolas, now riding beside him, tried very hard to cover his smile.

'You go on, General Avran! I don't want *it* thinking that it's in charge.' Oliver said.

Nicolas obeyed.

Oliver purposely slowed his horse down to try and hear what the soldiers were muttering to each other.

'Do you know they have been working together for seven years?'

'I heard he's plotting against General Avran.'

'The Agalit was only sixteen when she and Oliver...you know...'

'Enough!' Oliver screamed out, hearing enough. He turned towards Nicolas and the general of the Chamcoks who both halted.

The general sneered at Oliver.

Oliver gritted his teeth and clenched his fists.

'Steady yourself. You will rip his head off soon enough!' he told himself.

'What's the holdup?' Nicolas screamed over.

'Nothing, General Avran! We will be at the castle in less than half an hour!' Sedty said.

Nicolas nodded and then continued riding ahead.

Sedty turned towards the general of the Chamcoks and whispered, 'I don't like either of them any more than you do. Don't worry though, with my power now, we can make them suffer however we want!'

Meanwhile, up at the very top of the castle, all the Agalits were watching down on the army ascending the mountain.

Scarlet had summoned all the Greliks that were willing to fight to come up the mountain now.

'Of course, it would take them a while though! They are very stubborn creatures. When they are asked to do something, they take their time.'

'But are you sure they *will* come?' Gemma asked.

'Yes.'

Damon leant against the balcony with his arm all bandaged up. He looked over at Scarlet and after a few minutes he said, 'No animal would be able to say no to Scarlet!'

They all turned towards him, surprised at what he just said.

'Well... you know...' he mumbled to himself, looking down and fidgeting with his fingers.

They all looked back towards the army. It was only Juliet who kept her eyes on him.

The army was approaching the castle now.

'Can you hear anything they are saying yet?' Scarlet asked.

Athena shook her head.

'No! I can only hear some of them. But not all of them. I can hear that man on the horse, riding next to Nic—'

'Nicolas? You see him!' Juliet and Scarlet both said together.

They leant over the balcony to take a closer look at their only brother.

'He's changed so much! I hardly recognise him. It's like he is a completely different man!' Scarlet noticed.

Juliet nodded in agreement. 'If it weren't for his hair, I wouldn't be able to recognise him!'

Gemma peered over too and said, 'I know. It's sad how we haven't seen him for years and years. Maybe he is completely evil after all.'

Athena shook her head. 'No, I don't think he is evil. He is just under the influence of evil. I am sure that if he lived with us for a few months, he would be back to his old self!'

'I wouldn't count on it. Men are very stubborn creatures. If we wanted him to change, he would deliberately not change just to make sure we have no satisfaction. Men are just stubborn animals!' Juliet said.

Max and Damon waved at her to remind her that they were there.

'Of course, how silly of me. You, Damon, are an exception.' Juliet said, trying to flutter her eyelashes but failing miserably.

Max cleared his throat. 'What about me?'

Juliet turned to him and changed her tone of voice.

'What about you!' she said as she turned away.

'Oh no.' Athena groaned again.

'What is it?' Gemma asked, immediately as though she knew what Athena was going to say.

'The general of the Chamcoks. He knows about the caves!' Athena said, panicking now.

'What? He can't! Only *we* know about the caves!' Scarlet said in protest.

'We have to warn them.' Athena said slowly, looking at the army who were getting closer and closer to the castle.

She walked away but quickly turned to Scarlet and the rest.

'I have to warn father and our Army! Scarlet, I need you to ask the Greliks in the nicest way possible to hurry. To really hurry!'

Scarlet nodded.

Athena ran down the stairway and down to the bottom of the castle. She caught sight of Malo.

'Oh Malo!' she said panting.

'My dear Athena, what's wrong?' he asked, patting her shoulder.

'Nicolas and the army. They're here now and they know about the caves. They are probably in the gardens as we speak!'

'Oh no. There is only one passage to those caves. If they get there first...'

Malo didn't finish his sentence. Instead, he ran off to the main entrance of the castle, where all the other soldiers were.

He ran to Nathan who was beside the King.

'We have a problem! They know about the caves!' he blurted out.

Nathan's eyes widened.

'Where are they now?' he asked.

'In the gardens! Nathan, they are going to get there before you and I can. The soldiers should be prepared though, surely?'

Nathan and Malo shared their panic with each other. Nathan patted Malo on the neck. 'Let's run, Malo! We'll get there before they do!'

'Almost there!' the general of the Chamcoks said as they entered the gardens.

'Wait a minute! The girl. The Agalit. She can hear our thoughts. She will know that we know where the caves are!' the general said.

Oliver shook his head.

'Did you really think we would come to this war unprepared? How small you must think of us! For your information, I took care of that. Her sister reminded me of this little fact. So, when I got back to the headquarters, I gathered my scientists and together we produced a compound which blocks Athena's power to getting into our minds. I secretly poured it into my men's glasses for their 'Last Meal' and now, Athena cannot hear not any of my men's thoughts!'

The general was speechless.

'What about my men?' he asked.

'What about your men? They are ruthless, unintelligent and defenceless. They have no protection in them or on them. They only have weapons that can be easily taken away.

My men, on the other hand, are immune to the Agalits power and have their own unique vials around their neck. Can I assure you *now* that we have come prepared?' Oliver asked.

He flashed a quick smile and rode on.

Now, to find the right fountain!

'It has to be here somewhere.'

He rode on to the tallest fountain in the gardens. He got off his horse and paced around the circular fountain several times.

'Juliet, use your powers to stop them.' Gemma urged.

Juliet stepped forward and concentrated very hard. She lifted her right hand slightly, stared at the water fountain and made the water slowly rise up towards the sky.

After several seconds, the water stopped rising up. It stopped completely.

'That's making no difference, whatsoever!' Subo shouted.

Nothing happened for a minute or so.

'Found it!' Oliver said out loud as he bent down and rummaged his fingers around a loose marble tile.

'He found it. Juliet, do something. He found it! He is going to kill everyone in that cave!' Scarlet screamed in Juliet's ear.

Suddenly, all the water from every fountain in the gardens began to swirl around.

'What is she doing?' Damon asked.

'She's making a current.' Gemma whispered.

By now, the water in each fountain started to rise higher and higher, shaped as tornados. Juliet raised her left hand, completely parallel to her right and aimed all the water she controlled at Oliver.

Sure, the water violently washed Oliver away, but it also washed away the loose tiles which had now collapsed inwards. The entrance of the cave revealed itself.

A child who was playing with a wooden sword down below was instantly soaked.

His mother came to him and was almost hit with the huge marble tile, which was inches long in length and width.

She slowly looked up only to see daylight and the face of a horrid man peering down.

'Excellent!' Oliver said, the word echoing through the huge cave.

'The entrance of the cave is opened. How could you do that Juliet? They're all going to die, they're all going to *die*!!' Scarlet shrieked.

'I was only listening to you. Don't blame me! I didn't think that would happen!' Juliet said in her defence.

'Well, it did happen and now...' Scarlet stopped.

She felt something. She turned around to look at what was happening. The Greliks were on their way. There were so many of them.

'I never knew how many Greliks there were!' Max whispered, astonished by the sea of black creatures, of all sizes, sprinting up the mountain to their aid.

Being the fast animals they were, they would catch up with the army before too much damage was done.

Oliver looked upwards only to see the general of the Chamcoks standing over him, exposing his rotting teeth.

'You alright down there?' he asked, smiling.

'Come on. Get a move on! The soldiers are already going into the cave!' he said as he kicked Oliver in the ribs.

Oliver groaned.

'Oh, I am sorry! Did that hurt? I thought you said you and your army had protection inside and out,' he continued, flashing a quick smile like Oliver had done so previously.

'That's enough, Owen!' Nicolas said as he pushed the general out of the way to help Oliver up.

'Yes, Owen! That's enough. Now, why don't you go to your pathetic little soldiers and see what's taking them so long to get into the cave!' Oliver said in a hoarse voice.

The general snarled but obeyed.

'Why do you do this to yourself?' Nicolas asked him, as he put his shoulder under Oliver's arm to help him up.

'He asks for it! That general is one nasty piece of work!' Oliver said, forcing a laugh.

'You make it very easy for people to hate you, Oliver! You act like an evil, monstrous person who only lives to see harm done to the world but I am sure deep, deep, *deep* down…you are even worse.'

Nicolas walked away to get into the caves.

'You have no idea.' Oliver said to himself. He was about to walk over to the cave opening when he felt a tremor. He stopped straight away just to make sure it wasn't him but, once again, he felt another tremor.

He turned around only to see Greliks heading his way, running at full speed.

Without thinking he ran as fast as he could to the opening of the cave. He pushed his way through many soldiers and he ran down the steep stairs.

The soldiers looked behind them to see what was scaring Oliver, who almost risked his life by falling down into a huge cave, only to see Greliks running towards them.

The several hundred soldiers who wouldn't get a chance to get into the cave in time ran towards the castle.

They knew Greliks were ruthless creatures.

For the soldiers who neither made it into the caves nor ran towards the castle, their last glance was to see a huge Grelik with razor sharp teeth and green, merciless eyes storming towards them.

Some of us can't fit into that minuscule opening in the cave so those of you who can fit, go inside and kill as many soldiers you can! As for the rest of us…

The leader of the Greliks pointed his head towards the castle where the soldiers were running to.

'Nathan, we need to go and help the people! They are already in the caves. Who knows what will happen if we don't act fast!' Malo hissed.

Nathan nodded and whistled so loudly that all the soldiers stopped whispering immediately.

'Now, listen! The Blucks and Chamcoks are in that cave where all your children and wives are. Now, unless you all want to continue chatting, we need to get to those caves *now*!' Nathan screamed out sternly.

The soldiers stood firmly in their assigned places, feeling their blood boiling. This was the moment they had been waiting for.

The guards sprang open the huge wooden doors, and all the soldiers willingly ran out, with their swords held up high.

In the caves, the soldiers of both the Seven Hundred Army and the Chamcoks were fighting savagely against the Greliks. The older women were protected by the younger women and girls, while the old men were protected by the young boys. They were all bravely holding out their wooden swords with trembling hands, ready to fight any soldier that came towards them.

A Grelik jumped on three soldiers and ripped off their heads. Soldiers stabbed Greliks with their sharp swords and sharp pieces of crystal that had fallen off from the top of the caves.

There are too many of them!

Greliks thought out to other Greliks. However, none of them took notice and continued killing the soldiers. The general of the Chamcoks walked towards a little girl and kicked her wooden sword out of her hand. She slowly walked backwards and her mother grabbed her into her arms.

The general smiled evilly at the mother and grabbed the little girl from her arms. He drew out his sword with his other hand and said, 'if none of you surrender, this will happen to the rest of you!'

He pulled back the little girls head and was about to behead her when she suddenly screamed, looking at something behind Owen.

He turned around to see the biggest Grelik out of the whole group, exposing its razor sharp teeth, about to leap on him. Owen moved out of the way just in time, but the little girl suffered the consequence.

Oliver spat out blood as he and many other soldiers were fighting against a Grelik. He brushed his fingers through his hair only to find blood.

Lots of blood.

He took a deep breath and looked around. He saw Nicolas alone.

'I can kill him now if I want.' he mumbled to himself. However, he continued looking around and he saw Owen killing the smallest Grelik of all which was the size of a cat.

'I'll start with you though. I hate you more!' Oliver said, smiling. He spat out blood one more time.

Owen looked down at the dead Grelik and laughed. He suddenly heard someone call out his name. He looked around and saw Oliver panting and limping towards him.

'Owen! I think...' he trailed off and leant on Owen's shoulder.

'What happened? What's your problem?' he asked, looking at Oliver's head which was covered in much blood.

Oliver drew out his sword and stabbed Owen in the chest. Owen fell to the ground.

'*You're* my problem!' Oliver said as he wiped the blood off his sword with his clothes and spat on Owen face.

'One down, one to go.' he said, looking over at Nicolas.

A group of Chamcoks gathered together and were walking towards the helpless children, protecting their families.

The soldiers laughed at them but Oliver ran over to them.

'What are you doing?' he asked.

'Killing?'

Oliver didn't want them to kill the civilians. If he were to become King, then he would need people to rule over.

He drew out his sword and stopped them from walking any further.

'Do not take one step further.' he warned.

'Or what? Are you going to kill us? From the look of your sword, you've barely killed today! Look at mine!' the soldier said, showing his sword covered in blood. The blood even dripped onto the floor.

Mark walked over to help Oliver fight his case.

'Don't you dare kill one more child! They are the future of this kingdom.' he hissed.

'This is supposed to be a WAR! WHAT WAR DOESN'T INVOLVE KILLING?' the soldier screamed.

Suddenly, screams came from above. Everyone stopped fighting and gazed upwards to see who was coming. The sound was becoming louder and louder and the shadow became bigger. Hundreds of soldiers came running down the stairs and into the huge, hollow cave. Their screams were screams of enthusiasm. They were ready to kill.

Malo and Nathan were at the very front, running at top speed. It almost seemed as though they were gliding down the stairs.

Everyone came back to reality as they killed Chamcoks and Blucks in their way.

Oliver turned to the soldier and stabbed him in the heart. He fell down backwards.

The other soldiers who were with him ran away and Mark and Oliver smiled at each other.

Oliver looked away and saw Nicolas fighting two soldiers. He ran towards him.

'Nicolas.' he said as he made a small bow and killed one of the two soldiers.

General Avran killed the other soldier and turned to Oliver.

'Oliver.' he replied as he made a small bow as well.

'Oh Nicolas, Nicolas, Nicolas!' he said very loudly.

A soldier turned towards them on hearing that name.

Oliver patted Nicolas on the shoulder but looked away.

The soldier's eyes grew bigger. 'I know that look!'

Oliver looked at his shiny sword and saw Nicolas's reflection. Only, it wasn't Nicolas but a small boy: it was Nicolas as a young boy.

Oliver suddenly turned around but saw the present Nicolas.

'What's wrong?' General Avran asked.

Oliver shook his head and slowly walked away.

The soldier sighed with relief. He was, in fact, the King.

Athena was losing her patience. 'I can't do anything up here. None of us can!' she said, gripping hold of her long hair.

'Athena's right.' Scarlet said, getting up from the bench.

'I can't do anymore. I was to summon the Greliks. I have. Athena can't hear anything down there and-'

'That's not true, I hear some thoughts and none of them are pleasant. I know that father said we should stay here-'

'But we should go down there,' Scarlet finished for her.

Subo shook her head. 'What good could we do down there?'

Scarlet paused for a minute.

'You can move things with your mind Subo. What could you *not* do down there!'

Subo couldn't say anything in her defence, but she still didn't want to go down there. She shrugged her shoulders and took a deep breath.

Scarlet turned towards Max.

'You control metal. There's just as much down there as there is up here! Athena, you will definitely be able to hear more minds down there than up here. Gemma, you can change the speed of growth and Juliet, you can control the elements down there just as easily as up here as well!'

They all nodded in agreement.

'I can't come.' Damon said.

Juliet turned to him. 'Why ever not?'

'Because if I were to use my power, I would need to be in a calm environment otherwise everyone could end up being burnt alive. It's too risky!'

Scarlet nodded. 'Fine.'

She turned to Athena. 'So, we should all go down and-'

'Fine? What's that supposed to mean?' Damon asked, rather offended.

Scarlet rolled her eyes and turned to Damon.

'It means you can stay here!' she snapped.

'Well...' he began, not entirely sure where he was going with this.

'Because you might burn people alive, I think we all agree that's safer you stay here.'

She was about to turn back to Athena when he replied, 'so what! I should just wait here and hope for you to come back to me?'

Scarlet gave him a weird look.

He realised what he said. 'I mean... I can't just sit up here and do nothing. I want to *fight*!' he said sternly, hoping he wasn't flushing.

Scarlet nodded and gave an uncomfortable smile.

'You can fight! Just do what you think is best.' she whispered, looking away.

Juliet cleared her throat to break the awkward silence.

'Let's go to war!' she said.

The soldiers who hadn't made it into the cave were running for their lives. They were running as fast as they could to get away from the hungry Greliks, showing their razor sharp teeth and their green eyes, full of hatred.

By now, they ran around the castle twice and not one of the two hundred soldiers had collapsed yet. This was the plan of the Greliks: to watch each and every soldier suffer and eventually collapse from exhaustion.

It's only a matter of time.

The leader of the Greliks thought this and all the other Greliks responded with a low pitched whine. They were ready to fight and kill.

They could go far longer than any human without losing stamina or breath. They would continue running after the soldiers until every last one of them died.

One soldier finally collapsed from exhaustion after the fifth round around the castle. One Grelik stopped to kill him while the rest continued.

The soldier turned around and begged for mercy.

'Please... don't... kill me...' he said, panting, but the Grelik had no mercy and ripped his head off anyway.

The Agalits had reached the bottom of the castle and Damon began to open the two front doors only to see a huge group of soldiers running past.

A soldier quickly ran back a few steps to see the open door and the only path to freedom, away from the Greliks.

The soldiers behind him stopped and followed his gaze to see the open doors of the castle with only a few people inside, most of them women.

The soldiers, without thinking twice, made their way in.

A few of them shut the door with Damon so stunned that he couldn't move.

There were at least fifty soldiers in front of them.

What do we do?

Damon looked towards Athena and she shook her head.

'I'm not sure.' she said to herself.

Damon suddenly had an idea.

The Greliks continued chasing the other hundred soldiers around the castle.

Soldiers are missing!

Where do you think they went?

The Greliks looked around but saw them nowhere in sight.

They must be in the castle if they're not out here.

Once the soldiers had regained their breath, they looked at one another and after a moment of silence, they began to laugh.

One soldier, the one who had seen the castle door open first, looked at the Agalits. After the laughter had died down, the rest of the soldiers also stared at them.

'Well, look what we have here boys!' the soldier said, walking closer towards the Agalits.

He walked up to Gemma and slowly touched her cheek.

'I know you!' he said, examining her face.

Gemma flicked his hand away and replied, 'you must be mistaken!'

The soldier laughed and signalled the other soldiers to join him.

'No, I definitely recognise your face. Benny, don't you think she looks familiar?'

Benny came and stood beside the soldier and looked blankly towards Gemma.

Athena's heart missed a beat when she saw Benny.

'Oh no.' she sighed.

'You're right, Christiaan! I do recognise her face as I recognise this one,' he said, walking over to Athena who kept her head up high.

'Hello, Athena!' Benny said, flashing his yellow teeth.

'You two *know* each other?' Scarlet asked with disgust.

'Of course we do! And now I can finally have my revenge,' he said, remaining calm.

'You most certainly won't!' Max said as he pushed Benny away from Athena and punched him in the face.

Benny tasted blood dripping down onto his lips.

'You will pay for that.' he hissed as he lunged for Max.

Max was a huge Agalit. His arms were easily twice as big as Benny's and everyone knew that if it came to a duel, Max would evidently win, even if he was just a human.

'Calm down!' Twit said as he emerged from the crowd. He put his arm around Benny's shoulders.

'Relax, Benny. He can easily take you down. You know it!' Twit continued.

Benny took a deep breath. He punched Twit in the face and Twit fell backwards. Benny turned back to Max and wiped his face.

'This is between you and me!' he said, as he drew out his sword.

Max cracked his fingers and his neck.

'Do you not realise what I am, *Benny*?' Max asked, amused.

'You're an Agalit!'

'So, I have a power.'

'I know! Because you're an Agalit!' Benny said slowly.

'Well, I can control metal.' Max said, smiling.

Benny gulped as he suddenly felt his heavy armour weigh him down.

He slowly drew out his sword, his hands trembling and shyly pointed it towards Max's neck.

'Do you really think that's a wise decision?' Max asked, still grinning, folding his arms.

The sword in Benny's hand dropped to the floor and then slid to the other side of the hall.

Benny felt as though he was going to be sick. His hands were trembling even more violently.

'I am not afraid of you!' he kept telling himself over and over again.

'I don't want to kill you Benny, but if you do touch Athena again, then I will have to. I hope you understand that! My kind comes before yours.'

Benny slowly nodded and walked back to his comrades. He suddenly stopped and looked at Max, who already had his back to him. Benny realised this was an opportunity. He quietly and subtly bent down to retrieve a dagger that was hidden in his boot and silently walked towards Max.

He was a few feet away from him when he stopped. He took a deep breath and lunged on the Agalit.

Max turned around and stepped back, leaving Benny to fall hard on the ground. Max bent down and looked at the small dagger.

'Did you really think that small little thing could harm me? Make me bleed? Kill me?'

Max tutted. The dagger rose up from Benny's hand and rested in the air above it. Its tip turned towards Benny and slowly made for his neck. When the dagger touched his flesh, it moved no further.

'You have two choices here Benny. You either admit defeat and you live or you continue being a stubborn pain and die! Take your pick.'

Benny closed his eyes and spoke.

'I came into the army for one purpose and one purpose only: to fight in this war and die in this war if it would help the army come any closer to victory. I want people to remember me, knowing that I gave my life to give my comrades the knowledge that there is no mercy in war and we are only given one chance.'

He opened his eyes and said, 'so I choose to die!'

He spat on Max's face. Max slowly wiped off the spit and whispered, 'you chose death. You shall have it!'

The dagger started to make its way through the flesh and red blood tickled down his throat.

'Stop it.' Athena calmly said. 'Don't kill him.'

Max immediately obeyed and sure enough, the dagger fell on Benny's chest.

Athena walked towards him and bent down, next to his face.

'There is one thing I need to know. Why can't I hear any of your thoughts? Why can't I hear anyone's thoughts in your army?'

Benny remained silent. Max made the dagger point against Benny's neck once more.

'Answer the question, Benny!' Max snarled.

Benny could feel the dagger dig deeper and deeper into his skin.

'I don't know! I swear! I really don't know,' he said, honestly.

'Didn't your mother ever tell you not to lie?' Max asked as he controlled his anger.

'I don't think he's lying,' Athena said looking into Benny's face which was, by now, completely red and sweaty.

Max clenched his fists but made the dagger fall onto the ground. Benny fell back on the ground, panting heavily.

'But there *is* something you aren't telling me.' Athena said.

Benny unwillingly nodded.

Athena got up and stood behind Benny's face. He bent his head backwards to look up at her.

'I really can't tell you.'

'Why not? Is Oliver going to kill you?'

'He will if he knows I told you!'

'Please, tell me. He won't find out. There is no way out of this situation. You either tell me or you die.' Athena said bluntly. She knew that Benny would tell her.

'Okay. Your sister has been working with Oliver for the past seven years.'

Athena looked up and saw her three sisters, side by side. All three faces looked horrified.

Athena looked back at Benny.

'You're lying! None of them would betray our father like that. It's impossible!' she said, astounded.

'It's true! I promise you that I'm not lying.'

Athena realised he was telling the truth. She looked back at her sisters, fighting back the tears.

'Which one of you have been helping the Council?' she asked.

None of them replied.

'Which one?' she repeated, now with tears flowing down her cheek.

'It's not me!' Scarlet said as she stepped forward.

Athena trusted her. She looked back at Gemma and Juliet with both their eyes cast down. She walked towards them and whimpered the question again.

'Gemma? Would you really do that?'

Juliet and Gemma looked at one another and Juliet nodded her head.

'Athena, you have to understand that...'

Suddenly, the doors slammed open and the Greliks came running in, jumping on screaming soldiers who knew it was the end for them.

Nathan stabbed a soldier in between the eyes while Malo killed the soldiers who were trying to kill Nathan.

'We're outnumbered now. There is no way we can win without them!' Nathan said as he saw the number of dead bodies from his army. Malo knew he was referring to the Agalits.

Malo made his way to a few Chamcoks who were making their way to a group of young children, but suddenly caught sight of a young boy who seemed familiar.

It was Yan.

Malo continued running as there was nothing he could do for Yan. He knew he would be alright. Malo could see Yan was distressed by the number of dead Greliks around them.

'I know there are more Greliks elsewhere,' Malo murmured to himself.

Sedty and Oliver looked over at Nicolas who was wiping his sword.

'You must kill him.' Oliver demanded.

'Why not you?' Sedty asked.

'I have known Nicolas since he was a little boy. I can't bring myself to do it.'

'You stay here while I go ahead like a real man and kill the general of the victorious army. It's a shame you can't get the satisfaction!' Sedty said, smiling as he walked towards Nicolas.

'General Avran? Can I have a minute?' Sedty asked, completely serious now.

Nicolas looked around him and saw no one coming to kill him, so he gave a signal to Sedty to come forth.

Sedty turned around and winked at Oliver.

'We are winning the battle, general! There is no chance now that their army can beat ours. We are invincible!'

Nicolas nodded but continued wiping his sword.

Sedty cleared his throat and moved closer. He remained still for a moment but then drew out his sword and pointed it to General Avran's neck.

'Drop your sword.' Sedty said slowly.

Nicolas obeyed and felt the vibrations run up his spine when the sword hit the ground.

'I have been waiting for this since the day I met you! You never gave me enough credit. I am your best soldier. I have always been your best soldier. And you never noticed it! Well, I have had enough! Today, I take over the army as general!'

He was about to kill Nicolas when somebody else stabbed him in the back.

Sedty fell to the ground.

The soldier saw green blood drip from his weapon. It wasn't a sword or dagger, but something completely different. It was a small yet wide, beige instrument with twenty thick needles at the tip.

The soldier looked up at Nicolas.

'I saw Oliver trying to kill you before. I stopped him by using one of my small gifts to make him stop, but with this one,' he said looking down at Sedty, 'his powers were far too powerful that I had to kill him!'

Nicolas looked at the man, completely stunned. 'How did you kill an Agalit?'

The man smiled at him and said, 'many years ago, someone gave this to me and told me that it was able to kill anything magical. Agalits, for example. That someone was you, Nicolas.'

Nicolas studied his face and realised who it was.

'Father?'

'We have to run to the caves. Now!' Scarlet said as she was running towards the doors.

They ran, leaving Juliet and Gemma behind.

'I can't believe they would do that to us!' Scarlet said, outraged. 'I have known them all my life. I could never imagine either of them betraying father like that.'

'Maybe it's both of them.' Max suggested.

'What makes you say that?' Subo asked.

'They both looked at each other. They both knew what was going on.' Athena answered for Max.

'They may not be betraying father in the same way, but both have clearly done terrible things. Neither of them could tell on the other because then, everyone's secret would be out!'

'Now, I am confused,' Damon said.

'No, Athena's right! Todd happened to fly past Juliet's chamber the other day when both she and Gemma were having an argument. He also mentioned something about a huge book. A diary of some sort?'

'But one won't talk until the other does.' Athena said.

'And now we either have two confessions or no confession,' Subo realised.

'The other's secret must be really terrible! What could it possibly be?' Scarlet wondered to herself.

'For all we know, it could be that she stole the ice cream from a child or she clogged up the toilet and forgot to do something about it!' Damon suggested to lighten the mood.

Scarlet looked at him, unamused.

'I mean if one secret is helping the army for years, repeating every secret father had told and even revealing the entrance of the cave… that in itself is unforgivable. So, the other secret must be just as-'

'Unforgivable as well!' Damon finished for her.

Scarlet nodded her head at him.

They reached the entrance of the cave.

'How do we go in without being attacked almost immediately?' Max asked.

'We should wait for the Greliks to come and form a barrier around us,' Subo suggested.

'No, we can't wait any longer, we have to go now!' Scarlet said, stubbornly.

Max pointed behind her and they all turned around. The Greliks were running towards them. None of them were killed by the soldiers they had chased and eventually ate.

Without stopping, the Greliks ran straight into the cave.

'I guess we follow them.' Subo said.

Athena nodded.

Max and Damon went in first with Athena and Subo following.

Scarlet took a moment. She felt as though she was going to throw up again. Her head was pounding. She was afraid what she might see down there.

Athena came back up and hugged her, 'It's alright! I just caught a glimpse of Malo. He's fine, Scarlet!'

Scarlet sighed with relief. She took a deep breath and made her way to the cave's entrance.

She almost tripped over the first stair as she took a small glance around the cave and saw so many bodies and so much blood everywhere.

Luckily, Athena helped her up.

'Just relax Scarlet! You need to control yourself or you could get yourself hurt. Maybe you should go back to the castle?' she suggested.

Scarlet shook her head with her eyes fixed on Malo. She started walking down the stairs once more.

The King's army was heavily outnumbered by the Blucks and the Chamcoks.

'There's no chance we can win!' Scarlet said to herself as she felt her heart miss a beat.

A large group of Greliks had made an attack on a huge group of Chamcoks. No soldier came out alive. The Greliks were hungry for more blood and they charged towards a group of Blucks.

A Grelik suddenly rushed to Athena and Scarlet.

We have killed six hundred soldiers. We are on the way to victory!

The Blucks, however, were prepared and held out their swords and heavily wounded some Greliks at that moment.

Scarlet and Athena both shuddered from the agony the Greliks were enduring.

Scarlet tripped over again, but this time Damon caught her.

For a moment neither of them said anything. Scarlet just walked away, nodding her head to show her gratitude.

Damon smiled to himself.

Athena smiled at him as she walked past him. She knew exactly what he was thinking.

'Look at those girls over there! They are the daughters of the King. Agalits! I reckon it would be impossible to kill them with these swords!' a Bluck soldier from the Seven Hundred Army said to his comrade, pointing to Athena and Scarlet.

'Maybe if we were to put poison on the tip of the sword?' the other soldier suggested.

He removed the vial from his neck and squeezed five drops of his deadly poison onto the tip of his sword.

'Five drops? That's too much. That would kill her instantly. It should be three!' his comrade warned.

'We cannot kill the King directly because he is immortal, but I am sure it would destroy him if we killed a daughter of his. I want to kill that one!' he said, pointing towards Scarlet.

They both laughed and slowly walked towards the sisters.

'Wait!' said the soldier who wasn't holding the poisonous sword.

He looked at his friend.

'What if we were to kill them both? My vial contains a poison that only kills you after a few hours, leaving you in excruciating pain! That would be fun to watch,' he said as he looked over at Athena.

They both smiled and the soldier poured the dark, green poison onto the tip of his sword. Together, they walked towards their chosen victims.

In that moment, Athena walked towards Max while Scarlet ran to a small wounded boy who had blood smeared all over his face.

Malo, after killing five soldiers with one blow of his sword, looked over at Scarlet and saw her looking after the wounded child. His eye then caught two soldiers walking towards her.

He felt every inch of his body shake. He could sense something was going to happen. His heart began to beat so loudly, he could no longer hear anything.

'Scarlet, move out of the way!' he screamed at the top of his lungs.

She turned around and saw Malo running towards her. Both soldiers saw this and so they began to run as well. They were willing to die if it meant killing an Agalit.

Scarlet looked at Malo and then the soldiers. They were all charging towards her. She moved backwards but tripped over a dead body. She fell over one last time.

'You can make it!' the soldier said to his comrade as he headed towards Athena.

The soldier was only yards away from Scarlet. He raised his poisoned sword upwards, ready to strike down on her.

Malo lunged forward and fell on Scarlet. He put all his weight on his clenched fists against the ground so that he didn't hurt her.

'Malo,' she said, quietly crying.

'I love you!' he whispered as the soldier dug his poisoned sword right through him.

For a moment, Scarlet's heart stopped. She could no longer feel Malo's heavy breath on her.

She felt nothing.

'Malo?' she asked, crying so much now, no one understood could hear what she was saying.

'MALO!' she screamed.

Everyone turned to her.

Athena immediately ran to her sister. The soldier who was running to Athena with his poisoned sword stood no chance, as Max used his power to make the sword fall to the ground.

Soldiers eventually stopped fighting, hearing Scarlet's heartbreaking shrieks of pain. They heard Malo's name repeatedly and looked around to see what was happening. It was a name everyone knew of.

Scarlet hugged Malo's body and repeated his name over and over again.

'Out of the way!' the King shouted as he came through the crowd.

He saw his sweet Scarlet, underneath Malo's body.

He ran towards her.

'Are you hurt?' he asked, not knowing what else to say.

'Malo! He is dead! HE IS DEAD! I feel dead. I don't...I can't live without...' her words were completely muffled by her tears.

No one knew what to do. They all remained still and watched Scarlet cry in agony.

Nicolas, who was right behind the King, came forward.

'I might be able to help you!' he announced. He pulled the chain from his neck which contained his vial.

His vial was the only one in the army that contained a healing potion. He poured some of the crystal white liquid onto Malo's back, directly into the wound.

For minutes, everyone held their breath. Even Nicolas, who hated Malo, prayed to the Gods for him to return back to life.

After a while, Nicolas spoke. 'He was given far too much poison. Nothing can help him now. He is dead.'

Nicolas removed Malo's body from Scarlet so she could move again.

She didn't move at first. She just laid there, drowning in her own tears.

'Malo?' she whispered as she eventually moved over to him and held his cheek.

'Malo, don't leave me. Please...' she broke off once more.

Athena slowly walked towards her, her face completely red.

She bent down besides Scarlet and stroked her back. Scarlet took no notice of her. Instead, she controlled her tears and just looked at Malo's pale face.

She stroked his brown hair.

'Please, don't leave me.'

Everyone looked at each other.

Nicolas looked over at his father and then to the rest of the army. His army had won. Only a handful of Chamcoks had survived but over a hundred of the Blucks were still standing. Even though a few hundred men from the King's army were still alive, without the protection of the few Greliks they would be easily defeated.

Everyone was silent. No one dared to speak.

Nicolas cleared his throat and then looked at his army.

'We have all just lost a friend. Malo. In his honour, we shall stop this war. We are close to victory, so we shall spare the remaining soldiers. We should continue to let the King rule our country. We should all go back to our way of life and not let war interfere in our lives. This has been the war these lands have been waiting for. We have won it. We are victorious! Yet, we will not conquer. We have all just seen how war destroys lives. Not just of those who die but for those to have to suffer every day from their loss. Look around you. Children killed! The sufferance for the parents is unimaginable.'

He turned to his father.

'Thirteen years ago I was taken from my father, my future kingdom. Today, I ask my father for forgiveness from my evil actions.'

He bent down before his father.

'If you would allow me to re-join my family.'

The King held his head high up, 'I am not the one to ask, Nicolas. I am no longer the ruler of Fairoses.'

He turned towards Athena who was by her sisters side.

No one had the nerve to move. However, the Blucks found the soldier who had killed Malo and pushed him through the crowd until he was at the front.

'General, this is the man who killed Malo,' a soldier said.

Nicolas walked towards the soldier and studied him. He shook his head in disgust. He had no words to say to the soldier. He just simply gazed at him. The Blucks turned to one another, not knowing what was happening. The soldier who killed Malo whimpered and fell to the ground with his hands covering his face.

'Kill me already! The suspense is eating me alive. Kill me, KILL ME!'

Nicolas sighed out loud with no remorse. He helped the soldier up. 'If I were to kill you, you would not suffer very long. No, instead, I want you to kill yourself.'

'I don't have my sword with me, general!'

Nicolas gave an empty smile, with death in his eyes. 'Did I say I wanted you to stab yourself? No. You will suffer like Scarlet will have to suffer for the rest of her life. Kill yourself, slowly and painfully, by drinking three drops of the potion from your vial. You will be in much agony for a long time. It will give you time to regret your action. It will give you time to think about your short, pitiful life.'

The soldier, feeling everyone's eyes on him apart from Scarlet who was hugging the lifeless body of Malo, slowly ripped the chain from his neck and unscrewed his vial. With his hands trembling so violently, that some of the potion fell to the ground, he drunk three drops. Moments later, he began to shake uncontrollably.

Just as fast as he dropped to the ground, everyone turned their attention back on Malo.

'I can't believe Malo's dead! He escaped death so many times... for him to die in such a fast way, it's not fair to him.'

'He probably had the biggest sense of humour in the entire army.'

One by one, all the soldiers dropped their swords to the ground and kneeled down, in respect to Malo.

Athena and the other Agalits turned to see all the soldiers surrender and bow down to them. Scarlet, who was still hugging Malo, also turned to see this. She cried even more, knowing that he was loved. Not just by her but by everyone who he had once fought with.

Athena looked over at Malo's face. Tears began to blur her own vision as she bent down to kiss him on the forehead. For the next long minutes, she and Scarlet held hands as they both looked down at the lifeless body of the man they both respected and loved.

XXV

Scarlet refused to be walked back to the castle. She wanted to be alone. She slowly walked to her chambers and over to her bed.

At first, she just stared into thin air but quickly looked away as she could feel her eyes were watering again.

She laid face down on the bed and stretched her arms out. She looked over to the window and saw it was almost dark.

'Scarlet?' Todd whispered as he flew in.

She buried her head into the sheets.

'Please, Scarlet! I don't want you to block me out. I am your best friend.'

Scarlet started sobbing again.

'I'm sorry. I didn't mean to make you even more upset!' Todd said as he landed just next to her shoulder.

Scarlet lifted her head up, her eyes all watered.

'It's not you, Todd – it's the sheets. They still have Malo's scent. It just seems almost surreal that he's dead. Only this morning he promised me everything would be fine but...'

She shook her head and started crying uncontrollably. Todd gave her a tissue that he held with his beak and she happily took it.

'Listen. There's something Malo told me to tell you but seeing that you're so upset, I should-'

'No, tell me! What did he say to you, Todd?'

He looked down and fidgeted with his wings.

'Todd, what did he tell you?'

He looked back up into her bright blue eyes.

'He said you should go to the waterfall tonight, but I really don't think it's the best idea for you right now. You're so fragile!'

Scarlet shook her head again.

'I disagree. I think I should go. I need to feel close to him right now. I can't explain it but I need to feel his presence. From the look on your face, you don't understand. It's fine. I prefer it, in fact, that nobody understands.'

Todd was getting worried. 'Scarlet, let me come with you. I know, now that I told you, there is absolutely no chance you won't go to the waterfall. So, I think I should come with you. For moral support!'

Scarlet laughed as she tickled Todd's miniature face.

'Thank you, Todd!' she whispered.

Athena laid in her bath, her eyes swollen. She couldn't help but cry.

'Oh, Malo!' she sighed.

Nathan came in the bathroom and only saw a hint of Athena's face as the whole room was only lit by one small candle.

He kissed her hand and stroked her hair. 'It's silly but you can't imagine how attached you can get to someone within a few weeks. I remember the first time I saw him, it was on a volcano and I thought he was dead but he wasn't. But now...'

Athena started crying again.

Nathan decided to get in the bath with her, with his night clothes still on.

He drew her towards him and once again kissed her hand.

She smiled but continued to cry.

'Even though I knew so much about nature, he taught me new things. He showed me a piro leaf one time. He was always so kind. Immature but so funny. He and I even spent a night in the dungeons together, eating simbuy which I didn't even like!' she said, laughing at the last part.

'I am so sorry, Athena!' he whispered.

'Don't be! It's not your fault. It was mine. How could I not hear that soldier as he ran to Scarlet? I could have prevented the whole thing. I could have prevented Malo from dying, I could have prevented Scarlet's pain.'

'Is there anything I can do?' he asked, looking deep into her eyes.

She shook her head.

'I know that through this misery and pain we can't see the positives, but Malo's death stopped the war. He brought peace. We no longer live divided. Everyone obeys you now – their Queen! I am sure that Malo would have wanted that.'

Athena nodded as she bit her lip, trying to stop her uncontrollable tears.

'He would have sacrificed his own life just to see Fairoses as one again, just as he sacrificed his life for Scarlet. Oh poor Scarlet, I can't imagine her pain right now. She's all alone now. I have you and I love you!' she said as she quickly leant in to kiss him.

I love you more.

Scarlet waited till it was late at night. She suddenly opened her eyes and saw the full moon out. She looked over at Todd who was sleeping in the cage Malo had made for him.

She quickly and quietly got out of bed and made her way to the door. Once she was on the other side, she ran down the corridors and out of the castle as fast as she could.

She saw a group of Greliks about to leave and the biggest one offered to give her a ride on his back.

How are you?

'I need to get to the waterfall!' she ordered.

The Grelik could feel her pain so decided to leave it at that.

Once they had reached the bottom of the mountain, the Greliks separated and Scarlet and her Grelik were left alone. For minutes they said nothing and saw nothing but after a while, Scarlet could make out a light of some sort in front of her.

She heard the waterfall.

'Stop here!'

The Grelik obeyed and let her jump off.

Would you like me to stay here and wait for you to come back so I can bring you back to the castle?

Scarlet shook her head. 'That won't be necessary. Thank you!'

And with that, she ran to the source of light. She got closer and closer and could now see the source of light was coming from the waterfall. She began to run faster, feeling the warm, light breeze brush against her face.

She took a deep breath in as she arrived.

Candles were lit around the waterfall. There were even candles on the rocks in the waterfall pool.

The biggest rock, directly in front of the waterfall, was lit by several candles. Scarlet could see an object placed in the centre of it.

She quickly hopped on each rock to get to this object, but fell over as she underestimated the distance between one rock to another.

The water was warm and Scarlet was actually thankful for falling in. She swam deeper in the water and spun around with her arms out. She felt free.

She opened her eyes as she faced the sky. Her eyes shone and she could see the bright, white full moon above her. She stared at it for a moment, feeling it shine a light into her heart that she did not yet want. Scarlet then went back to closing her eyes. Back to the darkness.

After spending much time underwater, she came back up to the surface and swam to the rock. She carefully moved a candle so she could reach the object in the middle.

'I wonder what it is!' she said as she carefully picked it up.

She slowly unclenched her fist and saw a ring in the middle of her palm.

The ring was unique. It was red. Scarlet red. She gasped as she saw an inscription on the inside of the ring reflect against the moon.

She didn't want to read it just yet so she quickly clenched her fist again.

After a while, Scarlet placed the ring through her finger and it fitted perfectly.

She smiled as she took it off and looked at what was inscribed.

You are my light in shining armour.

She laughed as she wiped the tears from her eyes. How she suddenly loved those words! She decided then, she would never take off the ring. It was the last thing Malo had left her and she was going to hold on to it forever.

'We were supposed to be together, Malo. You said it yourself. We were supposed to live far away with our children. But you have gone too far! Too far away that these children of ours will never exist and too far away, even I won't see you again! I don't want to seem like the selfish one but you were supposed to be with *me*! And only *me*. You were not supposed to be anywhere else. Now, we will *never* see each other again,' she said out loud, her voice getting softer and softer until she could no longer speak.

Athena leant against her balcony, lost in her thoughts.

It was the next morning, before dawn, but the air was warm breezy.

Athena shuddered as she felt a leaf tickle her ankle and turned around only to see many leaves flooding into her chambers.

She followed their trail and saw that they stopped at the bottom of her wardrobe.

She bent down and looked under it. It was still quite dark so she couldn't see anything.

Athena slowly stuck her arm under the big wardrobe but couldn't feel anything.

'What's going on?' Nathan asked as he woke up, seeing all these leaves.

'I'm not sure. It could be a sign though that there's something underneath this wardrobe, but I can't find anything.'

'Try again.' he suggested.

Athena reached her hand out once more and this time, she did feel something. It was a small object made of wood.

She quickly grabbed the object and put it in the light where she could see what it was.

'Oh.'

'What is it?' Nathan yawned.

Athena showed him. 'I thought I lost this the day all four of us went down to the markets. I went back to find it but I couldn't. I wonder how it managed to get all the way over here!'

She felt the leaves brush against her ankle again as they returned to the balcony and then blew away into the sky.

Athena's eyes suddenly widened.

'You don't think that was Malo, do you?' she asked Nathan.

Nathan didn't say anything for a moment but then looked up at her and quickly nodded his head.

'It was for him we brought that down to the markets and he knew you were looking for it afterwards. Maybe now, that he is...he found it and placed it under the wardrobe as a joke?'

Athena turned back to the balcony to see if there were any more leaves left. There was one.

She leant over the balcony itself and bent down to pick up the leaf.

'It *is* you!' she whispered to herself, thinking of Malo.

She recognised the leaf. It was a piro leaf. She remembered Malo saying it was incredibly rare and if she was to ever see one, it would have to remind her of him.

She smiled as she looked down at the object in her hand. It was the pen she was given on the night of her birthday.

'Magic. Do you understand the logic now?'

As the day went on, everyone in the Flame tried to return to their routine, but it was almost impossible. Many women lost their husbands and husbands lost their children, killed by the Chamcoks and the Blucks. The sun hid behind heavy, dark grey clouds and the light breeze was slowly turning into a heavy wind.

In the late afternoon, everyone who was informed of Malo's funeral made their way to the river bank.

The King was the first one there, having helped a few of his soldiers place Malo's body onto a wooden raft made from branches and twigs. The King had the idea to place Scarlet flowers all over the raft. So, the remaining soldiers from the Seven Hundred Army as well as the King's army were called to help find the red flower.

Athena and Nathan came together, followed by Gemma and Juliet with Nicolas in between them. Subo, Max and Damon followed soon after.

Mark, too, came and was welcomed by the King with a pat on the shoulder. Even Todd was on a tree nearby.

'Where's Scarlet?' Athena asked as she looked around.

Nathan looked around but she was nowhere to be seen.

'Give her time!' the King said.

For a few minutes, everyone stood in silence, looking down and praying that Scarlet would arrive.

'My King, she is not in her chambers.'

'Give her time!' the King repeated.

Minutes passed and the King was starting to feel a bit uneasy. Rain began to fall.

'We should start now before we all get soaked.' Mark said, looking up at the sky.

The King felt a raindrop fall on his head but still wanted to wait for his daughter.

Scarlet walked away from the waterfall, looking back at it one last time.

She then looked down at the ring she wore on her fourth finger and then took a deep breath as she walked back to the Four Flames.

Scarlet started running so she could feel the strong breeze whip across her face. She dodged trees that had fallen onto the ground, the craters that had been created by Damon and the droppings from the horses of the Seven Hundred Army. She quickly stopped and leant against one of the huge trees. She was about to be sick again.

'Father, I don't think she is coming. She must be too upset!' Gemma said.

The King sighed and looked down. They had all waited long enough and now the rain was coming down faster.

The King nodded and they all moved forwards. 'Get the fire ready!'

Scarlet slipped over the wet soil and buried her head in her hands.

'Everything is falling apart!'

She rubbed the palms of her hands together and felt the ring. She suddenly remembered. She looked up and her ears pricked forwards. Yes, she knew she was late.

Scarlet quickly got up and started running as fast as she could to the river bank and from where she was, she could already see the fire starting up.

Everyone placed the tip of their long, beautifully carved wooden sticks into the fire. Then, they closed their eyes and made silent prayers.

'Wait!' Scarlet groaned.

Athena suddenly opened her eyes as she saw Scarlet running towards them.

'She's here!' she called out, pointing towards Scarlet.

Everyone opened their eyes and sure enough, saw Scarlet running towards them.

She didn't even stop and hesitate as she reached the water. She just continued running through the river, but as she got further in, she could no longer feel her feet.

She started feeling faint.

I have no more energy, Athena. I'm fainting.

'We have to help her!' Athena said, turning to those around her as she knew she couldn't help with her terrible swimming skills.

Damon immediately stepped forward and said, 'I will go.'

Athena nodded and watched Damon plunge into the water to save her sister.

After a few minutes, he came out of the water with Scarlet in his arms. He gently laid her on the river bank but continued holding her hand. She looked up at him, still panting.

'Are you alright?' Damon whispered.

She slowly lifted her head, her eyes still paralyzed with fear. The King walked over to her and with Mark's assistance, they helped her up.

Gemma passed Scarlet her piece of wood, lit with fire at the tip. Scarlet didn't accept it. She simply stared at Gemma with all the judgement in the world.

'Scarlet, my love, take it!' the King said, softly.

Scarlet shook her head and hissed, 'you are a *traitor*!'

With that, she walked over to the raft and looked down at Malo's body. She stared at his angelic face. His eyelids shut, his hair perfectly placed. However, his skin was much paler. She bent down and kissed his forehead. She then took one of the Scarlet flowers and placed it in between his hands.

'I love you. I will keep this ring forever and think of you every day. I promise!' she whispered, touching his cold cheeks as she silently began to cry.

Damon looked away.

Scarlet turned to Athena who was walking towards the raft. They gave their best attempt at a smile as they passed each other.

Athena took a deep breath before she bent down to say her last words.

'Malo, you saved my life so many times and for that, I am forever grateful. We both set out to the Four Flames for the same reason in the end. To find love. I wanted to find my family and you wanted to find your soulmate you had met at the tournament. We both succeeded. And the only comfort I have from this is that you will have died in peace. Because you met her. And you both fell in love.'

Athena had to pause for a moment as her tears were making it near to impossible to speak.

'I haven't forgotten our journey. And I most certainly haven't forgotten my promise I made to you about the Striberosse. I will put a stop to them. You died very young, but you accomplished so much! And

I am so proud of you.'

Athena wiped the tears from her eyes.

'I love you very much!' she whispered.

The King held her by the shoulder as she stood up. Everyone held out their long, wooden sticks with the tips on fire and walked towards the raft. Damon offered his to Scarlet and she accepted it.

After they pushed the raft into the river, they set fire to it. They watched it go down the river, slowly going up in flames.

Athena held Scarlet's hand and smiled at her.

'I need to be alone,' Scarlet whispered as she dropped her hand away.

She walked back to the Azul Flame with Todd on her shoulder.

'Shall I walk after her?' Damon asked, suddenly appearing behind Athena.

Athena shook her head and turned to him, 'I think she wants to be alone, but I do think it would be good for her to talk to someone about it. Go up to her chambers before dinner.'

Damon patted her shoulder, smiled, and walked off.

'May I come in?' the King asked, knocking on Athena's door.

'Yes,' Athena said as she opened up her door.

The King stepped in and looked around the room. Nathan was sitting by the fireplace and smiled as the King walked to him.

'My boy, would you mind giving Athena and me some privacy?' the King asked gently, holding Nathan's shoulder.

Nathan shook his head and stood up. As he walked to the door, he briefly brushed his hand against hers.

See you later, my love.

Athena smiled at him and walked over to her father.

For a moment, they stared at each other. Not saying a word, but just looking at one another.

'You were made to be a queen. You are elegant, quick-thinking and intelligent, and you have nothing but a beautiful heart, filled with only goodness.'

He walked up and down the room, pacing.

'Your coronation as queen will take place in two weeks. You do want to be queen?'

Athena took a deep breath and nodded, 'yes.'

'Do not feel obliged, my dear child. You can walk away from it all. Live far away with Nathan, in peace. I will give you as much money as you want so you will never have to endure poverty again.'

'I don't want money, father. I want to live here with my family. I want my children to grow up like I grew up for the first few years of my life. I loved my life back in Oakrose but too many nights did I go to bed with an empty stomach. I want my children to never have that sensation. Also, I want to help people. Help them and their lives. I want to eliminate the Striberosse. There are so many things I want to do. As queen, I would be able to do that. I would be of no use if I was in Clandon or Oakrose or anywhere else. Tatila is the place for me. The Four Flames is where I belong.

But, is it fair to Scarlet, Gemma and Juliet who have lived here all their life to not be given the throne? I didn't even know who I was until a couple of weeks ago. Is it fair to take one of their places as queen?'

The King laughed to himself.

'Ever since she could speak, Scarlet told me that she never wanted to become queen. Besides, she does not have the nature for a queen. She is a free spirit and at times, uncontrollable. Gemma does not have a heart like you. I know this because I have taught her how to master her gift since the age of four and I know that it is her nature to destroy things. Her gift is a dangerous one. And Juliet, she is very dear in my heart, but like Scarlet, she does not have the makings of a queen. Unlike, your other siblings, she does not know the difference between right and wrong. We have all discussed it years ago, and they all knew you would be made queen after this war.'

Athena nodded.

'What about Nicolas? In my memories, I could see that he was a wonderful person.'

'Yes, he was. He was perhaps the most well-behaved child.'

'Then, why not make him the next ruler?'

Her father sighed and looked down.

'The ruler of Fairoses *must* be an Agalit. It has been this way for many centuries. They must have a power and Athena, Nicolas no longer has a power.'

'But if he *did*, would he be made the ruler?'

The King shook his head.

'It would be debatable. If he had come from the same background as you, then maybe...but he didn't. He was raised in the foulest of places. Yes, as you mentioned, he was born to be great, but he has been exposed to too much evil, malice and torture. He even cut off Mark's hand in a moment of anger! He would be feared by everyone. That is the last thing I want – my country to fear its ruler.'

'Would you take offence, father, if I asked Nicolas to help me rule?'

The King didn't say anything for a moment but then looked into Athena's eyes.

'If you think it would be best.'

'I do.'

'Very well. I respect your decisions. You have grown a great deal since you arrived here. I know your mother would be proud to see her Atheneglary grow into the woman she was born to be.'

Athena hesitated for a moment. 'What was her gift?'

'Athena, do you remember what we did the first afternoon you arrived?'

'You looked into my memories with me.'

'Exactly. That was her gift. You see, Athena, it is very rare for two Agalits to marry one another. In a lifetime, it is rare to find another Agalit yet alone one that you love.

Well, that was your mothers gift. When she died, it was passed onto me. Being an Agalit goes far beyond having green blood, blue eyes and a power. I will teach you all about it over the next few years. You will understand everything. Well, everything I have learnt so far.'

'Will you explain why I have two powers?'

'You learn things very fast. That is a strand to your gift of hearing thoughts. Your second gift is to see people in the past and future. That is something I will help you control one day. It is the most confusing gift of all, in my opinion.'

The King paused for a moment.

'You also have a third gift, Atheneglary. You also have the power to look into memories. Why are you blessed not with two gifts but *three* gifts? I have no idea. It is something that I have been trying to figure out myself.

One day we will solve this mystery. However, that is not today.'

Her father walked to the door and opened it up.

'Where are we going?'

'We are going to your sister's room.'

Juliet, Gemma and Nicolas were all in Gemma's chambers. They were on the balcony talking to one another. As soon as Gemma saw her sister and father walking towards them, she stopped talking.

'My dear children,' the King started.

'Father,' they all replied at the same time.

There was a moment of silence.

'How did they know about the cave?' Athena blurted out, unable to not break the silence.

Juliet and Gemma looked at one another. Gemma looked up and started speaking.

'Before we tell you, you must not hate me for eternity, father,' Gemma said, looking at him.

'Why would I hate you in particular?' he asked.

Juliet made an uncomfortable laugh, expressing her anxiety.

Oliver and Mark walked in only to see a small reunion.

'Oh, I'm sorry! Are we interrupting?' Mark asked.

'NO!' Gemma exclaimed.

She ran to Oliver and held his hand. 'You are right on time!'

Gemma took a deep breath and started to talk.

'Ever since that day thirteen years ago, I have always tried to gain your love. No matter how hard I tried, though, it was never good enough. It was always about your precious Juliet. She was your favourite, along with mother and you were happy. If I ran away, it still wouldn't have affected you. So, I went down a different path. I wanted to be loved. I wanted to be useful for something. So, six years later, I saw Oliver on his horse and I recognised him from the battle. He told me I could see Nicolas if I went with him. I did. He made me feel so important and when he told me their plans for the war, I seized the opportunity to make myself useful. I told him everything I knew. For the next few months, I spent every day with Oliver and soon, we fell in love with each other.'

'So, you were the one who told the enemy about all our secrets,' Athena realised.

'Our father's secrets, not *your* secrets, Athena. You only showed up weeks ago. Don't start pretending like you've been here all your life!'

'But it *was* you who gave away all my secrets which were only supposed to be heard within the family,' the King stated.

'Yes, it was, but you don't understand! I *wanted* to give the information. Oliver was making me happy. He gave me gifts and I wanted to give something in return. Why is that so hard for you to understand?'

'Gemma, why should my secrets be the gateway to your happiness?'

Gemma didn't know what to say so Oliver intervened.

'Yes, she gave away your secrets to me. However, that didn't make me love her any more than I already did. I knew it was breaking her heart though, betraying you like this. However, I needed her help and to prove it, I *did* win the war!'

Nicolas shifted his body slightly.

'Oh please, Nicolas, I was the mastermind behind it all! If it weren't for me, we wouldn't have won. Not even close. They had the Greliks, the Agalits. It was *me* who gave that potion to our soldiers to make them immune to Athena's power.'

'Wait! I couldn't hear you because you gave all your men a potion that made me unable to hear them? Is that why I couldn't hear you thoughts either, Gemma? You took the potion too?'

'I didn't want you to suspect anything. I didn't want you to think you could control everything here. I also secretly poured the potion into Juliet's drink,' Gemma said coldly.

'I would never try to control everything here, Gemma. I just wanted to be part of the family again.'

'That's not entirely true. You have control over father, Scarlet and Nathan. I have never been able to do that in the space of many years. You know that's true! Didn't mother ever tell you it was bad to lie?'

Athena looked up at her in tears. With the death of Malo, tears were easily on the horizon. Gemma didn't reply, but instead buried her face into Oliver's shoulder. She spoke faster than she thought.

'One of our dear housekeepers told me she overheard you and Juliet arguing about whose secret was the worst. Now, Gemma, your secret was rather shocking.'

The King paused and then turned to Juliet.

'How bad can your secret be?' he asked.

Juliet bit her lip but knew there was no way she could keep the truth away from her father any longer.

She cleared her throat and was about to speak, but didn't.

'Spit it out! I told my secret! It's your turn.' Gemma said, infuriated.

Juliet nodded and began to speak.

'I have always adored you, father! I would have always gladly died for you. As mother was beginning to spend more and more time with you and less time at the market, I found that you didn't spend as much time with me. I admit I was jealous and at the time, I thought it was all mother's fault.

So, one day, I told her that I knew where Athena was living and it wasn't far from where Nicolas was. So, naturally, she set off to find her. It was just a guess. I had no idea where Athena was.

I knew from Gemma that the scientists were looking for Agalits to extract their blood for some particular reason. I knew that if they found her, they would kill her.

I didn't know what I wanted. I didn't know whether I wanted her dead or alive. The moment I found out she was dead, I realised I wanted her alive. I wanted her back here, reading a book by the fireplace in my chambers. I just wanted to spend more time with you, father. Be your absolute favourite! With mother in the way, that wasn't possible. I'm sorry and I have regretted it every day. I see how lonely and unhappy you are without her and I feel so guilty. The guilt was getting to my mind that I had to write it down. I couldn't tell anyone and that's how Gemma found out. She read my journal.'

The King froze and felt tears coming to his eyes. 'It is because of you my wife is no longer here?'

'Yes, but only because I wanted to be with you father. Spend more time with you. You spent most of the day with her by your side. I wanted you alone.'

The King looked up at the ceiling, trying to conceal his tears. 'You selfish girl! You ungrateful, jealous child! I spent "most of the day with her" because I loved her. I adored her and yes, the day I learnt about her death, was the worst day of my life. She was my wife and you are my first born child. I adore you both but in different ways. She was the love of my life. It took me more than six centuries to find her and when I did, I reached a level of happiness I never even knew existed! I didn't get to spend more than twenty years with her because of *you*. You are so selfish, Juliet. Well, congratulations, she is dead and she will never come back because of you.

You could have *told* me you wanted more time with me, rather than send your mother to her death! I would have gladly given it to you. Well done, now you have all the time in the world to spend with me. Very well done!'

The King didn't care that tears were flooding down his cheeks anymore. He had never felt so much anger. He turned around and left the room, slamming the door behind him.

'I didn't realise it was your mother at the time. Otherwise, I would have never let my scientists lay a finger on her.'

'Well, that won't bring her back now, will it?' Juliet snapped.

Gemma walked over to Juliet and slapped her with all her force.

'You are never to speak to Oliver like that! Besides, it was all your fault that mother died, you selfish person. Because of you, father is miserable. He has been ever since her death. If mother was to hear this, she would be absolutely disgusted and quite frankly, she would disown you. You are a disgrace to the family. Nobody likes you. Even Damon. He's interested in Scarlet. Can't you see it? Nobody goes for the favourite. Well, now that you are no longer the favourite, maybe your luck will change. I sincerely hope it doesn't. What I did was absolutely horrible but at least I can be forgiven. But *you*! You purposely killed our mother who had raised us so well and loved us unconditionally. I hope you never find love, Juliet. You truly don't deserve it!'

And with that, Gemma and Oliver left.

Juliet started crying but nobody comforted her.

'I feel like it is my turn to give an explanation,' said the most unlikely person to have a confession to make. Everyone turned to him.

'Nicolas, you are my godson,' Mark proudly announced.

Nicolas turned to him, shaking his head, as though he just woke up from a dream.

'I'm sorry?'

'That's why I stayed in the army's headquarters for so long, even though I detested that place. I wanted to protect you. Your father asked me to follow you no matter where you went. Since your birth, I swore to protect you.'

Nicolas looked at his arm with no hand. 'I cut off your hand. You cannot forgive me for that.'

'It wasn't easy, I admit, but it happened and I have learnt to accept it. I knew Oliver was plotting against you. I had to stay. He wanted to kill you and take over the army. I pretended as though I was on his side, but I was never going to let him hurt you. Not for one minute.'

Nicolas smiled to himself. 'So, if it weren't for you, I might be dead.'

Mark nodded.

'Thank you.'

Mark patted his shoulder.

'But if you knew where I was and my father knew where I was, then how come he never came to bring me back? Why was I forced to grow up in that horrible place?'

Mark gulped. 'It's how it was meant to be. If you would have returned, there would have been yet another revolt or battle just to get you back. You were always meant to lead that army over the hill. It was your destiny. If your father wasn't such a strong believer in Fate and Destiny, then of course, he would have come and got you himself. It just wasn't meant to be. And your father knew that when the time came, only someone with a heart as kind as yours would make the right decision. You did! You chose to surrender, even though you were so close to victory and had much resent and hatred built up in you over the years. You have no idea how much strength and goodness it takes to do what you did. All those horrific things you've done over the years was the persona of General Avran. You are free now. You are Nicolas. You no longer have to be a general and you never have to go back to that place.'

Nicolas took deep breaths and felt like he was going to be sick. All that anxiety he had felt from over the years had just vanished. He looked over at Mark, trembling.

'Thank you for telling me that. I needed to hear that. I could cry knowing I can sleep here tonight and not underground. I never have to do that again.'

He brought his hands to eyes to stop the tears from coming and sighed with utter relief.

Juliet sniffed out loud and knew there was nothing more to be said on her behalf, so she left without saying another word.

Athena slowly walked to Nicolas. Mark patted Nicolas on the shoulder once more and then left.

Athena waited till she was alone with her brother. She gave him the longest embrace and felt his body shake. After he calmed down, she whispered, 'I have many questions to ask you.'

Nicolas sat down by the window. He looked up at his sister and was ready to answer her questions. He couldn't smiling. He felt liberated.

'When we spoke in the dungeons, you told me you would "kill our father on the spot" if you ever saw him. You acted as though you didn't know who he was. Why did you lie to me?'

'Everything I said was true. I hated him so much. I was taken when I was six years old, Athena. I had more memories than you and I wasn't enchanted by a Wueltin. I still remember a lot of them to this day. That's why the betrayal was even harder. Every day, I wished for him to save me and bring me home.'

Athena sat down next to him.

'I'm sorry for what happened to you. I wouldn't wish that fate on my worst enemy.'

Nicolas laughed, 'You? Having enemies? Please...'

'I would say Benny got rather close to that.'

Nicolas shook his head and put his arm around Athena's shoulder.

'The reason why I didn't reveal the identity of our father was because I didn't want to take that surprise from you. I already took our mother away. I wanted you to still feel the thrill of searching for your family. How did you feel when you found out the King was your father?'

'To be honest, I thought it was too good to be true. It felt like the storyline of a fairy tale with a happy ending when the girl is finally reunited with her father. But I felt the connection. I was certain he was my father. *That's* what made it real and not a story.'

Nicolas smiled to himself.

'And finding out you had sisters? That must have been a great bonus, surely?!'

Athena looked at her brother. 'Just as wonderful as finding out I had a brother who didn't grow up with his family either. The fact that we were separated leads me to my next question. Would you like to rule together?'

Nicolas looked at her with a serious look.

'Excuse me?'

'Rule with me, Nicolas. You, Nathan and me. Let's rule together.'

'Has father agreed to this?'

'He says I should do what I think is right. I think this is right!'

Nicolas hugged her.

'Thank you.' he whispered.

'Are you ready?'

'Yes.'

'It's never too late to change your mind!'

Athena quietly laughed, 'I am sure, father!'

'Good, good.'

The music began to play.

'It's time!' he said.

They walked down the white marble stairs which led to the gardens. There were hundreds of people on either side of them who were standing up, gazing at their queen passing by.

There were white roses surrounding the altar where Nathan was standing by, admiring his future wife.

He smiled as their eyes finally met.

'You look absolutely beautiful!' he whispered as she stood by his side.

'Thank you. I am so exhausted though! I had to walk about four hundred yards to get to you in these heels, you know!'

'If that's not love, then I don't know what is!'

They both quietly laughed and turned to the priest as he began to speak, with the beautiful blood-orange sunset behind them.

XXVI

Nine months later

'Come on, Scarlet. Once again!' Athena said, feeling Scarlet's grip harden.

Scarlet pushed once again and soon, a cry was heard.

'It's a little girl!' Athena said, taking the baby from the midwife and holding the child in her arms.

Scarlet leant back against the wall, taking deep breaths and smiled.

'Would you like to hold her?' Athena asked, giving the baby to Scarlet.

Scarlet reached her arms out and held the child.

'She's so beautiful!' Scarlet cried as she kissed the child's forehead.

'Do you know what you are going to call her yet?' Athena asked, pushing back the strands of hair on Scarlet's face.

Scarlet looked into the child's face.

'Rebecca. Malo and I wanted to have a baby girl named Rebecca.'

Athena smiled as she looked into the child's face.

'It suits her perfectly.'

Scarlet unwillingly handed Rebecca back to the midwife who finished cleaning her off.

'You did great!' Athena whispered.

Scarlet smiled as she closed her eyes.

I am so tired.

'Don't you want to hold your beautiful Rebecca again?' Athena asked.

'I just want to... sleep!' Scarlet said as she drifted off.

After a few moments, she suddenly sat up and screamed, giving Athena such a fright.

The midwife turned around and asked what was wrong.

'I am getting those contractions again. They are coming back!'

Athena and the midwife looked at each other. Athena's eyes widened and she smiled. 'She's having twins!'

After half an hour, another baby was born.

Athena looked at the child, who was crying and smiled.

'It's a boy.' she whispered as she passed the child over to Scarlet.

Scarlet greeted the child with greedy arms and grabbed hold of him.

'Give me my daughter!' she ordered the midwife.

The midwife placed Rebecca into one arm and the boy in the other.

'My dear Rebecca and Jack.' she said, smiling down at them.

Athena bent down and looked at both children.

'Who would have known? Twins!'

'That finally explains why I was so big then!'

They both laughed.

Scarlet suddenly turned serious.

'I am leaving the Four Flames, Athena. I want to live somewhere far away with my two treasures.'

'When did you decide this?'

'Months ago. When Malo was still alive.'

Athena closed her eyes. 'If you think it is best.'

Scarlet nodded, 'I really do. Also, I want you to be both their godmother.'

Athena smiled and looked down at their faces.

'Rebecca and Jack. Such beautiful names.'

'I wonder if either of them are Agalits.'

Athena turned to Scarlet with a huge smile.

'We shall have to wait and see!'